4/11

DAUGHTERS-IN-LAW

JOANNA TROLLOPE

A Touchstone Book
Published by Simon & Schuster
New York   London   Toronto   Sydney

Touchstone
A Division of Simon & Schuster, Inc.
1230 Avenue of the Americas
New York, NY 10020

First Touchstone trade paperback edition April 2011

TOUCHSTONE and colophon are registered trademarks
of Simon & Schuster, Inc.

For information about special discounts for bulk purchases, please contact Simon
& Schuster Special Sales at 1-866-506-1949 or business@simonandschuster.com.

The Simon & Schuster Speakers Bureau can bring authors to your live event. For
more information or to book an event contact the Simon & Schuster Speakers
Bureau at 1-866-248-3049 or visit our website at www.simonspeakers.com.

Manufactured in the United States of America

10   9   8   7   6   5   4   3   2   1

ISBN 978-1-4516-1838-9
ISBN 978-1-4516-1840-2 (ebook)

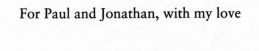

For Paul and Jonathan, with my love

CHAPTER ONE

From the front pew, Anthony had an uninterrupted view of the back of the girl who was about to become his third daughter-in-law. The church had a wide aisle, and a broad carpeted space below the shallow chancel steps, where the four little bridesmaids had plopped themselves down, in the pink silk nests of their skirts, during the address, so that there was a clear line of sight between Anthony and the bridal pair.

The bride, tightly swathed in ivory satin, seemed to Anthony to have the seductively imprisoned air of a landlocked mermaid. Her dress fitted closely—very closely—from below her shoulders to her knees and then fanned out into soft folds, and a fluid little train, which spilled carelessly down the chancel steps behind her. Anthony's gaze traveled slowly from the crown of her pale cropped head, veiled in gauze and scattered with flowers, down to her invisible feet, and then back up again to rest on the unquestionably satisfactory curves of her waist and hips. She has, Anthony thought, a gorgeous figure, even if it is improper for her almost father-in-law to think such a thing. *Gorgeous.*

He swallowed, and transferred his gaze sternly to his son. Luke, exuding that raw and possessive male pride that gives wedding days such an edge, was half turned towards his bride. There had been a touching moment five minutes before, when Charlotte's widowed mother had reached up to fold her daughter's veil back from her face and the two had regarded each other for several seconds with an intensity of understanding that excluded everyone else around them. Anthony had glanced down at Rachel beside him and wondered, as he often had in the decades they had been together, whether her composure hid some instinctive yearning she would never give voice to, and how her primitive and unavoidable reaction to yielding a third son to another woman would manifest itself in the coming months and years, escaping like puffs of hot steam through cracks in the earth's crust.

"Okay?" he said softly.

Rachel took no notice. He couldn't even tell if she was actually looking at Charlotte, or whether it was Luke she was concentrating on, admiring the breadth of his shoulders and the clearness of his skin and asking herself, at some deep level, if Charlotte really, *really* knew what an extravagantly fortunate girl she was. Instead of a conventional hat, Rachel had pinned a small explosion of green feathers to her hair, very much on one side, and the trembling of the feathers, like dragonflies on wires, seemed to Anthony the only indication that Rachel's inner self was not as unruffled as her outer one. Well, he thought, unable to gain her complicity, if she is absorbed in Luke, I will return to contemplating Charlotte's bottom. I won't be alone. Every man in the church who can see it will be doing the same. It is sheer prissiness to pretend otherwise.

The priest, a jovial man wearing a stole patterned with aggressive modern embroidery, was delivering a little homily based on a line from Robert Browning that was printed inside the service sheet.

Grow old along with me,
The best is yet to be.

This poem, he was saying, was not actually about marriage. It was about the reward experience can be for the loss of youth. It was a tribute to a Sephardic Jewish scholar of the twelfth century, but all the same it was relevant, it celebrated joy, it commanded us to call the glory from the gray, it urged trust in God. The priest spread his wide, white-sleeved arms and beamed upon Charlotte and Luke and Charlotte's mother in her lace dress and coat, and all the congregation. Anthony removed his gaze from what was about to belong to his youngest son and looked up at the roof. It had been heavily restored, the beams varnished, the ceiling plaster between them brilliantly whitened. Anthony sighed. How lovely it would have been if Luke could have been married, as his elder brother Ralph had been, in the church at home, and not in this cozily domesticated bit of Buckinghamshire with no marshes, no wading birds or reed beds or vast, cloud-piled skies. How lovely it would be if they were all in Suffolk, *now.*

The church at home would, of course, have been perfect. Anthony had no orthodox faith, but he liked the look and feel of churches, the dignities and absurdities of ritual, the shy belonging of English Anglican congregations. He had known his own village church all his life; it was as old as the rabbi in Browning's poem, even if no longer quite in its original form, and it was wide and light and welcoming, with clear-glass windows and a marvelous small modern bronze sculpture of Noah releasing the dove, to commemorate the first performance there of Benjamin Britten's church opera,

Noye's Fludde. That had been in 1958, when Anthony was eleven. He had heard all the church operas there, in the far-off days before the Suffolk coast had become a place of musical pilgrimage, sitting through them dressed in his school gray-flannel shorts and a tie, as a mark of respect to the music and to the composer. It was where he had first heard "Curlew River," which remained his favorite, long before he had dared to put drawing at the heart of his life, long before birds became a passion. It was the building where he had first become aware of the profound importance of creativity, and thus it was natural that he should want his sons to go through the great rites of life's passage there too. Wasn't it?

They had all been christened there, Edward and Ralph and Luke. Anthony might have preferred some simple humanist naming ceremony, but Rachel had wanted them christened in the church, baptized from the ancient and charming font, and she had wanted it quite forcefully.

"They don't have to stay Christian," she'd said to Anthony over her shoulder, as always occupied with something, "but at least they have the option. It's what you had, after all. Why shouldn't they have what you had?"

The christenings had been lovely, of course, and moving, and Anthony's sense of profound association with the church building had grown deeper with each one. In fact, so intense was his assumption that that was where the boys would marry—when, if, they married—that he was startled when his eldest, Edward, appeared with an elegant and determined young Swede, and announced that they were to be married, and, naturally, from her home, not his.

His fiancée, a laboratory researcher into the analysis of materials for museums and galleries, had been well briefed. She drew Anthony aside and fixed her astonishing light-blue gaze on him.

"You needn't worry," Sigrid said in her perfect English, "it will be a humanist ceremony. You will feel quite at home."

The wedding of Edward and Sigrid had taken place at her parents' summer house, on some little low, anonymous island in the archipelago outside Stockholm, and they had eaten crayfish afterwards, wearing huge paper bibs, mountains and mountains of crayfish, and aquavit had flowed like a fatal river, and it never got dark. Anthony remembered stumbling about along the pebbly shore in the strange, glimmering nighttime light, looking for Rachel, and being pursued by a rapacious platinum blonde in rimless spectacles and deck shoes.

The morning after the wedding Sigrid had appeared, packet-fresh in white and gray, with her smooth hair in a ponytail, and taken Ed away in a boat, not to return. Anthony and Rachel were left marooned among Sigrid's family and friends under a cloudless sky and entirely surrounded by water. They'd held hands, Anthony recalled, on the flight home, and Rachel had said, looking away from him out of the airplane window, "Some situations are just too foreign to react to, aren't they?"

And a bit later when Anthony said, "Do you think they are actually married?" she'd stared right at him and said, "I have no idea."

Well, that was over eleven years ago now, almost twelve. And there, on the carpet below the chancel steps, sat Mariella, Edward and Sigrid's eight-year-old daughter. She was sitting very still, and upright, her ballet-slippered feet tucked under her pink skirts, her hair held off her face by an Alice band of rosebuds. Anthony tried to catch her eye. His only granddaughter. His grave, self-possessed granddaughter. Who spoke English and Swedish and played the cello. By the merest movement of her head, Mariella indicated that she was aware of him, but she wouldn't look his way. Her job that day, her mother had said, was to set a good example to the other little bridesmaids, all Charlotte's nieces, and Mariella's life was largely dedicated to securing her mother's good opinion. She knew she had her grandfather's, whatever she did, as a matter of course.

"Concentrate," Rachel, beside him, hissed suddenly.

He snapped to attention.

"Sorry—"

"I'm delighted to announce," the priest said, removing his stole that he'd wrapped around Luke and Charlotte's linked, newly ringed hands, "that Luke and Charlotte are now husband and wife!"

Luke leaned to kiss his wife on the cheek, and she put her arms around his neck, and then he flung his own arms around her and kissed her with fervor, and the church erupted into applause. Mariella got to her feet and shook out her skirts, glancing at her mother for the next cue.

"In pairs," Anthony saw Sigrid mouth to the little girls. "Two by two."

Charlotte was laughing. Luke was laughing. Some of Luke's friends, farther down the church, were whooping.

Anthony took Rachel's hand.

"Another daughter-in-law—"

"I know."

"Who we don't really know—"

"Not yet."

"Well," Anthony said, "if she's only half as good as Petra—"

Rachel took her hand away.

"If."

The reception was held in a marquee in the garden of Charlotte's childhood home. It was a dry day, but overcast, and the marquee was filled with a queer greenish light that made everyone look ill. The lawn on which it was erected sloped slightly, so that standing up, complicated by doing it on rucked coconut matting, was almost impossible, especially for Charlotte's friends who were, without exception, shod in statement shoes with towering heels. Through an opening at the lower end of the marquee, the immediate bridal party could be seen picturesquely on the edge of a large pond, being ordered about by a photographer.

Oh God, water, Petra thought. Barney, who was still not walking, was safely strapped into his pushchair with the distraction of a miniature box of raisins, but Kit, at three, was mobile and had been irresistibly drawn to water all his life. Neither child, in the unfamiliarity of a hotel room the previous night, had slept more than fitfully, so neither Petra nor Ralph had slept either, and Ralph had finally got up at five in the morning and gone for such a long walk—well over two hours—that Petra had begun to suspect he had gone forever. And now, uncharacteristically, he had joined a roaring group of Luke's friends, and he was drinking champagne, and smoking, despite the fact that he had given up cigarettes when Petra was pregnant with Kit and, as far as she knew, hadn't smoked since then.

Kit was whining. He was exhausted and hungry and intractable. Keeping up a low uneven grizzle, he wound himself round and round in Petra's skirt, shoving against her thighs, disheveled and beyond being reasoned with. He had started the day in the white linen shirt and dark-blue trousers that Charlotte had requested, even though she considered him too young to be a page, but both had become so filthy and crumpled in church that he was back in the Spider-Man T-shirt he insisted on wearing whenever it wasn't actually in the washing machine. Petra herself, in the clothes that had looked to her both original and becoming hanging on the front of her wardrobe in their small bedroom at home, felt as out of sorts and out of place as Kit plainly did. Charlotte's friends, mostly in their twenties, were dressed for the mythical world of cocktails. She looked down at Kit. Intensely aggravating though he was being, he was to be pitied. He was her sweet, sensitive, imaginative little boy, and he had been plucked out of the familiarity that he relied upon, on an entirely and exclusively adult whim, and dumped down in an artificial and alien environment where the bed was not his own and the sausages were seasoned fiercely with pepper. She put a hand on his head. He felt hot and damp and unhappy.

"Petra," Anthony said.

Petra turned with relief.

"Oh, Ant—"

Anthony gave her shoulder a brief pat and then squatted down beside Kit.

"Poor old boy."

Kit adored his grandfather, but he couldn't give up his misery all of a sudden. He thrust his lower lip out.

Anthony said, "Might you manage a strawberry?"

Kit shook his head and plunged his face between Petra's legs.

"Or a meringue?"

Kit went still. Then he took his face out of Petra's skirt. He looked at Anthony.

"D'you know what they are?"

"No," Kit said.

"Crunchy things made of sugar. Delicious. Really, really, really bad for your teeth."

Kit pushed his face out of sight again. Anthony stood up.

"Shall I take him away and force-feed him something?"

Petra looked at her father-in-law, comfortably in his own father's morning suit, shabbily splendid.

"You're too clean."

"I don't mind a bit of sticky. Have you got a drink?"

"No. And I'm worried about the water."

"What water?"

Petra indicated with the hand that wasn't trying to restrain Kit.

"Down there. He hasn't noticed it yet, thank goodness."

"Where's Ralph?"

"Somewhere," Petra said.

Anthony regarded her.

"It's not much fun for you, all this. It is—"

"Well," Petra said, "weddings aren't meant for people of three, or for people with people of three to look after."

"Yours was."

She glanced down at Kit. He was still now, breathing hotly into her skin through the fabric of her skirt.

"Ours was lovely."

"It was."

"Perfect day, walking back from the church to your garden, all the roses out, everybody's dogs and children—"

Anthony smiled at her. Then he said casually to Kit, "Crisps?"

Kit stopped breathing.

"Maybe," Anthony said, "even Coca-Cola?"

Kit said something muffled.

"What?"

"With a straw!" Kit shouted into Petra's skirt.

"If you like."

"Thank you," Petra said. "Really, thank you."

"I am sitting next to Charlotte's mother at whatever meal this is. She's a noted plantswoman and amateur botanical artist, so we are put together at all occasions. I shall fortify myself by feeding Kit the wrong things first. Better eat the wrong things than nothing. If you don't come with me, Kit, I shall choose your straw color for you and I might choose yellow."

"No!" Kit shouted.

He flung himself, scarlet and tousled, away from his mother.

"Sam, Sam," Anthony said to him in a mock Yorkshire accent, "pick up tha' musket."

Kit grinned.

"You're a lifeline," Petra said.

Anthony winked at her.

"You know what *you* are."

She watched them walk away together, unsteadily over the coconut matting, hand in hand, Anthony gesturing about something, Kit as scruffy as a bundle of dirty washing in that sleek company. She looked down at the pushchair. Barney had finished the raisins and torn the box open so that he could lick traces of residual sweetness from the inside. He had faint brown smudges across his fat cheeks and on the end of his nose.

"Where," Petra said to him, "would we be without your granny and gramps?"

It was amazing, Charlotte thought giddily, to be so violently happy. It was better than waterskiing, or dancing, or driving too fast, or even the moment just before someone you were dying to kiss you actually kissed you. It was amazing to feel so beautiful, and so wanted, and so full of hope, and so pleased to see everyone and so awed and triumphant to have someone like Luke as your husband. Husband! What a word. What an astonishing, grown-up, glamorous word. My husband Luke Brinkley. Hello, this is Mrs. Brinkley speaking, Mrs. Luke Brinkley. I'm so sorry, but I'll have to let you know after I've spoken to my husband, my husband Luke Brinkley, mine. Mine. She looked down at her hand. Her wedding ring was brilliant with newness. The diamonds in her engagement ring were dazzling. The diamonds had come from an old brooch belonging to Luke's grandmother, and they had designed the ring together. Luke had actually done most of the designing because he was the artistic one, coming as he did from an artistic family. Charlotte's mother was an artist too, of course, but of a very controlled kind. The table where she worked at her meticulous drawings of catkins and berries was completely orderly. It wasn't like Anthony's studio. Not at all.

Charlotte loved Anthony's studio. She thought, in time, that she might rather come to love Anthony himself—oh, and Rachel, of course—but at the moment, with her own father dead only two years, it seemed a bit disloyal to think of loving anyone else in the father category. But Anthony's studio, in that amazing, messy, colorful house, was a perfectly safe thing to love, with all its painting paraphernalia, and sketches and pictures pinned up all anyhow everywhere, and the photographs of birds and models of birds and sculptures of birds and skeletons of birds on every surface and hanging from the beams of the ceiling in a kind of birdy flypast. She'd been there once—it was only her second or third visit to Suffolk—when Anthony and Rachel were looking after their little grandson, Kit, the one who was so shy and difficult to engage with, and Anthony had taken down the skeleton of a godwit's wing from a dusty shelf and drawn out the frail fan of bones so that Kit could see how beautifully it worked. Kit had been quite absorbed. So had Charlotte. When she mentioned, at work, that she had met someone called Anthony Brinkley, a boy looked up from the next desk in the newsroom and said, "*The* Anthony Brinkley? The bird painter? My dad's mad on birds, he's got all his books," and Charlotte had felt at once excited and respectful that she had been shown the godwit's wing by Anthony Brinkley. And now here he was, her father-in-law. And Rachel was her mother-in-law. How amazing to have parents-in-law, and brothers- and sisters-in-law, and to be going to live with

Luke, not in her cramped basement flat in Clapham but in the flat Luke had found two minutes from Shoreditch High Street. How cool was that? How cool was it to be married, well before she was thirty, to someone like Luke and to be so happy with everyone and everything that she just wanted the day to go on forever?

She looked at her champagne glass. It was full again. People kept giving her full ones; it was ridiculous, absolutely ridiculous, but wonderful too. Everything was wonderful. She caught Luke's eye across the heads of a group of people, and he blew her a lingering kiss.

"Quite soon," Charlotte thought, "quite soon, I'll be back in bed with him."

"Don't sit there," Edward said to Sigrid, "disapproving of English weddings."

"I'm not disapproving—"

"Well," Edward said, "you look like someone enduring something that you know you could do much better."

"I don't think," Sigrid said, "that we're being made to feel very welcome. Do you? This is all about the bride's family. If we were in Sweden, the groom's family are made to feel part of the wedding. Remember ours."

"Oh, I do—"

"Your parents were made to feel really welcome. My parents made a real fuss of them. So did their friends."

"You mean Monica Engstrom making a pass at my father—"

"He didn't mind! It's flattering to have a good-looking woman come on to you."

Edward looked round.

"Do you think that's what this wedding lacks? Randy women—"

"It would certainly loosen things up."

Edward nodded towards the group of Luke's friends, which had grown larger and noisier, and seemed now to be equipped with pint glasses of beer as well as champagne chasers.

"*They* look quite loose."

"Boorish," Sigrid said.

"Where's Mariella?"

"Organizing the little girls. She had them in an imaginary schoolroom just now having a lesson on the weather. She has just done weather at school, you see."

Edward was still looking at Luke's friends.

"Luke is only six years younger than me, but that lot feels like a different generation."

"They are single, mostly. Not married, anyway."

Edward took a swallow of his champagne. It was warm now, and faintly sour. He said, casually, "Do you like being married?"

"Mostly," Sigrid said again.

"Your candor. Your famous candor. I remember saying in my wedding speech that you were one of the most honest people I had ever met."

"And?"

"You still are."

"And?" Sigrid repeated.

"And now I sometimes wish you would temper it slightly even while I know I wouldn't believe you if you did."

"I think," Sigrid said, "that our new sister-in-law looks quite stunning, but that she is very young for her age. How old is she? Twenty-six? Twenty-seven?"

"About that. She's certainly a looker. D'you know, Ralph's in that gang over there. What's he doing? He hates all that heavy lad stuff."

"Weddings make people behave very strangely."

"You mean," Edward said, "English weddings."

"I didn't say so."

"But you liked *our* wedding—"

"It was Swedish."

"And Ralph's wedding—"

"That was charming," Sigrid said. "So simple. In your parents' garden and Petra taking her shoes off. Where is Petra?"

"Probably chasing her children."

Sigrid stood up.

"I shall go and find her."

"What shall I do?"

"Find your parents," Sigrid said. "See if your daughter has instructed those children properly about the effect of El Niño. Find out where we're sitting for the meal."

"Salmon," Edward said, "and strawberries. Pink food. Wedding food." He stood up too. "Dad's down there, by that pond thing. Kit's paddling." He paused. "Naked from the waist down."

Rachel had her eye on Ralph. He looked awful. Well, not ugly, Ralph couldn't look actually ugly, but gaunt and tired, with shadows round his eyes and his thick dark hair in tufts, as if he'd had a seriously bad haircut. Which he probably had, being, of all her boys, the least vain, the least worldly, the least concerned with appearances. Of course, all crammed together in a so-called family room at the hotel, they hadn't really slept the night before, any of them, Petra said at breakfast, and then Ralph had taken himself off to walk, just as he used to do when he was a boy, and he'd found some woods and come back looking wild and disorientated after struggling through bushes and undergrowth. Well, Ralph had never been easy to pigeonhole, never been orthodox, that was a great deal of his charm, but it was to be hoped—very much to be hoped—that he wasn't leading Petra too much of a dance by being too inaccessible and uncooperative.

When Ralph and Petra told them that they would like to get married, she and Anthony had been overcome with relief as well as happiness. Petra was exactly what Ralph needed, they told each other; Petra would give Ralph the stability and purpose that he seemed to find so hard to achieve while needing it so badly. And now, when Ralph looked as he did today, and left Petra to cope with the children on an occasion that plainly called for two parents, not one, Rachel felt clutches of the old intermingled anxiety and protectiveness that she'd felt since Ralph emerged into the world and arched away from her when she first tried to put him up against her shoulder.

He shouldn't, Rachel told herself, be in that crowd. Luke's friends were quite different from his brothers' friends, heartier, simpler, more conventional. Luke's stag weekend, a three-day affair in Edinburgh, where he'd been at university, sounded like the kind of thing Rachel could tolerate hearing about only because it involved Luke, her son. Ralph had gone for one night, out of brotherliness, and had then come back to Suffolk and said loyally but briefly that they were all having a good time but that it wasn't really for him. Petra reported later that a lot of drunken shaving of various bits of them had gone on, and that Luke was lucky to get away with saving his eyebrows. So what was Ralph doing, in the thick of that crowd, and was that a cigarette in his hand? Rachel had been so thankful when he'd given up smoking. Ralph was the only child she'd really worried over when it came to drink and drugs; he was the only one inclined to see the possibility of addiction as a challenge rather than a threat.

Perhaps, Rachel thought, she should go and talk to Petra. She could see Anthony and Kit down by the pond— Anthony was now drying Kit off with his handkerchief before persuading him back into his pants and shorts—and presumably Petra would have found a quiet spot in which to spoon another meal into Barney. Barney loved meals. His enthusiasm for food made Rachel and Anthony laugh, although Petra said it sometimes amounted to a tyranny. Rachel, who had been a professional cook all her life, made soups and purées for Petra's freezer, and no doubt it was one of those that Petra was now feeding to Barney somewhere, openmouthed in his buggy like a rapacious little fledgling.

She stood up and smoothed down her skirt, green linen bought in a sale in a dress shop in Aldeburgh, and, as it happened, a good contrast to Charlotte's mother's old-rose lace. Such an odd woman, Charlotte's mother, and anally tidy. Well, at least Charlotte wasn't that. Even by Rachel's standards, Charlotte and Luke left their bedroom in Suffolk in an award-winning state of chaos.

As she moved to start her search for Petra, Ralph materialized beside her. He was holding a bottle of lager and he smelled of cigarettes.

"You okay, Ma?"

She looked at him. He was her adored son, but she had Petra to think of now, too.

"I'm fine," she said. "What about you?"

"What d'you mean, what about me?"

"I mean, are you okay? Is everything okay with you?"

"Of course," he said. He tilted the beer bottle, as if toasting her. "Of course everything's okay. Why wouldn't it be?"

CHAPTER TWO

When Anthony was a boy, the building that was now his studio had been a decayed barn, used for storing the lawn mower, and various defunct pieces of semi-agricultural machinery, and nameless old sacks, and coils of baling twine and rusty wire. It had been a dim and dusty place, with barn owls nesting precariously on the beams and colonies of bats and swifts swooping wildly about in the summer dusks. It was known to Anthony's parents as the Dump, and every year it shed a few more huge slates from its sagging roof, and settled itself more deeply and crookedly into the earth, so that its doors no longer corresponded to their frames, and the small windows at one end had ejected their cobwebby glass into the bed of nettles below.

It was Rachel who had thought of rescuing it, and making it into a studio, Rachel who had come from the Welsh hills and who had such profound misgivings about the flatness of Suffolk and—even more—about moving into the house where her fiancé had grown up.

"God," she'd said to her sister, "you should see it. I mean, it's a lovely house, but they've lived there since the dawn of time. *Everything*'s sacred, everything. Anthony thinks it's all perfect."

Rachel's sister, married to a dedicated inner-city teacher and struggling in a council flat with a splintered front door where someone had kicked it in, didn't much want to hear about huge, if decrepit, Suffolk houses that you were being given—*given*—however much ancestral baggage was inconveniently attached.

"I think you're bloody lucky, Rach."

"Well, yes. It's lucky not to have to *buy* anything. But it isn't lucky to inherit a moldering old heap you're expected to *revere*, rather than restore."

"Balls," said Rachel's sister.

"What's balls?"

"Of course you can restore it. It's your home, isn't it? Give Anthony his bit and make it plain that you've got as much right to the rest of it as his mother had or his granny or his great-granny or whoever."

"What d'you mean, his bit?"

Rachel's sister sighed. She tried not to notice that the aquamarine on Rachel's engagement finger was the size of a Fruit Gum.

"Oh, you know. The shed thing. The place where men go and mess about making things that don't work so that they have to unmake them again. Doesn't Anthony draw?"

"Actually," Rachel said proudly, "rather well."

"There you are then," her sister said. "Give him somewhere to draw. I wish Frank drew. I wish Frank drew or collected beetles or belonged to a cycling club. I wish Frank did anything, *anything*, rather than think it's up to him to save every delinquent kid in Hackney."

"It could be a studio," Rachel said, some days later, to Anthony.

"What could?"

"The Dump."

"But it's always been the Dump."

"Well," Rachel said, squinting up at the enormous East Anglian sky, "it isn't going to be, anymore."

Anthony looked hurt.

"Mum and Dad liked it like that."

Rachel went on gazing upwards.

"Mum and Dad are in heaven, Anthony."

"They didn't believe in heaven. They didn't believe in the supernatural. They thought the mind of man was paramount. As I do. They were pragmatists."

"The Dump," Rachel said, "is not pragmatic. The Dump is a collapsing waste of space. It would make a wonderful studio. It even has a big north wall, for a window. You could paint in there and draw, and make models of birds the size of airplanes. There's enough room in there to *build* an airplane, even."

Anthony sold a piece of his parents' old and unproductive orchard to the neighbors, for the price of turning the Dump into a studio. He put in windows and skylights, and a wood-burning stove, and laid old bricks on the floor and tongue-and-groove paneling against the walls. He brought in old kitchen tables, and battered armchairs from the tobacco-stained snug where his father used to spend long afternoons working on his complicated cross-referenced systems of racing form, and rugs that had worn down to the canvas after a lifetime on stone-flagged floors. He put up his easels, and lines of shelves, and old saddle brackets on which to hang frames. He added books, and the decoy birds carved out of wood that the fishermen once made on Orford Quay when the weather was too rough to put the boats out. And then, in pride of place, he hung a reproduction of Joseph Crawhall's *The Pigeon*, a gouache on Holland cloth, painted in 1894 by one of the Glasgow School, which he had taken Rachel all the way to see, in the Burrell Collection.

"He's my hero," Anthony said.

Rachel had gazed at the pigeon, its white plumage flecked with gray, its pale-coral beak and feet, its hard, wild, small eye.

"It's wonderful," she said. "Why is it so wonderful?"

"Because," Anthony said, "because you feel the inner life of the bird." He took her hand. "In early Chinese culture, bird painting was very important. Not just because birds are so decorative, but because they are wild, inhabitants of the world of air and freedom. The Chinese thought you should observe a bird intently, for ages and ages, and then paint it from memory, making it as vital as possible. They thought that was one of the finest expressions of the human mind, to observe, and then paint like that. Crawhall painted from memory, as he had been taught as a boy. I wasn't taught like that, but I've taught myself. I'd rather there was life and truth in a painting, than romance. I want an emotional charge."

Rachel had slipped her hand out of his, still looking at the pigeon.

"Yes," she said respectfully.

The studio, even separated as it was from the main house by a stretch of weedy gravel, became as significant to their lives as Rachel's kitchen. All three boys had their babyhood daytime sleeps in there, tucked into the huge old coach-built pram that had once been Anthony's, and then, as time went on, brought their homework in, to sit at one of the cluttered tables, and kick the chair stretchers and complain about fractions and French vocab and Mrs. Fanshawe, who went through every head in the school with a nit comb she doused in Dettol.

It was years, though, until the studio, and what Anthony produced in it, made any money. During those years, Rachel cooked for local people's parties and held small informal cooking courses in the kitchen she had made by knocking a warren of little domestic offices into a single space. Her efforts were supplemented by Anthony's part-time job teaching at a big art college fifteen miles away, a job he kept, out of habit and affection, even after his work began to be exhibited, and widely sold, and he was made a Royal Academician. It was a job that had led to his encountering Petra.

He had noticed her, at first, because she never said anything. She sat at the back of the class, dressed in the whimsical and bohemian rags that most of Anthony's students affected, and took notes. When he looked over her shoulder as he strolled, talking, up and down the aisles between the students, he saw that she was writing in pencil, with a strong and characterful script, in a notebook so artisan that she could only have made it herself. Her hair was twisted up in a bit of rough blue muslin patterned with gold spots, and her hands—her nails were bitten, he saw—were half shrouded in torn black-lace mittens. She went on writing as he paused beside her, and he could see that she was writing exactly what he was saying.

"I want to say this to all of you as gently as I can, but correctness can become a terrible inhibition. You see, there's the truth of what we observe, and then there's the truth of how we *interpret* what we've observed. When you're painting a bird, say, you want to give the sense that you were there, that you are responding to that moment in the life of a living bird. Do you see?"

Petra had underscored "terrible" and "interpret" and "there," following his vocal emphases. And later, when he had made them loosen up their drawing arms by sweeping charcoal across great sheets of drawing paper, he saw that she was either a natural, or had been very well taught already, and that she was far, far better than anyone else in the class. But she would not look at him, and she did not speak, and Anthony, feeling as he did when watching the incipient apprehensions of wildlife, did not oblige her to either.

"There's a girl at college," he said to Rachel. "Odd girl. I should think she's nineteen or twenty. Never speaks. But she draws like an angel. It's years since I've had anyone who draws like her."

Rachel was grinding pine nuts for a pesto.

"What's her name?"

"Petra something."

"Petra?"

"That's what it says on my class list. I've never heard her say it. I've never heard her say anything. She's completely mute."

"How peaceful."

"And intriguing. I'm intrigued by her."

Rachel began to drip olive oil into the green sludge of basil leaves and pine nuts.

"Ask her here. I miss all the boys' friends coming round. I used to love that, when the kitchen was full of them and they were all always so starving."

"I can't ask her anything," Anthony said, "until she speaks."

Rachel put a finger into the sauce to taste it.

"Perhaps she'll do for Ralph. He doesn't speak much, either."

"He wouldn't accept any choice of ours—"

"Probably not. Is she pretty?"

Anthony thought.

"Yes—"

"You sound doubtful."

"Well, she's not Sigrid kind of pretty. She's not—not *organized*-looking—"

"Okay," Rachel said, spooning the pesto into a pottery dish they had brought back from a bird-watching holiday in Sicily. "When she speaks and you like how she sounds, ask her here anyway. I could do with more young."

22

"I know."

"D'you remember that poem? 'How Can That Be My Baby'?"

"Pam Ayres."

"Yes. Well, that's me. 'What happened to his wellies with the little froggy eyes.'"

A month later, Petra spoke. Anthony had been talking to the class about the importance of never having an eraser—"Keep going, as fast as the bird moves. Soft pencils, 4B to 6B, pencil sharpener vital but no eraser. Never"—and Petra had looked up and said in a voice presumably hoarse from lack of use, "Is the angle of the bird's body more important than its outline?"

The whole class had turned to look at her.

"We thought you was mental," a boy two seats away said to her, not unkindly.

Petra went on looking at Anthony for an answer.

"Yes," Anthony said.

Petra glanced at the boy two seats away. Then she looked back at Anthony.

"That's what I thought," she said, and went back to her drawing.

Two weeks later, Anthony said to the class, "I wonder if you would all like to come and see my studio?"

It was evident that they all would, and had no idea how to say so.

"Good," Anthony said. He smiled. "All of you?" They nodded. He looked at Petra. "Even you?"

"Yes," she said, and then, "Please."

They came on the local bus, as exotic-looking as a troupe of Shakespearean traveling players. Petra was wearing small, studious-looking steel-framed spectacles, and her hair hung down her back, almost to her waist, over a paisley shawl and purple Turkish trousers gathered at the ankle.

"I'm not going to ask your names," Rachel said, "because I won't remember any of them. But I'm Rachel and he's Anthony, and those are scones I've just made, and that's a chocolate cake. Obviously."

The food released them. They ate with the focused concentration of babies, and then they began to talk. Anthony let them into the studio, and they all gasped and began to chatter and point things out to one another, and Rachel said to Petra, "Do you go bird-watching?"

Petra took her spectacles off. Her eyes were greenish, with a definite dark rim to the iris.

"Not really—"

"Well, you should," Rachel said. "Anthony thinks very highly of your drawing, but you need to observe, like he does."

Petra nodded.

"What about your family? Does anyone in your family draw?"

Petra cleared her throat.

"I don't really have a family—"

"Oh," Rachel said. She waited a moment, and then she said, "Meaning?"

"It all kind of fell apart," Petra said.

"Fell apart?"

"My mother died and my father went, ages ago. And now my grandmother's gone to Canada."

"Why did she do that?"

"Because most of her grandchildren are there. I suppose."

"Leaving you all alone?" Rachel demanded.

"It's okay," Petra said. "We weren't close. I've got somewhere to live."

Rachel looked at her intently.

"What are you doing in Anthony's art class?"

"It's what I want," Petra said. "I work in a football-club bar weekends, and a coffee place weekdays except my college day."

"How old are you?"

"Twenty," Petra said. She put her spectacles back on. "It's okay. I'm okay. I'm used to fending for myself."

Later that evening, Rachel said to Anthony, "I think we should help her."

"In what way?"

"I'll teach her to cook. You take her bird-watching, to Minsmere."

"Rach—"

"She's a brave child," Rachel said. "She reminds me of me at that age, somehow, all stubborn and independent without quite knowing how to do it. And she's got no one."

"Rach, I can't go round rescuing students. You know I can't. Especially girls. You're regarded as an old perv if you even look at a girl student while you're talking to her."

Rachel sighed.

"I'll ask her. I liked her. She's not ordinary."

"Certainly not—"

"And then, after a bit, you can take her bird-watching."

Petra, it turned out, could cook. She'd never made bread, or a white sauce, but she knew what to do with chillies and lemongrass and fish sauce. She had several ingenious ways of turning a budget tin of baked beans into something interesting and surprising. And she was a quick learner. She watched, with the concentrated silence Anthony had noticed in his classes, while Rachel demonstrated various knife skills, and then she did it herself, with considerable competence. Rachel liked having her in the kitchen. In fact, she would have liked her to be in the kitchen far more often, but Petra was working, always working.

"You have to," she said simply. "On the minimum wage. You have to."

"What is the minimum wage?" Anthony said to Rachel.

"Under six quid an hour—"

"Poor child—"

"I know. But she'd rather do it herself. She'd rather be independent."

"Who's this Petra person?" Edward said to his father on the telephone.

"What?"

"Someone called Petra. Mum keeps talking about her. Is she a new cleaner? Wonderful to have a cleaner called Petra."

"Actually," Anthony said, "she's one of my students. A seriously good draftsman. With not a bean and no family. Mum has rather taken to her."

"And you?"

"I don't want to be thought weird—"

"Dad!"

"But I think she's great. She's a bit peculiar and very talented and she's only twenty and she's great."

"Are you grooming her for Ralph, by any chance?"

"They haven't met—"

"Don't dodge the question."

"It has crossed our minds," Anthony said, "that they might have something in common. Yes."

"So you're sort of keeping her on ice?"

"I'm taking her bird-watching," Anthony said slightly stiffly.

"Ah," Edward said affectionately, from his office in London with its view of another office. "Minsmere. The East Hide at Minsmere. The Garden of Eden."

"Exactly," Anthony said, and smiled into the telephone. "Exactly."

He had driven Petra, on one of the rare weekend days she allowed herself off, down the long wooded entry to the nature reserve. She was, as usual, silent, looking about her at the spreading oak trees, the pairs and groups of quiet, earnest bird people, the view out across the marshes to the white dome of Sizewell, like some exotic temple on the skyline.

Anthony had hired her a pair of binoculars, and taken her out among the whispering reed beds, past wooden seats dedicated to the memories of ardent bird-watchers—"He loved all living things"—to the East Hide to see, he said, because it was summer, the avocets in their precise black-and-white plumage, stalking about on their long gray legs with their shiny, upturned black bills questing for worms and insects.

"Avocets," Anthony said, "and, over time, sandpipers and spotted redshanks and black-tailed godwits. All we have to do is wait, and watch. Watch and watch."

It was the first visit of many. They spent, over the subsequent months, hours in the East Hide overlooking the shallow lagoon of the Scrape, with binoculars, and sketchbooks balanced on the wide ledge below the low window that, except when it was very cold, was opened to let in the sounds of the reeds sighing, and the gulls, and the not far-off sea. Sometimes, Anthony left Petra there alone, and took himself off to the bittern hide, to wait for a rare glimpse of the big striped birds stealing through the reed beds and uttering their peculiar booming call. And when he came back to find her, she would never have moved, and the pages of her sketchbook would be filled with the rapid, energetic drawings that gave him such satisfaction to see.

"I wonder," Rachel said, "if it would have felt like this, if we'd had a daughter?"

"No."

"Why d'you say no?"

"Because it wouldn't have felt so friendly. There'd have been baggage. There always is."

"So—"

"So," Anthony said, "we mustn't rock the boat."

Then Ralph came home. Ralph had been traveling. Ralph

had been sent, by the American bank that had, to his parents' surprise, hired him, to Singapore. He had not fitted in to Singapore. He sent e-mails describing his weekend escapes, to islands, to the hills, to stretches of coast not groomed as playgrounds for Westerners who liked their adventures sanitized. He said he would stick it for three years, until he had made enough money to come home and buy a cottage in Suffolk and start up some business of his own, that didn't mean wearing a tie and being a habitué of airports. He gave no hint of what was going on in his personal life, and slid past all Rachel's questions with the ease of practice.

"He'll come back," Rachel said, "married. Or not married. But with a Malay girl or an Indonesian girl. And a baby. There's bound to be a baby. And she'll hate Suffolk and be miserable and cold and then she'll want to leave him and go home."

"Probably."

"Don't you care?"

"Desperately," Anthony said, "but what can we do? What have we ever been able to do, about Ralph?"

Rachel looked at him quickly, and then looked away, but not before he had seen tears spring to her eyes. Rachel had never been tearful, had never resorted to weeping when upset or frustrated—except where Ralph was concerned. Ever since his babyhood, ever since his complex and elusive childhood, Ralph had presented Rachel with a conundrum she could neither solve nor relinquish, an Achilles' heel that she could bear only if she kept him close to her, supervising, involved, worrying. Sometimes Anthony had tried to say that it was perhaps not a good idea to indulge Ralph in his persistent oddness, but Rachel, instantly protective of her own acute vulnerability, as well as of Ralph himself, would fly to his defense.

He was so clever, she'd say, so talented, so unusual, it was really unimaginative, as well as depressingly orthodox and limited, to expect Ralph to conform to mere convention. Anthony seldom argued. Not only did he see how deeply Rachel felt her defensiveness, but he also, to some degree, shared it. When Ralph announced, without preliminaries, that he was off to Singapore, Anthony's guilty relief was tempered by a very real anxiety. Would Ralph ever come back? Or would he, like a character out of a Somerset Maugham short story, go native, and end up in some decayed ex-colonial outpost, soaked in arak and reading ancient Greek philosophy in the original by the light of a kerosene lamp? Or would he, as Rachel had suggested, come home, as ever unannounced, with a girl and a baby, whom he would proceed to dump, without explanation or apology, on his parents?

But then Ralph did come home, alone. He had resigned from the bank. They had begged him to stay, but, despite the fact that many of his colleagues were being sacked, and he was regarded with a fierce envy for being considered worth keeping, he persisted in his resignation. He told the manager of his department that, although he could go on doing what he was doing perfectly competently, he imagined, his heart wasn't in it and he wanted to feel engaged. His manager asked, with some force, if the money he was being offered wasn't pretty engaging, and Ralph said that how he felt wasn't much affected by money, and he'd made enough for now, and he needed to get out of all this tropical tidiness and do his own thing.

"I don't get it," his manager said. "I simply don't get people like you."

"No," Ralph said, "you wouldn't," and then he took his tie off and dropped it in a corporate waste bin with the bank's logo embossed in silver on the side.

He looked, Rachel thought, very well. The bank had required that he have regular and conventional haircuts, and the weekends of hiking and snorkeling had honed him and tanned him. His eyes were clear, and his teeth, courtesy of some skillful Singaporean cosmetic dentistry that he had agreed to, because the bank had paid for it, were a marked improvement on the slightly ramshackle mouthful of his adolescence. He settled back into his old bedroom with complete nonchalance, bundling his business suits on to dry cleaners' wire hangers at the back of his wardrobe, and emerging, as he had done all his life, at random times of the day and night in search of cornflakes or coffee or the sports section of the newspaper.

"Do you have any kind of plan?" Anthony said.

Ralph was hunched over a sudoku, nursing a mug of soup. He glanced up briefly but didn't speak.

"Well," Anthony said, "I don't want to play the heavy father. Or even the especially conventional one. But you are not far off thirty, and have had a thriving, if brief, career, and sitting about in your mother's kitchen in a sweater you have had since school doesn't appear to me to be a very satisfactory way to live."

Ralph regarded his father.

"I've bought a cottage."

"What!"

"I've bought a cottage."

"When—"

"The other day."

"Ralph—"

"It was easy," Ralph said. "I heard about it, I saw it, I liked it, I bought it."

"Where is it—"

"Shingle Street."

"Oh, Ralph—"

"It's cool. It's in a little terrace. Right on the shingle."

"But what will you do, in Shingle Street, how will you earn a living, away from everything?"

There was a pause. Ralph took a noisy swallow of soup and looked back at his puzzle.

"Leave that to me," he said, "why don't you."

When Petra next came, Ralph was out at his cottage, which he had so far declined to let his parents see.

"Why not?"

"I'm painting it."

"Are you? Inside or outside?"

"Inside."

"Oh, lovely. What colors?"

"White," Ralph said.

"Would you like some help? Would you like curtains and things? Why don't you make a list of furniture you need—"

"No, Mum," Ralph said. "No. Thank you."

Neither Rachel nor Anthony mentioned to Petra that Ralph had come home. Petra made a seafood lasagne with Rachel, and then she went across to the studio and watched Anthony experimenting with a brush drawing using black watercolor. He was drawing vultures, angrily squaring up to each other, wings up, heads jutting. Petra sat beside him, like a pianist's page turner, and watched his brush intently. Occasionally he said things like, "Sometimes directional lines are useful," or, "D'you think that's better because it's more a diagram than a drawing?" but mostly they sat in silence broken only by the faint hiss and crackle of the wood-burning stove.

When Anthony finally said, "Tea?" Petra said, "Oh, yes," in a tone that sounded pleased, but also indicated that she could easily have waited, hours if necessary, and then they left the studio and crossed the gravel to the house, and there was Ralph in the kitchen, with white splashes of paint on his hands and clothes. Anthony did not catch Rachel's eye.

Rachel said, "Petra. This is our middle son. This is Ralph."
Petra looked slightly past Ralph.

"Hi."

"Hi," Ralph said. He waited a few seconds. Then he said, "Why are you called Petra?"

"After the ancient city in Jordan," Anthony said, too heartily.

"No," Petra said. She gave Ralph a quick glance. "After the dog. The dog on *Blue Peter*."

"The *dog*—"

"My mother wouldn't have known about Jordan—"

Anthony opened his mouth again.

"Shut up, Dad," Ralph said. He smiled at Petra. "Ignore him."

"It doesn't matter—"

"She was a famous dog—" persisted Anthony.

"Dad says you draw. You draw birds."

"A bit."

"I made a gingerbread," Rachel said. "Tea and gingerbread."

"I'm so sorry. I really am. I should have known about the dog—"

"When I was away," Ralph said to Petra, "in Singapore, the birds were quite different. Utterly different. Very brightly colored. And raucous."

"Yes."

"Mugs or cups?" Rachel said.

Ralph pulled a chair out from the table and gestured at the seat.

"Have a chair. Petra."

She sat down wordlessly.

"Well, mugs, then," Rachel said. "They hold more tea and it stays hotter."

Ralph took the chair beside Petra's. He had, Anthony noticed, paint in his hair as well as on his hands, and a splash above one eyebrow.

"Were you born in Suffolk?" Ralph said to Petra.

"Yes, Ipswich."

"I missed Suffolk. When I was away. I thought I wanted to get away, but I was so relieved to come back."

Petra accepted a mug of tea.

"I've never been away."

"D'you want to?"

"What—"

"Go away."

She looked at him properly for the first time. Rachel risked a lightning glance at Anthony. Surely, surely Petra would be struck by Ralph's looks, only enhanced by old clothes and whitewash?

"No," Petra said. "No, I don't. I think—I think I'd pine."

"Pine," Anthony said. "What a good word. Pine. Like a longing dog—"

"Give dogs a rest, Dad."

"Gingerbread? It's got dates in it—"

"I've bought a cottage," Ralph said to Petra. He took a mouthful of gingerbread.

She waited.

"It's right on the sea," Ralph said, "practically in it. Just down the coast from here."

"Really?"

"It's so bleak, it's thrilling—"

"I—like bleak," Petra said nonchalantly.

"We haven't been allowed—" Anthony began.

Quiet, Rachel signaled, cutting more cake, *quiet*.

Ralph put another wedge of gingerbread into his mouth. Round it, he said, "Like to see it?"

She put her mug down.

"Yes."

"C'mon then," Ralph said, getting up, still chewing.

"But it's getting dark!" Anthony said. "You won't see any-thing!"

Petra rose too. Ralph put out an arm, as if he was going to encircle her, steer her.

"There'll be light enough, off the sea," Petra said.

Ralph smiled down at her.

"I know."

Petra half turned. She said to Rachel, "Thank you. Thank you for tea."

Rachel nodded. Then Ralph almost pushed Petra through the kitchen door and out into the stone-flagged passage beyond. Anthony and Rachel heard the outer door slam, and then the sound of Ralph's car starting up, and the crunch of gravel.

Anthony looked at Rachel. They were both smiling.

"*Well*," Anthony said.

Rachel held up both hands, her first and second fingers twisted together.

"Fingers crossed!"

CHAPTER THREE

Luke took Charlotte to Venice for their honeymoon. The man who had preceded Luke in Charlotte's life had worked in the City, on a busy and hugely successful trading floor, and his taste in holidays ran to Thailand and the Maldives, just as his leisure tastes had included cross-dressing and cocaine. His cocaine habit had, in fact, and finally, put Charlotte right off both him and drugs. She regarded herself as perfectly freethinking in all sorts of social areas, but she was very clear about drugs, and when Luke first asked her on a date she said no, with a vehemence that took him aback.

"What d'you mean, no? Why d'you have to say no like that?"

"Because I saw you," Charlotte said, "I saw you last week, at Julia's dinner party. I don't want to have anything to do, again, with anyone who has their dinner off a mirror."

"It was just a line—"

"People who do coke," Charlotte said, interrupting, "are boring. Really, really dull. They're either jittery because they've just had a fix, or jittery because they want one. Their noses run and they think they're fascinating, but they are so, so boring. Gus was unbelievably boring. I thought I could put up with it for the Club Class flights to Sri Lanka, but I couldn't. So, until you clean up your pathetic little act, you'll have to look for dates anywhere but me."

Luke had been fired right up by this speech. He knew Gus, the City trader, slightly, and he knew that Gus made the kind of money that bore no resemblance to the money that anyone in Luke's family had ever, or would ever, make, even Ed, even Ralph in Singapore, even Dad in his best years. And Gus was not only wealthy, but personable, and athletic, with a flat in Clerkenwell and a brother in a rock band. But if he couldn't keep Charlotte, if Charlotte wasn't prepared to tolerate or join in a habit that was significant in Gus's life, then Charlotte acquired, in Luke's eyes, a particular luster that went way beyond her looks and her energy and her undoubted popularity.

He began to make real efforts. He started going to the gym more often and he stopped using cocaine, even when nursing a Coke Zero in a room full of insanely, irresponsibly hyped-up people made him feel he'd landed on another planet. After a while, he even stopped going to parties where he knew what the menu would include, and instead started taking Charlotte's friend Nora out for coffee and pizzas and other fraternal little meals so that Nora could relay to Charlotte what an impressively changed character he was. He had no idea if this clumsy reformation was working, he only knew that he wanted Charlotte in a way he had never wanted anything in his life before, and whenever he saw her, across a room at a party, he could think of absolutely nothing else whatsoever then, or afterwards. Charlotte, quite simply, filled his head.

And then Gus began to try to win Charlotte back again, and Luke heard unnerving rumors of promises of private planes to

Paris and a chartered yacht in the Caribbean, and he lost his head and hard-won self-discipline and rushed over the river on impulse to the basement that Charlotte shared in Clapham with Nora, and a great many wood lice and silverfish, and found Charlotte on the sofa, in a vest and pajama bottoms, with her shorn fair head unwashed, eating toast and jam and watching *Big Brother* on the television. He stood there, unable to proceed further in any way, and burst into tears, and Charlotte had got up off the sofa and leaned against him, and he had smelled her hair and a faint synthetically sweet whiff of strawberry jam, and had thought he would simply like to die, right then and there, of sheer happiness and relief.

But a year later, and with an engagement ring securely on Charlotte's finger, there was still to be no question of honeymooning in any place that was remotely reminiscent of a tropical spa. There would be no orchids and no Singapore Slings or infinity pools or flawless room service. Gus, poor guy—it was safe just to pity him now, for most of the time, anyway—might be wealthy and hunky and worldly, but he was a philistine. There was no getting away from that. He knew about consumerism, but he hadn't the faintest idea about art, or theater, or literature, or any music that wasn't whatever was playing that week in Mahiki. Luke was going to show Charlotte something different, reopen her eyes to a world she had been kind of brought up to, but had neglected when the buzz of life in London had drowned out all other sounds.

Anthony and Rachel gave Luke some money for the honeymoon. Luke wasn't earning enough to allow for ten days in Venice in the kind of hotel that was expensive enough to be glamorous. With his parents' contribution, he could afford a hotel just behind the Accademia, with polished-black-marble bathrooms and electric window blinds and wide pale beds heaped with pillows. They could have breakfast in their room and glasses of Prosecco on a little roof terrace among the seagulls from the lagoon, and walk out one way to the sunlit Zattere with its air of cultivated seaside, or the other over the Accademia bridge to the *campi* and *calli* that would finally lose them in a labyrinth of bridges and blind alleys and decayed, romantic beauty.

Charlotte was bowled over. She had never been to Venice before. She had never been in an art gallery where pictures on the walls, painted hundreds of years before, showed scenes that she could still walk through, right now, hand in hand with history. She had never eaten tiny soft-shelled crabs out of a paper cone in a fish market, or ridden a water bus, or sat in a hot, dim, late-afternoon church, her bare shoulders swathed in a required paper shawl for decency, and thought about the Virgin Mary as anything more than a sort of sacred cipher that belonged to the Catholic girls at school, and not to anyone else. She had never, either, imagined that she might be married to someone who she not only loved, and fancied so much she sometimes had to lean against something when looking at him, but who knew so much more than she did.

"I don't, you know," Luke said. "I just know about different things."

"But they're important. I mean, Titian, and Carpaccio, and the Venetian Empire, and things. They're important."

"The doges would be so chuffed to hear you say that."

"Are you patronizing me?"

"Only," Luke said, "a little bit."

"I don't mind," Charlotte said, "I really don't. One day I might, but I love it now, it just makes me feel—" She stopped.

"What?"

"That I can do no wrong," Charlotte said, and laughed.

Luke reached across the café table and gripped her wrists.

"You can't," he said.

They had a pact that, in order to preserve the extraordinary and magical bubble in which they were briefly living, they would turn on their mobile phones only once a day, in case there was an emergency. There was never an emergency. There were texts hoping they were happy—cheerfully, rudely expressed from most friends—and a few from Luke's partner in the little graphic-design studio they shared in a shabby building not far from St. Leonard's Church in Shoreditch, but there was nothing that couldn't be ignored, or replied to in moments; nothing, certainly, that needed them to speak to anyone except each other, beyond ordering Americanos and glasses of wine, and little cups of green-tea ice cream from a specialist shop off the Campo di San Tomà. It was only on the last day but one, chugging back across the lagoon from a slow and languorous day on Murano, that Luke held his telephone out to Charlotte and said, "What d'you think?"

There was a short text on the screen. It read, "Bro. Things tricky. Need to talk. Ring? R."

"Ralph?" Charlotte said.

"Mmm."

"Something that can't wait till we get home?"

"Sod him," Luke said. "Why can't he wait till I *am* home?"

Charlotte squinted at the hazy blue outline of Venice advancing towards them across the glittering water.

"Maybe he's forgotten we're still away—"

"Typical."

"I don't," she said, "know them very well. Your brothers, and sisters-in-law. It didn't occur to me, it didn't seem to matter—"

"It doesn't matter."

She transferred her gaze to look at him.

"It kind of does, now. It's not just a you thing, it's an us thing. Your brother sends a text like that, and you begin to look all preoccupied and distant, and I'm your wife now, so I'm in the loop, too."

Luke put his phone in his trouser pocket. He leaned forward, pinning Charlotte against the rail of the vaporetto, and put his chin into the angle of her neck and shoulder.

"Wife—"

"Don't change the subject."

"I'll ring him later. When I don't want to thump him for being so thoughtless."

"*Is* he thoughtless?"

Luke took his chin away, and stared past Charlotte at the cemetery walls of San Michele as they slid by.

"By normal standards, yes. But Ralph isn't normal. He's brilliant and he's impossible. I missed him like anything when he was away, and it was so peaceful at the same time. You are so bloody gorgeous."

Later, while Charlotte was showering in the black-marble bathroom, with the window open to the warm, bell-haunted sounds of early-evening Venice, Luke rang Ralph. Charlotte knew he was ringing, so she had the shower turned on full, and she sang as well, for good measure, in order to indicate to Luke that she was in no way going to influence or preempt any reaction Luke might be having in response to whatever it was that Ralph had to say. When she had finished, she wrapped herself in a large white towel, ran her hands through her hair so that it stood up in the soft damp spikes Luke seemed to like so much, and went through to the bedroom. Luke was lying on the bed with his shoes off. His phone was some distance away, on Charlotte's side of the bed, as if he had just chucked it there.

Charlotte sat down on the edge of the bed beside him. She waited for him to ruffle her hair, or untuck her towel, or slide his hand underneath it. But he lay there frowning, looking ahead at the silvered wooden cabinet that housed the television.

"Is he okay?"

Luke went on staring ahead. He said shortly, "He's losing his business."

"*What?*"

"The bank won't either extend his credit or lend him any more, despite him offering their home as collateral, so he'll lose the business."

"Oh my God," Charlotte said.

Luke took her nearest hand.

"He said he suspected it would be that bad, at our wedding. He said he was sorry he was a bit weird, but he couldn't help thinking about it."

"Was he weird?"

Luke sighed.

"He got plastered. He was smoking. Mum and Dad were furious with him."

"Do—do they know?"

Luke raised Charlotte's hand to his mouth and looked at her over it.

"No. They don't. Nobody does, except Ed, and now me. He hasn't told anyone. He hasn't told Petra."

Charlotte felt a clutch of panic. She wanted to say, "You'd tell *me*, wouldn't you? You'd always tell me everything. Wouldn't you?" but sensed that if she did she might not get any answer that reassured her. So instead she said, "So, even if he'd offered their house to the bank and they'd, say, accepted, Petra wouldn't have known anything about it?"

Luke regarded her solemnly.

"Yes."

"But that's awful—"

"It's to protect her."

"What?"

"Not telling Petra is protecting her. So's not to worry her."

41

Charlotte took her hand out of Luke's.

"That's not right—"

"Petra's got no family," Luke said. "We've all sort of become her family, so there's this unspoken thing about looking after her. She's only twenty-four, or something."

"Two years younger than me."

"Not a real comparison, angel."

"But," Charlotte said, "she's his *wife*. They've got *children*. It's a thing you do *together*, bad times."

Luke sighed. He twisted himself round, and lay so that his head was in Charlotte's lap. Then he reached up to untuck the towel across her breasts. Charlotte put her hand on his.

"Don't—"

"Why not?"

"The mood's not right—"

"Bloody Ralph."

"It's not Ralph," Charlotte said, "not really. It's Petra. It's this Brinkley thing of treating Petra like a child."

"Well, she is in a way—"

"Only if you all make her like that. She was managing okay on her own, I gather, before she met Ralph—"

"Just."

Charlotte looked away. She said, "It's like Ralph found her under a hedge or something, like an abandoned kitten."

"She was in Dad's art class. He said she never spoke but she was brilliant. She is brilliant. At drawing, I mean."

Charlotte looked down at Luke. She began to stroke his thick hair back from his forehead.

"And then Ralph fell in love with her—"

"Well," Luke said, gazing upward and thinking how amazing Charlotte looked, from every angle, even when foreshortened from underneath, as she was now, "I suppose he did. I mean, he liked her, he really liked her, but I'm not sure getting married was ever top of Ralph's to-do list."

"Did she ask him, then?"

"Oh no," Luke said. He caught Charlotte's hand and put it sideways, lightly, between his teeth. Then he took it out again, and said, still holding it, "She got pregnant."

"Wow," Charlotte said. "So he felt he had to marry her."

Luke ran his tongue along the edge of Charlotte's hand.

"Well, not really. And I don't think Petra would have expected him to, either. She wasn't conventional, any more than he was. She'd probably just have shrugged and got on with it, taking the baby to art classes in a basket, that sort of thing. It was Mum and Dad that wanted the wedding. They wanted them married."

"To be respectable?"

"Not really," Luke said. He heaved himself upright and ran his hand through Charlotte's damp hair. "They're a cool old pair in some ways; they don't mind about how things look, how conformist things are. It was more that they didn't want to let Petra go. They'd kind of adopted her. So they couldn't lose her after all they'd invested, all they'd got used to. At least, that's what I think."

Charlotte was very still.

"Are you shocked, angel?" Luke said.

"No—"

He peered into her face, his eyes an inch from hers.

"What is it?"

"It's a bit silly—"

"What is?"

"How I feel," Charlotte said. "I mean, I've got my own family, who are lovely, and your parents who've been really sweet to me, but when you describe how they feel about Petra, I— well, I feel a bit—" She stopped.

"What?"

"Jealous," Charlotte said.

Luke took his face away a little.

"You are one idiot of an adorable girl."

Charlotte bent her head. She said, "There's Sigi, you see, all groomed and professional and clever and detached, and she's been in your family forever, and then there's Petra, who everyone treats like a daughter, like a little sister, and it's a bit much, sometimes, to have to compete with all that, especially when you've been competing with sisters all your life and you're not academic or talented or anything—"

"Shush," Luke said loudly.

Charlotte didn't look up. Luke put his hand under her chin and tilted it until her gaze was level with his.

"It's only what I think that matters," Luke said. "And you know what I think. And when the family know you better, they'll think it too, which I suspect they do already because nobody could know you and not think it."

He leaned forward and kissed her, without hurry, on the mouth. Then he said, "Bugger Ralph and bugger his problems. We've got far more important things to concern ourselves with," and he smiled at her, and, with a single, deft movement, he took her towel away.

The flat Luke had found for them in London was at the very top of a tall and elaborate brick building in Arnold Circus, a stone's throw, as Charlotte excitedly told Nora, and all her other friends, from Columbia Road flower market, from Brick Lane, from—oh my God—*Hoxton*. The building, like all those that ringed the Circus like a circle of great ships, had been designed as part of a grand nineteenth-century philanthropic project for public housing, to provide light and air and sanitary living conditions for people who had known nothing previously but teeming slum life. The Circus was impressive, built of red brick banded, here and there, with peach brick, like a kind of architectural Fair Isle jersey, and in the center, on a mound flanked by flights of steps and planted with enormous plane trees, was a folksy little bandstand under a pointed roof where Charlotte had, on her very first visit, seen a pair of thin boys picking at guitars and singing raggedly to an audience of mothers with babies in buggies, and neat old men in kurtas and embroidered caps. It had seemed to her wonderfully vivid and wonderfully exotic. She'd bought take-away falafel and a sun-dried-tomato salad from an engaging little place on Calvert Avenue so that they could have a picnic in the empty, dusty flat that Luke had just signed a lease on, and felt the future unrolling before her like a fairground ride, sparkling with lights.

The flat had two rooms, with a kitchen under the eaves and a bathroom with a huge window from which you could see, giddily, far, far below, the decayed strip of low buildings, which now housed a series of artisan workshops, including Luke and Jed's studio. You could even, Charlotte discovered, pick out the very skylight of the studio, and she imagined how, in the winter dark, she could look down there and see, with lovely wifely exasperation, that the lights were on in the studio, which meant that Luke was still down there working, when he should have been up in the flat eating the kind of delicious nourishing supper she was going to practice cooking until she was as good a cook as Luke's mother was. She thought that, what with the number of commissions Luke was now getting from the music industry, as well as the new sidelines he was developing in film, and lighting design for concerts and things, there might be quite a lot of evenings when she would be looking down at that skylight, and seeing the lights still on. She vowed she would not nag. She vowed she would stay as pleased and excited at his growing career as he was, as she was at the moment. She vowed that she would never give him cause to feel that she had to be protected from hard times, like

Petra. She had no idea what Ralph's business was, except that it was some kind of online financial thing, investment advice or something, and she had no inclination to ask further since the whole situation around Ralph and Petra and the little boys and Anthony and Rachel made her feel strangely unsettled, however many times Luke told her that no one mattered to him like she did. She wished she hadn't told Luke she felt jealous. She wished she'd just navigated the whole topic with the kind of grown-up poise that indicated that she was naturally concerned by Ralph's news, but not in the least personally ruffled by it. And so, to make amends to herself for an adolescent moment of vulnerability, she said to Luke, when they returned to the flat from Venice, "Do ask Ralph up here, if you want to talk or anything. He can christen the sofa bed."

And she'd been rewarded by Luke putting his arms round her and saying, his mouth against her ear, "You are a complete doll."

So here she was, getting wedding-present sheets out of their complicated packaging of cellophane and cardboard, and pulling a new duvet out of its box, in order to have them ready, later that day, to make the sofa up for Ralph to sleep on. It was seven in the morning, the sun was out, Luke was showering in the bathroom, and Charlotte, in a denim miniskirt, tight striped vest, and shrunken military jacket with huge brass buttons, was all ready to leave for her job in a local radio station located on Marylebone High Street. In the fridge sat salad ingredients and pieces of salmon to grill, and she would pick up bread during the day, and cheese and strawberries, and Luke would get wine and beer, and she would light candles later and not tell Ralph that he was their first guest ever. He might also turn out to be rather an appreciative guest. Luke said he'd leapt at the chance of coming to London for the night.

"Actually," Luke said, "he asked if it was okay by you. A

first for Ralph, I should think, wondering if he was being a nuisance."

Charlotte banged on the bathroom door.

"I'm off, babe!"

There was a pause while taps and Luke's iPod were turned off, and then he opened the door. He was naked, and wet. He looked her up and down.

"Don't go to work, angel—"

She giggled.

"I've got to. I'm on the eight o'clock shift, which means being there at seven forty-five. You know that."

"I'll be thinking about you all day. All day."

She blew him a kiss.

"Me too. When's Ralph getting here?"

Luke stepped forward and enfolded her in a wet embrace.

"When he gets here. Miss me. Miss me all day."

"Promise," Charlotte said.

Luke's studio was approached along a broad asphalted path behind the Arnold Circus buildings. It was in a long, low line of what might once have been mews, or garages, brick-built with sizable sections of metal-framed windows, broken where the studios behind them were unoccupied. The ground-floor walls were punctuated by battered black-painted doors that, when you pushed them open, gave on to steep, narrow stair-cases that led up to small landings illuminated by dirty windows, floor to ceiling. In Luke's case, one of the two doors on such a landing had been newly painted, in dark-gray matte paint, with a brushed-steel plate fixed slightly to one side of the center eyeline, which read, in black sans serif lower-case lettering, "Graphtech Design Consultants."

Ralph had only been to Luke's studio once before, when Luke and Jed were in the process of moving in, and long before

Luke met Charlotte. They'd borrowed the money for the initial payment on the lease and down payments on their computers from Jed's father, who was separated from Jed's mother and spent most of his time and money restoring classic motorbikes. Luke, who had always been good with his hands, was building drawing boards and installing overhead lighting while Jed sanded the floorboards with a gadget that looked like a giant hair dryer. It had made Ralph think, with some emotion, of how he had intended his Suffolk cottage to be, a private space in which to live and to work without the distraction of obligation to anyone else. It was going to be him, and the white walls, and the uncompromising coastal light, and the sea, and the shingle, and the development of his idea to extend the ease and intimacy of Internet banking into the limitless world of the small investor.

But, of course, it hadn't turned out like that. He had been in the cottage a few months, four or five maybe, with Petra undemandingly there, now and then, drawing gulls on the beach and doing remarkable things with tins of baked beans and sharing his bed with the same absence of claim, or right, that she brought to most things, when she said, quite baldly, that she'd missed two periods, and she thought she was probably pregnant. He had been stunned, then rather overwhelmed and almost tearful, and then asked her, clumsily, what she would like him to do about it.

She'd stared at him.

"Nothing."

"I mean, d'you want to live here? D'you want to come and live here with me?"

"I might."

He'd held her. He thought that if this was love, he liked it. He imagined a baby in his bare sitting room, Petra holding a baby, him holding a baby and showing it the sea, out of the window. But then, impelled by something he could not explain or really remember, they had gone to tell Anthony and Rachel, to *tell* them, not to ask them anything, and from then on everything changed, everything was not only different from how he'd imagined it, but hardly his and Petra's anymore, either.

The cottage had gone. It went almost at once. It was replaced by a little terraced place in Aldeburgh, with a small garden but no view of the sea. Ralph had a good room to work in, but it looked out over sheds and other people's gardens, and a random parking space, not shingle and sea and sky. Rachel made sure it was comfortable for him and pointed out how much better the Internet connection was than it had been at the cottage, and then there was a wedding—which he'd liked, he'd liked a lot—and there they were, living in a little house, in a little town, and the baby turned out to be Kit, two months after they were married. None of it, Ralph thought, standing outside Luke's studio on a summer evening in Shoreditch, was remotely, *remotely*, what had been in his head or his imagining when he had last stood there. And that had been no more than four years ago.

Not only had the studio changed, but Luke and Jed had, too. The studio looked very together, very monochrome and modern with sophisticated track lighting and computer screens set at angles, like drawing boards. Luke and Jed were wearing a similar nonchalant kind of nonuniform: black T-shirts, combat trousers, carefully designed trainers, and Luke had a wedding ring now, a flat band of white gold that made his left hand look weirdly grown-up. He gave Ralph a rough hug, and Jed high-fived him and said he'd got to go, good to see him, take care, man, and had hooked a black leather jacket over one shoulder and loped out of the studio and down the stairs, whistling. And then Luke said, "You don't look too hot, bro."

Ralph perched on one of the black stools by the computers.

"How's Charlotte?"

"Great."

"And Venezia?"

"A-mazing."

Ralph took a pack of cigarettes out of his jacket pocket and held them out to Luke.

"Smoke?"

"No thanks," Luke said, "not anymore. No drugs but alcohol. And not in here."

"Come *on*—"

"You can smoke outside. Not in here."

Ralph shrugged. He dropped the pack back in his pocket.

"Tell me," Luke said.

"What, now? At once?"

"I don't want you boring Charlotte later. I don't want Charlotte thinking my brothers are tedious and problematic."

"Okay then," Ralph said. He stuck his hands in his jacket pockets and stared at the ceiling and the skylight.

"Bad, bad, bad?" Luke said.

"Yup."

Luke said nothing. He glanced at his watch. Charlotte would be home in ten minutes.

"I've had my small-business account closed," Ralph said.

"Ouch—"

"Sometimes I have to wait up to six months for commission on something I do. Sometimes even longer. That means I need a good overdraft facility, it's important. No, it's crucial. And four months ago, the bank just raised the interest rate. Bang. Just like that. Five percent to 9.9 percent, take it or leave it. And—" He stopped. He looked at Luke.

"What?"

"There was my personal overdraft rate. It was bad enough, anyway. It was 9.9. And they upped it, no arguing, to *19.9* percent even though I'd never exceeded the limit. And when I objected, they said I'd only get a better rate when there was more money going in. So I pointed out that more money was hardly likely to go in if I was being caned for my necessary, and *agreed*, business account, and they said tough. I have no assets they seem interested in, so it's the end of the story. Except that my investors, the friends from Singapore who helped me set this up, aren't happy. You can imagine the e-mails I'm getting."

Luke said softly, "It's scandalous."

"Too right."

Luke sighed. He scratched the back of his neck. It wouldn't help Ralph if he said how sorry he was. Ralph never liked people being sorry for him.

"Have you told Mum and Dad?"

"Not yet."

"Petra?"

"Nope. Just Ed. And you. Like I said on the phone. I wouldn't have done that, if I didn't need you to know before Mum and Dad do."

Luke jammed his fists into his trouser pockets. He felt terrible about Ralph, but he wanted to be up in the flat before Charlotte got home. He said, scuffing at the black floorboards with the rubber toe cap of his boot, "What are you going to do?"

CHAPTER FOUR

E very weekday morning, Sigrid bought coffee from an Italian who ran a tiny stall, not much more than a cupboard, opening out onto the pavement not far from the laboratory where she worked. The Italian, a voluble man from Naples whose English had hardly improved in thirty years of speaking it, preferred blondes, and every so often he insisted on either giving Sigrid her coffee for nothing, or adding a café-style biscotto as a present, dotted with almonds and chips of bitter chocolate. Sigrid liked all this. It was one of the bonuses—the many bonuses—of living in London. In Stockholm, where she had grown up, true blondes, like her, were two a penny.

Sigrid's laboratory, independently funded but loosely affiliated with London University, was tucked into the basement of a building in Bloomsbury, behind the School of Hygiene and Tropical Medicine. In the mornings, during school terms, and when it wasn't her turn to drive a carload of small girls to their junior school in Highgate, Sigrid tidied the house, then walked the length of Upper Street to the Highbury and Islington Tube Station, and caught a Victoria Line train to Warren Street.

Then, via Marco and his coffee stall, she walked down Gower Street, to work.

Sigrid's father was an engineer, and her mother a doctor; Sigrid had one brother, who had become an avant-garde composer and wrote scores for cult movies, largely made in Berlin, where he now lived. Sigrid herself had taken a master's degree in computational science at the University of Uppsala, followed, through English student friends she made there, by research at the faculty of engineering at the University of Loughborough, which was where she had met Edward, who'd gone there to celebrate an old school friend's birthday. What a weekend that had been! Even twelve, nearly thirteen years later Sigrid couldn't recall that weekend without smiling.

And now here she was, thirty-eight years old, Edward's wife, Mariella's mother, and in command of her own particle accelerator, which could analyze materials without destroying them and was thus invaluable to museums and art collectors alike. Her triumph, the year before, had been to examine a sixteenth-century pen-and-ink drawing for a private collector, and establish that both the ink and the paper had come from the same time period, and geographical location, as Leonardo da Vinci himself. The collector had been beside himself with excited gratitude. He had wanted to give Sigrid and her family a skiing holiday in his chalet in Gstaad. But Sigrid had declined graciously. In her lab coat, with her hair tied back and her spectacles on, she was not the blonde in knee-high boots whom Marco wanted to give free coffee to. And as far as her professional life was concerned, it was the lab-coat Sigrid who prevailed.

Walking into the building off Gower Street, holding her coffee and her briefcase, Sigrid thought gratefully of the prospect of her lab coat. The head of the laboratory was away at a conference in Helsinki, and whenever he was away the assumption was that Sigrid was in charge, an assumption that nobody in the laboratory seemed to question except for a clever, ginger-haired boy called Philip who craved Sigrid's attention and believed that challenging her authority was a successful way of getting it. Yet this Monday morning, even the prospect of batting Philip's tediousness away was attractive; better anyhow than spending the weekend listening to Edward on the telephone to his parents, or his brothers, or his parents again, in an endless cycle of anxiety and suggestion and countersuggestion and exasperation, that had finally driven her to take Mariella, and her three best friends for that week, to eat immense pastel-colored cupcakes at an American bakery that seemed to be the current nirvana for the whole of Mariella's class.

"So bad for you," Sigrid said, watching them eat. "All that fat and sugar. Empty calories, every mouthful."

Mariella's friend Bella had held out an alarming deep-red cake, iced in buttercream. Her mouth was frosted with it.

"Red velvet," she said. "Taste it. You'll see. Worth getting fat and spotty for."

In the evening, after Mariella was in bed—accompanied as she was every evening by her iPod and seventeen stuffed animals, all of whom would be offended, Mariella said, if they were anywhere but on her bed at night—Sigrid laid out their customary Sunday-night supper of Matjes herring, black bread, and pickled-cucumber salad, and then took a glass of New Zealand Sauvignon Blanc to the small room off the kitchen where a big plasma television screen had been fitted into a wall of bookcases. Edward followed her. Sigrid sat down on the sofa opposite the screen and aimed the remote control at it. Edward leaned forward and took the remote out of her hand.

"Please don't," Sigrid said.

Edward sat down close to her.

"I need to talk to you."

"You've been talking all weekend—"

"Yes," Edward said, "but not to you. I've been talking, as you well know, to my fucking maddening family, and I need to talk to someone with some sense."

Sigrid sighed. She put her wineglass down on the nearest pile of magazines and turned to face him.

"Okay."

"*Please* don't say it like that."

"Well," Sigrid said, "I know your family. And I know how you all operate. So I can't feel very hopeful, now, can I?"

Edward reached across Sigrid for her wineglass and took a swallow from it.

He said, "I cannot believe the fuss they are making—"

"Can't you?"

"No," Edward said. "I mean, Ralph has lost his company, which is very sad, but not really surprising when you look at the high-handed way he's behaved to his bank all along, and they're all reacting as if one of the children had been run over. I kept saying to Mum it's only a *job*, Mum, and she said, oh, he'll never find another one in this climate and what about the mortgage, they can't afford that and Dad and I can't help them at the moment and Petra is distraught—"

"Is she?" Sigrid said.

"Is she what?"

"Is Petra distraught?"

"Well," Ed said, shrugging, "when I spoke to her, she sounded as if she was doing the usual Petra thing of being all vague and unconcerned till everything had blown over and someone else had thought of a solution."

"Well then."

Edward put his hand out again for Sigrid's glass. She moved it deftly out of his reach.

"Get your own."

Edward sighed.

"It isn't Petra. I mean, in a way it is because she's such a professional eternal child, but it's also Mum and Dad panicking and Ralph at his most unhelpful because he feels he's handled it all so badly, and he has."

Sigrid took a sip of her wine and offered the glass to Ed. He looked at her gratefully. He said, "I could cheerfully strangle the lot of them."

"Have you spoken to Luke?"

"Yes."

"And?"

"He's still on honeymoon. In his head, anyway. He says it's rotten for Ralph and scandalous of the bank, but Ralph's got to deal with it."

"He has," Sigrid said.

Ed took another deep swallow of Sigrid's wine.

"I'm the eldest, Sigi. I feel I have to prop up the parents and help the brothers."

"Only up to a point. You can't choose their lives, you can't live their lives for them, you can't stop your parents having the priorities they have."

"You mean Petra."

"Only partly," Sigrid said.

Edward put the wineglass down and took Sigrid's nearest hand.

"The geography doesn't help. All of them living so close and being so involved with each other. I said something so stupid to Mum—"

"What?"

"I said," Ed said unhappily, "I said, because she said she was really wound up about it all and wasn't sleeping and stuff, I said just leave it to me and I'll think of something and ring you tomorrow, and you know how pseudo-tough she is and never cries and all that, and she did cry, well, nearly, and she said, oh thank you, darling, thank you, in a way she never does normally, and now I'm in a hole because I'm exhausted by it all and can't think how on earth I'm going to come up with anything constructive by tomorrow."

Sigrid let a silence fall, but she didn't take her hand away. Instead, she let her gaze travel along the lines of family photographs in their glass-and-chrome frames, which sat on the front edges of some of the bookshelves, her parents on their boat, her parents dressed up for some formal occasion at the Grand Hotel in Stockholm, her brother in a leather coat and dark glasses on a Berlin street, Mariella in a tutu, on a bicycle, in a playpen, on a beach, Anthony and Rachel on Ed and Sigrid's wedding day, his brothers and their wives on theirs, Ralph and Petra's little boys posed on a hearthrug with some colored wooden bricks. Then she looked back at Edward.

"I can think of one thing. One thing you could do."

He sighed again. He said, despondently, "What?"

"Well, Ralph is clever, isn't he? He was successful in Singapore—"

"Yes—"

"They wanted him to stay."

"Yes—"

Sigrid moved to the edge of the sofa, preparatory to getting up and returning to the kitchen for supper.

"Well," she said, "why don't *you* offer him a job?"

It was only much later, Sigrid thought now, pulling off her boots and sliding her feet into the ergonomic molded clogs in which she worked, that Ed had confessed that he thought Ralph—even if work could be found for him—would be very difficult to work with. So difficult, in fact, that he, Edward, wasn't at all sure he could do it. It was at that point that Sigrid had lost her temper. She said a great deal about Edward's attitude to his family, and contrasted it with her attitude to her family, and then she said that she, too, would find working with her own brother difficult, but if she decided to do it she would just *do it*, for family reasons, and not go complaining on, as all the Brinkleys did, and all the time, about everything, *everything* was a drama with them, and then she had gone into the bathroom and locked the door and, staring at herself in the mirror while she brushed her teeth, told herself that tomorrow she would be in her laboratory, with interesting, impersonal work to do and, even if there was irritating Philip, there would be no Brinkleys, and no circular conversations, and nobody asking for advice in order to ignore it.

And here she was now, clogs on, hair tied back, ready. In a sealed box, wrapped in acid-free paper, on the bench by her accelerator and microscopes, lay a fragment of medieval textile, sent from a significant church in Florence, about which Sigrid had all the interested skepticism of the cradle atheist. She opened the door to the lab, almost humming in anticipation of a day ahead free of all the clinging tendrils of family preoccupations, and saw at her bench, actually sitting on her particular stool and peering into one of her microscopes, ginger-haired Philip.

Mariella liked her rare journeys to school with her father. She liked her father being tall—taller than most of the other fathers—and she liked his black car with its blond interior, and she liked being able to talk to him when she had his individual attention. His attention, at the weekend, had been all over the place, which meant that her mother had been distracted too, although she would have denied it, which rather diminished the eventual victory about the American bakery and the cupcakes. They had gone, certainly, but Sigrid hadn't been wholehearted. Like most only children, Mariella was aware of every nuance in parental mood.

"Daddy," she said, buckling herself into the front seat of the car beside her father, "are Ralph and Petra going to have absolutely no money at all, not even enough money for cornflakes?"

"*Uncle* Ralph," Edward said automatically. "*Aunt* Petra."

"Petra said to call her Petra. What do you do if you have absolutely no money, not even enough to buy a tiny little piece of cheese that would be too small even for a mouse to live on?"

"They aren't like that," Edward said. "They have plenty of money for cheese and cornflakes."

Mariella spread her hands. She had a tiny blue daisy transfer on her smallest left fingernail, which she had daringly left on for a school day.

"So they're okay?"

"Exactly."

"You go jabbering on," Mariella said, "all weekend, and then you say there's nothing to worry about."

Edward turned the car expertly away from the curbside and into the traffic along the street.

"It isn't quite as black-and-white as that. Uncle Ralph needs to find different work to do."

"For when the money runs out?"

"Well, yes, kind of—"

"He could be a doctor," Mariella said, "or a weatherman. Or he could be in the post office, selling stamps. Mummy says there are never enough people in the post office, and the queues are terrible."

Edward slowed the car at the first traffic lights.

"It takes six years to train to be a doctor."

"Wow," Mariella said admiringly.

"And you need a science degree to be a weather man, and selling stamps might not produce quite enough money to look after them all."

"Petra could work," Mariella said. "Like Mummy does.

Mummy says it's good for women to work. She says look at Bella's mother spending her whole life having her toenails painted."

"I don't think she said that—"

Mariella tossed her head and felt her school-day plait thumping against her neck.

"Well, she *looked* as if she was going to say it."

"Maybe she just thought it."

Mariella stared out of the car window in silence.

"Or, maybe," Edward said, "*you* thought it, looking at Bella's mother, and then you just found you'd said it."

Mariella inspected her daisy transfer.

She said, "D'you think we should spend next weekend making food and putting it all in a basket and driving to Suffolk to give it to Ralph and Petra?"

"That's a very nice idea."

"Shall we ask Mummy?"

"Let's."

Mariella glanced at her father.

"If you and Mummy run out of money, Daddy, you're to tell me. Okay? At once."

"Really? Why? Suppose we want to protect you?"

Mariella snorted.

"If I don't *know*, then I can't do anything about it, can I?" She kicked at the rubber mat that protected the carpet in the floor well under her feet. "That's not protection."

"Oh?"

"No," Mariella said firmly. "That's just daft."

Edward rang Sigrid at lunchtime. He told her about his conversation with Mariella and said he hoped she was having a good day untroubled by human provocation, and that he was going to talk to his managing director about Ralph because even though the bank wasn't much in a hiring mood, there were still some opportunities in the analysis team. Sigrid told him about Philip.

"And he'd brought me flowers."

"What? *Flowers?*"

"Cornflowers. Really rather pretty."

"Fuck Philip—"

"I was so cross," Sigrid said. "I was so cross that he tried to disarm me with flowers. I've put them in a mug in the little place where I eat lunch sometimes. I hope he gets the message."

"As long as you don't like them—"

"Oh, I like *them*," Sigrid said, "I just don't like being given them."

Edward said, "I'm really sorry about the weekend—"

"That's okay."

"Mariella wants us to bake cookies and stuff for Ralph and co."

"At least she's practical," Sigrid said.

"I'm trying to be, too. Just one thing—"

"What?"

"I quite understand," Edward said, "why you said a lot of what you said, last night, and you were right about most of it. But—"

"But what—"

"It's much easier," Edward said, "to be detached and grown-up about your family, if said family is safely in another country. That's all."

"Is that a judgment?"

"No," he said, "it's an observation."

"Then you said it in the wrong tone of voice."

"Sigi—"

"I would like," Sigrid said, "to see more of my family than I do. I would *like* the chance to get as exasperated with them as you do with yours."

There was a brief pause and then Edward said shortly, "See you later," and put the phone down.

Sigrid's colleagues—three girls, a quiet and competent middle-aged man, and Philip—were either eating various forms of lunch in the cubbyhole adorned with the mug of cornflowers, or out. Sigrid wrote a note to deter any further interference during her absence—"Please do not touch under any circumstances"—and weighted it under a stapler on her bench, and then went out of the lab to retrieve her boots and have half an hour in a café to settle her thoughts and her temper. As she passed the cubbyhole, Philip looked up from the tub of pasta salad he was eating with a plastic fork, but did not speak. She dared to hope she had quelled even him into silence.

Walking briskly, she crossed Tottenham Court Road and made for Charlotte Street, and the lounge of a hotel where she could be sure of coffee and a sandwich and the brief peace of anonymity granted by a public space. The hotel was unaggressively hip, with most life in it being concentrated in its brasserie, so Sigrid found an armchair in a corner, ordered a smoked-salmon sandwich, put on her spectacles, and opened a book to deter interruption—there was a breed of men who seemed to believe that any blonde alone in a bar or hotel lounge had been left there like a parcel, expressly to be collected—and applied herself to straightening her thoughts.

It was not, she told herself firmly, that she did not like Edward's family. She had always liked them, from that first visit to Suffolk when Ed wanted to show her off to his parents as the prize he had secured, and now she was used to them. She had grown up in a first-floor flat in a good part of Stockholm, furnished with pared-down modern furniture interspersed with elegant gray-painted Gustavian pieces inherited from her father's mother, and the color and sprawl of Anthony and Rachel's house on the flat Suffolk coast had been a great surprise to her. But she was accustomed to it now, as she was to Rachel's robust cooking, and Anthony's energetic emotions, and the expectation that anyone who came in from the outside would acknowledge, as a matter of course, that they would be subsumed into the Brinkley way of thinking, the Brinkley way of doing things, because the Brinkley way was— well, the best way.

Her sandwich arrived, on a square white-china plate, garnished with frondlike pea shoots. She regarded it. Smoked fish. Her parents probably ate smoked fish at some point every day. If they—she and Edward and Mariella—lived in Stockholm, would there be a quiet but determined pressure on them to eat smoked fish, too, on a daily basis? Would her parents, unshowily preoccupied with their own lives and professions as they were, be insistent that Sigrid and her family lived their lives by the same rules and expectations as they did themselves? Was Edward right? Had she somehow idealized her parents because they were tidily in Sweden, and not messily right here? She bit into the sandwich. Was she being unfair?

She leaned back in her chair, chewing, and closed her eyes. I have been here in England, she told herself, for fourteen years. I have been in London for twelve years. I like it here, I like London, I like England, I don't want to go back to Stockholm. But—she took a little breath, as if to give herself the energy to pursue the thought right through to the end—although I am not an outsider to Edward, to Mariella, to most people I meet and work with, I am still a foreigner to my parents-in-law. To them I am Our Swedish Daughter-in-Law. I may be made welcome and made at home and invited to help Rachel in the kitchen, but I am always a little bit the stranger, the one who captured their son before he could meet an English girl, and married him in a place that wasn't their place, and in a way that wasn't their way. And nothing can ever change that, because I was born in Sweden, and however good my English is—and it is good—I speak with a slight singsong, as Swedes do, and so every time I open my mouth I remind them.

And then there is Petra. I don't mind Petra. I am quite fond of Petra, in fact. She is not, perhaps, a natural fit for me as a person, but she makes no difficulties, she is not jealous or possessive or unpleasant; in fact, she is sweet in her odd way, and Mariella loves her and loves to help with the little boys. But she is treated differently from me. Nothing is said, but it is in the *attitude*. Petra is English, Petra is an artist, Petra has no family to support her or look after her, Petra is something they can own, and shape, and make think like they do. And what they don't remember, Sigrid thought suddenly, angrily, is that every time they pull Petra a little closer they make a little more distance between them and me, and, because I don't have my family in this country, I feel that distance, and when I feel it I am sometimes cold to Edward, to punish them through him, and then I am sorry, and angry with myself, and with them, and end up crying in hotel lobbies and not eating my expensive sandwich.

She opened her eyes, sniffing, and sat upright, pulling a pack of tissues out of her bag. She blew her nose decisively. This was ridiculous. She was a grown woman, a scientist, a wife and mother. Her English parents-in-law were not unkind to her. She had a lovely house and enough money and a husband and daughter who thought the world of her. Her job was to support Edward through family crises, especially when he felt, as the eldest son, that everyone was turning to him in the hope of a solution, and he could not think what that solution could be. It was not her job to isolate him, and refuse to help him, or listen to him, and then shriek at him when he touched a raw nerve in her, which he never did out of malice, but only because he was a man and therefore sometimes clumsy.

She picked up her sandwich. There was something else now, too, to add to the mix. There was Charlotte. Gorgeous Charlotte, the baby of her family and plainly babied by them, especially by her mother who had, since the death of Charlotte's father, devoted herself to her maternal and grandmaternal roles. How would Rachel and Anthony turn out to be with Charlotte? Would Luke stand up to them, in her defense, if she wanted him to? How was Luke going to manage, balancing the expectations of the Brinkleys? And how would Charlotte relate to Petra, and to the place Petra had at the heart of the Brinkley family? Sigrid swallowed her mouthful. Somehow, the thought of Charlotte made her feel better, less excluded, more able to look at the situation as something that could be perfectly well managed. She blew her nose again, and smoothed her hair back, and looked up to ask someone to bring her some coffee.

There was a man standing in front of her. He was about her age, in a dark suit, and he was holding a glass of wine and a bottle of water. He had a black-leather satchel slung over one shoulder, and with the hand holding the wine he made a little gesture towards the armchair beside Sigrid's.

"Mind if I join you?" he said.

She gave him a minimal smile.

"No, thank you," Sigrid said, "I am just about to make a call to my mother in Sweden. And then to my sister-in-law. If that answers your question?"

Mariella was sitting on the stairs. She had been about to go into the kitchen, on the pretext of wanting someone to hear her spelling list, but in reality to nail her mother for a while before she was sent to have a bath, but had been deterred by discovering both her parents in there already, with their arms around each other.

When Mariella was younger—much younger—she had hated finding her parents embracing without her, and had always fought her way in between them so that she became the focus rather than they to each other. But now, although she was relieved to see them behaving in a way that meant they probably weren't going to get divorced, thank goodness, she found she wished they'd just get it over with, and be like normal, because it was a bit embarrassing, really, and made her feel weird. So she had retreated to the stairs with the cat's cradle someone at school had shown her how to do, made out of a length of purple wool, and she was singing to herself to cover any potentially disconcerting sounds that might emanate from the kitchen, like kissing, when the telephone on the hall table rang.

"I'll go!" Mariella shouted.

She scrambled off her step and down to the hall to seize the telephone. She was supposed to say, "The Brinkleys' house," when she answered the phone, but she always said, "Hello?" on a rising note instead, because that's what her parents did.

"Mariella?"

"Yes—"

"Mariella, it's Charlotte."

Mariella thought.

"Charlotte! Your new aunt, Charlotte."

"Oh!" Mariella said, beaming. "Oh, *hi*."

"You were such a cute bridesmaid," Charlotte said. "You looked so great. Everyone said so. I really liked having you as my bridesmaid. What will you do with your dress?"

"Mummy says she has no idea," Mariella said truthfully. "You can't exactly go Rollerblading in pink silk, can you?"

"Did she say that?"

"Oh yes," Mariella said.

"Oh."

Mariella took the phone back to her seat on the stairs. She said confidingly, "Everyone's really worried now about Ralph and Petra."

"Yes," Charlotte said uncertainly.

"Daddy says they've got enough money for little things, like cereal, but not the big stuff. We're going to make a huge load of food and take it to them at the weekend. Are you coming?"

"No," Charlotte said.

"Why not?"

"We're going to see my mother," Charlotte said. "You remember my mother?"

"Yes."

"Well, she's doing a big lunch for me and Luke and my big sister Fiona and her husband and my other big sister Sarah and her husband, and all the little girls you were bridesmaid with."

Mariella settled herself more comfortably.

"So it's going to be a party?"

"Yes," Charlotte said. "My family is big on parties. We have parties whenever we can. When you come to our next party, you can wear your bridesmaid's dress, can't you?"

"Okay," Mariella said.

"Is Mummy there?"

"Well," Mariella said, "she is, but she's doing something with Daddy."

Charlotte began to giggle.

"They'll be finished soon," Mariella said. "They're only in the kitchen."

Charlotte was laughing.

"Don't interrupt them—"

"No, *thank* you," Mariella said.

"Could you give Mummy a message?"

"Okay."

"Could you tell her that we'd love to meet up, as she suggested, sometime. Love to. But at the moment, we just haven't a minute, we're flat out, hardly even time to brush our teeth—"

She sounded, Mariella thought, a bit overexcited, as if she wasn't breathing properly.

"I'll tell her."

"Thank you," Charlotte said, "thank you. Give them my love. No, give them *our* love. Byeee!"

Mariella clicked the phone off and sat looking at it for a while. Then she lifted her head and called out to the kitchen, "Mum! Charlotte's too busy to see you at the moment, but she'll see you sometime!" and then she untangled the cat's cradle from her fingers and went slowly up the stairs to her bedroom, singing a cheeky song they'd made up at school, about some of the teachers, that was supposed to be a complete and utter secret.

CHAPTER FIVE

W hen Ralph was in a mood, Petra had learned, it was better not to be in the house. She thought of his moods like
fog, or dark smoke, drifting silently under the closed doors of
his office and seeping into all the corners of the house, so that
every room was invaded, and affected, and even Barney, who
was the epitome of straightforward good cheer, looked at her
with anxious eyes and an unsteady lower lip. On such occasions, she had discovered, the best thing was to bundle Barney
up into his buggy and collect all the paraphernalia necessary to
nourish and change both little boys, and just leave quietly, no
notes, no door banging, just a swift, undramatic, unremarkable
exit.

In the winter, she usually turned towards the High Street—
past all the cottages with their seaside names, Shrimper's
Cottage, Mermaid Cottage, Gull Cottage—because Kit loved
the shop windows. She hardly ever bought anything, largely
because she had never been in the habit of shopping, but
she liked grazing along the windows at Kit's pace, past the
ceramic curlew in the little gallery window, which was priced

at a fantastical—to Petra—two hundred pounds, and the dentist with a plaque of a buxom mermaid coyly brandishing a toothbrush while reclining carelessly on a row of teeth fixed to the wall, and the pharmacy, which sold buckets and spades in summer, to the amber shop, where Kit yearned for the tiny seals and elephants carved out of amber the color of barley sugar. And then, for Barney's especial delight, they would trail slowly down the other side of the High Street, and stop, for ages, outside the sweet shop, which had huge, foil-wrapped sweets in the window, through which you could see pretty jars on white shelves and more sweets than you could dream of. Barney never made a sound outside the sweet shop. He simply craned forward in his buggy, his arms and fat little hands held out towards the window in rapture, like someone prostrating himself before an altar.

But in summer, as it now was, their walks went the other way. They would turn out of their scrap of front garden—Kit pointing out, every time, that it was so sad that they didn't have a name, only a number, 31, on their house—and go past the primary school, where they would always stop for Kit to admire the bas-relief of a ship at sea on the gable end, and the fence made of giant colored pencils that divided the playground, and then they would proceed, very slowly, on account of all the things that needed to be examined on the way, down the King's Field footpath to Petra's allotment.

Kit approved of the allotment. He liked the way other people in the allotments flew patriotic flags, and he liked Petra's little shed, where she kept her tools, and the elder and lilac bushes that hung over it, and the special wicket gate you went through, from the path. He kept some toys—a plastic digger, a dumper truck, a tractor—in the shed, and he would get these out with a workmanlike air while Petra settled Barney, and found a hoe and straightened bean canes. He was, Petra often reflected and sometimes pointed out to Ralph—even if it was hard to tell how much it registered with him—very contented when he was in her allotment, and seemed to be free of most of the cares and apprehensions that stalked his waking hours.

"Perhaps," she said to Ralph, "he likes being in a sheltered space. He likes knowing where the edges are."

Ralph gave a little bark of laughter.

"Then he's not like me—"

But nobody, Petra reflected, peering under the stiff, abrasive leaves for new courgettes, was much like Ralph. That was what she had liked about him, apart from his looks, when she first met him; she'd liked his difference, the way he came from quite a posh background, but you'd never know it from the way he talked, or dressed, or thought. He'd been a banker once, after all, in a suit and tie, and even, he told her, with manicured nails because his Singapore office required you to have that done because your hands were on show at meetings, and bitten nails and ragged cuticles gave an impression of insufficient professionalism.

Well, everything about Ralph was a bit ragged now. He needed a haircut, he shaved in a haphazard way that made him look worse than if he hadn't shaved at all, and he wore the same T-shirt every day unless Petra actually picked it up off the floor and put it in the washing machine. Petra didn't mind Ralph looking untidy—heavens, untidy was a natural and proper state to her way of thinking—but grubby and neglected was another matter. And even if Ralph had been the kind of person you could tell off, or try to change, it wasn't in Petra's nature to do either, even if it occurred to her, now and then, that Ralph was the least susceptible-to-change human being that she had ever met in all her life.

Rachel had often tried to talk to her about this aspect of living with Ralph. She was sympathetic to Petra, Petra knew that, and anxious to help and even to ameliorate some of the exigencies imposed by sharing your life with someone who could take imperviousness to extraordinary levels. But Petra, who had never experienced the smallest element of emotional possessiveness until she had children, was aware that she owed at least the courtesy of gratitude to Rachel, but saw no need to oblige Rachel by minding the way Ralph was, more than she did. She didn't want to interfere with the way Ralph lived or made money for them to live on. She didn't want to change him any more than she wanted him to change her.

Except—well, now she *had* changed. Having Kit and Barney had changed her. Things that would never have crossed her mind as worrying were now troubling her, mundane things like security and fatigue, and the sharing of anxious, fragile burdens like Kit's propensity for unhappiness. She didn't know if she felt like this because of hormones and motherhood, or because Rachel and Anthony's concern for her had infected her and made her believe things were the matter that would never have entered her head to matter if left to themselves. She just knew, with a heavy heart, as she laid a shiny little row of courgettes on the grass strip that edged her allotment, that Ralph's current money and employment worries and his family's urgent and vocal concern were getting to her in a way that nothing had ever got to her before, and were knotting her stomach, and her mind, and making her look at her children as if her urgent and only duty towards them was to shield them from harm.

And Ralph would not talk to her. He was the same as he always was with the children, affectionate and even interested in his intermittent way, but he would not discuss any of his business troubles with her. Petra, who had never even had a bank account before she met the Brinkleys, knew that the bank had refused Ralph something he could not operate without, which was presumably a loan, but she did not know why this refusal spelled disaster, or what degree of disaster it meant. When she thought about having, perhaps, to leave their house, she only felt fear that Kit and Barney would lose the familiarity of their shared bedroom, but when she had tried to voice this alarm to Ralph, he had simply said, hardly looking at her, "You can always go to Mum's, can't you? Take the boys to live with Mum and Dad."

She straightened up and looked across the allotment. It was a bright day with a nursery-rhyme sky of small, solid white clouds decorating an expanse of satisfactory blue. Kit, squatting beside his truck, was filling it with pebbles, which he was piling in carefully, one by one. Barney, under the dappled shade of the lilac bush, was asleep, his hands clasped comfortably on his belly like a caricature alderman. It was lovely, peaceful and contented and safe. Petra looked down at her sneakers, stained where Barney had dropped a buttered cracker upside down. It was perfect, yet she could see only how frail it was, how temporary, how susceptible to being destroyed by the prospect of going home to Ralph's silent fury with himself for having let them all down. She wondered, with a sudden wild pang of nostalgia, where the peace of mind she used to have when there was only a fiver in her pocket, and a drawing class in prospect, had gone.

She crossed the allotment and crouched down by Kit.

"What are those for?"

Kit didn't look at her.

"To make a wall."

"What kind of wall?"

Kit went on piling.

"So the bad guys don't get in."

"What bad guys? What do you know about bad guys?"

Kit shrugged.

"There aren't any bad guys," Petra said. She leaned forward.

"There aren't any. And if there were, I'd look after you. I wouldn't let them come."

Kit gave her a quick glance and went on with his pebbles.

"I'm sorry," Petra said, "but we've got to go now. We've got to go home—"

Kit got up abruptly. He drew his right foot back and then kicked his truck hard so that the pebbles sprayed out across Petra's strawberry bed, among the canes that held up her sweet peas.

"NO!" Kit yelled.

Rachel was in their kitchen when they got home. Ralph was there too, in his half beard and usual T-shirt, and he had made Rachel a mug of tea, and was holding one himself with the air of doing something strictly for politeness' sake only. On the kitchen table, which still bore the remains of the children's breakfast, was moussaka in a pottery dish and a plastic box of nectarines and a chocolate cake dotted with Smarties.

"Boys!" Rachel said.

She put her tea mug down and darted round the table, kissing Kit and swooping Barney out of his buggy. She held Barney so that he could see the cake.

"Look!" she said. "Look! Look what Granny's brought you!"

Barney curved himself over her arm and leaned down towards the table.

"Where's Gramps?" Kit said.

"Painting," Rachel said. "Where d'you think? Gramps is always painting, isn't he?"

"That's kind," Petra said. "I mean, the food—"

"We aren't actually short of food," Ralph said.

"Well," Rachel said, jiggling Barney, "you won't be, after this weekend. Mariella's baking for you. She rang to tell me.

She's having a bakeathon, and they're bringing it all up on Sunday."

"Mariella's coming?" Kit said.

Ralph moved to take Barney out of his Rachel's arms.

"Mum, we aren't refugees, you know—"

Barney flipped himself round so as not to lose sight of the cake.

"No, of course not. But food never comes amiss. Does it, Barney?"

"Who's coming?" Ralph said. "Are they all coming?"

"Well," Rachel said with a slightly dangerous emphasis, "Ed and Sigi and Mariella are. But not Luke and Charlotte."

"Why not?" Ralph said sarcastically. "Why aren't they all coming, bringing cast-off clothes and blankets and unwanted toys?"

"Don't be difficult," Rachel said. "They aren't coming because Charlotte's *mother* is having a lunch party—"

"So?"

"Luke," Rachel said, "is needed *there*."

Kit stood on tiptoe, holding the edge of the table, and quietly, slowly pushed his forefinger into the chocolate cake until stopped by his knuckle.

"Kit!"

He did nothing, but merely stood there with his finger in the cake. Rachel seized him and pulled him back. Petra gave a little scream, half a sob, and fled from the room. Rachel looked at Ralph over Kit's head.

"It's all too much for her—"

"Of course it is," Ralph said savagely, "if you all behave as if it's the end of the world."

Rachel said nothing. With a knowledge of the kitchen that caused Ralph to exclaim under his breath and Barney to regard his father's furious face, three inches from his own, with grave alarm, she opened a kitchen drawer, took out a long-bladed knife, and said to Kit, "Let's cut it properly, shall we? Let's cut it and then you and Barney can both have some."

"A *huge* piece," Kit said.

"Magic word?"

"Huger," Kit said.

"What about please—"

"Please," Kit said.

Barney lurched forward in his father's embrace.

"It's okay, Barneykins," Rachel said, "there'll be cake for you."

Ralph pulled out a kitchen chair and sat down, confining Barney with one arm. Rachel said, "Shouldn't you go and see if Petra's okay?"

"No."

"Ralph—"

"She's okay. She's by herself. Being by herself is what she does when she needs to."

Rachel put two slices of cake onto plates. Barney was purple with desire.

"Are you sure?"

"Yes, Mum!" Ralph shouted.

Kit jumped. He shot his father a fleeting, terrified look. Rachel lifted him onto another chair and put the cake in front of him.

"Don't shout," she said to Ralph.

"Don't make me shout."

"There, Barney, there. Just stop him putting the whole thing in at once! No hurry, Kit darling, try to eat slowly. I actually had a purpose in coming."

Ralph broke off a piece of Barney's cake and ate it.

"I bet you did."

"It's about Petra," Rachel said.

"Oh yes?"

"When did she last do any drawing?"

Barney pushed his plate slightly to one side out of Ralph's reach, and hung over it possessively.

"I don't know," Ralph said. "Ages ago, months, before Barney maybe—"

"That's what we thought. We thought that what she needs while everything is so up in the air is the chance to do some drawing. To have a bird day."

"It's not up in the air," Ralph said.

Rachel ignored him. She fetched a cloth from the sink and began to dab at the chocolate smeared on her grandsons' faces.

"We thought we'd take the boys next week, for a day or so, and then you and Petra can have some time together, or Petra can go off and draw."

"Okay," Ralph said. "Great. Fine. You can do it on the Wednesday."

Barney stretched out, removed the cloth from Rachel's hand, and dropped it neatly on the floor. Then he put his whole face down into the cake.

"Barney!"

"Wednesday?" Ralph said, pulling Barney back but making no attempt to wipe his face.

"Why Wednesday?"

"Because," Ralph said, "I have an interview next Wednesday."

"Darling!" Rachel said. "Fantastic! What amazing news."

"It's an interview, Mum. Not a job. An interview."

Rachel came round the table and put her hands on his shoulders.

"Where is it? Where is this interview?"

Ralph looked across the table at Kit. Kit had picked the Smarties off his piece of cake and was arranging them on the rim of his plate. He glanced up at his father, as if to check that there would be no more shouting.

"London," Ralph said.

77

*   *   *

When Petra had first gone to Rachel and Anthony's house, as a student in a group of students, it had struck her as being a wonderful place. It looked quite formal outside, with its soft old bricks and defined white windows, but inside it had been only comforting, random and colorful and warm, with crooked floors and sudden steps and beams and odd patches of paneling. She had been bowled over by Anthony's studio, by Rachel's kitchen, by the easy authority they both exercised in their particular spheres. But back then, of course, on subsequent visits and until Ralph came home, she had been alone with Rachel and Anthony, the only child, as it were, and she was lapped about with the privilege of being the only young thing in a place that had largely evolved for the nurture and stimulation of a family. Nowadays, however, what with her own family, with Ralph's brothers and their families, with so many diverse claims upon the house and its chief occupants, going there no longer had the luxury of the past, or the sense of individual significance. Sometimes going there now, being there, she even forgot to speak, she forgot to claim the right to be spoken to, included. Sometimes, too, Ralph said to her on the way home, "Are you sulking?"

It had been like that today. The house had felt as if it was roaring with people. Mariella, a lock of her long hair carefully wound with colored threads, and bead bracelets on her wrists, had dumped a huge baker's basket on the floor of the sitting room, and proceeded to give a kind of performance of benefaction, producing biscuits and buns and cake out of it to the exclamations and applause of everyone. Except Petra. Petra was very fond of Mariella, and very touched by the fact that this baking bounty had been entirely her idea, and partly her achievement, but, in that rowdily enthusiastic company, she found she simply could not speak because she felt she in no way belonged to what was going on. It was too *much*. And Ralph looked mutinous.

Lunch was, if anything, even worse. Rachel had cooked superbly, as usual, and lavishly, as usual, and Kit had eaten three roast potatoes, with gravy, and asked for a fourth, and Rachel had been delighted. And, when Luke's absence had been mentioned, and mentioned again, and analyzed, and discussed, and Charlotte's mother had been relegated to being the inevitable reason for his not being there, the conversation had turned to Ralph, and the prospective interview, which was apparently at Edward's bank, by Edward's connivance, and everyone was extremely pleased with him for engineering it and equally certain that Ralph would acquit himself well because he was, after all, so clever, wasn't he?

"What if you get the job?" Anthony said.

"What do you mean, what if I get it?"

"Well," Anthony said, "it's City-based, isn't it. You can't commute from the Suffolk coast to the City every day. Can you?"

"Of course I can."

"No, you can't," Rachel said. "You'll be exhausted. You'll never see the children."

And then Ralph had said calmly, not looking at his parents, not looking at Petra, "We'll have to relocate then, won't we?" and then, as an answering hubbub rose around the table, he lifted both his hands in the air and shouted, "No more speculation! No more discussion! Stop!" and Petra had a distinct sensation that, if she just gradually pushed her chair back to the wall, she could melt into it somehow, and vanish, and escape through it into the air and freedom the other side, and nobody—except Kit—would even notice that she was no longer there.

"Are you sulking?" Ralph said on the way home.

"No."

"What is it then?"

"I'm stunned," Petra said.

"What by? That I've got an interview?"

Petra glanced over her shoulder. Both boys were asleep in their car seats. Barney's mouth was open.

"No. Of course not."

"What then?"

"You said," Petra said, "you said that we might have to leave Suffolk."

"No," Ralph said, "I didn't. I simply said that if I couldn't manage the commute, we might have to relocate."

"I can't do it."

"I'm not asking you to leave Suffolk. Maybe we just move nearer Ipswich."

"No."

"You used to live in Ipswich. You *know* Ipswich."

"That was before," Petra said.

"Before what?"

"Before you. And the boys. And being by the sea, and everything."

Ralph said nothing for a mile or two. Then he said, "Nothing's happened yet. Why are we crossing bridges we haven't even got to?"

Petra stared out of the car window.

"There's always new bridges. I liked it at Shingle Street. I've got used to it at Aldeburgh. I don't want to get used to something else."

Ralph turned the car into their little street. He said, "You may have to."

Petra said nothing.

Ralph said again, louder, putting the brake on decisively, "You may have to."

"No," Petra said.

*　*　*

Later, when the boys had been bathed and Barney was in his cot under his dinosaur mobile, Petra said she was going out.

"Where?" Ralph said. He was reading to Kit.

"Just to the allotment—"

Kit began to scramble out from under his duvet.

"I want to come—"

Ralph put restraining arms around him.

"No."

"Yes, yes, I want to—"

"No," Petra said. She bent and smoothed Kit's hair back. "I'm just going quickly. By myself. I'm going to pick the strawberries."

Kit began to cry.

"I'll come and kiss you when I'm back. See if you can still be awake when I come back, see if you can stay awake that long."

"Stay with me," Ralph said.

"Are you talking to me?"

"No," Ralph said, "I'm talking to Kit."

Petra let herself out of the house, and turned towards the footpath. It was a calm, sweet evening, with an apricot light from the sinking sun, and a little sharp breath of air coming up from the sea. Petra went along the road past the school, and then crossed to take the path down towards the allotments, remembering that she had forgotten to bring something to put any ripe strawberries in and wondering if she could balance them in a courgette leaf, or make a pouch out of the hem of her sweatshirt. She'd never owned a sweatshirt before she had children; she'd never considered anything so practical and comfortable and washable. She hadn't needed to.

A little way down the path, there was a lowish wall with a flat top, the boundary of the garden of a house that Petra fantasized about. Often, on the way home from the allotment, she would put the brake on the buggy and lift Kit onto the wall, and they would gaze together in silence, and Petra had the sense, as she so often did, that Kit understood something in her because that same element was in him, and thus entirely a matter of course. There was a grassy stretch below the wall, running away to a big, still pond edged in shrubs, some with lime-green-and-purple leaves, and then beyond that the ground rose sharply and dramatically in a little cliff, at the top of which sat the house. It wasn't a beautiful house, it was simply a big, friendly house, commanding the garden and land in front of it from its wonderful position, surveying the marvelous trees below it, and then the marshes and the reed beds, and beyond that the sea, glimmering away in the distance. The house gave Petra a feeling of something more profound than calm, a sense of fitting in, of homecoming, of being a ship at last in safe harbor. It gave her, in fact, the very opposite feeling that being in Rachel and Anthony's house today had provided. Just looking at it made her feel better, and it wasn't even hers. And never would be.

She squinted up at the sky. A few geese were crossing the far horizon, faintly honking, and there were swallows diving in the soft air. She would see, she told herself, what happened after Wednesday, and at least Ralph knew now what she couldn't do, what she wouldn't do, and how she wasn't so stupid that she couldn't see when support segued into suffocation. She took a few deep breaths, her hands flat on the wall top. She didn't belong to anyone, not even to Kit and Barney, any more than they belonged to her. She was, however overlaid she had become by the kindness of expectation, the benevolent burden of obligation, still her own person.

In her allotment, Kit's dumper truck still lay where he had kicked it, on its side, spilling pebbles. Petra got down on her hands and knees and gathered up the pebbles, and mounded them up neatly because Kit would need them next time he came, with the intensity peculiar to childhood. Then she dusted out the truck with a dock leaf, and began to pick the strawberries, one by one, carefully, laying them in rows in the truck with their green stalks all facing the same way, as she knew Kit would like her to do. And when she had picked all the ripe ones, she took her penknife out of her pocket and cut a fat bunch of sweet williams, dark red and striped white, and laid them on top of the berries. Then she stood up and looked down at the truck. It was the most satisfactory and healing sight of the day.

CHAPTER SIX

Charlotte was, as usual, home before Luke. Her shifts at the radio station were long, but they were regular, and when they were done they were done, and someone else came in to take over the things Charlotte did, like greeting and shepherding guests, and fetching cups of coffee and glasses of water, and organizing taxis to take the more important guests to wherever they were going next. She liked it that a lot of the guests, especially the regular male ones, either asked for her specifically or made a flattering fuss if it wasn't her shift, and it was Ailsa instead, who was attractive but small and slight and inclined to a more classic wardrobe than Charlotte's. Sometimes, of course, the guests went too far and demanded Charlotte in a frankly sexist way, like the well-known actor who'd said loudly that day, "Where's Miss Well Stacked and Wonderful?" but mostly it was just gratifying to be asked for.

"You *are* well stacked, of course," the female producer of the afternoon show said, not looking at Charlotte but at the computer printout in her hand. "And it's a great pity that, as far as he's concerned, you can't return the compliment, and point out his pitiful inadequacy."

"Oh, I wouldn't do that—"

"I know," said the producer, looking up, "you wouldn't. That's why we put up with you. If you weren't so good-natured, we'd be obliged to detest you."

Now, standing in her own bathroom in the flat, Charlotte opened her shirt and surveyed her bosom. She'd had quite big breasts ever since she was thirteen, but were they now even bigger? And were they, when she unhooked her bra, and pressed the sides tentatively, slightly tender, in the way they sometimes were just before she got her period? That is, when she last had a period. She hadn't, actually, had a period for almost two months, not since before the wedding, when she had done some calculations to see if she was going to have a period either on her wedding day or—worse almost—on her honeymoon. But, as it happened, she hadn't had a period for— she paused and ticked off the dates on her fingers—nearly eight weeks. Which she hadn't made too much of, in her own mind, because her periods had been so irregular since she stopped taking the Pill, as the doctor had warned her they might be. She looked at herself in the mirror with a kind of awe and instinctively laid one hand flat across her stomach.

It was Luke who had said she should stop taking the Pill. She'd swallowed it, almost without thinking, ever since she was in the sixth form at school, and Luke had said to her one evening, very seriously, looking at her across a supper table while they were both eating a Thai green curry, that he thought, now that her future was with him, she should give her body every natural chance and stop putting chemicals into it, however sophisticated and finely judged those chemicals were. He said he was very happy to take contraceptive responsibility, in fact he would like to, so could she please go home and flush the remainder of the month's supply down the lavatory and give her amazing body the chance to do its own wonderful thing.

Charlotte had been enchanted by this speech. It was thrilling

JOANNA TROLLOPE

to have Luke be so mature, and so masterful, and to see her body as something that needed respecting, and taking care of. When she had thrown away the pills—Luke had remembered the effect of contraceptive pills on the potency of the male population via a contaminated water supply—she felt unbelievably womanly and fertile and powerful, and this had been very satisfactory for both of them to the point where Charlotte supposed that, if you were quite simply happy enough, you didn't really need to sleep. Nor did you need to think too urgently about the precise and efficient use of contraception if your husband had told you, in his alluringly commanding way, to leave it all to him.

So she had. And now she was standing in her bathroom, with her shirt unbuttoned, and her bra loosened, just wondering. That's all—just wondering. Her breasts might not look *much* bigger, but they certainly didn't look smaller. And they were tender, just very slightly tender. Charlotte licked her lips. She found she was holding her breath. And then she remembered, with a sudden, joyful rush of relief, that if in fact she *was* pregnant it didn't actually matter, this time, however much they had planned to give themselves two years of freedom before they even considered a baby. This time, Charlotte thought, there need be no frantic rushing to the chemist for a pregnancy-testing kit, no anxious furtive sessions in a shared bathroom, no three-in-the-morning silent rehearsals of how she was going to tell her mother, should the test be positive. This time if—*if*—she really was pregnant, it would be something to celebrate.

She pulled her bra back into place and fastened the only two buttons on her shirt she considered necessary, tucking it into the top of the skirt, which had caused Ray, the black guy on reception at work whom everyone loved, to say he didn't know why she didn't stop pretending and just come to work in her knickers. Then she went across the sitting room to the kitchen, and the bag she had left on the worktop containing the ingredients—chicken pieces and a pot of hot salsa—for supper. She would put the pieces of chicken to marinate in oil and lemon juice, as her mother did, and wash the salad leaves and measure out the couscous she'd decided on to accompany the chicken, and only when that was done, and the table was laid, would she ring Luke in his studio and ask him—without telling him her simmering suspicions—when he thought he'd be up for supper.

Luke had some new graphics software. It enabled him not just to view things three-dimensionally, but to design in three dimensions too, and the afternoon had been extremely absorbing in consequence. He had a new commission, to design the logo and publicity material for a small chain of spa gyms in Essex and East London, and the software was enabling him to come up, even at this early stage, with some amazing ideas that he was certain the marketing team for the gym would really like. So when his phone rang, and he knew it would be Charlotte, he picked it up and said, "Swing down here, babe, I've got something to show you," even before Rachel had time to say, "Darling?"

"Mum," Luke said, in quite another tone of voice.

Rachel said, "I don't think it's me you want to hear—"

Luke tucked the phone in between his ear and his shoulder.

"I've got a new toy I want Charlotte to see."

"A work toy?"

"Oh *Mum*," Luke said, laughing. "Of course—"

"I won't keep you," Rachel said. "It was just that you hadn't rung since the weekend, and as we didn't see you I wondered how things were?"

Luke kept his eyes on his screen and his hands on his mouse and keyboard.

"Great, thank you."

"Did—did you have a nice weekend?"

"Fab," Luke said. "Five-star lunch, played tennis—we won—with my new brothers-in-law and Char's sister Sarah, who has a momentous backhand. Terrific."

"Oh, good," Rachel said without enthusiasm.

"It was such a lovely day," Luke went on blithely, "that we stayed for supper. Char's mother—I mean Marnie, I keep forgetting to call her that—gave us loads of fruit and veg. We're eating raspberries twice a day."

"I have a marvelous crop here," Rachel said. "You could have picked all you wanted and hardly made a difference."

"Everyone okay?" Luke said.

"Who exactly do you mean—"

"Well," Luke said, "you and Dad, Ed and Sigi and Mariella, Ralph and Petra and—oh, what about Ralph and Petra?"

"Ralph has an interview."

"Wow. Fantastic. Well done him. Who with?"

Rachel said, "Haven't you spoken to your brothers either?"

Luke shifted his phone a little.

"Nope. Haven't spoken to anyone. Too busy with work and marriage, Mum. Just too busy."

"Ralph has an interview Ed got for him. Ed's been wonderful. And Mariella baked the little boys a basket of cookies and things. We had a wonderful day all together."

"Good," Luke said.

"We missed you."

Luke shut his eyes for a second. He removed the phone from his neck, and put it against his other ear and said, "What a relief about Ralph."

"It's only an interview—"

"But it's a start."

"Why don't you ring him? To wish him luck—"

"Mum," Luke said, "I'll make my own decisions about who I call—"

"Ralph's your brother—"

"I know."

"And he's in trouble."

"I know that, too."

"It would have been supportive if you'd come at the weekend."

Luke closed his eyes again. He remembered Marnie handing him the basket of raspberries on Sunday night, and giving him a quick kiss, and a pat on the shoulder, and saying how glad she'd been to pass the care of her Charlotte to someone like him. He thought of saying to his mother that he had another family in his life now, as well as his own one, and although his priorities would never change they were priorities and not the only pebbles on the beach. But then he thought, immediately, of how the conversation might develop in consequence, and so he contented himself with saying good-humoredly, "Cut it out, Mum," and then adding straight afterwards, "We'll be up in Suffolk soon, I promise. Char's longing to show you the wedding pictures."

"Lovely," Rachel said flatly.

"You can see them all on the website now, if you—"

"I'd rather you showed them to me, darling."

"I will, Mum. And I'll ring Ed and I'll ring Ralph, and now I must go and find Charlotte."

"Give her my love—"

"Sure will. Love to Dad."

"Love to you, darling," Rachel said. "Love to you."

Luke pressed the end button. The phone rang again at once.

"You were engaged," Charlotte said reproachfully.

"It was Mum—"

"For *ages*."

Luke sighed.

"Oh, you know. Rabbiting on about last weekend—"

"What about last weekend?"

"We didn't go to Suffolk—"

"Of course not," Charlotte said, "we went home. We had a lovely day at home."

"We did have a lovely day. Babe, I miss you."

Charlotte giggled faintly.

"Come on up, then."

"You come down here."

"Why?"

"I've got something to show you."

"Will I like it?"

"You will," Luke said, "be very impressed by it."

"So will you."

"I'm impressed already—"

"No," Charlotte said, laughing. "No. Not about that, whatever it is, but about me. About something I've got to tell you."

"Tell me now—"

"No."

"Go on—"

"No," Charlotte said. "It's the kind of thing you have to tell in person."

"Then you get your person down here!"

"Okay—"

Luke blew a kiss into the phone.

"Can't wait to see you," he said. "*Hurry.*"

Luke was awake. Wide awake. It was two forty in the morning and Charlotte was beautifully, profoundly asleep beside him, her pale head almost on his bare shoulder. What she had told him that evening in his studio had been momentous, even more momentous, in a way, than when she'd agreed to marry him, because it was such a surprise and such a responsibility and such a change and such a joy. Luke moved a hand and laid it on Charlotte's nearest thigh. He felt flooded with the most enormous and primitive sense of sheer potency.

He hadn't really taken much notice when Sigi was pregnant. He'd been on his gap year, in South America, when Ed and Sigi were married, and although there'd been a huge amount of communication about the wedding and offers of airfares, Ed had telephoned Luke, when Luke was by Lake Titicaca, and said look, we're fine about you not coming back for the wedding, it's only Mum and Dad fussing really, you stay in Bolivia and we'll get together after you're back. So Luke had remained, and made his way down to the Chilean coast and then across to Argentina, where he stayed with a friend from school, whose parents had an estancia near Rosario, and rode out every morning through fields of wild parsley. And when he finally got home a few months later, he discovered that Ralph hadn't turned up for the wedding, either, and that Ed and Sigi were living in a flat in Canonbury in conditions, it seemed to him, of impressively grown-up settledness, as if they'd been married for years.

Sigrid had got a new job then, in a laboratory attached to a police forensic unit, and she did that job for a few years before announcing, in her steady, undramatic way, that she was pregnant, and by then Luke was deep in life at uni, and this pregnancy was not much more than another cheerful piece of news to be slotted in among all the other buoyant preoccupations in Luke's mind at the time. Petra, of course, had made more of an impact, because she was not conventional, like Sigrid, and nor had Ralph ever been, and the responsibility for their future, and their baby's, never seemed to be permitted to be their own, but became a Brinkley family project, which sucked them all in, however often Luke said to Ralph, "You don't have to do this, bro. You don't *have* to get married if you don't want to. It won't stop you being a good father, if you aren't married."

But Ralph had been like a sleepwalker. Ralph, who had always been perverse and willful and recalcitrant, seemed almost paralyzed by the thought of this baby, but happy paralyzed, as if he wanted to do whatever would be best for this baby who was going to be, he said in marveling and uncharacteristic tones to Luke, someone of his *own*. And when Luke had talked to his parents, he discovered that they didn't want a marriage in order to be socially acceptable, but because they thought Petra was the only person who could understand Ralph's singularity, and who would be prepared to support him in it, and that—although this was never expressed openly—they had invested too much in this child who had softened the blow of their own children leaving home to want to let her go.

Luke turned to look at Charlotte's sleeping face, at the thick fans of her eyelashes resting on her cheeks. There'd been so much agitation around Ralph and Petra and their wedding that poor Kit's arrival had been almost incidental, brushed over like the final scene of some uncomfortable drama. Luke had driven up to Ipswich to the hospital, to see Petra and Kit. Petra was lying in bed, looking about fourteen, with her hair tied up in a bit of brocade, and her black-lace mittens on, and Kit was parceled up like a solid white grub in a Perspex cradle, red-faced, with an explosion of dark hair. Luke remembered bending over him and thinking, funny little tyke. Looks like Ralph already, but he hadn't thought, oh wow, this is a new life, this is a real person that Petra and Ralph have made between them, this is the *future*.

Which is what he was thinking now. His hand was warm on Charlotte's warm leg. Just a few inches above where his hand lay, something now—probably—stirred, some as yet small collection of cells that would evolve to become a baby, with ears and fingers and toes and, above all, a mind of its own. Tears began to fill Luke's own eyes, brimming up, and spilling over, and running unchecked down the sides of his face into his ears. Please let it be true, Luke said silently into his dim bedroom, please let it be true. Please let there be a baby.

The doctor had confirmed that Charlotte was, indeed, pregnant. About nine weeks pregnant. She'd looked at Charlotte over the top of her reading glasses, and said that Charlotte's age was an excellent age to have a first baby. She made it sound as if Charlotte had done something especially clever, and she smiled broadly and said, well, looking at the two of them, this was going to be a lovely child, and then she stood up and shook their hands warmly, and they went out in the street in a glow of self-congratulation and apprehensive excitement, to celebrate in a coffee shop, which was the limit of the stimulation that either of them were going to allow into Charlotte's system from now on.

In the course of drinking their flat whites—decaffeinated in Charlotte's case—they discussed the advice the doctor had given them about waiting to tell their families until the three-month mark of pregnancy was passed, and Luke had said, "Well, while you ring your mum, I can ring my parents, can't I," and Charlotte had spooned some of her coffee into her mouth and said, "No, after."

"What d'you mean, after?"

"I mean," Charlotte said, "that I'll ring my mother and my sisters first, and when I've done that you can ring your family."

Luke put his coffee cup down.

"Why not at the same time?"

"Because," Charlotte said, as if what she was saying was perfectly obvious, "the mother's mother is always the first to know. The mother's family comes first."

"*What?*" Luke said.

"The mother's mother," Charlotte said, "is the first grandmother. That's how it works. My sisters told my mother first, and then their mothers-in-law."

Luke leaned forward.

"But this baby is half me, half mine. It's as much Mum and Dad's grandchild as it's your mother's."

Charlotte looked at him. Her gaze was clear and confident.

"No, it isn't."

"But it'll be called Brinkley—"

"Don't be so old-fashioned," Charlotte said. "It's not about names. It's about—about the natural order."

"Well, it's the first I've heard of it—"

"You haven't got sisters," Charlotte said, "and your parents have been very lucky, because Sigrid's family live in Stockholm and Petra hasn't got any."

Luke thought for a moment. Then he said, "Are you *sure*?"

"Oh yes."

"It doesn't seem at all fair—"

"Nature isn't fair—" Charlotte said severely.

"Could you—could you consider defying this natural-order whatsit and doing our own thing and ringing our parents together? For me?"

Charlotte took a swallow of coffee.

"No," she said firmly, and she didn't add, "Sorry."

Luke had been strangely unsettled by this exchange. He was besotted with Charlotte, and thought her family were terrific, and refreshingly different from his own, with their sporty, clean-limbed approach to life, and his mother-in-law's neat painting confined to an ordered table in the sitting room, where it made no mess and left no smells or atmospheres. But all the same, they were very other than his family, and his family was as deep-rooted in him as his own DNA, however exasperating and demanding and disordered they might be, and when he thought of how his parents might feel if they ever knew that the accepted grandparental pecking order put them firmly in second place, his heart simply smote him.

Luke knew without a shadow of doubt, and had known it all his life, that his parents were on his side, as they were on Edward's side, on Ralph's. At school, and later at uni, he'd seen friends who were not unreservedly loved and supported as he and his brothers were, and if he ever reflected on his child-hood, he recalled a period of unquestioned security, even if not, both inevitably and properly, of improbable unalloyed happiness. He also thought, now that he came to consider it, that his parents were pretty good grandparents, indeed wonderful grandparents to Kit and Barney and as wonderful to Mariella as distance and differing ways of life permitted. Thinking of the injustice implicit in Charlotte's attitude, Luke grew quite heated, and although it was almost impossible to imagine get-ting angry with Charlotte herself, it was very easy indeed to get angry about the stupidity of a social class or habit that had allowed such thinking to harden into an apparently perfectly acceptable custom.

It was at the end of a long day churning these thoughts about in his mind that Rachel rang again.

"I just wondered," she said, "if we could make a plan for you to come up to Suffolk?"

"Oh sure—"

"We're sitting at the kitchen table," Rachel said, "with the diary, and it looks as if the next three weekends are free, give or take the odd minor thing, so pick any—or indeed all—of them, why don't you?"

Luke said guardedly, his eye on Jed, absorbed in his screen across the studio, "Can I call you a bit later?"

"Why not now?"

"Well, I'm working, and I'd also like to consult with Charlotte."

There was a fractional silence at the other end of the line. In it, Luke heard his father say, "Leave it, Rach," and then his mother said to Luke, "Let me just pencil something in—"

Jed raised his head and shot Luke a swift glance.

Luke said, "Okay. Pencil in two weekends from now. I'll call you later."

He put the phone down. Jed said, his eyes back on the screen, "You should have stayed single, mate."

"Oh no I shouldn't. Nobody in their right mind would have passed on Charlotte—"

"True. But there's all the baggage. All those mummies and daddies and competition."

"There's no competition," Luke said. "I won't let there be."

Jed smiled at the screen.

"Good luck, dude."

Later, up in the flat, pouring out water for Charlotte and Coke Zero for himself, Luke told her he'd agreed that they'd go up to Suffolk for the weekend in a fortnight's time. Charlotte was on the sofa, with her feet on the coffee table, looking as relaxed as some syrupy African wild cat lounging nonchalantly along a branch. She accepted her water, to which Luke had added ice cubes and a slice of lime.

She said, "It'd be more fun to have them here."

Luke settled himself beside her and laid an arm along the sofa back behind her shoulders.

"You're sweet. But they want us there to feed us, and have an ooh-and-aah session with the photos."

Charlotte took a big swallow of water. She said sweetly, "But I don't want that, angel."

Luke put the back of his hand against her nearest cheek.

"I thought you liked going to Suffolk."

"I do. I love it. I especially like your dad's studio."

"Well, then."

Charlotte turned her face slightly towards him. She said, "I want the first time we see them when we're married to be here."

"Why?"

"I want to be here in charge of it—"

"What do you mean?"

"I want them to see that I can do it. That I can make a home for you. I want your mother to see that I can cook."

Luke took his hand away. He said cautiously, "That might be a bit difficult."

"Why?"

"Well, we didn't go there that last weekend, and we've been married five weeks, and there's been all the Ralph stuff. And I think Mum wants to welcome you there as her definite daughter-in-law and spoil you a bit and all that. I think, in her way, she wants to make a fuss of you."

Charlotte said, looking straight ahead, and lightly, "She hasn't done much of that yet—"

"No, but now you're *married* to me, you're a done deed. It'll be different, you'll see. It's only fair to give her the chance, babe, especially as we went back to yours. We've got to be fair."

Charlotte moved fractionally away from him. She said, "My mother doesn't ask."

Luke gave an ill-judged hoot of derisive laughter.

"Oh come on, babe! She doesn't ask outright like Mum does, but she implies and hints all the time—"

"Shut up!" Charlotte said sharply.

There was a sudden and alarming silence. Luke took Charlotte's hand, the one not holding her water glass. She snatched it back. He waited a few seconds and then he said in a low voice, "Sorry."

Charlotte said nothing.

"Sorry," Luke said, "sorry. That was completely uncalled for."

"Yes," Charlotte said with emphasis.

"We can't fight about this. We mustn't. We mustn't let this family competitive thing get in the way of you and me—"

"No," Charlotte said, her voice still distinctly unfriendly, "we mustn't. Which is why I am not going to Suffolk before your parents have come to London to see where and how we live, and celebrate us being married and in charge of our own lives."

Luke said unhappily, "Dad hates London."

"Well, he'll have to get used to it. Doesn't he ever go to Ed's house?"

"Not often," Luke said. "Usually Ed and Sigi go to Suffolk."

Charlotte turned slightly so that she could look directly at Luke. She said, "We're going to be different."

"I hope so—"

"We're going to do things *our* way. We're going to establish *our* lives."

Luke said cautiously, "Does that apply to your family too?"

Charlotte took a deep breath. She leaned forward and put her tumbler down on the coffee table. Then she turned to look at Luke again.

"I don't think you get it. My family wouldn't ask me to behave in a way I didn't feel was right for me. They just wouldn't."

"Oh."

"I expect it's being all girls," Charlotte said. "Daddy always said we belonged to him and Mummy only until we belonged to someone else."

"Are you implying something? About my parents?"

"I'm just saying," Charlotte said, "that now we're married we don't belong to our parents the way we did before we were married. And I want to establish that by having your parents here, and cooking them a lovely lunch and showing them the photographs and, if it's a Sunday, taking them to the flower market."

Luke slumped against the sofa back.

"I don't know why that doesn't make me feel better—"

"It doesn't make *me* feel better that you don't want to show your parents our home and how we're living."

"I didn't mean that—"

Charlotte pushed herself off the sofa and stood up.

"It's what's happening."

Luke looked up at her. She looked astonishing, seen from his position on the sofa, tall and powerful and more than a little terrifying. He had got out of the habit of being terrified by Charlotte, since those seemingly long-ago cocaine-argument days, and he was horrified at the thought of going back to it. A clutch of panic seized him.

He said, not wanting to sound appeasing but conscious that he did, "Why don't we just do one weekend in Suffolk to satisfy them, and then we'll do it our way from then on."

"No," Charlotte said. She folded her arms.

"But we went to your mother's—"

Charlotte almost shouted, "I *told* you why! I *told* you that it's different for the girl's family! We aren't going to keep going there any more than we're going anywhere, but I am not going to Suffolk until your parents have seen us in our own home and that's *final*."

"Final—"

JOANNA TROLLOPE

"Yes," Charlotte said. She unfolded her arms and put her hands to her face and Luke realized that she was crying. He leapt to his feet and pulled her into his arms.

"Don't, angel, don't, don't cry, please don't cry—"

Charlotte said something indistinct.

"What? What, tell me—"

"She thinks I'm such an airhead—"

"Who does? Who thinks anything like that?"

"Your mother," Charlotte said. She pushed her damp face into his shoulder.

"She doesn't, she couldn't—"

Charlotte said unfairly, "Don't make me go there—"

Luke sighed. He kissed the side of her head.

"We've got to, sometime—"

"I know. Just not this time."

"Okay."

"Please ring them. Ring them and ask them here. Say it would mean so much to us."

"Okay."

Charlotte took her face away from Luke's shoulder and looked at him. She gave him an uncertain smile.

"If you ask them in three weeks' time," she said, "I'll have had my twelve-week scan and we can tell them about the baby."

"I can't ask them to wait three weeks—"

Charlotte paused a moment and then said, "Why not?"

"It'll be two *months* since the wedding!"

"Yes," Charlotte said, and then she paused again.

Luke's arms loosened around her. He looked past her for a while and then he let his eyes travel back to her face. He attempted a smile.

"Okay," he said.

CHAPTER SEVEN

In his studio, Anthony was drawing with a 4B pencil. He had passed a cottage near Woodbridge a few days earlier, and had seen a dozen bantams pecking about in a patch of worn grass outside it, and had stopped the car and gone to knock at the door and ask if he could watch and sketch the hens for a while. There'd been an elderly couple in the house, looking after a toddler grandson, and they had said, yes, yes, of course, in a harried way, as if they couldn't actually be distracted from their custodial task to take any interest in other people's requests or pursuits. So Anthony had climbed over a battered wire fence and crouched down beside the bantams with his sketchbook, and the birds had gone on muttering about around him and stabbing at the earth, as if he was of no more consequence than a tree.

Anthony still taught his art classes. He taught only a day a week now, but he was reluctant to give it up and face the end of the teaching chapter of his life. And it had struck him, often, that domesticated birds were perfect models for new students to use when learning to draw birds, because their outlines were so solid and their movements were much easier to follow than something that was balanced in such a variety of extraordinary ways, like a godwit. Also, hens were comical and characterful, and allowed one close to them, as Anthony had been then, with two or three bantams coming right up to him, an especially bold one even investigating his shoelaces, seizing them in her beak and then dropping them with little exclamations of exasperation. And now he was back in his studio, working up a series of sketches that he would take into the first class of the new academic year after the summer and hand round among the students, some of them surly with apprehension, as an icebreaker.

Anyway, hens were soothing. They weren't romantic and wild and free-spirited like his beloved waders, but they were comforting and familiar, and comfort was what Anthony sought this particular afternoon after a miserable lunchtime conversation with Rachel. It had literally been lunchtime, not lunch, because, although Rachel had made one of her magnificent salads, scattered with seeds and nasturtium flowers, Anthony had not, on account of their altercation, felt like eating it, and the rejection of prepared food had been, of course, the last straw.

The heart of the trouble had been Anthony's standing up for Charlotte. Rachel had been full of indignation at the idea that a whole weekend in Suffolk was to be rejected in favor of an exhausting, unwanted, and unnecessary drive to London to have lunch, amateurishly cooked, in a poky flat, and then to be required to admire the trendily insalubrious area in which Luke and Charlotte had incomprehensibly elected to live. And Anthony had then said mildly, "I think we should go."

"What?"

"I think we should accept with enthusiasm and go with a good grace."

"You are so perverse—"

"No," Anthony said. He looked at the salad in front of him, decorative and colorful in its pottery bowl, and thought that it suddenly looked impossible to eat. "They want to show the flat off to us, they want us to see the flat—"

"I've seen the flat," Rachel said crossly, interrupting. "I saw it when Luke first found it—"

"Which they have now settled into, as their first married home, and they want to show it off."

Rachel did not reply. She took a pair of black wooden African salad servers out of a drawer and slammed them down in front of Anthony.

"They want," Anthony said, "to be seen to be married. They want to be taken seriously now they are married."

"You mean *she* does—"

"Possibly. More than possibly, as far as you're concerned."

"Meaning?" Rachel said dangerously.

"Meaning," Anthony said, not caring now, "that you don't think Charlotte has the first idea how lucky she is."

Rachel took a breath. Then she sat down at the table opposite Anthony, and said, glaring at the salad rather than at him, "You are an old *fool*. Just because she is pretty."

Anthony had pushed his chair back then and stood up. Rachel said, "And don't imagine I went to the trouble of making this lunch for *fun*." Anthony waited a second or two, to see if any helpful riposte came to him, but nothing did, so he had gone out of the kitchen and the house, and across the gravel to his studio, to the solace of a 4B pencil and the prospect of hens. Rachel did not follow him. He had not expected that she would.

What he did expect was that she would still be in the kitchen, feeling awful. She was no good—never had been—at subduing fierce primitive impulses and converting their natural energy into something more measured and constructive. She had been

103

a tiger mother when the boys were young, not necessarily overprotective but savagely partisan if they came up against the smallest hint of injustice or disloyalty. It had made her, for sure, a trustworthy mother, but, at the same time, a disconcerting prospect for potential friendship among other mothers. She hadn't cared, she often said to Anthony. She hadn't wanted friends just for friendship's sake; she hadn't been interested in anyone who couldn't see that her boys came first with her as an instinctively justifiable matter of course. She was amazed, astonished, gratified to have sons, three of them, coming as she did herself from a small family with only one rather older sister. It had been evident from Edward's birth onwards that Rachel could not help but feel that being the mother of sons conferred upon her a peculiar and visceral consequence. She loved it, and had striven to be, as she saw it, worthy of it, by not insisting on an exaggerated femininity or caprice, by being supremely welcoming to all their friends, by continuing to support them through all the changeableness and experimentation of their adolescence. But girls—the boys' girls—were another matter. Girls demanded her boys' loyalty, just as she had expected—and got—Anthony's. Sigrid and Petra had, for completely different reasons, somehow managed to sidestep any confrontation about who belonged to whom, but Charlotte was not going to be as easy. Anthony sighed and added a small beady eye to the nesting hen he was drawing. Charlotte was used to having her own way with family, and Luke was top of her family list now. Rachel was going to find that the newest of her daughters-in-law was not in the least afraid of standing up to her.

The door to the outside opened. It was a warm day, and usually Anthony would have left it ajar, but the altercation with Rachel had led him, instinctively, to close it.

"I've just been talking to Petra," Rachel said from the doorway. Anthony didn't turn.

"Oh?"

"She'll bring the boys about half nine tomorrow. Barney has to be kept off the bread, apparently. He ate half a loaf yesterday and she said his tummy was as distended as if he was pregnant."

"Loves his nosebag—"

Rachel came quietly across the brick floor and stood looking at Anthony's drawings.

"Those are great."

"Good subject."

"Yes," Rachel said. "I wonder why we never kept hens—"

"Because of Mr. Fox?"

"Maybe."

Anthony drew a hen running, her legs splayed out sideways.

"That's exactly right," Rachel said, watching him.

"They can be so funny—"

"I'm just—worried at the moment about Ralph—"

"I know," Anthony said.

"And you think I'm taking it out on Charlotte—"

"Mmm."

"She isn't very bright—"

"You don't know that."

Rachel sighed.

"I know she's got Luke so's he can't think straight."

Anthony drew on.

"Well," Rachel said. She touched his arm quickly and lightly. "It's the little boys tomorrow, and Ralph's interview, and a day off for Petra. Thank God for Petra."

Anthony shaded in some neck feathers.

"Yes," he said. "Amen to that."

Petra didn't think she had been to Minsmere since before Kit was born. Ralph would always have looked after the boys if she'd wanted to go, and so would her parents-in-law, but somehow another part of her brain had taken precedence since motherhood, and when she thought about drawing, she visualized it as belonging to that other Petra, the Petra who had worked in the football-club bar and the coffee place, in order to pay for her rent and her strange and inventive food and her drawing classes. She had not been brought up to regard art as vocational, as central to anyone's existence. Indeed, until she met Anthony, she'd encountered no one who thought art was anything more than a self-indulgent privilege granted to very few. So when art got overlaid in her life by babies and keeping house and adapting to the arbitrary demands of living with Ralph, she had accepted it, just as she had accepted the hand-to-mouth condition of her student days in Ipswich.

But now, suddenly, and because of this interview of Ralph's, which seemed to her to be as full of things to dread as to hope for, she had a day to herself, a day she was to spend, it had been firmly indicated, sketching. The boys had been dropped off— no frantic screeching from Kit, she was thankful to note—and she was heading north, in the secondhand car Anthony and Rachel had given them to replace Ralph's unsafe old one, and which Anthony had taught her to drive, as her twenty-first birthday present. She was a good driver, better than Ralph, but it was difficult to concentrate alone in the car, without the chatter from the backseat, without Kit asking how birds did flying or could she stop Barney touching him. She should, she supposed, be exhilarated to be free for a day, but instead she felt only lost, and slightly naked, as if she had come out unprepared and undefended.

Her sketchbooks were in a canvas bag on the passenger seat. Anthony had slipped a couple of pencils into her pocket, and Rachel had produced a picnic, in a cloth bag printed with ecological slogans, and they had waved her off, each holding a small boy, with a vigorous enthusiasm that made her feel guilty. There was a strong temptation not to go anywhere near Minsmere, but simply to wander off down an unmarked lane and find a gateway big enough to park the car, and then just go and lie in a field somewhere, and stare at the sky and let all the fretting about Ralph and Kit and money and expectations seep out of her mind and into the air, where it would dissolve of its own accord.

But Minsmere had to be done. The boys were being looked after on the unspoken but firm understanding that Petra would be drawing, all day, with an absorption that would energize and revitalize her. She had no option but to take the car down Minsmere's long wooded entry and leave it in the sloping car park above the Visitor Center, and hire binoculars for two pounds fifty, and set out into the marshes and the sighing reed beds to the East Hide, where she might—just might—find consolation and distraction in watching the avocets picking their fastidious way around the Scrape.

The reserve was busy. It was summer, and the school holidays were in full swing, and there were children scuffing along the sandy paths towards the sea. Petra thought that, if she were them, and used to the restless drama of computer games, a day out in a bird sanctuary, where shouting and racing about were forbidden, and all adults were weirdly distracted and slow-moving, would be very bewildering. Even frustrating. In fact, she thought, pausing by the ingeniously secluded entrance to the East Hide, I'm not sure I can do it today. I'm not sure I can go in there, and find a place on the bench, and sit there in silence with my binoculars and watch and wait and wait and watch until my hand goes to a pencil almost without thinking and I find I'm drawing away, as if I'd never stopped. Maybe I can do it later. Maybe I'd better walk a bit, and get rid of some of this restlessness. Maybe I'll go down to the sea, too, and sit in the dunes and look at the sky and empty my head a bit.

It was calming, down by the sea. Petra crossed the soft, deeply sandy path that ran parallel to the shore and climbed up the sliding sides of the shallow dunes until the water was visible, shifting and blue-gray under a cloud-streaked sky. There were a few people scattered about, their binoculars trained upwards, and over to one side a young man in an RSPB sweatshirt was rolling up lengths of netting that had evidently been stretched along an area of the beach. Petra sat down to watch him. He moved slowly and steadily, unhurried, bending down to add stakes to a pile, straightening up to pull the netting towards him. It was peaceful to watch him, a stocky, competent figure against a background of sea and sky, his head and shoulders now silhouetted against the shining water, now almost invisible against the sand and the clumps of marram grass. Petra remembered a visit to Minsmere with Anthony in the spring. There'd been purple orchids then, and yellow flags, and she'd seen a little egret, as elegant and exotic as a Japanese print, hunting for frogs among the shallows.

She lay back in the sand. It was warm on the surface, but cool if you dug your fingers in deeper. The sky above her was divertingly striped with tatters of pale cloud, and there were the steady, unchanging, insistent sounds of the sea and the wind and the gulls, although the air was still down there, flat on the dunes. Petra wriggled her shoulders to make comfortable dips for them in the sand, and breathed deeply, in and out, in and out. Then she relaxed down into the hollows she had made and closed her eyes, and slept.

Steve Hadley finished rolling up the nets and stacked them in a loose pile that he would collect later, after the punters had gone and the reserve was empty. The nets had fenced off a few areas of the beach, during the early summer, to stop visitors accidentally treading on the little terns' nests, which was particularly heartbreaking when it happened, as the little terns often laid only two eggs in the first place. And the terns themselves were so tiny too, barely twenty centimeters or so, with their black-tipped yellow bills and sleek black heads in the winter. Steve loved them. But then, he loved most birds, otherwise why would he be here, working with them in all weathers, instead of joining his father and brother in the thriving family opticians' business in Birmingham?

He paused to take a gum packet out of his pocket. He'd been all over the beach to check all the nests were clear, that every healthy egg had been hatched, and now he was going back up to base, to get a coffee and something to eat before he went off to check the handrail on one of the tower hides on the canopy walk. There'd been some kids—big, heavy kids—swinging on it yesterday, and even though they'd stopped when they were told off they'd been seen there again, later, just to show authority, Steve supposed, that they didn't give a stuff for it. It was interesting on the canopy trail, but it wasn't like the marshes and the shoreline. Steve was never happier than when he was within earshot of the sea.

On his way up the dunes to the path, Steve passed a girl asleep in the sand. She was deeply asleep by the looks of her, her hands were entirely relaxed. She was wearing the usual bird-watching gear of T-shirt and pocketed drill waistcoat and trainers, and she had RSPB binoculars slung round her neck, and a canvas satchel beside her with the corner of a sketchbook sticking out, but there was something about her that struck him, something more than the little swallow tattooed on the side of her neck or the jumble of colored ribbons tied round one wrist. It wasn't really, he thought, her appearance, it was more her attitude. She looked utterly comfortable, lying there in the sand, completely at home, entirely natural. She looked as if she had come to Minsmere with the express purpose of falling asleep there, in the dunes, above the sea.

He thought he really ought to wake her. She wasn't being a

nuisance or anything, and she certainly wasn't disturbing the birds, but this was a nature reserve, not a place of recreational relaxation, and the visitors were supposed to be here for bird-watching, not slumbering. He bent down, intending to put a gentle hand on her shoulder and wake her, and found that he couldn't do it. She wouldn't, after all, be sleeping like that if she didn't need to. She looked as if this was the best and most restorative sleep she'd had in ages. In any case, someone would come tramping through the dunes quite soon, as a matter of course, and she'd get woken anyway, so no need for him to get all officious and jobsworthy and wake her for no good reason. Steve straightened up again. He'd probably tell the other guys he worked with about her. "I found Sleeping Beauty down on the beach today," he'd say. Except she wasn't really a beauty. Nice face, he liked it, but not a beauty.

"Sleep well," he mouthed down at her silently, and tramped on through the dunes to the path.

Later Petra bought a cup of tea from the Visitor Center's café and took it out to one of the picnic tables on the grass. She unwrapped the foil packets Rachel had given her and found egg-mayonnaise sandwiches and cucumber batons and flap-jacks and dried apricots. She spread these out on the table and looked at them. Very delicious. Very thoughtful. The reward for a long morning's sketching. Except that she hadn't sketched a thing, she hadn't even taken one of Anthony's pencils out of her pocket, she had not done anything except sleep in the warm sand until she was woken by two children stamping past and inadvertently spraying sand in her face. It had been a won-derful sleep. She didn't think she'd slept like that in years, not since she used to stay with Ralph in his bare cottage at Shingle Street, and slept with the window open to the sounds of the sea, and the wind and the gulls, just like here.

She yawned. She must have slept for two hours or more, in

broad daylight. She felt much lighter and clearer as a result, almost happy. She certainly felt—there were hours of daylight yet—that she could draw, after she'd eaten, she could draw enough to demonstrate to Rachel and Anthony that she had fulfilled the terms of the unspoken bargain, and earned her day off. She took her phone out of her pocket and looked at it. There was no signal. A small feeling of relief stole over her. She couldn't check on the children, and she couldn't check on Ralph. She couldn't, in other words, pick up all the responsibilities concerning other people, which colored her life and sometimes burdened it to an extent that she found very hard to bear. If Ralph was in a mood, for example, she knew it was neither her fault nor her problem, but she could not evade being associated with it somehow, and thus implicated and involved, so that she could feel the energy draining out of her, leaching out into the ground under her feet. But today, sitting in the intermittent sun at a warmed wooden picnic table eating Rachel's delectable sandwiches, she was having a little holiday from all that, a brief respite in which the mobile-phone company's signal capacity had kindly conspired.

She finished the sandwiches and cucumber, and her tea, and wrapped the foil round the remainder. Barney would be pleased later to see the dried apricots, and thrilled to see the flapjacks. Kit would whimper over his supper as he did over most meals, put off by any food that was new, or bright, or natural in shape. But she didn't need to think about that just yet nor, even, about Ralph's interview. She didn't need to think about anything except a few slow, quiet hours in the East Hide with her binoculars to her eyes, and her sketchbook open on the wide shelf below the window where Anthony had first shown her, drawing rapidly and in complete silence, how the beginning of bird drawing lay with the triangle.

She settled herself at the very end of the bench, to give herself a good view to the left as well as straight ahead. There was an absorbed man with a camera on a tripod, and a few people with notebooks, but apart from them the other visitors slipped in and out of the hide with all the respectful lack of obviousness of people visiting churches and cathedrals. In any case, Petra soon forgot to be aware of anyone coming and going, forgot even to notice the bodies that briefly sat on the bench next to hers. It took her only half an hour of sitting and watching and breathing with increasingly slow, deep breaths before she had a pencil in her hand, and she was drawing.

She was drawing a redshank, marveling at its brilliant orange legs, when a voice behind her said, "Sorry to interrupt, dear, but it's five to five."

Petra looked up, startled. An elderly man with an enamel avocet pin on his pocketed gilet, and thick glasses, stood beside her, notebook in hand.

He said, "I've been watching you. My wife, too. We come here every week when the weather's good; we love it. And we're very impressed." He indicated Petra's sketchbook.

"Oh—"

"But maybe you've forgotten that it closes at five? I said to Beryl, was I being an old fusspot, telling you, and she said better have me tell you than one of the staff, and anyway then I could tell you how good we think your drawings are."

Petra looked down at the page. Her male redshank was in flight, showing the white edges to his wings.

"Thank you—"

"That's all right, dear. There's nothing like birds, is there, nothing. We've found them such a comfort since our daughter died."

Petra stared at him.

"Oh, I'm so sorry—"

"It's something to do with wings, I expect. Birds and angels. Beryl says it doesn't do to make too many links like that, but I find it helps."

Petra began to gather up her drawing things, shoveling them into her canvas satchel. She couldn't look at the man.

"Yes," she said, "yes. I'm sure it does." She slung the satchel over one shoulder. "Thank you for telling me. About the time I mean. Thank you."

And then she pushed past him, through the door into the reed-lined corridor that led back to the pathway, and fled.

In the car park, she couldn't find her car keys. She turned the satchel out, and her waistcoat pockets and the picnic bag, and there were no keys. She jumped up and down experimentally, to see if anything jangled in a pocket she'd forgotten, but there was nothing, not even in the buttoned pouches of her combat trousers. She looked at her watch. It was five fifteen. Rachel and Anthony would be expecting her back about five thirty, and she had no phone signal to tell them she'd be later. She raised a fist and hit the car, pointlessly and impotently, on its roof.

She must have lost the keys down among the dunes. They must have slipped out while she lay sleeping in the sand, their chinking obscured by the sound of the gulls and the sea. She would have to go back, running past the pond and along the North Wall to the point where the path turned south, parallel to the sea, and find the spot where she had—so carefree then, so untroubled by any preoccupation—lain down and surrendered her gaze to the wide and empty sky.

She put the canvas bag down beside the car and then, on second thoughts, pushed it underneath, with the picnic bag. The car park was almost empty now, with only the cars belonging to the few paid staff still standing close to the entrance to the Visitor Center. Petra set off at a run, thinking she would ask at the center, to see if anyone had handed in her keys, but the center was shut, its huge glass door closed upon all its goods and services for another day, and no sign of life within, or at

113

the café, where the tables and chairs had been rearranged with a businesslike regard for symmetry.

Petra ran on, her mind jerked out of the serenity of the afternoon and scrabbling to find a solution to the problem of a locked car and a useless telephone and two little boys needing collecting half an hour away. When she reached the dunes, she found the spot where she had slept, and fell to her knees, raking through the sand with her fingers, hoping and hoping for a glint of metal.

Then someone called. It was not a shout, but more the sound of someone trying to attract her attention in as discreet a way as possible. She looked up. Away down on the edge of the beach, a quad bike with a trailer was parked, and the trailer was piled with rolls of netting, and the young man Petra had seen earlier was waving at her, gesticulating with his hand.

Petra scrambled to her feet. She began to run towards him, stumbling in the sand, and he was moving too, and when he was only twenty feet or so away, she could hear that what he was saying was, "I've got them, I've got them."

He held the keys out to her. She was breathless, and beaming. She said, gasping, "Oh thank you, thank you, you can't imagine, I thought I'd lost them, I can't phone, I didn't know what I'd do—"

He said, "I saw them when I came down on the bike. They were just lying on the sand." His voice was easy, with a Midlands accent. "I passed them, on the bike. I thought they must be yours. I was going to hand them in, tomorrow." He smiled at her. "I saw you asleep earlier."

Petra nodded. She held the keys hard against her. She said, "I don't know how to thank you—"

"You don't need to—"

"You saved my life," Petra said.

He shrugged. He said, "Glad to help. Just luck, really."

"*So lucky—*"

"It looked a good sleep—"

She nodded.

"It was wonderful."

"It's the best, sleeping in the open air. By the sea."

Petra looked past him, at the water. She said, "I love the sea."

"Me too. And seabirds."

There was a small silence. Then she said, "What can I do, to say thank you?"

"You don't need to."

"I'd like to."

"Well," he said, putting his hands in his pockets, "you could make a donation, I suppose."

"Yes," Petra said, "yes. I'll do that. I'd like to do that. Who shall I say helped me?"

He looked at his feet.

"No need for that—"

"Yes, there is."

He shrugged. He glanced at her. She was breathing more evenly now, and her hair had escaped from her scarf thing and had fallen round her face.

He said, "I'm Steve."

She nodded. She said, "I'm Petra."

"Unusual name—"

"I live in Aldeburgh," she said, "and I've got two little boys." She held the keys up. "Who I've got to collect now. Thanks to you." She took a step or two back, towards the path behind the dunes. She said, "Where d'*you* live, Steve?"

He looked up at the sky for a moment. Then he looked briefly at Petra.

"Shingle Street," he said.

CHAPTER EIGHT

Ralph, Edward gathered, had done well in his interview. Which was a relief. In fact, it was an enormous relief since Edward, having arranged the interview, had had severe subsequent apprehensions about the way Ralph might put himself across, and simultaneous pangs of guilt for his disloyalty in fearing that his brother might let him down. Ralph could not, in truth, be relied upon to be orthodox, or even, on occasion, particularly polite. He might turn up unshaven and unironed, in sneakers, and behave as if he was auditioning for an edgy indie band rather than the analysis team of a small, Swiss-owned bank that had managed to keep its sober nose clean during all the upheavals caused by what the French-speakers among Edward's colleagues called *la crise*.

But Ralph had worn a suit, and a tie, and the clarity and speed of his thinking had distracted Aidan Bennett, who was his principal interviewer, from the fact that his hair was over his collar and oddly rough, and his shirt cuffs seemed to have neither buttons nor links. Ralph had also, Aidan indicated to Edward, been extremely candid about his past history, explaining that he had put most of the money he had made in Singapore into his Internet business and had lost it, partly, he said frankly, because of the downturn and his bank's behavior, but also partly, he thought, because his skills were intellectual and catalytic, rather than managerial. He had admitted that he liked problems, he liked unraveling difficulties and discovering the reasons for their having happened. Problems, mental problems, suited him, he said.

"I liked him," Aidan said to Edward.

Edward nodded, trying to look as if he'd been quietly certain of that all along.

"He'd fit in well with the Southeast Asia analysis team, especially in relationship to business in the U.S.," Aidan said. "We could do with that sort of sudoku mind." He glanced at Edward. "It would be long hours, of course. Not really possible to do daily from the east coast unless you're a travel junkie."

"I don't expect," Edward said untruthfully, "that that'll be a problem—"

"He's not at all like you."

"No—"

"In any way."

Edward said, faintly nettled, "What's that supposed to mean?"

"Only that he wasn't what I was expecting."

"Is that a compliment? To me, I mean?"

Aidan surveyed him for a second or two. Then he put a well-cared-for hand briefly on Edward's shoulder.

"Not really," he said.

Edward found Ralph in the wine bar next to the bank, with two junior members of the analysis team. They were drinking Peroni out of the bottle, and Ralph looked as easy with them as if they'd been working together for years.

"How'd it go?"

Ralph tipped his bottle towards his brother.

"Good. I'm good."

"Ade liked him," one of the juniors said. "He didn't bother with the charm. That's Ade all over. Only charming when he's about to give you the hair-dryer treatment."

Edward nodded. He said to Ralph, "Well, I don't think you should count yourself in just yet—"

"I don't, bro."

"It may take a few days. There are other people to ask—"

"I know. Want a drink?"

"Well," Edward said, "I was thinking of heading home. Are you coming back for the night? I think Sigi's expecting you."

Ralph put his bottle down.

"Sorry—"

"Have you got to get back?"

"Later," Ralph said.

"Come back for supper at least," Edward said.

One of the other men signaled to the barman for another round.

"I think," Ralph said, "I'll just stay put for a while. Thank you, though, and all that."

Edward hesitated. He wanted to ask Ralph if he didn't want to tell him, in some detail, about how the interview had gone. He also wanted to say, don't you want to see your sister-in-law, and your niece, but felt too exposed, especially in front of two men who were both in Aidan Bennett's team, and also very much junior to him. He looked hard at Ralph.

"Sure?"

Ralph smiled at him. He seemed like someone who had come through a considerable crisis and been rewarded by the assurance of an unexpectedly good future.

"Quite sure. Thanks, bro."

118

Edward took a step back. Were the thanks for the interview, or for the supper invitation—or for neither? Was Ralph, in fact, telling him to leave him alone? A small spurt of fury at his brother's lack of grace flared inside him.

"I'll leave you," he said, glaring, "to your new friends."

"The minute I was out on the pavement," Edward said to Sigrid an hour later, "I wished I'd pushed him. I wished I'd made him come home with me."

Sigrid was laying the table. On weekdays, in term time, Sigrid tried to insist that Edward was home by seven thirty so that Mariella could eat supper with them and they could ask her about her day. Not that she wanted to tell them much. For Mariella, school was still something that you just had to do, every day, like brushing your teeth, or feeding your goldfish, but not something that constituted your real life, which was waiting for you outside school hours. And in the holidays, as it now was, Mariella spent the days with her friend Indira, whose mother also worked full-time, being looked after by a student earning some vacation money, and devising the kind of elaborate and inconsequential games with Indira that did not, definitely, stand up to parental examination over supper. All Mariella wanted to know, every evening, was whether her mother was going—as she occasionally did—to take the day off from work and devote herself to Mariella, all day, from waking up to going to sleep again, and with her mobile phone on silent into the bargain. If one of those rare days was promised, Mariella was all animation over supper, and invented extraordinary adventures and conversations that she had shared with Indira, despite the oppressive presence of Tanya, who only wanted to be back in Leeds with her boyfriend, and not tediously in charge of two conspiratorial little girls who insisted that they were never obliged by their parents to eat meals at a table. But if Sigrid was working the following day, as usual, Mariella simply watched her steadily throughout supper to see if, somehow, she might change her mind.

Sigrid said, placing the candles, which were an integral part of her table laying, "I hadn't really expected him—"

"I just rather hoped, you know. After I'd got him the interview. Is that Mariella practicing her cello?"

"Arpeggios," Sigrid said briefly.

"Ralph—"

"Is rude," Sigrid said.

Edward shrugged.

"Maybe he was just relishing not being around at home for tea, bath, bed. Time off."

Sigrid put clean cotton napkins beside their three plates.

"He had the same upbringing as you. But he is not the same."

"Not conventional—"

"Not connected," Sigrid said. "A little bit autistic, I would say."

Edward opened the fridge door and took out a half-empty wine bottle. He held it up inquiringly.

"Please," Sigrid said.

"If Mum rings," Edward said, opening a cupboard door in search of glasses, "I'll simply say that she'll have to ask him how today went."

"Or not answer the phone—"

Edward turned to look at her.

"Oh, I couldn't do that—"

Sigrid sighed.

"You've done enough. You got him an interview for the right kind of job, and he seems to have done quite well, but he has not thanked you and he has not wanted to talk to you about it; he would rather drink with two strangers."

"Are you cross?"

"With him, yes," Sigrid said. "With your family sometimes. With your mother more than with your father."

"Because of—?"

"Maybe."

"Sigi," Edward said, "that was such a long time ago. And we never told them. Not properly, anyway. You can't blame them for not knowing something they were never told."

The sounds of the arpeggios in the sitting room stopped suddenly.

"She has done fifteen minutes," Sigrid said, "as I told her."

The kitchen door opened.

"Finished," Mariella said triumphantly.

"Some scales now?"

"Completely not."

"Five minutes—"

"Oh no, please, oh please no, oh no, *no*—"

"Five minutes," Sigrid said. "I am coming in, to hear you."

"Will you stay the whole time?"

"Yes."

"Every second till I stop?"

"Yes," Sigrid said.

Mariella looked at her father. "If she comes back in here," she said sternly, to him, "send her *right* back to me."

Edward took his wine to the glass doors at the back of the kitchen that led out onto a deck above the small paved garden where Mariella had a netball hoop screwed to the wall that backed onto the house behind them. When she was a baby, they had discussed the possibility of moving farther out to a bigger house in a suburb, where there would be a lawn for Mariella to play on, and maybe a tree for a swing, and even bushes, to make camps in. But Edward had soon seen that such

121

a project would never be more than a topic to play with, that Sigrid was, in a way, humoring him, trying to be normal, trying to persuade him—and herself—that she hadn't spent the first year of Mariella's life battling with the most profound and frightening of depressions, but had managed instead to take every change easily in her stride, as she would have wished to have done.

The glass doors stood open to the deck. There were a couple of wooden armchairs on the deck, but Edward stayed in the doorway, leaning one shoulder against the frame, the hand that wasn't holding his wineglass in his trouser pocket, restlessly sifting his change. He took a swallow. That had been a terrible year. Well, more than a year, really, if you took into account the end of a difficult pregnancy and the slow unhappy settling of Sigrid's hormones, and her insistence, her absolute insistence, that Rachel and Anthony should not know what was the matter, should not know what a bungled and appallingly prolonged birth Mariella's had been, ending in an emergency Caesarean operation because the heart monitor showed—had shown for far too long, in Edward's view—that the baby was becoming acutely distressed.

"Never again," Sigrid said.

She was lying on her side in the hospital bed, turned away from him.

"No—"

"I may be a coward, but I cannot do that again, I *cannot*—"

The obstetrician had told Edward that a complicated first birth seldom affected subsequent births. But this, Edward felt, was no moment for pointing this out. Sigrid was weeping. She did not seem to want to try to feed Mariella. She wept and wept and told Edward that she was a bad mother, she knew it, she was bad through and through, a bad mother was the worst kind of badness there was, and there was nothing she could do about it, nothing, and please don't give her the baby, don't, because it just made her feel worse, just made her realize how bad, bad, bad she was.

Sigrid's mother, the doctor, had arrived from Stockholm. Edward had been thankful, just thankful, to see her. She had been very kind to Edward, and steady, and very firm with the hospital, and she had put Sigrid and Mariella on a plane and taken them both back to Stockholm, where they had stayed for three months. Edward had flown out most weekends to hold his daughter and feed her and change her and to have Sigrid tell him that he must not come near her, and that she was a bad mother.

"Never again," she said, over and over.

And all the time, all during those alarming months, Edward was faced with protecting Sigrid from his parents knowing what was the matter, and with protecting his parents from knowing that they were being excluded from what was the matter.

"It's that mother of hers," Rachel said. "Chilly woman. She was chilly at the wedding, remember?"

"It's hard to have a baby in another language, especially a first baby—"

"She has us," Rachel said. She looked at Edward. "She has you."

"Childbirth is different—"

Rachel had looked at Anthony.

"What do you think?"

"I hope," Anthony said, "she'll come home soon. We can look after her here. We'd love to look after her here. We'd love to have the baby."

"I expect she's jealous," Rachel said. "I expect she resents Sigi marrying an Englishman and having an English family. Not that Sigi seems to want an English family much. She seems to insist on being so Swedish when's she's with us—"

"She *is* Swedish," Edward said. He thought gratefully, and with simultaneous regret, of the ordered calm of the flat in Stockholm, of the long windows and the pale floors and furniture, and the quiet, decided way that Sigrid's mother spoke to her daughter. It was so different from the house he had grown up in, so different from his parents' random, enthusiastic hospitality to all his friends, so different from the color and chaos and opinionated, loudly expressed conversations. He longed for Sigrid to be home, yet he dreaded her leaving Stockholm. He looked at his mother, ladling a Spanish-inspired stew into pottery bowls, and wished urgently that he could tell her that Sigrid was very ill, and had forbidden anyone in England but him to know.

"He thinks we don't know," Rachel said to Anthony later.

"Well, we don't *know*—"

"*I* know," Rachel said. "We're forbidden to go to the hospital, Sigrid gets carried off to Stockholm, Edward looks like a ghost and plainly wants to tell us things he's been forbidden to mention. What on earth could that be, unless Sigrid had an awful time and now has severe baby blues?"

"Maybe," Anthony said reluctantly, "there's something the matter with the baby."

Rachel shook her head.

"Nope. It's Sigrid. It hasn't gone as she thought it would, and she doesn't want us to know."

Anthony got up from where he was sitting, and came over to Rachel and planted his hands on her shoulders.

"Rach—"

"What?"

"Rachel, if Sigrid and Edward make it plain that they don't want us to know, we *don't* know it. D'you hear me? We don't know a thing."

Rachel sat very still.

"We do not know," Anthony repeated.

"Okay," Rachel said reluctantly. And then, "Even if Edward obviously wants us to know?"

"He doesn't," Anthony said.

"I don't," Edward said a week later, when his mother confronted him.

"It's nothing to be ashamed of," Rachel said. "More women feel like that than don't, after babies. It's absolutely normal. It's hormones. It shouldn't be called depression."

Edward looked away from her. He was consumed by a violent need to protect Sigrid and a dual fury with himself for letting his anxiety show and his mother for not keeping her mouth shut.

"There's nothing the matter," he said. "She just wanted her mother there after Mariella was born, and now she wants to be with her a bit longer. It's what Dad said, about having your first baby in another language. That's all."

Rachel gave a small smile.

"I don't believe you," she said and Edward, goaded out of self-control by her astuteness and her refusal to restrain it, had yelled, "Mind your own bloody business!"

It might have been all right, Edward reflected now, drinking his wine and jingling his change, if the matter had been left there, if Rachel had been content with her definite if unacknowledged victory. But she had been unable to restrain herself, unable not to make it plain to Sigrid, after she and the baby were back from Sweden, that Sigrid's parents were not the only grandparents, and furthermore that Mariella, being the first grandchild on either side, was of particular importance and significance. Then she had gone on to offer help, and support, and babysitting, and Sigrid, adamant with fury, had told Edward that if his mother didn't leave the house instantly, and possibly forever, she would go straight back to Stockholm, taking Mariella with her. And then, after Rachel had finally gone, Sigrid turned on Edward and accused him of disloyalty, and of telling his mother things he had promised her he would never tell anyone, and of being more attached to his family than he was to his wife and child.

So he hadn't confessed. He hadn't told her, then, that he had been so frightened by her suffering, so desperate not to add to it or be the cause of its ever happening again, that he had, when Mariella was ten weeks old, booked himself a vasectomy with Marie Stopes International and handed over his three hundred pounds with a determined conviction of doing the right thing for the right reasons in the right way.

The procedure had taken ten minutes.

"Your sex drive will be unaffected," a doctor about his own age said to him. "You will produce the same amount of fluid, but devoid of sperm. We will test you in six months."

After six months, he had still not told Sigrid. He had, in truth, no need to, because she came to bed in uncompromising pajamas and made it unequivocally plain that she did not want to be touched. He bore it until Mariella was almost one, and until sessions in the shower with himself had reached a pitch of disgusted pointlessness, and then he told her in a rush, blurted it all out, told her his sperm count was nil and that he was going mad.

She cried. She'd cried so much since Mariella was born that at first Edward thought exhaustedly, distractedly, that this was just more of the same. But she was smiling. Or at least, she was trying to smile, and she said a whole lot of stuff to him in Swedish, and then she said, in English, that he was wonderful, that she so appreciated what he'd done, but at the moment she had all the libido of a floorcloth. He could do what he liked, Sigrid said, laughing, sobbing, but he'd have to put up with her just lying there, a fish on a slab, a fish with a scar across its belly.

He finished his wine. God, it had taken ages. Years,

probably. Years of patience and frustration and knowing that seeking sex elsewhere would provide the brief heady release that comes with, say, losing your temper completely, only to be followed by a long, gray drag of remorse and regret and self-disappointment. He'd tried not to remember the Sigrid he'd met at that wild party at the University of Loughborough, the Sigrid who'd caused him to say, happily amazed, "Is it normal—I mean, is it okay—to have as much sex as this?" He'd tried to concentrate on love, on loving her, on adoring Mariella, on being a man who was not, as someone once said of persistent sexual desire, chained to a lunatic.

And now, here they all were. Mariella was eight and practicing the cello. Sigrid was the number two in a serious and highly regarded laboratory. He was well paid, professionally well thought of, and their marriage, if not what it had initially promised to be, was something he could not visualize being without. Maybe that was habit. Or maybe it was just . . . marriage. Maybe the seismic shocks of it left a kind of emotional scar tissue, but the body kept on functioning over and around the lumps and bumps with a dedicated optimism peculiar to the human race.

Edward turned back to the kitchen. Sigrid was by the sink, washing lettuce, and Mariella was leaning up against her from behind, as if to make sure that she couldn't go anywhere. He felt, abruptly, rather unsteady, and that if he said anything his voice might come out choked, and a bit ragged, so he just stood there, holding his empty wineglass, and thinking that if all you really needed was love, then that was actually a very demanding and complicated recipe for human survival.

Later, Mariella summoned him to say good night to her. She was going through a phase of nagging for a dog, and had bought a dog whistle with some of her pocket money, which she had attached to a glitter shoelace and hung from one of the knobs of her white-painted Swedish bedhead, and when she was ready for a good-night kiss, she blew it peremptorily.

She was sitting up in bed in spotted pajamas with her hair brushed into a smooth fair curtain. Her bed was full of her plush animals, and a revolving night-light was casting starry shapes across the walls and ceiling.

"Daddy," Mariella said.

Edward sat down on her bed.

"Ouch," she said, moving her feet.

"Wouldn't you like to lie down?"

Mariella slid gingerly down in bed, in order not to disturb the animals.

"Daddy—"

"Yes."

"This dog—"

"Darling, we've explained. Over and over. It wouldn't be fair on a dog, with all of us out all day. Dogs hate it, being without company."

"Okay then," Mariella said, clasping her hands together, "we'd better think of something that'll make you stay at home. Let's have a baby."

"Darling—"

"Look," Mariella said, "I know what you have to do. I'll go for a sleepover at Indira's and you can just do it, you and Mummy. I really, *really* want a baby."

Edward put a hand on the duvet over her stomach.

"Darling, it isn't as simple as that—"

"You always say that."

"Because," Edward said, "it's true."

"Mummy said she didn't have any more baby eggs—"

"That's about it."

"What if I don't like being an only child?"

"Then," Edward said unfairly, looking straight at her, "I would be very sad indeed."

Mariella sighed. She lifted her hands and interlaced them in front of her face.

"Do you *have* to tell your parents everything?"

"When you're a child, it's quite a good idea to tell them most things. So they can help."

"But you don't really help," Mariella said. "You just say no, no, this won't work, that won't work, you don't do things that I know would help *me*."

Edward leaned towards her. He put a hand either side of her head, sinking them into the pillow.

"You are a baggage, Mariella Brinkley."

She glimmered up at him.

"When I'm big—"

"Yes."

"I'll have babies and dogs and probably a monkey."

"Will I want to come and stay with you?"

Mariella raised her chin for a kiss.

"You'll have to. To babysit everything while I go to work."

Edward paused in the downward movement to kiss her.

"*Work?* Are you going to *work*?"

Mariella closed her eyes briefly, as if he was too tiresome to be borne.

"Of course I am," she said.

In the kitchen, Sigrid was standing with the telephone in her hand.

Edward said, "Mariella is bent upon a career, and we're going to look after her monkey while she does it."

"I'd be glad to," Sigrid said. She dropped the telephone back into its charger. "That was Charlotte."

"What was—"

"On the telephone. While you were with Mariella."

"Oh?"

Sigrid said, "She wants us to go to lunch. When your parents are there, the weekend after next."

"Goodness. Not what we're used to—"

"She sounded very excited."

"What, about having us all to lunch?"

"Well," Sigrid said, "about something. I don't know what. It can't have been about Ralph."

"Why Ralph?"

Sigrid began to clear plates from the table.

"Ralph was there."

"With Charlotte and Luke?"

"Yes." She glanced at him. "I think he was a little bit drunk."

Edward put his fists up against his forehead.

"Give me strength—"

"Charlotte said they would make him a bed on the sofa. She seemed to think it was funny."

"I wish I did—"

The telephone rang again. Edward moved to pick it up, but Sigrid darted ahead of him, laying a hand on his arm as she passed, to deter him.

"Yes?" she said into the receiver and then, in a carefully neutral voice, "Oh. Rachel."

Edward put his hand out automatically for the telephone. Sigrid smiled at him and turned her back.

"I'm afraid I don't know," Sigrid said to her mother-in-law. "No, Edward is at a business dinner, and Mariella is in bed . . ."

There was a brief pause and then Sigrid said, "Edward worked so very hard to get Ralph this interview. It was not easy, in this climate."

Edward came up behind Sigrid and slid his arms round her waist. To his relief, after a moment or two, she relaxed against him. He could hear his mother's brisk tones from the telephone, as if he was listening to her through a wall, or from under bedclothes.

"I'm not aware," Sigrid said, "that he has thanked Edward. I'm not aware that he knows the favor he has been done."

Edward put his face into the angle of Sigrid's neck and shoulder.

"I can't help you, I'm afraid," Sigrid said. "I'm sorry Petra is in the dark, too. I'm sure he'll turn up. Maybe he is celebrating. Yes, yes, of course. I will tell Mariella. She would send kisses too, if she were awake. Yes, thank you. Love to you, love to Anthony."

She clicked the phone off.

"You saved me," Edward said into her neck.

"Only a very small save—"

"Why didn't you suggest she ring Luke?"

Sigrid turned round in his arms.

"Because," she said, "I didn't feel like it."

CHAPTER NINE

On the way to London, Rachel said she would drive. Anthony agreed, as she had known he would, so that he could sit silently beside her, half listening to Classic FM, and gazing out of the window at the clouds, and the passing landscape—even the townscape of northeast London—and she could drive and think.

She needed to think. She had tried to think for days, either alone, or out loud to Anthony, but Anthony had not wanted to participate in her thinking, and had evaded her, either, she supposed, because he didn't know what to think himself, or because he was not of a mind to sympathize with her and had no inclination to fight about it. Anthony had never liked analysis, anyway. All their lives together, whenever there was a problem involving relationships, Anthony had worn the hunted expression of a dog required to walk on its hind legs, a bemused, slightly oppressed expression, and made for his studio. The most he would ever say, if Rachel pursued him with her need to dissect and ferret out an explanation, was, "Can't we just see what happens? Can't we just wait?"

Rachel knew she was bad at waiting. All her life, ever since the first self-awareness of childhood, she knew that the flip side of her marvelous energy was her impatience. Problems had the effect of firing her up like a rocket, impelling her to chase about in her mind, mentally darting hither and thither, to seek a solution that invariably involved her own zealous participation. Rachel's mind and body thrived upon activity, upon practical and immediate answers to even intractable-seeming dilemmas, and, when she was thwarted of the opportunity to offer instant resolution, she found herself utterly devastated by her own helplessness. It was then, even after almost forty years of disappointed experience, that she turned to Anthony, and he, as usual, made it abundantly plain that he couldn't help her.

It was always worse when the trouble was Ralph. Edward's comparative orthodoxy and Luke's relative youth and optimism made them both less of an anxiety to Rachel than Ralph. But Ralph was designed to cause anxiety, and was also designed to be completely oblivious to his capacity for being a constant small nagging worry to her, like an emotional toothache, bearable much of the time but with a propensity to flare up without notice and cause agony. He had caused a bout of agony when the bank foreclosed on his borrowing, and, although the agony had abated at the prospect of a job interview, it had flared up again when Ralph had gone missing after being offered the job, and nobody had thought to tell Rachel that he was sleeping off a drinking binge on Luke's sofa, and that he had no idea whatsoever how he was going to manage a working life that expected a minimum of twelve-hour days in an office that was almost three hours' traveling time from his wife and children.

Rachel had tried to talk to Petra. Petra had been, to say the least, detached about the job interview in the first place. She stood in her kitchen, making tea for Rachel with maddening abstraction, while Barney crawled peaceably about the floor putting unsuitable bits of detritus into his mouth and swallowing them.

"I don't mind about the money," Petra said. "I've never minded about money. I'm used to not having money."

Rachel had taken a deep breath and averted her eyes from Barney on the floor.

"That was then," she said to Petra. "You were a student, and only had yourself to think about. You have children now. You have a house. You have responsibilities. You aren't free to indulge yourself by saying you don't care about money."

Petra didn't reply. She put Rachel's tea down in front of her, and then bent to extricate a plastic bottle cap from Barney's mouth, but without hurry. Her whole posture, her every movement, indicated to Rachel that she was not going to pursue this conversation, any more than she had engaged in the one about possibly having to move nearer a station, to enable Ralph to commute more easily.

"I can't leave the sea," Petra said. "Once I could've, when I hadn't lived by it, but I can't now. The best place I ever lived was Shingle Street. It was the best place for Ralph too. We were really happy at Shingle Street. The sea was almost *in* the sitting room."

Rachel had felt her whole body clench with tension. She had so much to say, so much to point out about practicality and common sense and responsibility and maturity, and there was no point in uttering a single syllable of it. She had drunk her tea, and gone to find Kit sitting staring and rapt in front of the television, in order to kiss him good-bye, and had then driven home in an advanced state of agitation, to find Anthony determined not to engage with her either.

"We are talking about your *son*!" Rachel had shouted. "Your son and your daughter-in-law who are declining—no, *refusing*—to face the practicalities and consequences of how their life will be!"

Anthony was in his studio, drawing a dead mole he had successfully trapped as it flung up its chain of miniature mountains across the lawn. It lay on a piece of yellowish paper, quite unmarked, its purposeful front paws half curled, as if still in the act of digging.

"It's their life," Anthony said, drawing on.

"But they have *children*, they can't ignore that, and if they don't move Ralph will never get home at night and then—"

"Stop it," Anthony said.

"I can't believe you don't care—"

Anthony smudged his drawing with a forefinger.

"I care. I care quite as much as you do. But caring confers no right to interfere."

"How dare—"

"I am not," Anthony said, "discussing this further. Not now, not tomorrow, and certainly not in the car going up to London when I am trapped beside you."

So, here they were, in the car together, with the radio on to neutralize the atmosphere, and Rachel at the wheel, driving in a way she knew Anthony would both observe and decline to comment on. She had decided not to speak, being well aware after all these decades of living with herself that fear only made her sound angry, and, if she added the anger caused by her anxiety over Ralph and Petra to the resentment she felt at being forced to have Sunday lunch in Shoreditch rather than at her own large and familiar kitchen table, she knew she couldn't trust herself to say anything of which she could subsequently be remotely proud. So she drove furiously, and beside her Anthony sat striving to distract himself from her violent silence, and his own inner turmoil at the storms threatening his family life, by examining the cloudscapes and

135

wondering how Constable, or Turner, or Whistler might have painted them.

Luke had made a table large enough to accommodate seven people for lunch by overlaying their small black dining table with a piece of MDF left over from his office conversion. Charlotte had wanted there to be eleven people, not seven, but Luke had grown tired, after Ralph's second night on their sofa in a reek of alcohol, of pursuing Ralph and Petra for a sensible answer to their invitation, and had said that they'd just go ahead without them.

"But I want the children," Charlotte said.

"No, you don't. Barney will wreck the flat at floor level, and Kit will whine and make a fuss about eating."

"I don't mind—"

"I do," Luke said.

There was a short pause, and then Charlotte said accurately, "You're worried about your mother coming."

"I am not—"

"Lukey—"

"I have never," Luke said, "had my parents to a meal. Not ever. In my whole life."

"Well—"

"We always went home. We went home to eat. That's what we did. Always."

"That's why it's worth making an effort—"

"I *am* making an effort!"

Charlotte waited a few seconds, and then she said, "Don't take it out on me, babe."

Luke looked at her. He gave a little bleat of exasperation, and flung his hands out.

"It's not you—"

"Well?"

"It's—well, it's just all this stuff recently. Ralph, and us not going to Suffolk and not telling Mum and Dad about the baby—"

"We'll tell them today. They'll know today."

Luke said sadly, "You told your mother last weekend."

"I saw her," Charlotte said. "I wanted to tell her in person, and I saw her."

"Three weekends running, seeing your mother—"

"Are you counting?"

"No," said Luke, "but Mum will be."

Charlotte unfolded a white double sheet, and billowed it out over the table. She said, "Did you get Coke or something, for Mariella?"

"Are you changing the subject?"

Charlotte bent across the table to smooth the sheet out. She was wearing a short gray gauze smock over white-lace shorts. Her legs were absolutely amazing. Luke had a sudden vision of those legs stalking past his father and his elder brother. He said, "Is that what you're planning to wear?"

Charlotte straightened up. She had smoothed her hair close to her head and added enormous pearl earrings.

"Of course. It's new."

Luke sighed unhappily. "It's gorgeous. You look gorgeous. It's just—"

Charlotte began to giggle. She came round the table and put her arms round Luke's neck.

"It's to distract them all from how disgusting lunch is going to be. D'you think it'll work?"

"If there are no babies at lunch," Mariella said, "I will have completely nothing to do."

"Bring a game," Sigrid said, "or a book."

She was standing in her bathroom, putting her makeup on, and Mariella was sitting, fully dressed, in the empty bathtub beside her, on a stool she had brought in for the purpose.

"If we went to Suffolk," Mariella said, "I'd have heaps to do. I'd always have heaps to do in Suffolk."

"Well, Aunt Charlotte—"

"She said to call her Charlotte—"

"Charlotte wants us to see her new flat and to cook for us."

"It'll be weird," Mariella said.

"Not necessarily."

Mariella squinted up at her mother.

"Indira's mother paints lines on her eyes all the way out like little wings. Little flicky wings."

"Indira's mother is very dramatic."

"She has a million bangles," Mariella said, "all up her arms. She lets us play with her jewelry; she lets us put on her toe rings and the ankle things and everything, and whoosh about in her saris. She never says, oh what a mess please tidy up don't jump on my bed careful you don't get nail varnish on the carpet. She never does."

"Why don't you spend more time there then, instead of bothering me."

Mariella put her head on one side.

"I like bothering you."

"I noticed," Sigrid said. She leaned forward towards the mirror, holding her eyelash curlers.

"Why can't we have a baby?" Mariella said.

Sigrid applied the curlers to one eye, and squeezed. She said, "I'm afraid I'm not very good at it."

"You are," Mariella said. "You had me."

Sigrid opened the curlers for her other eye.

"I did. But not easily. Some women have babies easily and are very good at it. Their bodies are very good at it. We are all designed a bit differently, you see."

"But," Mariella said reasonably, "the doctors would help you. The baby doctors. That's what they're for."

"Even so."

"Which bit of you didn't work?"

Sigrid put the curlers down and picked up her mascara.

"My head, darling."

"You don't have babies in your head."

"But you have," Sigrid said, "thoughts and feelings in your head. Especially when you are growing a baby. You are never just a body, you are a head too. After all, you have thoughts all the time, don't you? And you have to remember that some people have difficult thoughts and feelings, which you might not have yourself, and you have to be sympathetic to them, all the same."

Mariella stood up, and climbed out of the bathtub. She said quite casually, "Like Granny?"

Sigrid stopped applying mascara. She turned round.

"What?"

Mariella bent to pick up the stool. She said, "Well, Granny had three babies, so she must have thought it was easy."

"I think she did."

Mariella put the stool on the bathroom floor. Then she climbed on it, so she was taller than her mother. She looked down at Sigrid, smiling at her own superior position.

"So," she said, "Granny forgets sometimes to be sympathetic to someone like you. Doesn't she?"

"Well," Charlotte said, "we've got something to tell you."

She was slightly flushed. Lunch had been pretty successful, considering, and even though Rachel had hardly commented on it she had eaten everything on her plate and even said, "Oh, chervil!" in a tone of pleased surprise when she saw the garnish on the potato salad. Mariella had been adorable and funny and kept them entertained with improbable stories about her friends, and Anthony had drawn cartoons of them all as

birds—Charlotte was an extremely pretty ostrich with false eyelashes and fishnet stockings—and everybody had exclaimed at the flat and the wedding pictures and Charlotte had caught Luke's eye and felt him acknowledge that she had been right to insist on hosting lunch, right to demonstrate to his parents that successful family occasions could happen away from the familiar base in Suffolk. So she tapped a stray spoon against her water glass and said in a slight rush, "Well. We've got something to tell you—"

Rachel, who was sitting next to Luke, put a hand out to touch his forearm. She said, too fast, "Oh, darling. A work breakthrough—"

Luke was staring at Charlotte. He looked slightly pent-up, as if he was holding something in that it would be a relief to release.

Charlotte, in turn, stared at Rachel.

"No," she said decidedly.

Rachel turned to regard Charlotte.

"Not—"

"Not what," Charlotte said dangerously.

"Please—" Anthony said to Rachel across the table.

"Not a baby," Rachel said recklessly.

"Rachel!" Anthony shouted.

Charlotte stood up. She had lost her temper in an instant.

"Yes," she yelled. "A *baby*! We're having a baby! What's wrong with having a baby?"

Rachel said unflinchingly, "You've only been married ten minutes. Couldn't you have waited?"

The noise erupted. Luke got up, overturning his chair in his haste to get round the table to Charlotte, but Sigrid was there before him, her arms round Charlotte. Edward and Anthony turned on Rachel.

"How *could* you?"

"What are you *thinking* of? Have you lost your *mind*?"

"What business is it of yours—"

"God, you are a liability—"

Mariella was watching. She stayed in her chair across the table from her grandmother, and watched. She saw her mother and her uncle Luke with their arms round Charlotte, and, even though she could only see Charlotte's hair and Charlotte's legs, she knew she was crying in there, in all those arms, and she was crying because Granny had said something that she shouldn't have said, and Granny was now sitting there, staring at her lap, while her father and her grandfather shouted at her in angry whispers. Mariella wondered if Granny would like to say sorry, and then she wondered if her mother was comforting Charlotte because of all the baby-in-your-head stuff, and then she remembered that Charlotte had started all this by saying she and Luke were going to have a baby, and a surge of delight lifted Mariella clean off her chair to stand on it, so that she was taller than anyone else there, just as she had been, in her mother's bathroom, a few hours before.

She clapped her hands.

"Stop, everyone!" Mariella shouted.

No one took any notice.

"Shut up, shut up!" Mariella shouted. She looked down at her father. He had stopped ranting at Granny, and was sitting with his head in his hands. Mariella took a deep breath, then she yelled, "There's going to be a *baby*!"

Anthony said he would drive home. He had taken the car keys from Rachel's bag, and then he held the passenger door open for her, and she had climbed in wordlessly, and buckled her seat belt, and not looked at him as he settled himself into the driving seat and adjusted the mirrors. She asked if he would like to be directed towards the A12, and he said thank you, but there were perfectly adequate road signs, and then he turned on the radio, quite loud, and they drove in wretched silence, all the way back to Suffolk.

It took two and a half hours. For most of the journey, Rachel lay back against the headrest, with her eyes closed, and her face turned away from Anthony. She could not think how to initiate conversation, and Anthony looked as if such an idea was the last thing he would have welcomed. She had seldom seen him so angry. He wasn't a man given to anger, least of all with her. In fact, she had grown, over the years, to accept that, as far as Anthony was concerned, she could get away with almost anything, that he not only valued but also depended upon her particular variety of vitality and certainty, her frankly partisan championing of the men in her life, her ability to take action. Her mind roamed over events in their life together where Anthony had sought her for reassurance, for sympathetic companionship, events like Edward's wedding, or Ralph's disappearing to Singapore, or Luke's uncommunicative gap-year wanderings, and she tried to console herself by telling herself that Anthony had needed her then, had relied upon her for her good sense, her candor, her capacity not to be spooked by imaginings. She tried to tell herself that what she had said today was no more than the common sense that everyone else was thinking, and dared not say, and failed. She tried to tell herself that Anthony's reaction was exaggerated and unjust and colored by his tragic male infatuation with Charlotte's looks, and failed. She told herself that, whatever she had done, and whatever Anthony's reaction had been, she would not cry in front of him, and succeeded. And so, through mile after mile of the long road out to East Anglia in the tired sunlight of a summer Sunday afternoon, Rachel sat with her face averted, her eyes closed, and her thoughts teeming behind them like a scuttling plague of vermin.

* * *

In the drive at home, Anthony waited for her to get out before he put the car into the small barn that served as a garage.

"Actually," Rachel said, "I'm taking the car."

"Taking it?"

"Yes."

"Where?"

"To Aldeburgh," Rachel said.

Anthony said, staring ahead through the windscreen, "Do you imagine you will get a more sympathetic hearing there?"

"It's not that—"

"No?"

Rachel said, slightly desperately, "I need to talk to someone. I need to talk. And I can't talk to you."

Anthony opened the driver's door and got out. He said, "No. You certainly can't do that."

Rachel slid inelegantly across the gear shift and into the driver's seat. It was still warm from Anthony's body, and the warmth abruptly made her want to cry, more than any of the thoughts she'd had on the way home. When she had turned the ignition on and inched forward, she realized that the seat was too far back, and the mirrors were at the wrong angles, so she had to stop a yard from where Anthony had halted the car, and adjust everything, with him standing there watching her, his expression inscrutable but not in any way encouraging. She crept forward over the gravel and out of the drive gates to the road, and only when she was out of sight of the house and Anthony's still and silent figure, did she give way to tears.

Anthony had grown up with dogs. His father had been a spaniel man, liver-and-white springer spaniels, who were either flat out racing about or flat out fast asleep, and Anthony had assumed that all households, all families, had dogs, the way they had refrigerators and cars and early television sets. But Rachel had, as a child, been bitten, badly, by a dog, an elderly half-blind old Labrador who had believed Rachel to be obstructing her access to her supper, and had never recovered her ease around dogs in consequence. She had tolerated the last of Anthony's springers, to the point of sitting up with him during the final long wheezing nights of his life, on an old quilt in the kitchen, but had then said she would be grateful for a dog-free spell, which had lengthened because of Edward's arrival, and then lengthened again when Ralph came, and so on until being without a dog was something even Anthony came to accept. In fact, he hardly thought about dogs now, and it was only on an occasion such as this, walking down to the quay, and along the river parallel to the sea, that it occurred to him that a dog would be comfortably companionable and an uncomplicated distraction from the inside of his own head, and that one could safely say, out loud, to a dog all kinds of things that were clamoring to be expressed and would only make everything considerably worse if uttered to another human.

The footpath ran along a dike between flat land to the left of the path, and the flat River Orde to the right. It was a walk Anthony had known all his life, starting by the quay with its quiet stretches of sheltered water, and spits of low land, and clusters of small sailing boats, moored and clinking in the soft wind. From the quay, the path ran on past wooden sheds selling fresh fish on weekdays and a neat little tea room with a veranda, and the small white cube of the sailing club—all familiar, all timeless, as timeless as, farther on, the outline, if he looked inland, of the church and the castle among the trees and hedgerows. The boys had all loved the castle when they were younger. Ralph had chosen it for a school project, and had written a careful and measured essay on it, which began, "The castle was built, AT GREAT EXPENSE, by Henry II." Luke had moved on to Second World War stories, and was keenly envious of the excitement Anthony had known as a boy of the dismantling of beach defenses, the removal of mines, and unexploded bombs. Edward, now so urban, so cosmopolitan, had been the one who was interested in the natural history of the place, the collector of samphire and sea pinks, the identifier of gull types by the color of their legs, the one who would crouch for hours in those flat fields by the dike waiting for brown hares to engage in the remarkable boxing matches of the spring mating rituals.

Well, Anthony thought now, descending the steep inland side of the dike and turning to look at the white blade of a sail serenely passing on the far side of it, there was nothing to be gained by comparing those days with these. Those days involved three boys under twelve. These days involved three boys almost all over thirty. Little children: little problems; big children: big problems. He felt disgusted by the day, by the drama of it, by the wearisome drives, by Luke and Charlotte's contraceptive carelessness, by Ralph's selfish self-involvement, by Rachel's inability to control her thoughts and her tongue and her conduct. He felt dirtied by it all, soured and sullied, and longed for that mythical dog, racing ahead of him along the wheat-field path in utterly focused pursuit of a scent so compelling that nothing else could be heeded. It would be a comfort in its sheer simplicity. It would remind Anthony that life didn't consist only of crossed wires and lost tempers and injured feelings.

From the wheat about a yard away came the sudden sharp drawn-out fall of a bird call. Anthony stopped and stood motionless. There, on a wheat ear, rather than the reed top of its usual choice, sat a reed bunting, smaller than Anthony's hand, with its boldly striped and speckled body and its coal-black head, garnished with a white collar and a comedy moustache. Anthony waited. The bird had surely seen him. It would have a nest nearby, close to the ground and cup-shaped, with maybe half a dozen eggs in it, which would hatch into brown babies with black-and-white moustaches above their tiny beaks. The bird and the man were quite still together in the summer evening for what seemed like a miraculous number of seconds, and then the bird uttered its curious little cry again and took off without hurry towards the reed beds beyond the dike. Anthony watched it go. He took a breath.

"Thank you," Anthony said to the empty air.

Rachel did not return until after dark. Anthony had poured himself a tumbler of whiskey and water, and had carried it across to his studio, intending to immerse himself there, in his usual way, and found that he couldn't do it, so he had returned to the kitchen and spread the Sunday newspapers out and tried to read them, and not look at his watch too often, and not to pour a second whiskey.

Rachel threw the car keys on to the kitchen counter with a clatter. She said, not looking at Anthony, "I am very sorry."

He stared at the newspapers. He said, "So am I."

"I don't really want to talk about it—"

"I thought you did—"

"I did want to," Rachel said, "but it kind of died out of me. Standing in their kitchen, I was just tired of it, tired of myself, tired—oh, tired of behaving like that. Which was just as well."

Anthony looked up. Rachel was standing where she had halted when she came in. She looked exhausted and rumpled, and her hair was sticking up here and there as if she'd slept on it while it was damp.

"What d'you mean?"

Rachel turned slowly to look at him. She was smiling reluctantly.

"Well, they weren't interested, were they—"

"What—"

"I got there just as bath time started. Ralph was doing bath time. So I helped with this and that and then I read to Kit and then I went downstairs, and Petra was drawing at the kitchen table and Ralph was in his office. And I told Petra about the baby and she didn't look up, she just said, "That was quick." And I said stupidly, "So were you," and she didn't reply, and she just went on drawing, and then Ralph came down and said, thanks for coming, Mum, and I realized I was being—I was sort of being *dismissed*."

Anthony got up slowly from the table.

"So where have you been?"

"Down by the sea—"

"Where—"

"Parked," Rachel said, "at Shingle Street. Where Petra said she and Ralph were so happy."

Anthony came and stood beside her. He said, "A wrong-footed day—"

"Sure was—"

It occurred to him to say, "You have to let it go," but then he thought that they were both too tired for what would inevitably follow, and maybe Rachel knew that anyway, and didn't want to face it, or couldn't face it at the end of such a day. So he stood and half looked at her, and after a while she said, "Did anybody ring?"

"The boys? No."

"I thought Luke might."

"No."

"Or Edward."

"No."

"Sigi—"

"Stop it," Anthony said. "I'm drinking whiskey. D'you want some?"

Rachel shook her head. She glanced round the kitchen, at

the colors, at the accumulation of objects, the rows of mugs on the wooden pegs, the great pottery fruit bowl, the scarred chopping boards.

"This all looks pretty dated, doesn't it—"

"Rachel, don't start. It's too late. We're too tired—"

She gave him a quick look, and he caught a sudden glimpse of the girl to whom he'd given the aquamarine ring that had once belonged to his grandmother, the girl who'd known what to do with him, with the Dump, with his parents' quietly collapsing house.

"Bed," Anthony said. He put a hand on her shoulder. "There's nothing more to be done about today but end it."

Rachel moved away so that his hand slipped from her shoulder. She picked up the car keys and threw them into the fruit bowl among the bananas.

"Okay," she said.

CHAPTER TEN

W hile Petra was out at her allotment with the boys, Ralph got all his old suits out from the back of the cupboard in their bedroom. He had never moved his suits from his old bedroom in his parents' house to the cottage at Shingle Street, but when the move to Aldeburgh came Rachel had arrived with all his suits, in an assortment of plastic and canvas covers, and said that, as he was now embarking on family life in earnest, he should house his own property.

Ralph had been mildly surprised. Rachel had brought his suits, but not his childhood books or his toy fort or the key rack which had been Woodwork Job One at his secondary school. He had accepted the suits, supposing that she was signaling that impending fatherhood required a seriousness of approach, and had stuffed them at the back of the too-small wardrobe that he and Petra shared, haphazardly, and forgotten them, as he had forgotten the childhood possessions that his mother seemed still to wish to keep. In fact, he had forgotten them so thoroughly that he had hired something to wear to Luke's wedding before Petra said quietly, "But you've got a suit. You've got several suits."

And there they all now were, dark blue and dark gray, squashed on inadequate hangers, bearing the labels of Singapore tailors who had copied so beautifully the two English suits he had arrived with. They did not look good, his poor suits, creased and neglected, with grubby linings and stuff in the trouser pockets and cuff buttons missing. Ralph dropped his jeans to the floor, and picked up the top pair of fine-wool gray chalk-striped trousers. He stepped into them, pulling them up over his elderly boxer shorts and thin market-stall socks. He fastened the waist and zipped the fly. They fitted perfectly, flat across his belly, skimming his thighs, roomy enough to put his hands in his pockets, where he found half a boarding pass for Singapore Airlines and a crumpled fifty-Singapore-dollar bill. He looked at the bill in his hand, remembering. He thought about his flat, in an immense block on Orchard Road, with a vast, shining atrium floored in polished stone and a lift in a glass column that rose silently up among the brilliant-green trees of an indoor jungle. He thought about the dealing room at the bank, where they had all screamed into headphones for ten hours a day. He thought about the beaches at the weekends, where he had sat alone on the sand, watching the sun go down, suddenly, into the Straits of Singapore, thinking that, out there, across the indigo sea, lay the first of the immeasurable islands of Indonesia. He closed his eyes. A sudden yearning for freedom struck him so forcibly that it almost took his breath away.

He put the fifty dollar bill back in his pocket and opened his eyes. He looked at himself in the narrow mirror he had nailed up behind the bedroom door, and whose bottom edge Kit had decorated with Bob the Builder stickers. He looked quite different in suit trousers, despite a much laundered and stretched dark-green T-shirt, and two days' worth of stubble. He found the jacket belonging to the suit trousers and put it on too. Even with the T-shirt, and the crumpled condition of the jacket, the suit was impressive. He straightened his shoulders. The suit gave him definition and authority. He breathed in. He wondered if he still had any shirts—and shoes. He had sworn he would never wear a tie again, but there was something ties did for a shirt, a sort of finishing something. Like cuff links. Were people wearing cuff links? Did he still own any?

In his socks and his suit, Ralph padded down to the kitchen. He filled the kettle. He wasn't exactly hungry, or thirsty, but he felt a definite stirring of recollection, of remembering something which was—had been—not without excitement, and stimulating, which ought to be celebrated with, at least, coffee. He thought about how carefree it had been in Singapore, how easy it was to exercise his talents but not to be responsible for doing anything more than exploiting what he was naturally good at, and then to be turned loose, in the evenings, at the weekends, and allowed to run free. He wondered now whether he believed that it had sated him, bored him, and how he had been able to turn his back on it all so deliberately. He recalled dropping his tie—he thought it might even have been an Hermès tie, acquired at Changi Airport—into a company wastepaper bin, and marveled at his lunacy. What could he have been thinking of?

He stared around him at the kitchen. It wasn't Petra's kitchen the way his mother's kitchen was his mother's kitchen. It was, in a way, their kitchen, or at least the kitchen that he and Petra had allowed to evolve out of a pleasant square room with a sink and a cooker in it. He had painted the walls blue so that Petra could add birds, and clouds, and constellations, and they had arranged the pieces of furniture they had nonchalantly acquired from here and there in a way that was comfortable if not especially aesthetic, and then they just lived there, and the laundry pile acquired its place just as the kettle did, and the cereal boxes and the plastic mugs the boys used. Would he, Ralph wondered, miss it? If they had to leave this kitchen, this house, and move somewhere so that Ralph, in this suit plus shirt and tie and cuff links, could travel on a train every day to a world of glass and steel that held for him, at this precise moment, all the nostalgic glamour of Singapore, would he really care?

The kitchen door to the outside opened. Kit, in his Spider-Man T-shirt, came in holding an earthy carrot and a stick. He held out the carrot.

"Look!"

"I'm looking—"

"I pulled it," Kit said.

"Well done. Will you eat it now?"

Kit dropped the carrot on the floor.

"No."

"Wow," Petra said from the doorway. "Look at you—"

Ralph struck an attitude.

"What do you think?"

Petra was holding Barney. She bent to deposit him on the floor. He made straight for Kit's dropped carrot.

"Not really my kind of gear," Petra said. "But cool."

"Can you iron it or something?"

"Okay—"

"I don't have any shirts—"

Petra went back outside and reappeared with a trug of vegetables.

"Look."

"Kit said that to me—"

"Kit just yanks them. I grew them. Carrots, spinach, radishes, lettuce."

Ralph came across the kitchen and peered into the trug.

"Very impressive."

"I like it," said Petra.

"The allotment?"

"Growing things."

Ralph went back to the kettle.

"Maybe we'll find a house with a garden. A garden big enough to grow stuff in it."

"I like the allotment," Petra said.

Barney was eating Kit's earthy carrot. Kit was standing by the table, his stick between his legs, like a hobby horse, wedging pieces of Lego into a toast rack. The table had Petra's sketchbook on it too, and several newspapers and jars, and a carton of milk and a hammer and some bowls left over from breakfast with cereal dried to their sides. Petra put the trug down on her sketchbook. She said, "This house is okay."

Ralph tipped coffee out of a foil packet into a cafetière. He added boiling water from the kettle and replaced the plunger on the cafetière. Then he pushed it down, slowly and carefully, before he said, "I'll be earning at least sixty grand. Just for starters. More after a three-month trial."

"I can't think about that much."

"Well," Ralph said, "you should."

Petra bent down, took the carrot out of Barney's grip, wiped off most of the earth on her T-shirt hem, and gave it back to him.

"It doesn't matter."

"What doesn't?" Ralph said.

Petra rubbed her hands against the front of her T-shirt.

"The money," she said.

Ralph left the coffee and came across the kitchen so that he was standing close to her. He said, "We need the money, hon."

"Only a bit—"

Ralph put out his arms and turned her to face him.

"Petra. Lesson one. If you don't have money, you don't have

somewhere to live, you don't eat, you don't have clothes. Lesson two, if you don't have work, you don't have the money for the above. Okay?"

Petra didn't look at him. She nodded.

He said, "You're not working—"

"I could. I did."

"Yes. But you're not working now. You haven't worked since Kit. I don't mind. I don't mind if you don't work. But one of us has to. I was, and I'm going to again."

"Yes."

"And I can't work from this house anymore."

Petra said nothing. Ralph bent down to look in her face. He said, "I've got to go *out* to work now. I've got to go to *London*."

Petra took a step back, out of his grasp. She said to Kit, "Eggy toast for supper?"

Kit was focusing on his Lego, breathing heavily. He took no notice.

Ralph said to Petra, "It's just going to happen."

Petra climbed over Barney to get to the fridge and opened it in search of eggs. She said, without heat, "Why do we go on liking things that hurt us?"

Ralph went very still.

"D'you mean me?"

Petra didn't reply.

"D'you mean," Ralph said, "that I'm trying to hurt you?"

Petra straightened up, a carton of eggs in her hand.

"Not trying. But it's happening."

Ralph said tensely, "How else do you suggest I support you all?"

"There'll be something—"

"But not something I want to do."

Petra found a bag of sliced bread under the newspapers on the table.

"D'you want to do this, then?"

"Yes," Ralph said.

She looked at him. She wore an expression of complete bafflement.

"You *want* to wear a suit and go to London on a train and work all day in an office and never see daylight in winter?"

"Yes," Ralph said.

"You want it to be like it was in Singapore?"

Ralph picked up the cafetière and started to pour coffee into a mug.

"Yes," he said.

"What's happened to you?"

"I've been given another chance to do something I'm good at doing."

"We had money before—"

"But I couldn't manage myself," Ralph said. "I thought I could, but I couldn't. I'm not a manager. I'm good on a team; I'm creative when I don't have to be in charge. I'll be a bloody nuisance, but I'll get results. I'll get results if I'm free."

"Free—"

"Yes."

Petra pulled slices of bread out of the bag. She said, "You'd better *be* free then."

"Thank you." He held up the mug he had just filled. "Coffee?"

Steve Hadley had got to know Aldeburgh quite well. Ever since Petra's card had arrived—a card on which she'd painted a male lapwing with its spiky crest, and in which she'd enclosed a ten-pound note—he'd spent a lot of his spare time in Aldeburgh, looking out for her. She'd said she had two little boys, and although he saw quite a number of smallish young women with children, not many of them seemed to have only boys.

But Steve was in no hurry. He'd got all summer to patrol the coast through Aldeburgh, from the great scallop-shell sculpture to Benjamin Britten, all the way to the southern point of the town, where the tall seafront terraces petered out into the marshy stretches of mingled river and sea. He had Petra's card in his pocket. She'd sent it to the director of the nature reserve, with the money as a donation, and the director had given the card to Steve, saying as you're the only Steve she can have meant you'd better have it, nice little painting. It was a nice little painting. Without it, and the trouble she'd plainly taken to do it, Steve doubted he'd have bothered to try and find her. But the painting and the memory of her sleeping in the sand combined to lodge her in his mind in a way that was pleasantly intriguing. So, after work, and on his days off, Steve ambled about Aldeburgh and ate fish and chips sitting on the shingle, and waited.

He finally saw her just as he was about to go home, one afternoon of a day off, and he was standing looking at the primary school, admiring the little bright boat modeled on to the white wall, when she came past, with a buggy containing a big baby and a little boy beside her, dragging a bit on the buggy and emitting that kind of low-grade steady whine that Steve recognized from his brother's children.

He stepped off the pavement into the road in front of her.

"Hi," he said.

Petra looked uncomprehendingly, and then her expression cleared. She smiled at him. She was wearing an Indian embroidered tunic over jeans, and sneakers, and her hair was tied over one shoulder in a long ponytail.

"Hi—"

He put his hand out.

"I'm Steve. From Minsmere. Remember?"

She nodded. She said to the little boy, "I went to sleep in the sand and my car keys fell out of my pocket. This man found them."

Kit paused in his whine. He looked uncertainly at Steve. Steve squatted down in the road in front of him.

"I've got nephews your age—"

"I'm three," Kit said guardedly.

"I bet you are."

"I've got a digger."

Steve stood up.

"Lucky man."

Petra said, "Why are you in Aldeburgh?"

He smiled at her.

"Looking for you."

"Were you?"

He pulled the card with her little painting out of his pocket.

"Been carrying that around for weeks—"

"I don't want you stalking me," Petra said.

"No," he said, "I was just waiting. Hoping a bit. You know." He looked back at Kit. "What's your name?"

"Kit."

"And his?"

"Barney," Kit said, and then, "He's always eating."

Steve laughed.

He said, glancing at Barney, "Looks it."

Petra was studying him. She said, as if she had suddenly decided something, "We're going to my allotment."

Steve nodded. He said hesitantly, "Can I come along?"

"Okay—"

He motioned to Barney's buggy.

"Shall I push him?"

Petra moved sideways.

"Okay," she said again, and then, "I'm married."

"I thought you would be."

Petra took Kit's hand.

"Four years—"

"It's not a problem."

"A problem?"

Steve began to push Barney towards the footpath to the allotments.

"I mean, I like you anyway. I like you for going to sleep in the sand and painting the lapwing. You're different."

"It's not a help," Petra said, "being different. Kit's different, too. Aren't you, Kit?"

Kit looked across his mother at Steve pushing the buggy. He thought that he couldn't usually hold her hand because of the buggy, and he liked holding her hand and he liked it that there was nothing in her other hand either. He regarded Steve with approval.

"Yes," he said to his mother.

"I don't want to talk about liking," Petra said to Steve. "I don't want anything like that. I'm not in a good place right now. I was just going to the allotment because I feel better there, it settles me."

"Fine by me," Steve said.

Barney twisted round in his pushchair and noticed that his mother had been replaced by this stranger. He began to roar.

Petra bent sideways. Kit could see where her free hand was going. She said helplessly, "Oh Barn—"

"Come on," Steve said suddenly. "Tally-ho! Race you!"

He set off at a surprisingly fast run down the path, neatly skimming and swerving the buggy to avoid the bumps. Barney's roars almost immediately subsided into squeals and then shouts of delight.

"Come on!" Kit cried to Petra. "Come on, come *on*!"

And he began to run forward, tugging her, and she came stumbling behind him, and he knew she could feel his excitement because she was laughing too—in his charge, and laughing.

Steve was very helpful in the allotment. He mended the bolt on the gate, and dismantled the canes supporting the sweet peas that had died from lack of water, and dug a root or two of early potatoes, and stopped Barney from eating some woodlice, and made Kit a track for his digger with a line of old bricks he found on someone else's allotment, which they plainly didn't want, he said, because the whole thing was so overgrown and gone to seed. He didn't bother Petra with talking, he just took the fork from her to dig the potatoes, and mended the gate with the screwdriver on the Swiss Army knife he had in his pocket, and crouched down wordlessly beside Barney and fished the woodlice out of his mouth without drawing attention to what he was doing. When they left at last, Barney without protest allowed him to strap him into the buggy and steer him out through the gate, and Kit waited until Petra was through before he slid the mended bolt into place, and took her hand again, and this time her free one held a bunch of sweet williams, which was fine, because they were only flowers.

And when they got to the school, Steve stopped pushing, and said, "Well, I'll say good-bye now."

"D'you want a coffee?" Petra said.

He shook his head.

"I'll be on my way, thanks."

She held out the flowers. He shook his head again.

"I'm not much of a flower man, me—"

Petra laid the flowers across the handles of the buggy. She said, "Thanks for your help."

"Thanks for your company."

Steve looked down at Kit.

"See you, digger man."

Kit said, "Are you coming to my house?"

"No, mate. I'm not."

"Yes!" Kit said.

"Tell you what," Steve said, still looking at Kit and Petra, "you could come to mine, though. You could come to my house."

"Yes!" Kit shouted.

"There's enough stones at my house," Steve said, "to fill a million diggers."

He glanced at Petra. She was looking at the sweet williams.

"How about it?"

She lifted one sneakered foot and kicked off the brake on the pushchair.

"Okay," she said.

Rachel sent Ralph the particulars of a house in Ipswich, by e-mail. It was semidetached and unremarkable, but it had three bedrooms, a hundred-foot garden, and was seven minutes from the station. She attached, also, a train timetable of services from Ipswich so Ralph could see how early he might get into the office and how late he might be able to leave, since the journeys either end of the train travel were negligible.

Ralph thought the house looked fine. It had probably been built between the wars, but it had the space, and the location was perfect. Rachel said, in her accompanying e-mail, that she and Anthony could probably find a way to help with any shortfall in buying a house more expensive than the one they were selling. They hadn't discussed it yet, but she was sure that it wouldn't be a problem, Anthony could sell some paintings or sign a new contract, Ralph wasn't to worry. And she'd researched schools and there was a good Church of England primary half a mile away, and two preschools nearby with vacancies for the autumn term. The garden had plenty of space for Petra to grow vegetables. Should she go and view it, on his and Petra's behalf?

"Do. Thanks," Ralph replied laconically, and clicked "Send." Having been so hard, and painful and frustrating, life suddenly seemed to be smoothing out, rolling away in front of him in a manner it hadn't done for ages. He didn't actually want to live in a semidetached house in a featureless street near Ipswich station, but that prospect, at the moment, seemed merely dimmed by the brightness of all the other things on offer that were suddenly, wonderfully, making him feel that he was being released into an immense space of brilliant blue air, where he could soar and spin and dive. He thought that, with lungfuls of that liberty and energy and chances for achievement inside him, he could well endure reducing himself to weekends in a mildly unsympathetic place. Anyway, there was a hundred-foot garden. In Aldeburgh, they had no more than a scruffy little yard, backing onto a pebble-dashed garage wall. A hundred feet of garden was enough to kick a ball, hit a ball, have more vegetable space than there was in the allotment.

He put Rachel's e-mail printout down in front of Petra.

"What d'you think?"

Petra peered at it.

"It's okay—"

"It's seven minutes' walk from the station."

Petra nodded. She stopped looking at the house particulars and picked up her trug. There were new potatoes in it, whitish yellow and the size of walnuts.

"There's a hundred-foot garden," Ralph said. "For a football goal. And veg. South-facing."

Petra tipped the potatoes into the sink.

"Nice," she said.

"Want a beer?"

"No thanks."

"It's not especially attractive, I know, but the location's perfect. Schools, station, everything."

Petra ran water into the sink. She said, "Have you said good night to the kids?"

"Yes," Ralph said.

Petra turned round.

"You haven't—"

"Okay," Ralph said, "but I will."

"Stop looking at that stuff—"

"I was just thinking—"

"Don't," Petra said. "Go and see Kit. He's in bed. He'll be waiting."

Ralph stood up. He was wearing, Petra noticed, a T-shirt she had never seen before. It was bright white, with a little discreet dark logo on the left breast. And he'd shaved. Petra hadn't seen him this clean-shaven in months.

"Hon, just think about this—"

Petra turned back to the sink. She said, "We had a good end to the day. At the allotment. It was a relief, after what happened."

Ralph wasn't listening. He was standing by the table, in his white corporate T-shirt, lost in some place other than the one he was actually in.

"Kit pulled my hair," Petra said, rumbling the potatoes round the sink to rinse off the earth, "really hard. I mean, it really hurt, he pulled it so hard. I don't know if he meant to, maybe he just wanted to see how you get hair out of a head, or something, but I screamed, and I must have frightened him because he rushed across the room and pulled Barney's hair, and then Barney screamed. So I picked Barney up and cuddled him, and I ignored Kit, and then Barney got furious and I could see he was furious with me for not punishing Kit, just ignoring him. What do you think I should have done?"

"Um?" Ralph said absently.

"I mean," Petra said, "you could see Barney wanted justice, you could see he really wanted it, he wanted me to—to *stab* Kit, or something."

There was a silence. Then Ralph said, from far away, "You could hardly do *that*, could you?"

Petra pulled the plug out of the sink.

"I went on cuddling Barney and then Kit started whining. He whined all the time, for hours, until we went to the allotment. Then he was okay."

"Oh, good," Ralph said.

Petra picked up a tea towel draped across the back of a chair. She said, looking at the e-mail printout on the table, "It's no good."

"What isn't?"

"I'm not living there."

Ralph gave her a wide smile.

"It's pretty ordinary, I know. I'm sure we can find something else—"

"I'm not living in Ipswich," Petra said.

Ralph said patiently, "I need to be near a station."

Petra dried her hands. Then she draped the tea towel back over the chair.

"I can't," she said.

Ralph looked right at her.

"Can't what?"

"I can't," Petra repeated. "I can't leave it. I can't leave the sea."

CHAPTER ELEVEN

C harlotte's mother was at her painting table, with a dahlia. Dahlias had fallen so far out of fashion, it seemed, that they were now on trend, bang on trend. At least, that's what Charlotte had told her when she brought a bunch of them the day before, a gaudy strident bunch of them, orange and purple and scarlet and yellow. Charlotte had bought them, she said, in the flower market near their flat, which was apparently a famous Sunday flower market where you could also buy the world's best bread, and coffee, and cupcakes, and Charlotte said she couldn't get enough cupcakes just now, and Luke had bought her a whole box, and then a hat from the next-door shop because he said a hat would still fit her, however huge she got. And then Charlotte had burst into tears all over her mother and told her what Luke's mother had said to her, and how she hadn't been able to sleep the night after, and she still didn't know whether to be more hurt than angry.

Marnie had, after giving the dahlias a long drink, laid a single yellow one on a piece of white paper in order to examine the extraordinarily precise structure of its petals. It was as if it had been made of origami, so symmetrical and deeply three-dimensional was it. It would be a challenge to draw it, but a pleasurable challenge. When she had had a long and careful look, she would put the dahlia into the special small bronze clamp that Charlotte's father had designed and had made for her, and begin on the lengthy and exact process of drawing the flower before she painted it. She had been painting flowers since before Charlotte's sisters were born. She had started because Charlotte's father, although generous to a fault, had preferred to support her entirely, but had also acknowledged that she must, of course, have a life of her own outside the house and garden. Marnie, pregnant with Fiona, who was now thirty-five, had enrolled in a course that taught botanical drawing. She had been the best in her class. Charlotte's father had been so very proud of her. He had also, Marnie was aware even if she did not say so, felt justified; if she had been working, she would not have had the chance to be the best botanical artist in her area. Would she?

Charlotte's father was called Gregory, and he had been ten years older than Marnie, and a partner in a local firm of solicitors that he had joined as soon as he qualified. He was eager to have children but disappointed not to produce sons. He was extremely kind to Marnie after each of his three daughters' births, and gave her carefully chosen special pieces of jewelry to commemorate the occasions—garnets, for Charlotte, which were possibly Marnie's least favorite stone—but she knew he was disappointed. He never said so outright, but he was the kind of man whose conduct and vocal inflections carried far more meaning than his words, and Marnie knew that he was longing for another Gregory to take his place, as he had taken his father's, and his father had taken his own father's: four generations of Gregory Webster-Smiths with deep and affectionate links to the beech-covered hills of Buckinghamshire.

Even during his long last illness, during which Marnie had nursed him tirelessly, he repeated frequently that he was dying a happy man, in the tones of a defiantly dissatisfied one. He even said, once, after a day in which the pain had been hard to manage and they were both worn out by it, that he knew that it was not her fault that all their children had been girls. But he managed to say it in a way that induced only guilt and regret in Marnie, and she had wept helplessly into the chicken consommé she was heating up for him in the hope that he would accept even a spoonful of it.

She had wept a great deal too after he died. She had been married for almost forty years, and he was leaving her with a pleasant house and enough money, which she had done nothing to earn, even if she had contributed immeasurably in less quantifiable ways. She was used to him, used to being a wife, and she wasn't at all sure how she would—even could—make the transition to being a widow. Apart from anything else, she was bone-tired after three long years of steady nursing, and seemed to have lost herself in the process of sublimating herself to Gregory's personality in illness. For well over a year after his death, she moved about the house mindlessly, forgetting what she had gone upstairs for, carrying a ball of string pointlessly from room to room, gazing out of the window down the lawn to the pond without taking anything in. And then Charlotte, her lovely, adorable Charlotte, who had been such an anxiety to her father because he believed her looks could only spell trouble, came home one weekend, lit up like a Christmas tree, and said, almost before she was in the door, that she had met someone. Seriously.

Her announcement had the effect of waking Marnie from her post-Gregory trance. It galvanized her. Both Charlotte's older sisters, Fiona and Sarah, rang each other constantly to say what a relief, isn't it amazing, can you believe, have you *ever* seen Mummy like this? Everybody adored Luke of course, so good-looking, so tall, so besotted with Charlotte, so sweet to Fiona and Sarah's children, so polite to Marnie, such a good tennis player, so interesting to have Anthony Brinkley as a father. Marnie's house ceased, almost overnight, to be a place resonant with Gregory's powerful ailing presence and the girls' long-gone childhoods and became the energetic headquarters for a wedding. Charlotte wanted everything—frock, marquee, cake, flowers, speeches, champagne—that Marnie could have wished, that she had had herself, that Fiona and Sarah had had, although in modified form, since Fiona's husband had been on brief leave from the navy, and Sarah's husband had refused to be married in anything but specifically secular circumstances. The registry office in Beaconsfield had done the ceremony beautifully, of course, with great dignity, but Sarah wore a short dress and her husband was in a lounge suit and there was a distinct absence of—well, magic was the word, really. But Charlotte wanted magic. She wanted magic by the sparkling bucketload, and she had looked to her mother, as trustingly as she had looked to her for praise or comfort when she was small, to give it to her.

And she had. She knew she had. Marnie could still look back on Charlotte's wedding day with complete satisfaction, just as she could look back on the months that preceded it with the pleased certainty that the house had come alive again, that the children and their children were constantly there, that the tradition of Webster-Smith hospitality—Gregory had been famous as a host—was as vigorous and welcoming as ever. It had been a wonderful summer. The spare beds hardly seemed to have had time to cool between occupants. The fridge was full of beers, and there was a liter bottle of vodka in the freezer. Guiltily, Marnie sometimes wondered if she had ever been so happy.

But now this. Now Charlotte—who it transpired had already been pregnant even before her wedding day—was sobbing in Marnie's arms about how unkind Rachel had been to her. Marnie didn't know Rachel very well—there had been only a couple of elaborately orchestrated meetings before the big day—but she had struck Marnie as the kind of person she would expect Luke's mother to be. In Marnie's experience, mothers of sons were, broadly speaking, either excessively feminine or forthright and capable. Rachel had seemed to fall into the latter category, and although Marnie had never seen her house she knew Charlotte was impressed by its bohemian ease and color and the way life revolved around cooking and painting. Charlotte was awed by Anthony's studio. Marnie had never ever considered a studio. Gregory had bought her a pretty rosewood table—reproduction, but beautifully made— that fitted into the deep bay window of the sitting room. He said that, while he was watching racing, or golf, or cricket on the television, in the afternoon, as he liked to do, she could paint at her table, across the room from him, and that way they could be together.

Rachel, Charlotte said angrily, had asked her if they couldn't wait to start a family.

"She didn't say it in a nice voice," Charlotte said. "She said it as if she was furious. As if she was . . . *disgusted* with us. She thinks we're careless. She sounded as if we'd kind of insulted her, let her down."

"I expect," Marnie said carefully, "that it wasn't what she'd planned for you—"

They were together on the big sofa in the sitting room, Charlotte half lying against her mother. The sofa was in a different place from where it had been in Gregory's day, and so was the television and the chair he used to sit in to watch it, which now had a new cover in a bold russet check, which

Fiona had chosen for her, advised by a friend who had a small soft-furnishings business.

"She had no business to make plans for us!" Charlotte cried. She blew her nose and pressed her face against her mother's arm. "It's not her life! It's ours! And . . . she sounded so horrible. Her voice was horrible."

"Oh dear," Marnie said, as lightly as she could.

Charlotte took her face away from her mother's arm and stared at her.

"Aren't you angry with her? Don't you hate her for speaking to me like that?"

Marnie was conscious of a warm glow, induced by being the parent who was behaving well, the parent who was seen as the ally, not the enemy.

"I'm trying not to, darling."

"Why? Why aren't you angry? Don't you believe me?"

"Utterly, darling."

"Well, then—"

"The thing is, she feels about Luke as I do about you. Luke is her son—"

"Luke is *mine*," Charlotte said, blowing her nose again. "Luke is my husband. *First*."

"Sometimes people take a while to get used to that."

"That what?"

"That . . . transference of allegiance."

"Well, she'll bloody well *have* to. He's not her little boy anymore."

Marnie waited a moment. She pulled a clean tissue from the box and expertly wiped mascara from where it had smudged below Charlotte's eyes. She said, "Of course he knows you're here."

Charlotte looked past her mother at the wall behind the sofa.

"Not . . . actually."

"Luke doesn't know? Where does he think you are?"

"Work."

"And where does work think you are?"

"In bed. With a tummy bug."

"Oh, Charlotte," Marnie said.

Charlotte looked back at her. Her lower lip was very slightly pushed out. She said, "Why d'you say it like that?"

Marnie hesitated. The truth would have been to say, "Because that's the first lie of marriage that you've told Luke. And it'll be followed by years of half-truths. Years," but Charlotte did not look as if she could either hear or accept that. So she said instead, "It doesn't make muddles better if you muddle them further," and Charlotte said loudly, "I didn't *start* this."

"I know you didn't—"

"Rachel did, Rachel ruined my lunch party, Rachel's the one treating us as if we were stupid little kids. Luke and I are *married*."

"Marriage doesn't change how you feel about your children," Marnie said. "Maybe it does, in time, in your head. But not in your heart, really. You go on feeling just the same, and maybe some of those feelings are not as reasonable as they might be."

Charlotte sniffed. She said, "Did Daddy feel like that?"

Marnie laughed. She had a fleeting image of how Gregory would have reacted to Charlotte's story, storming out of the house to get the Mercedes out of the garage and roaring off to Suffolk.

"Daddy, darling, would have been ten times worse."

Now, examining the dahlia—it really was a rather awful color, like cheap butter—Marnie reflected, with more relief than guilt, that Gregory would have been no help in a situation like this. He would have shouted, "I told you so!" when he heard of the unintended pregnancy, and then he would have got very sentimental over Charlotte and unhelpfully defensive of her outrage at being spoken to without the customary admiration and approval.

Charlotte had been a willful little girl. Fiona and Sarah had been nine and seven when she was born, and she had been pretty from her first breath, her little round head thatched with thick primrose-colored down. Probably we spoiled her, Marnie thought, probably all four of us did, and she thrived on being spoiled except that she can't take anything other than praise, she can't deal with opinion that doesn't coincide with what she wants to do anyway. And yet, Marnie told herself, putting the flower down and picking up her 3B sketching pencil, she had agreed—or, at least, not disagreed—when Marnie suggested she go straight home and tell Luke where she had been. She'd stood in the doorway, jingling her car keys, and said, "Well, I'll try. But she made us quarrel! Can you believe it? She actually made us have a row!"

"Then don't let her."

Charlotte glanced at her mother.

"D'you really feel that calm? D'you really feel it's okay for her to talk to me like that?"

Marnie smiled at Charlotte.

"Actually," she said, still smiling, "I want to kill her," and she could still hear Charlotte laughing. She'd laughed all the way across the drive to her car, and then she'd got in and turned on the ignition, and music suddenly belted out of the car's speakers, and Charlotte drove away in a whirl of noise.

Marnie bent over her paper. The thing was, with parenting grown children, you had to learn to hold your tongue. If you wanted them to tell you anything, that is.

"It's Luke," Luke said into the intercom.

"Luke!" Sigrid said, surprised.

She was in the kitchen, ironing. Mariella was in bed, and

Edward had gone out to meet Ralph, who had suddenly appeared at his office that afternoon and said that he needed help.

"What about now?" Sigrid demanded.

"I don't know. He wouldn't say till we met later. I'll buy him a beer and a steak and put him on a train back to Suffolk."

"Your family—"

"I won't be late. Kiss Mariella for me. And count your blessings."

"What blessings?"

"The loving-family-in-another-country one—"

"Are you okay?" Sigrid said now over the intercom to Luke.

"I'm fine. Can I come in?"

Sigrid pressed the door-release buzzer. She heard the door slam behind Luke, and then his rapid footsteps on the stairs down to the basement kitchen.

"Hi," he said, coming over at the same speed to kiss her cheek.

"Where's Charlotte?"

"At a girl movie. With mates. Is Ed here?"

"He's with Ralph," Sigrid said. "Didn't you know?"

"I don't know anything," Luke said, "except that since that Sunday Char can't seem to calm down and I'm going mental."

Sigrid switched the iron off and motioned to a chair.

"Have a seat. Coffee?"

"Better not," Luke said, "I've drunk too much today, I'm twitching. I'd love a beer."

Sigrid crossed to the fridge. She said, "So you wanted to see Edward?"

"Well, sort of. Either of you. Both of you. I just need a bit of help—"

Sigrid handed a bottle of beer across the table to Luke.

"That's what Ralph said to Edward—"

"Can we not think about Ralph?"

Sigrid took a chair on the other side of the table. Luke looked very young and very tired, and she noticed that his nails were bitten. She didn't think she'd ever noticed before.

"Are you a nail biter?"

Luke took a swallow of beer from the bottle and rumpled his hair with his free hand.

"I'm everything right now. I'd be a pusher's dream market if I dared!"

Sigrid picked a grape off the bunch in the fruit bowl in front of her. She said, "Is it the baby? Are you worried about having a baby?"

Luke closed his eyes briefly.

"I am absolutely ecstatic about the baby. I don't care that we've only been married a couple of months. I'm thrilled. It's not that. It's . . . well, it's Mum and Charlotte of course, and Charlotte thinks Mum despises her because (a) she's pregnant so soon and (b) she isn't Petra, and she doesn't live in Suffolk and can't draw. And now—" He stopped.

"Now," Sigrid said. She ate another grape slowly.

"Now," Luke said wearily, "she wants Mum to apologize."

Sigrid laughed.

"Why are you laughing?" Luke demanded.

"That's not going to happen!"

"No."

Luke said despondently, "She told her family about the baby two weeks before she told mine. She said that's what you do. She says the mother's mother is different from the father's mother, and now she says that the way Mum behaved just proves it, and if she is going to have any kind of relationship in the future with Mum, Mum has got to say sorry."

He tipped up his beer bottle to his mouth and drank. Sigrid went to the fridge and took out a second one. She put it down on the table near Luke. She said, "What do *you* think?"

Luke sighed. "I think Mum was well out of order, but it's kind of time to forgive and forget, now."

Sigrid said, "Not so easy—" and stopped.

Luke looked at her. He said, "You haven't had a run-in with Mum, have you?"

"It was a long time ago—"

"I didn't know—"

"And you won't know now," Sigrid said. "Maybe we just say that sometimes your mother is careless, a little."

"Are you angry with her still?"

Sigrid hesitated.

"Wow," Luke said, and then, after a moment, "Aren't you going to have a drink too?"

"Maybe some tea," Sigrid said, moving towards the kettle.

"Charlotte's got a bit fixated on this Petra thing now, too. It's not just Mum, saying what she said, but also how can anyone compare to Petra."

"Yes," Sigrid said.

She took a mug and a packet of valerian tea bags out of a cupboard. Luke said, "*You* don't feel that, do you?"

"Yes," Sigrid said. She turned round to look at Luke. "It's a problem."

"But Petra's like . . . like a kid, like a kind of half sister—"

"She had the seal of approval," Sigrid said.

"But she was pregnant when they married."

"Logic isn't a part of this. And your Charlotte isn't used to family difficulties, she isn't used to being anything except the center of the family."

"She's the center to *me*," Luke said.

"Tell her that."

"I do. I do, but she says I can't mean it if I go on defending Mum."

Sigrid came back to the table.

"Do you defend her?"

Luke glanced at her unhappily and then looked away.

"I can't . . . attack her. Can I? Does . . . does Edward?"

"There is something between the two," Sigrid said, sitting down again. "Not defending, not attacking, but not leaving your wife to feel alone, either."

There was a pause. Then Luke said, half appalled, "Do *you* feel alone?"

Sigrid looked at him. He seemed suddenly too young to be anyone's husband, sitting there with his clear complexion and his bitten nails.

"Sometimes," she said.

When he had seen Ralph off in the direction of the station, Edward went back into the pub where they had had supper and, on impulse, ordered a brandy and soda. He carried it across the room to a small table in a corner with a single chair next to it, customers having taken all but that one to other tables. The table was full of dirty glasses with empty crisp packets wedged in them, but Edward didn't mind. He sat down with his back against the wall and tipped the whole bottle of soda water into the dark puddle of brandy at the bottom of his glass.

In some ways, Ralph had been quite restrained. He'd drunk a single pint of beer, eaten his steak with salad and without chips, and he'd worn a suit and a shirt, which must have been new since Edward could see the sharp horizontal creases where it had been folded round its packaging. He also made Edward quite a civilized speech of gratitude about helping him to obtain this new job, and said, unexpectedly, that he wouldn't let Edward down, and, in fact, he hoped that Edward would come to feel pretty pleased about his performance. He said he was feeling really fired up about starting employed work again, and that he knew he was bloody lucky. He then put his knife and fork down and said that there was a problem.

"I was waiting, actually," Edward said.

"It's Petra."

"Yes," Edward said.

"I can't talk to her. She says that the money means nothing to her and that she can't, now, live anywhere except by the sea."

Edward sighed.

"Oh God—"

"I've explained how life and money works. I mean, she knows that, she's not a fool, but when things get rough, or she doesn't like something, she goes into inert mode, sort of eludes facing the problem, till it's over. But this one won't be over until she looks at it."

"Have you told the parents?"

Ralph fiddled with a side plate.

"Don't really want to—"

"Wouldn't they help? Wouldn't Petra listen to them, especially Dad?"

Ralph said, "I've let Mum in too far already. She's beavering away finding houses and schools and stuff. I shouldn't have allowed it. I think it's put Petra's back up, although she won't say so. She won't say anything much. She's gone silent on me. It's the way she thinks she'll get me to change my mind."

"Or," Edward said, "she's genuinely withdrawn. She's always done that. Dad said she never spoke at all, the first year he knew her. She's probably miserable."

Ralph took a swallow of water.

"She doesn't have the option to be miserable."

"Hey, steady on—"

"She hasn't contributed anything much since the boys were born. The sale of the odd painting, maybe, but nothing significant. If she wants to go on playing with the boys and growing vegetables, then she has to accept some compromises in return for that freedom."

Edward leaned forward.

"Ralph, she's never known you in a suit. She's never known you commuting, with a regular pay slip and long working days. You've been a superannuated hippy ever since she's known you. You can't blame her for being a bit thrown by the change."

"It's exciting—"

"Exciting can also be frightening. Can't you just battle with a long commute for a few more months until she gets used to this zoot in a suit?"

There was a pause. Then Ralph said, "No. Not really. I want to do this properly. With all my energy."

"So you want to move into Ipswich—"

"Hell, that's a compromise!" Ralph said. "I don't want to live in a suburban street either, but I'm prepared to do it so that I can walk to the fucking station!"

"And if Petra won't budge?"

Ralph leaned back in his chair. He looked directly at Edward. He said, "That's why I'm here. I thought maybe you'd have the answer."

Edward stared down at his plate. He had a sudden mental image of Petra on her wedding day, taking her shoes off and running across the gravel of his parents' drive in bare feet, as easily as if she were running on a carpet.

"Well," he said slowly, not looking up, "I suppose you could just not live together for a while. Leave Petra and the boys where they are and rent a room here for the week? Go home at weekends. For now, anyway. Till things settle?"

Now, Edward drank several satisfying mouthfuls of his brandy and soda. A girl came from behind the bar to collect the dirty glasses on his table, standing as close to him, in her miniskirt and knee-high boots, while she stacked the glasses on a tray, as if he had been merely a piece of furniture. At one point, her black-mesh-covered thigh was practically touching his arm, but she took no notice of him whatsoever. Would she, he wondered, have behaved with such supreme indifference if he had been ten years younger? He watched her walk back to the bar. She was a girl so different from Sigrid, so different from Petra, who were in turn so different from each other, that it was hard to believe that they were all of the same gender. The girl from the bar would probably have thought Petra was insane. Pass up the chance to live in a city? Mental.

It might be mental in its way, Edward thought, but Petra was only being true to herself, however inconvenient and weirdly adamant that self was. He was delighted to see Ralph's enthusiasm for this new job, and relieved to see what looked like a real determination to make something of it. But he felt deeply, deeply uneasy that he had suggested that they lived temporarily apart. He shouldn't have done it. The moment the words were out of his mouth, and Ralph was eagerly, energetically seizing upon the idea, Edward had felt his heart sinking in that inexorable way hearts are prone to, in the aftermath of the wrong impulse.

"Just an idea," Edward had said hastily. "Only a notion. Think about it—"

But it was too late. Ralph said he must get his train, but his eyes were bright and, when they stood up from the table, he put his arms round his brother in a way he hadn't done in years and hugged him hard.

Edward said, trying to temper his enthusiasm, "I'm not trying to split you up, mate," and Ralph had laughed and said that wasn't a problem, they both knew what to do with freedom, no worries there, and had gone swinging out onto the pavement and into a taxi, leaving Edward feeling that he had, inadvertently, put something intrinsically pretty fragile even further into jeopardy. He stood there for a moment or two, watching the taillights of Ralph's taxi diminishing, thinking that he would go straight home and dump himself and his regrets on Sigrid, and then he thought that that was exactly what he should *not* do, that he should instead work through his remorse on his own, and go home at least on resolved terms with himself.

So here he was, halfway down a brandy and soda, wondering if the person he should actually talk to was not Sigrid, but Petra.

Luke prayed that it would not be his mother who answered the telephone. He was dreading the call in any case, but it was also imperative that he speak to his father alone, and in private, and as his father only used his mobile phone intermittently, and in art-college-term time, Luke's only choice was to try the home landline at a time when he thought his mother might be out, or in the garden, and his father alone in his studio.

"Hello?" Anthony said.

"Dad—"

"Luke," Anthony said, his voice full of warmth. "Great to hear you, lad—"

"How are you?"

"Good," Anthony said heartily. "Good. Drawing some sparrows. The Royal Mail might be doing a series of bird stamps. I love drawing sparrows, so sociable."

"Lovely—"

"And how are things with you two? I loved your flat."

"Well—"

"Well, what?"

"That's why I've rung. Things with us. It's a bit difficult—"

Anthony's tone altered to deep concern.

"Oh no—"

"I mean," Luke said hastily, "*we* aren't difficult, we're fine. It's just that there's a problem. I'm trying to sort it, for . . . Charlotte, well for us, really. Which is why I'm ringing."

"Tell me," Anthony said.

Luke paused. He was alone in the studio, Jed being out looking at a new project. It was just as well he was alone, because he'd been so jangled up all day after Charlotte had told him, when they woke up, that she hadn't been to work the day before, but instead had been to see her mother, that Jed would have been bound to notice something and Luke would probably have told him a bit, at least, and then wished he hadn't because Jed, though a really nice guy, thought people who got married needed their heads seeing to. And anyway, he could never have told Jed how horrified he'd been to realize that Charlotte had told him a lie, and that he'd believed her. The horror had deepened because Charlotte didn't seem to think she'd done anything very awful; she was far more concerned, still, with Rachel's awfulness, which she seemed to think justified all aberrant conduct on her part. He was now appalled to find that his father's voice, sympathetic and encouraging, made him feel distinctly unsteady.

"I don't know how to say it, Dad."

"Try just starting."

"It's . . . well, it's about the other Sunday."

"Yes."

"And what Mum—"

"I know—"

"The thing is, Dad, that Charlotte is still really upset."

"Poor girl," Anthony said sympathetically.

"I expect it's pregnancy and hormones and all that, but she doesn't seem to be getting over it."

"Give it time," Anthony said. "It's only ten days or so. I

know Mum felt terrible afterwards. I'm not saying she didn't need to feel terrible, but I know she did. They've both got to let it just bed down, and become not such a big deal."

"I don't think that's going to work—"

"Oh? Well, I'm not sure there's another viable option—"

"Dad, I think there is. Charlotte thinks there is. She's very clear about it."

There was a tiny pause. Luke wondered if Anthony was still drawing with the hand not holding the phone.

"Which is?"

"Oh God," Luke said, "I don't know how to say this, so I'll just say it. Charlotte wants Mum to apologize to her. Could you . . . could you ever ask her to do that? For . . . for Charlotte? For me?"

The pause was much longer this time, then Anthony said less warmly, "No, lad. No, I couldn't do that."

"Couldn't you?" Luke said, aware his voice was shaking.

"No," Anthony said, "no, she was very much in the wrong, she knows that, I know that, you know that. And she's paying for it internally, if you know what I mean. But I'm not asking her to make a public apology, I wouldn't ask her to do that." He stopped and then he said firmly, "She's my wife."

CHAPTER TWELVE

Steve Hadley's cottage at Shingle Street was sunk deeply into the beach. It was brilliantly whitewashed—Steve's landlord repainted the exterior every spring, after the winter storms—and stood with its narrow gable end facing the sea. From a distance it looked almost as if it was plunging through the shingle towards the shore, but when you got nearer you could see that a concrete gully ran round the house, wide enough for a water butt and a dustbin, and for entry by the only door Steve and his fellow tenant ever used, facing inland, away from the east wind.

Steve shared the house with a man who worked in a fish smokehouse near Woodbridge. They had met online, both seeking short, cheap lets on the coast, and although the landlord of the cottage could have leased it profitably as a holiday rental, he was a man opposed to holidaymakers, a man who preferred to let his few properties to people who worked in Suffolk and were therefore likely to contribute to its economy. So he was pleased to find Steve, and Terry from the smokehouse, who were not only locally employed, but who also would not mind the antiquated hot-water system or primitive kitchen. There were two small bedrooms, a shabby sitting room with a leatherette sofa and chairs, and a television of similar antiquity, and a bathroom where towels never dried and the walls were always sweating.

But there was the beach. Crunching across it, with Barney heavily on her back and Kit slipping and sliding and squealing by her side, Petra wondered how she could ever have borne to be away. The shingle itself—so much of it, so clean and smooth—the flatness, throwing the immense blue dome of the sky into even greater relief, the symmetrical mounds of blue-green sea kale, the creeping skeins of sea pea with its bright-purple flowers, the air, the space, the wind, it was all exhilarating, and at the same time profoundly consoling. I'm home, Petra thought, I'm back. This is the place.

"What d'you think?" she called to Kit. "What d'you think of it?"

He was scrambling through the stones, pink with exertion.

"Windy!" he shouted happily. "Windy!"

"Do you like it?"

He nodded furiously, bending down to seize handfuls of pebbles and throw them, clattering, down again. Petra laughed. Kit glanced at her, and laughed too, hurling pebbles about.

"Careful—"

"Look!" Kit shouted, pointing.

Petra looked. Steve, having seen them approaching, was coming across the shingle to meet them.

"Look!" Kit shouted again to Steve, chucking pebbles. "Look!"

"Hi there," Steve said to Petra.

She stopped walking.

"Hi—"

Steve indicated Barney.

183

"Shall I take him?"

"Yes," Petra said gratefully. "He weighs a ton—"

"I'm throwing!" Kit shouted to Steve. "I'm throwing!"

"I can see you," Steve said, deftly taking Barney. "I'm watching—"

"I'll have to watch," Petra said. "He's a shocker for water, Kit."

Barney looked at Steve calmly, without dismay. Steve said to him, "Hello there, big boy. The sea's not like other water."

"It's bigger," Petra said.

"You have to handle it differently," Steve said. "I'll take him down to the sea. I'll show him the sea. I'll explain." He smiled at Kit.

Petra glanced at him. Barney was lolling back in his arms now, like a pasha, and Kit approached to stagger round his knees with handfuls of stones, chattering and chirruping. She said, "You're a natural, with kids."

"I like them—"

"Have you—"

"No," Steve said, "but my brother has. And there's all the schools who come to the reserve. I like the primary schools a lot. I like it when they still want to please you. They're a nightmare when they start wanting to impress each other."

Petra nodded. Steve said, "Shall we go down to the water?"

"Okay—"

Steve looked down at Kit, still chanting and stamping round him in the pebbles.

"Come and meet the North Sea," Steve said to Kit, and he set off through the shingle, carrying Barney, with Kit tagging along beside him, still clutching his stones.

Petra watched the three of them for a moment, standing where they had left her. The day was bright and clear, so she put up her hand to shade her eyes a little as she followed their uneven progress towards the sea. Barney flung his head back in

Steve's arms, and closed his eyes in rapture against the sun and air, and then Kit, stumbling, put a hand out and grasped at the nearest leg of Steve's jeans, and Petra saw Steve detach his own hand briefly from supporting Barney, and touch Kit's head with it, and something inside her, something knotted and strangulated that had been there for weeks now, slipped and smoothed and untied itself. She took an immense involuntary breath of relief, and released it out into the huge blue space above the sea.

Later in his dank kitchen, with its view along the beach to the little terrace of houses where Petra had lived when she was first with Ralph, Steve made toast for the boys, and tea for himself and Petra. He spread the toast with brilliantly red jam of a kind Petra thought Rachel would never have countenanced— "Chemicals and colorings and synthetic pips—a complete *travesty* of jam"—and cut it into strips without Petra assisting him, or even suggesting it. The boys were entranced.

"*White* bread," Kit said reverently.

He picked up strips of toast in each hand. Barney was cramming toast into his mouth with his fist.

"Steady," Petra said to him, but not as if she meant it. Steve had put a mug of tea down in front of her, and a bag of sugar with a spoon stuck in it, and then he held out more toast and red jam inquiringly towards her and Barney lunged at it, grunting urgently through his packed mouthful, and they all began laughing, even Kit, sitting on plastic garden chairs round a rickety table in Steve's kitchen. It was then that Steve said to Petra quietly, under the laughing, "Who knows you're here?" and Petra said, intending only to be factual, "There's no one to know."

"You sure?"

"Ralph's in London for the day. He's at . . . at an induction meeting, he said. Whatever that is."

"I wouldn't want any sneaking," Steve said.

185

"No—"

"But I wouldn't want you not to come. Either."

Petra looked at her children, gobbling and giggling and sticky. She wanted to say something of what the afternoon had been like, how it had made her feel, how the gritty, abrasive things that had been inside her recently, like little balls of pumice, maybe, had dissolved out there on the stones by the sea. But she couldn't think how to put it; she couldn't think how you described a sensation of finding yourself back in place, in a situation which exactly fitted you, and suited you, so she just reached across Kit to remove a fragment of toast glued by its jam to Barney's thigh and said, for all three of them, "We've had a great time. Haven't we?"

Steve didn't say anything in response, but he was smiling. He collected up the mugs and the mess on the table, and put it all in the chipped Belfast sink by the window—Petra's nan had had a sink like that, veined with ancient cracks—and then he produced a flannel and ran it under the tap, and squeezed it out, and attacked the boys' hands and faces with it, and they loved it, and shrieked, and squirmed to get away and then thrust themselves back at him for more.

He was not, Petra thought, surveying him, good-looking. He wasn't tall enough, or well formed enough; he was too stocky and his eyes were too small and his ears were too big, but he was pleasing to look at all the same, because he inhabited himself so comfortably, he moved so quickly and nimbly, he had an air of flexible practicality. He turned from a deliberately exaggerated swipe of the cloth across Kit's face and caught Petra's eye. He smiled again easily. Petra smiled back. Then he threw the cloth towards the sink, and came round the table to where Petra was sitting and, without making any kind of drama out of it, leaned down and kissed her lightly on the mouth.

* * *

Charlotte's sister, Sarah, said that she would come to London. She made it sound as if she was doing Charlotte a favor, but in truth she loved the chance of a day in London, and she especially liked Marylebone High Street, where Charlotte worked, because it had, she said to her husband, not just a fantastic bookshop, but an amazing charity bookshop too. Her husband, practiced over the years at hearing "books" and understanding "shoes," nodded and said, have a good day anyway, and offered to collect the girls from school. He had just taken up flying lessons and was anxious to build up credit with Sarah for the hours and the expense that the new enthusiasm was going to require.

Sarah had agreed to meet Charlotte in a French café, with scrubbed tables and an acceptable Continental menu. Sarah had been to the bookshop, and had then bought a necklace and a sweater from the other shops, which she had added to the bookshop bag, which she hoped that Charlotte, who was notorious in her family for not reading anything other than magazines, would notice. But Charlotte, gorgeous in a small white skirt and a black smock top, with bell sleeves and a plunging neckline, was not in the frame of mind to notice anything except that she had an ally in the form of her sister. She came flying into the café and embraced Sarah with a fervor that suggested that they hadn't seen each other for a year.

"Sarah, I am so pleased to see you, you can't think what it's been like, and I am absolutely starving. I'm absolutely starving *all* the time."

Sarah, although joining in much of the family adoration of Charlotte in the past, took a more objective view of her younger sister these days. Charlotte, it seemed to her, had a propensity to go on trading on her small-child charms to an unacceptable degree, and it was time Charlotte realized that twenty-six wasn't, actually, very young anymore, and that marriage wasn't just a continuation of a pink-glitter wedding day, but a serious undertaking involving adult conduct and compromise. She surveyed Charlotte across the table. Not only was her cleavage much on display, but she was wearing a large jeweled cross on a long chain round her neck, which only drew attention to it.

"You might thank me," Sarah said, "for coming to London all of a sudden, to suit you."

Charlotte looked up from the menu. Her eyes were huge.

"I do thank you—"

"I may only work part-time," Sarah said, "but it isn't always easy to get away, all the same."

Charlotte took one hand away from the menu and put it on Sarah's.

"Please don't tick me off—"

"I'm not ticking you off, I'm just saying—"

"I know I've been a bit one-track-minded," Charlotte said, "but it really got to me, it really did. And when people can't be supportive, I just kind of crack up. That's why I rang you. I rang you because of Luke. After . . . after, well, after he called me a nut-nut diva."

Sarah stared at her.

"He *didn't*—"

Charlotte paused. She took her hand off Sarah's and looked down at the table.

"Well—"

"Charlotte," Sarah said warningly.

"He didn't . . . disagree—"

"He didn't disagree with what?"

Charlotte put her hands on either side of her face, and stared hard at the table.

"Well, I was really upset, really crying after Luke told me that his father refused to ask his mother to apologize, and I lost my cool a bit, and I said to Luke that they were all ganging up on me—which is what it feels like, Sarah—and treating me as if I was a nut-nut diva, and he didn't contradict me. I mean, he said they weren't ganging up, that he wasn't ganging up, but he didn't say I wasn't a diva, he wouldn't. He just went down to his studio, and when I went to the loo in the night and looked to see if the studio light was still on, it was, and it was two in the morning."

"Char," Sarah said.

Charlotte looked up slowly.

"What—"

"You are—"

"I'm what—"

"You are being a diva."

Charlotte cried, "But you weren't there; you don't know what she said, how she sounded—"

Sarah leaned forward.

"Look, Char. I don't know the woman, but she's a mother-in-law. Nobody will ever be good enough for her boy. She's really tactless, but she was just doing what people like her do. Remember our wedding? Chris's mother wouldn't even come, because it wasn't in a church, and she insisted I'd bullied him out of a church wedding. I'd have been fine in a church; it was Chris who wouldn't have it. He said he'd had enough of church in his childhood and he didn't believe in God anyway. But he wouldn't stand up to her, he let me do that. So I was the witch. It's what happens. It's what it's like for lots of daughters-in-law."

Charlotte regarded her solemnly. She fiddled with her cross. She said, "Mummy said she'd like to kill her."

"That's what she would say. That's Mummy all over. That's how I feel if anyone's unkind to the girls."

Charlotte said sadly, "What are you saying?"

"Just that you're making too big a deal of it."

"But—"

"But what?"

Charlotte leaned to meet her sister and said in a loud whisper, "I didn't mean to get pregnant."

Sarah waited a second, and then she said, "I know."

Charlotte's eyes filled with tears.

"Don't cry," Sarah said. "It's not perfect. But it's got some pluses. Two babies before you're thirty, family done and dusted, get on with your life."

Charlotte said, leaning back a little, "I don't think Luke feels the same way about me—"

"What do you mean?"

"Well," Charlotte said, looking back down at the table, "I sort of could do no wrong in his eyes. I mean, I held him off till he sorted the coke thing and he had to wait till I was finished with Gus, and everything. And now I haven't got that . . . power anymore. He looks at me as if I'd disappointed him, as if he'd opened a Christmas present and found something that wasn't what he'd been hoping for."

Tempting though it was to say "Nonsense" in a brisk voice, Sarah found herself softened. She said, "He loves you, you know. Really loves you. This baby's probably a bit of a bombshell for him too."

"He hasn't got to have it—"

Sarah looked at her sister. She said, "I was just beginning to feel sorry for you. Don't spoil it."

Charlotte smiled weakly. She said, "I'm a right mess, aren't I?" She picked up a paper napkin and blotted her eyes. "I'm supposed to be a grown-up married lady, and I'm a mess."

"Don't bleat."

"I'm not—"

"Charlotte," Sarah said, "we're all thrilled you married Luke, we think he's lovely and the wedding was wonderful. But marriage isn't just more of the same. And most of all, marriage doesn't happen in *public*. It's not a sort of performance where you can ask the audience for help when you feel things aren't going your way. You've got to sort it, together. You have no idea about my relationship with Chris, have you? It's never entered your head. Well, it's not a picnic, but we manage. And you'll have to manage. You've got a nice guy and a nice place to live and you're not on the breadline. Deal with it."

Charlotte sighed.

"Okay," she said.

"And now," Sarah said, picking up the menu again, "let's order lunch."

Ralph had found a room to rent. Someone who was about to be a colleague had a flat off Finsbury Square that he wanted to himself at weekends when his girlfriend came over from Dublin, but which had a small second bedroom that he was happy to let out during the week. He said that, if Ralph just had showers, and only used the microwave, he thought fifty quid in cash, for four nights a week, would be fine, utility bills and council tax thrown in, no paperwork, no questions asked, how about it? Ralph looked at the room, decorated and furnished to be as impersonal and modern as a hotel, and thought it all looked more than acceptable. He lay down on the bed and looked up at the ceiling, with its tiny brilliant recessed lights, and felt a little thrill of excitement at the prospect of liberty. He had no intention of misusing it, he reassured Edward on the telephone, no stupid bad-lad behavior just because he was off the lead, but there'd be films, and reading, and working late, and a gym membership, and going to see his brothers, and all that good stuff, wouldn't there? Edward, at the other end of the line, had not sounded convinced or reassured.

On the train back to Suffolk, Ralph thought about the room off Finsbury Square. Fifty quid a week was an amazing bargain, especially for a power shower and a ten-minute walk to work. He thought about Kit and Barney, and how odd it would be without them, and how wonderful it would be to see them at weekends, and how he would make up for his week-night absences by getting them up, so that Petra could have a lie-in, and taking them out to do things that he never seemed to do at the moment, because every day was just an ordinary day, and one day was really indistinguishable from another. He marveled at how his energy and optimism had returned and how, instead of floundering through life like a half-dead zombie, he was now alert and eager for what lay ahead. At Ipswich station, he bought packets of chocolate buttons for the boys and looked for flowers to buy Petra. There were none. Never mind, he told himself, she grows flowers anyway, I'll stop on the way home and buy a nice bottle of wine. We'll have wine tonight and I'll cook for her. In fact, I'll cook at weekends from now on; we'll have a whole new regime and outlook, and the money to pay for it. It'll be like starting again.

Petra was in the bathroom when he got back, kneeling by the bath in order to soap Kit, who was sitting in four inches of water playing with a wind-up plastic frog. Barney, swaddled in an endearing hooded towel with ears, was sitting beside Petra on the bath mat absorbed in a cloth book whose pages squeaked when he pressed certain places. Ralph heard their voices as he came up the stairs, and he could tell they were happy from the sound of them, and, when he came in, and they all looked up and saw him, and the boys squealed, he felt an elating rush of certainty that life was going to stop being a trudge across a plateau, and transform itself instead into a gallop across a plain towards a mountain range of sheer promise.

He bent, holding his tie back with one hand, to kiss Petra and Kit, and then he picked Barney up from the floor and sat down with him on his knee on the closed lid of the lavatory.

"Good day?" Petra said.

"Very. And you?"

"We went to the sea!" Kit said, scrambling to the end of the bath to be near to his father. He spread his arms. "It was this big! And full of stones!"

Ralph laughed. He said to Barney, "What about you, fat Buddha?"

Barney offered him his book. Ralph accepted it and began to press the pages obediently.

"Lots to tell you," he said to Petra.

"Great. When the boys are in bed—"

"Read to me!" Kit commanded. He dropped the frog and began to scramble out of the bath. "Read to me, Daddy, read to me, read to me—"

"Of course I will—"

"My digger book—"

"Could we have a change, maybe, from the digger book?"

Petra wound Kit into a towel.

"Give Daddy a break. Give him a break from the digger book, hey?"

"Nah!"

"No!" said Barney delightedly. He gazed up at his father. "Nah!"

Ralph looked down at him. He looked completely winning, beaming up at his father, displaying his tiny perfect teeth from under his pointed toweling hood. Ralph felt a rush of love for him, for all of them, for his whole little family, gathered safely round him in their shabby bathroom. He dropped a kiss on Barney's head.

"Of course I'll read the digger book," he said.

Later, in the kitchen, he unwrapped the wine from its cocoon of brown paper.

"Wow," Petra said. "What are we celebrating?"

"Lots of things," Ralph said. "And I'm cooking."

"I've done it—"

"Done it?"

"Almost. Just a risotto."

"I love risotto," Ralph said. "I love your risotto. Of course, I'd have cooked, but really, I like your cooking."

Petra put two wineglasses on the table.

"So the meeting was okay?"

"It was more than okay. I met all the analysis team, all good, all seemed fine, and one of them offered me a room. Fifty quid a week! Ten minutes from the office. Perfect."

Petra stopped moving. She was tipping mushrooms onto a board from a paper bag, and she stopped, the bag in her hand with most of the mushrooms still in it.

"A room?"

Ralph looked up from inserting the screw of the corkscrew into the top of the wine bottle.

"Yes, babe. A room. Like we agreed."

"Did we?"

Ralph began to turn the corkscrew.

"You know. You said I'd better have my freedom—"

"Yes."

"Well, you meant it, didn't you?"

"Yes," Petra said.

"So I'm taking a room on the edge of the City during the week and I'll be back at weekends, and you can stay here with the boys, like you wanted."

He pulled the cork out and straightened up, smiling at her.

"So we can work this thing out, and you can have what you wanted, can't you?"

Petra tipped out the rest of the mushrooms. She picked up a knife. Ralph said, "Are you with me?"

She said, not looking up, "I . . . suppose so. I'm . . . just a bit surprised about the room—"

"Why?"

"So quick—"

"Babe, I start work in two weeks."

"Yes—"

"What did you think would happen? How did you think we'd work it?"

"I didn't," Petra said truthfully. "I just thought I'd wait till you decided something, and then I'd see what to do."

"Well, I have decided. I've got a room."

Petra looked at him. She smiled.

"Good," she said.

"And you can go on with your life here. Doing what you like doing. Like going to the sea, like you did today. Wasn't the beach crowded?"

"We didn't go there—"

Ralph began to pour the wine.

"Where'd you go then?"

"Shingle Street," Petra said, slicing mushrooms.

"Shingle Street? How did you get there?"

"Taxi—"

Ralph stopped pouring.

"A *taxi*? Both ways?"

"No," Petra said calmly. "My friend brought us home."

"What friend?"

"He works at the bird reserve."

"*He?*"

Petra looked at him.

"Yes."

Ralph said, "How do you have a friend, a man friend, from the bird reserve?"

Petra put her knife down.

"He found my car keys when I lost them the day I went drawing there, when you had your interview, when your parents had the boys."

"And now he's a friend."

Petra said, "He lives at Shingle Street. It was amazing to be back there. Amazing. The boys loved it."

There was a silence. Ralph looked at the wine in the glasses, then he looked at Petra. He said, "You took the boys—"

"Of course. What else would I do?"

"Is—is that why you're so happy? Is that why the atmosphere here's so good tonight? It's not that you've come round to my point of view, my point about the future, is it, it's because you've had an afternoon—"

"It was the beach," Petra said.

"An afternoon," Ralph said, rushing on, taking no notice, "with some guy who you let be with my children and God knows what else you let happen, it's that, isn't it, it's that—"

He stopped suddenly. He tried to gauge, looking at Petra, what she was thinking. She was standing on the other side of the table, one hand lightly on the pile of sliced mushrooms, the other lying on her knife, quite still and alarmingly composed. She was looking back at him, and although her gaze was veiled she didn't look as she usually looked when things got difficult and she was trying to evade being involved in a resolution. She looked more as if she'd decided something and then pulled back into herself, decision made.

"Petra?"

"Yes."

"Petra, are you happy, not because of me but because you've had a good afternoon with this guy?"

She gave him a faint smile and picked up her paring knife again.

"Yes," she said.

CHAPTER THIRTEEN

Sigrid put down the telephone. She had called her mother in Stockholm, at a time she knew her mother would be at home after her surgery, and before her father returned and, in a way Sigrid was sure was unintentional, exercised a quiet but definite background restraint upon her mother's responses to what Sigrid was saying. Sigrid had meant—had wanted—to tell her mother about all the Brinkley family upsets, and had gone so far, on her journey back from the laboratory, as to plan how she would describe the lunch party, and Rachel's manner, and Charlotte's reaction and subsequent behavior: but when it came to it, she discovered that the flavor had quite leached out of it all, to the extent that she felt, oddly, that she ought to protect the Brinkleys in a way, she ought not to expose their inadequacies, even—or maybe, especially—to her mother. So they had an affectionate and anodyne call instead, so anodyne that Sigrid could sense her mother was only just managing to refrain from asking her if anything was the matter.

Sigrid picked up the mug of green tea she had made to accompany the phone call and looked at it. It was cold now, with a rim of brown sediment at the bottom, and looked as appetizing as a mug of pond water. She went over to the sink and poured it away, and then refilled the kettle. Coffee was the answer. Coffee, in her upbringing, had always been the answer. Green tea was no substitute. Just as, Mariella frequently pointed out, water was no substitute for juice. Or a smoothie. Mariella had been promised some vanilla smoothie—her favorite—when she could not only spell out loud all the words on her summer-holiday spelling list ending in "ough," but could write them down too. She had been shut in her room for hours, so she had probably abandoned spelling for playing, and her bedroom floor would be covered with the families of tiny anthropomorphized toy woodland animals whom she would be putting to bed, in nests of paper tissues, in all her shoes. Sigrid was not going to interrupt her. Absorbed playing with miniature mice and badgers had to feed the inner life more richly, surely, than learning why "cough" and "rough" and "bough" all looked the same but didn't sound it. English! What a language.

Edward's key scraped in the front-door lock, followed by a bang as he swung it shut behind him. He came rapidly down the stairs to the kitchen, as was his wont, and kissed her— rather absently, she thought—and went straight to the fridge.

"A bit desperate, aren't you?" Sigrid said.

"Water," Edward said shortly. He took out the filter jug Sigrid kept in the door of the fridge and poured out a large glass, which he then drank, straight off. Sigrid watched him.

"Is something the matter?"

Edward went on drinking.

"Please," Sigrid said. "No dramas. Have you had a bad day?"

Edward put the glass down and refilled it.

"Yes."

"Would you like to tell me about it?"

Edward nodded, drinking again.

"Is it your family?"

Edward stopped swallowing long enough to say, "Why should it be them?"

"It usually is."

"Whereas—"

"No," Sigrid said, interrupting. "No, not in comparison to mine, if you must know. I have just had a very inadequate talk to my mother."

"Inadequate?"

"I talked to her in a completely pointless way. As if I didn't really know her—"

"Why?" Edward said.

Sigrid let a small silence fall and then she said evasively, "I don't know. Maybe I was tired."

Edward sat down heavily on a kitchen chair, with his third glass of water.

"I *am* tired."

Sigrid waited. Edward said, "I am especially tired of Ralph. At least, poor bugger, I'm not tired of *him*, but I'm pretty tired of the complications he seems to attract."

Sigrid took a chair across the table from Edward. She said cautiously, "What now? Is he reneging on the job?"

"Oh no," Edward said. "Nothing like that. Heavens, he starts in a week."

"Well, then?"

Edward sighed. He said, looking at the tabletop rather than at Sigrid, "It's Petra."

"Petra!"

"He rang today. He sounded in quite a state. He said he'd been sitting on something for about a week, and he had to tell someone. It seems that Petra has . . . well, I don't know how far it's gone, I mean, I don't know if they're sleeping together or anything, but Petra's got another man."

Sigrid gasped. She held on to the table edge and leaned forward. "*Petra?*"

"Yes," Edward said. He got up. "I'm going to get something stronger. You want a drink?"

"Sit down," Sigrid said. "Sit down. We'll get a drink later. Sit down and tell me. Who *is* this man?"

Edward leaned against the table. He said dully, "He works at the nature reserve."

"He—"

"Outside. He's a kind of—maintenance man, I suppose. I couldn't really tell. He looks after the infrastructure, fences and steps and handrails, that sort of thing. Petra met him there."

"But she hasn't been there lately—"

"Once," Edward said.

"Once!"

"She lost her car keys. He found them. It was the day Ralph came up for the interview."

Sigrid put her head in her hands.

"Oh my God—"

"He's got a place at Shingle Street," Edward said. "Where they used to live. Petra takes the kids there, they love it, they— well, Kit anyway—want to tell Ralph about it, they want to take him there."

"Don't—"

"Ralph said that she doesn't seem to get what she's doing. She just doesn't. They agreed he could live in London in the week, so that she and the boys didn't have to leave Aldeburgh, and she seems to think that gives him a freedom that she's entitled to, too, so she's got this bloke."

Sigrid said, "I think I'd like that drink. *Petra.* I can't believe it—"

Edward turned towards the fridge.

"Ralph said he can't talk to her. He simply can't. She won't discuss it. She just looks at him, and smiles, and says she's okay now, so she's fine with him doing this job in London. She doesn't seem to understand that working in London to support your family doesn't exactly equate to unbounded freedom for Ralph. And it *certainly* doesn't give her permission to embark on an affair with someone else."

"*Has* she?"

Edward opened the fridge and took out a wine bottle.

"I don't know. Ralph doesn't know. She just says it's the sea, it's the sea, which is plainly utter rubbish. How can it be the *sea*, for God's sake? There's sea all over the place in Alde-burgh!"

Sigrid got up to fetch two glasses. She said, "It's always been . . . a bit funny, that relationship—"

"All relationships look funny from the outside."

"Goodness, Ed, that's very philosophical, for you—"

Edward put the wine down on the table, and picked it up again.

"I told him to tell the parents. He said he couldn't face it. He asked if I would."

"Will you?"

Edward began to pour.

"When I know more. When I know what I'm telling them, maybe." He pushed a glass towards Sigrid. "Stupid bloody girl."

Sigrid said nothing. Edward sat down again. He took a swallow of wine. He said, suddenly angry, "I know Ralph is a pain, I know he isn't the easiest person to live with, but he's doing this for his family and, however stupid and pigheaded he is, he isn't a player, he doesn't play around with other women, he doesn't drink or gamble, he's just Ralph, like he always was.

201

And Petra isn't exactly a picnic, is she, drifting about, refusing to grow up, all daffy and artistic. Honestly. *Honestly.*" He raised his voice and said again in almost a shout, "Stupid bloody woman!"

"Who is?" Mariella said from the doorway.

Charlotte lay in bed on her back. Luke was asleep beside her, his right arm across her thighs, where she had moved it, from being across her belly. She had been assured by everyone—her mother, sisters, friends—that if she felt sick (not everyone does, promise, Char, I mean, I nearly died from nausea but lots of people don't even feel a *thing*) it would be in the morning, early, and would be enormously helped if Luke brought her tea in bed, and a plain biscuit or something, before she even put a toe out. But the mornings were fine. Really fine. It was the evenings that Charlotte dreaded. In the evenings, she was beginning to find that not only could she not face food, she couldn't even face the *thought* of food, let alone the smell, and she daren't even think about coffee or brown bread, for example, without having to race for the bathroom. Luke had been so sweet. He'd had something to eat, the last week or so, in the studio before he came upstairs, and he'd brushed his teeth, too. She'd really appreciated that, and she really appreciated that he wanted to sleep with his arms round her. It was just that she couldn't bear the weight of his finger, let alone his arm, across her belly, but if she merely lifted it away he put it back again, at once, in his sleep, as if it was absolutely vital for him to be connected. So she had, the last few nights, just pushed his arm down her body a little, and that seemed to content him, while she lay waiting for either sleep or sickness to gain the upper hand.

Of course, tonight there was another reason to stay awake, a reason beyond that of simply wondering whether she was going to throw up, or just feel that she might. Luke had come up from the studio, touchingly redolent of toothpaste over pizza, and said that Ralph had rung him to tell him that Petra was seeing someone else. Luke didn't seem very clear about any of it, not who the guy was, or whether Petra was going off with him, or whether Ralph was going to do anything about it, but it was more that he, Luke, was in a stumbling sort of rage on his brother's behalf who, he said to Charlotte, was, he knew, not the easiest bastard to be married to, but hell, he was doing his best with a new job and all that and anyway, Petra hadn't exactly pulled her weight the last few years, and he now saw why she, Charlotte, had always had a bit of a down on Petra, and he should have taken her opinion on Petra more seriously, he really should, because she'd been proved spot-on right now, hadn't she?

Charlotte had wanted to feel the glow of satisfaction at having been so right and had failed to. When she questioned Luke further about exactly what Petra had *done*, he said he didn't know details and for God's sake didn't *want* to, but that Ralph had been most upset about the fact that Petra was perfectly happy for him to go to London and earn money to keep them all, now that she'd found someone to amuse herself with, who was also prepared to play with the boys.

"That's what really gets him," Luke said, standing over her as she lay on the sofa, his thumbs hooked in the belt loops of his jeans. "The kids really like him. Kit talks about him a lot, like Ralph's supposed to join in all this. It's gutting him." He gave an enormous sigh, and then he said, "I'd better ring Ed. Ralph rang Ed two nights ago and told him not to tell me till he'd told me himself. He said he'd meant to do it at once, but he just couldn't face saying it all over again right then. Poor bloody guy. I know he's a menace, but he doesn't deserve this, not on top of his business going belly up and everything, he really doesn't."

Then he had bent down, with the grace and ease Charlotte appreciated so much when she wasn't feeling so grim, and kissed her, and said he wouldn't be long. He was half an hour in their bedroom. Charlotte didn't move, on account of not wanting to alert the nausea in any way, but she knew he'd be lying on their bed with his shoes off, his mobile on his chest with the earpiece in, and the television at the foot of their bed on, with the sound turned off. Luke couldn't be in a room with a television without turning it on. He said it was what came of being a third child, that you liked company but you didn't always want to be part of the noise and energy of a family, you just wanted to be on the edge of company you could watch but didn't have to be part of. Television was perfect for that, Luke said. There was even one in the studio, which he had on the minute Jed left the room, just as if, Charlotte thought, he was afraid some dark spirits might sneak in, if there was only solitude and silence to contend with.

At first, she tried to hear what Luke was saying, but he was not quite audible, and the sounds from the street, even if far below, muffled his voice even further. So Charlotte rolled cautiously onto her side, holding a cushion against her, and attempted again to feel the satisfaction of having been justified in her reaction to Petra in the past. It wouldn't come, any more than even a shred of understanding of Ralph and Petra's relationship, which seemed to Charlotte as weird and unsatisfactory as an apparently grown-up relationship could be, based as it was on the proximity and support of Ralph's parents, Petra's parents-in-law. Even if everything her sister Sarah had said about Rachel had taken the white heat out of Charlotte's indignation and upset, it had done nothing to endear Rachel to Charlotte. Mothers-in-law are like that, Sarah had said. They just are. They'll never forgive you for marrying their boys, you'll just have to accept it. Your mother-in-law is no different.

Charlotte thought about her wedding day, and how she had felt about Rachel that day, how she had been ready to love everybody, almost ecstatically, and she remembered Rachel kissing her, in the vestry of the church while they signed the register, and she remembered that she had had to stoop a bit, because of her height and her heels, and how Rachel's cheek had been light and dry against her own, and that she hadn't said anything, she hadn't said, "I'm so happy for you," or, "Luke's a lucky boy," or anything like that. And then later, Charlotte had seen her with Petra, feeding the little boys, and she'd taken off her green-feather hat thing and she was laughing, really animated. And now? Would she be laughing now? Grimly—and at last with some sense of satisfaction—Charlotte didn't think so.

When Luke came back to the sitting room, he sat down on the edge of the sofa next to Charlotte.

"You okay, angel?"

"Ish," Charlotte said.

Luke took one of Charlotte's hands.

"I'd feel sick *for* you, if I could—"

"I know," Charlotte said. She looked at him. "How was your phone call?"

Luke said, "Ed feels like I do. We just went round the houses. You know, like you do when there's not enough to put your finger on."

"What if Ralph stays in Aldeburgh?"

"Char, he can't. He's got to work—"

"But your parents would help, they're always helping them anyway."

Luke put Charlotte's hand between both of his.

"Ed asked me if I'd go with him actually."

"Go where?"

"To Suffolk," Luke said. "To tell them."

Charlotte sat up slowly. She said, "The two of you, driving all the way to Suffolk? Why can't you tell them on the phone? Why can't Ralph tell them?"

"He can't," Luke said unhappily. "He asked Ed, and Ed asked me. It's . . . it's not something you can say on the phone, because, well, because of—"

"Petra?"

"Sort of," Luke said.

Charlotte swung her legs round and put the cushion in her lap. She said, "Aren't you all making a big deal out of this?"

"Well, what if it was one of your sisters? What if Sarah suddenly said she was playing around because she didn't like Chris's flying lessons? Wouldn't you want to tell your mother in person?"

Charlotte gave a tiny shrug.

"Maybe—"

Luke pressed her hand between his.

"I know you're fed up with Mum. And Dad. I know you feel let down and everything. I know what you think of Petra. But . . . they're my family. They just are. And the parents are going to be devastated."

Charlotte was silent for a moment, staring at her hand sandwiched between Luke's. Then she said lightly, "Oh, they'll forgive Petra—"

Luke looked across the room. Then he looked back at her intently, and he said, "I'm not so sure," and suddenly something shifted in Charlotte's mind and heart, something that wheeled the image of Petra into her mental vision, dressed in the funny little knitted dress she'd worn to the wedding, holding Kit in his Spider-Man T-shirt, both of them whey-faced with fatigue, out of their own context, out of their depth.

Charlotte had returned Luke's look then. She'd smiled at him.

"I'll come," she said.

"What?"

"I'll come with you," Charlotte said. "I'll come to Suffolk with you, at the weekend. With you and Ed. Of course I will."

He'd given a little exclamation and put his arms round her, holding her hard against him. He said, "You are a star, a complete star, but suppose Ed and I kind of have to do it alone?" and she'd said, into his shoulder, "It's fine. I'll be fine. I'd just like to be there, to support you," and then there'd been a few moments when she'd wondered if he was crying.

He kept thanking her. He'd thanked her so much while they were moseying round each other, getting to bed, that Charlotte had had—laughing—to tell him to stop, because what kind of gratitude would he have left for the really big stuff? And he'd said solemnly, "That *is* big stuff. For me," and she'd felt a mingled rush of remorse and relief, remorse at how she'd behaved recently, and relief that she was back where she'd been, on the pedestal of She Who Can Do No Wrong, to the extent where she was overtaken suddenly by a flood of inappropriate gratitude towards Ralph and Petra, which was as disconcerting as it was powerful.

Now, lying in the dim glow of a city night, with the nausea gradually subsiding, and Luke's arm heavy across her groin, Charlotte considered the journey to Suffolk. Luke had said that Sigrid and Mariella wouldn't be coming, so that left her alone with Edward and Luke. She thought she would offer to do the driving. She liked driving, she was a good driver, and she could tell the boys she'd feel sick if she wasn't driving and that way, when she'd dropped them off at Anthony and Rachel's, she'd be free to do as she chose.

"I should paint those," Anthony said.

He was standing by the kitchen table, which was covered with late-summer vegetables, runner beans and courgettes and a basket of spinach and a great heap of carrots, trailing their feathery green tops over the edge of the table, like hair. Rachel had been in the garden all afternoon, since it was the day the gardener came, the gardener who had started in that garden as a boy, wheeling barrows and raking leaves for Anthony's parents, and was now a stubborn old man with poor vision and a bad back. He and Rachel tolerated one another, no more, and an afternoon in Dick's company was guaranteed, Anthony knew, to test Rachel's temper.

She was making tea. She cast a glance over her shoulder at the green pile on the table. She said, "Can't think why I bother."

Anthony said nothing. His age-old instinct was to say something soothing like, "Oh, but I love spinach," but experience had taught him that this would not have a mollifying effect, and, in any case, Rachel had sounded more sad than cross. He regarded her back view, switching on the kettle, stretching up to the cupboards for tea bags and mugs. She was as trim in outline as she had been when he first saw her; in fact sometimes, now, catching a glimpse of her digging in the garden, heaving something out of the car, bending to pick a towel off the bathroom floor, he couldn't believe she was any older, any different from the girl he'd met on a walking holiday in North Wales. She'd had hair almost to her waist then, and a slight Welsh accent. She hadn't got the accent anymore, and her hair was cut to her jawline, but there was still a great deal of her that was the same—exaggerated maybe here and there, but the same.

She turned round and put two mugs of tea on the table, the swollen tea bags bobbing faintly obscenely on the surface. She said, not looking at Anthony, "Please don't behave as if I'll fly off the handle."

Anthony said reasonably, "Well, you might."

Rachel opened a drawer to find a teaspoon.

"I'm more likely to cry."

"You hardly ever cry—"

"Lately," Rachel said, "I've done rather a lot of crying. I don't like it, but it keeps happening. It happened this afternoon again, pulling those bloody carrots. I don't think Dick saw. He can't see anything smaller than a bus these days anyway, and I had my back to him."

Anthony said cautiously, "Why were you crying?"

"You know—"

"I don't. I mean, I don't exactly. Was it . . . Charlotte still? Or the carrots?"

Rachel pressed a tea bag against the side of a mug, and flicked it out.

"The carrots."

Anthony waited again. Rachel said, "Once I couldn't grow enough vegetables. Once we had sackloads of the things at the back of the garage, and it was a triumph if the potatoes lasted till after Christmas. We were pretty well self-sufficient, weren't we, and it *all* got eaten, all of it."

She stopped and dredged out the second tea bag.

Anthony said, "That was ages ago. Years. You're thinking of the boys' school days. As far as Ed's concerned, that's about twenty years ago."

Rachel took a big plastic carton of milk out of the fridge and splashed some into the tea.

"I know."

"Well, then—"

"It wasn't really then that I was thinking about, it was now, it was what's happening now—" She stopped.

Anthony went round the table and put his arms round her. She didn't respond, but she didn't resist him, either. She said, into the dark-blue drill of his shirt, "Nobody's been here, all summer."

Anthony bent a little.

"What?"

Rachel raised her face slightly and said more distinctly, "The family. No one's been here, all summer."

"Yes, they have, we saw the little boys—"

"Weeks ago," Rachel said. "Not long after the wedding—"

"And the day everyone came to lunch, when Mariella had done all that baking—"

"One Sunday," Rachel said. She put up one hand, and blotted her eyes with the back of it. "Other summers, they've all been in and out, all the time. Last year Mariella stayed for a week, by herself. And the little boys were here all the time, we got the old pram out, you remember, for Barney. And Luke was here, a lot, he went sailing, didn't he, he brought Jed down and they went sailing, and then he brought Charlotte to introduce her. But not now. Nobody's been, now. I mean, I expect them to have their own lives, of course I do, I just don't expect them to stop seeing us, so completely, so suddenly. And Ralph and Petra being in Ipswich won't make it better. Will it?"

Anthony took one arm away and reached across to rip a piece of kitchen paper from the roll on the wall.

"Here. Blow."

He looked down on the top of her head as she blew her nose. He said, "It's been a worrying summer for Ralph. And then the wedding. It's probably just a one-off, you know."

Rachel sighed. She pulled herself out of his arms and looked up at him. Then she patted his chest.

"You don't believe that any more than I do. This is *change*. This is a different dynamic altogether, and I don't like it." She blew her nose again. "It frightens me."

"Why?"

"Because nobody wants me to do something I'm good at anymore."

"I do—"

She smiled weakly.

"Ant, you aren't enough people. And you've got painting and the college still."

"Go back to your cookery courses, then—"

She sighed.

"I'm not sure I've got the heart—"

Anthony picked up the nearest mug of tea.

"Shall we start by turfing over the veg garden, so that you aren't oppressed by all this produce with no one to eat it?"

The telephone began to ring. Rachel said, crossing the kitchen to answer it, "I'd rather find a solution that didn't look as if I was giving in," and then she picked up the phone and said, "Hello?" into it, as she always did, and then Anthony saw her face lighten into a wide smile and she said, "Luke!" with emphasis.

He walked past her, carrying his tea, saying, "Send him my love," in a way that made him feel ashamed of his mild cowardice, after his last conversation with Luke, and then crossed the gravel to his studio. It was always a relief to open the door, always a pleasure, a sensation of both security and possibility to be back in that huge, cluttered space under the dusty, ghostly flypast of bird skeletons suspended from the beams. "Never pass up the chance to draw a newly dead bird," an old naturalist had said to him, and he had obeyed, stripping the carcasses afterwards to see how the feathers grew, how the wings and beaks were attached. They were all there, his birds, wired up and flying, even a wren, whose bones you could have fitted into a matchbox. It had looked so round, that wren, almost solid, like a little feathered walnut, but once it was a skeleton it was as small and fragile as the stamens of a flower.

Anthony stood in front of his easel, drinking his tea. On it was propped the beginnings of a drawing of a crane, a

European crane, startled into sudden takeoff with its big gray wings and long legs awkwardly splayed, its head just turned enough to show the red patch on the back of it. He'd been lucky to see it, because they were so rare in England, preferring Scandinavia and central Europe and liking great stretches of marsh and bog in which to make their precarious nests. He thought that, beyond the central crane, he might add some more, in flight, wings spread, to suggest the dance for which they were so famous. He put down his tea and picked up his pencil. Crane, he said to himself, Latin name, *Grus grus*. Like the sound they make.

The door to the drive opened.

"Guess what!" Rachel said from the doorway.

"What?"

"Luke and Ed are coming on Sunday. For lunch. Together. Isn't that lovely?"

CHAPTER FOURTEEN

Charlotte had never been to Aldeburgh before. When Luke asked her how she would spend the time while he and Edward were with their parents, she'd said airily that she thought she'd just go and be by the sea.

"Probably sleep," she said. "Eat an ice cream. Time off everything." She'd leaned sideways to kiss him. "Don't fret, babe. I'll be fine."

Luke was reluctant to get out of the car.

"This feels really weird, you driving us up here and not coming in. Leave your phone on. All the time. I'll text you when we're through."

Edward, climbing out of the backseat of the car, squeezed her shoulder.

"You're a heroine, Charlotte."

Then they had trooped away together, towards their parents' house, and Charlotte had thought how young they both looked suddenly, unformed, more boys than men, and she had put the car in gear and set the TomTom on the dashboard for Aldeburgh, and driven off without looking in the rear mirror to see if Luke was still watching.

The road led her north-westward, through woodland, before she turned right towards Snape, and Aldeburgh. She had been to Suffolk several times before, of course, but driving through it alone, with her own purpose, and no requirement to admire it for Luke's sake, made the journey extremely interesting to her. It was so different than the Buckinghamshire of her upbringing that it felt almost like being abroad, somewhere designated as foreign, and in consequence slightly exotic. Aldeburgh itself, with its main street still full of summer visitors, and the sea only yards away behind the houses and the shrieking gulls, was like nowhere familiar to her, and this was pleasurably exciting.

She left the car in a back street outside a shuttered house that looked as if its residents were not there to object, and walked down to the sea. It was a cool, fair day, and the beach was dotted with families, and plastic windbreaks, and the immense blue-gray sea was heaving and sucking at the pebbles with a relentless rhythm that might, Charlotte thought, drive you nuts if you weren't a sea person. She wondered if she was hungry and decided that she was too strung up by what she was about to do to be hungry, so she turned inland to the High Street, where she thought she would stop someone who looked local—holidaymakers from London were amazingly easy to spot—and ask them how she could find Ralph and Petra's house.

Ralph, holding the front door open wide enough to see out but not wide enough to admit her, looked as if he could hardly remember who she was.

"Oops," Charlotte said, "did I wake you?"

Ralph passed his hand over his chin, as if to check the time by whether he had shaved or not. He was wearing cutoffs and a sagging T-shirt. Charlotte, in a short summer dress and wedge-heeled espadrilles, thought he looked terrible.

"No," Ralph said. "No. I . . . it's just, I wasn't expecting you—"

"I didn't say I was coming," Charlotte said, "so you couldn't." She smiled at him. "I dropped Ed and Luke off at your parents'. Then I thought I'd come."

Ralph didn't open the door any wider. He looked past Charlotte rather than at her.

"I'm afraid this . . . this isn't a very good time—"

"I know," Charlotte said. "That's why I'm here."

Ralph sighed. He said, "I don't want to be rude to you, but I can't talk to you, really. I don't know you . . . well enough—"

"No," Charlotte said. She found that the sight of him gave her confidence, his beaten appearance made him no longer the slightly disconcerting, unpredictable brother-in-law who came to doss down on her sofa every so often, but hardly spoke to her, only to Luke.

Ralph said with evident frustration, but not specifically, apparently, to Charlotte, "For God's sake, what did I *do*?"

Charlotte shifted a little on her wedge heels. She thought of taking her sunglasses off and decided not to. She said, as nonchalantly as she could, "Actually, I came to see Petra."

Ralph said wearily, "They aren't here."

Charlotte felt a little clutch of excited panic. Where were they, then? Were they with *him*?

"Oh—"

"They're at the allotment," Ralph said. "You'll find them there."

He plainly, Charlotte thought, couldn't say Petra's name. She said, "Can you show me?"

Ralph lifted an arm. He pointed vaguely to the right. He said, "Down there, and then right past the school, then left to the footpath."

"Has Petra got her phone?"

Ralph looked at her with sudden focus. He said crisply, "I have no idea."

"Sorry," Charlotte said, "I'm sorry. I'm sorry about all of it," and before the words were fully out of her mouth, Ralph said emphatically, "Me too," and slammed the door shut in her face.

Petra and Kit were kneeling on the ground together, examining something in the earth. They had their backs to the gate. Opposite them, strapped into his buggy, with a carrot in either fist, was Barney. He gave an energetic wriggle when he saw Charlotte and gestured vigorously with his carrots.

"Gah!" Barney said loudly.

Petra lifted her head.

"What, Barn—"

"Gah," Barney said again. He looked over his mother's head at Charlotte, standing by the gate, her hand on the latch. Petra turned.

"Oh!" Petra said, scrambling to her feet.

Charlotte opened the gate.

"Surprise!" she said. She bent forward slightly, as if to kiss Petra. Petra stepped back.

"I didn't expect—" Petra said.

"I know. That's why I didn't tell you. I thought if you knew, you wouldn't see me."

Kit got up from where he had been kneeling, holding a snail.

"It's gone in again," he said to Charlotte. "It came out, then it went in again."

"Yes—"

"It doesn't like noise," Kit said sternly.

Charlotte crouched down beside him.

"I'll try to be quiet."

Kit nodded. Petra moved to stand beside Barney's buggy.

She said in a neutral voice, "I know where Ralph's brothers are today. They told him."

Charlotte glanced up from Kit's snail.

"How'd you know that?"

"Rachel rang," Petra said in the same neutral tone. She stooped and released Barney, heaving him into her arms. From behind him she said, "She asked us to go over. Because the others were coming. But we couldn't go." She paused and then she added, "So I knew you'd be there."

Charlotte stood up slowly.

"I didn't go in. They don't know I came. I just drove the boys down, and left them there. At the gate." She stopped, and then she said with much less assurance, "They were . . . going to tell them—"

"Yes," Petra said, "that's why we couldn't go."

"Look!" Kit shouted excitedly. "Look! He's done his horns out!"

Charlotte looked down. The snail withdrew sharply.

Kit said, "Don't look at him!"

Petra sat down on the strip of turf between the vegetable beds, holding Barney on her lap. She said into Barney's hair, "What d'you think will happen?" Charlotte sat down too, the other side of a bed of big, fierce marrow leaves. She tucked her legs to one side and leaned on one hand, looking down at the grass and ripping up single blades with the other.

She said cautiously, "What *is* happening?"

"What?" Petra said.

"With . . . with you. With you and this man—"

"He's great," Petra said. "He's easy. He just lets things be. He's called Steve."

"Have—" Charlotte said, and stopped.

"Have what?"

"Have you slept with him."

Petra brushed something off the top of Barney's head.

"Not yet."

Charlotte's head snapped up.

"But you're *planning* to?"

Petra shrugged.

"It might happen—"

"But you're *married*!"

Petra looked entirely unoffended. She said, glancing at Charlotte over the marrow leaves, "He said he had to be free."

"Who did?"

There was a beat, and then Petra said, her voice suddenly catching, "Ralph did."

Charlotte got up and went round the marrow bed, Kit following. She knelt on the grass by Petra and, to her delight and surprise, Kit lowered himself onto her knees, still holding his snail. Charlotte said with feeling, "Oh, Petra—"

Petra said, her voice shaking, "He said he had to be free, for all of us. So I let him! I couldn't stop him anyway, so I let him. And I thought that if he was free, then I was free too. Not from the boys, not ever, but from him, kind of, if that's what he wanted. Because . . . because, whatever I think of him, whatever I want from him, he . . . well, he doesn't really want me to *be* anything, he just doesn't want me to stop him. So I haven't."

Charlotte said nothing. She put her arms round Kit and held him, and he leaned back against her, peering into the snail shell, warm and solid and unspeakably reassuring.

"And there's the sea," Petra said. "I know everyone thinks I'm a flake about the sea, but it matters. It matters to me, and it matters that Ralph gets it, and he used to get it, and now he doesn't. Now he wants to be like he was before he met me. He got all his suits out again. Nobody gets what I'm doing, nobody thinks I have any right to live like I need to. They never have. I thought Ralph did, sometimes, but he doesn't. Not even

Ralph. He wants me to be like he wants me to be. Like everyone does."

"Not me," Charlotte said.

Petra sighed. She said, "You don't really know them yet."

"I know enough—"

"Not to stand up to them—"

Charlotte rested her chin on the top of Kit's head. Her gaze
went past Petra to rest on Petra's shed, which was open, reveal-
ing all the tools inside, ranged on hooks like a tidy kitchen.

She said, "That's why I've come." She held Kit a little
tighter. He was really relaxed against her now, almost sleep-
ily, and although her knees hurt from being bent under his
weight, she would not have dreamt of moving. "I don't know
what'll happen today," Charlotte said. "I don't know how
they'll react, but all I can say is that so far the boys are sticking
together. Brother stuff. So—so I don't know how they'll, well,
put it. I don't know how they'll tell the story—"

"It won't be good," Petra said.

"No. I don't expect it will." Charlotte paused, and considered bringing Rachel, and her own abiding grievance, into the
equation, and then, buoyed up by the sense of maturity she
was experiencing in this whole escapade, told herself not to.
Instead, she said, "I just came to say that not everybody doesn't
get it. I do. I mean, I might not understand about the sea, and I
don't know Steve, but I'm kind of here, if you need me."

Petra said into Barney's hair again, "I'm not in love with
him. Or anything."

"Steve?"

"No."

"Then why—"

"Because he helps me," Petra said. "He knows what I know.
About the sea and stuff. He likes what I like. He likes the
kids." She glanced at Kit. "He's asleep."

Charlotte looked down.

"What a compliment—"

"He likes women," Petra said.

"Does . . . does he like his grandmother?"

There was a tiny, significant pause, and then Petra said, "Yes. He does," and then she said almost inaudibly, "She's not going to like me, though. Not now."

Charlotte smiled at her. She said, "She doesn't like me, either," and Petra looked up at her, straight at her, and smiled back.

Anthony said, for the fiftieth time, "I cannot believe it."

Rachel was lying back in one of the sagging old armchairs in the studio, with her eyes closed. They had been in the studio for hours now, ever since the boys had gone, driving away with Charlotte at the wheel—Charlotte, who they hadn't even known had come to Aldeburgh, and who didn't get out of the car to greet them, but just sat there, smiling, with the window rolled down, the car engine still humming.

"Come in," Rachel had said, stooping to speak to her. "Come in, at least, and have some tea, before you go back."

Charlotte hadn't even taken her sunglasses off. She gave Rachel her wide, white smile and said thanks, but they really had to get back, work tomorrow and all that, and Ed and Luke had got in beside her docilely, as if somehow suddenly obedient to her rather than to their parents, and Charlotte had put the car in gear, and driven off, waving and smiling, and they had watched it go, desolate and disorientated, and then turned, as if by unspoken mutual consent, and retreated to the studio.

Anthony was standing by the easel. His drawing of cranes was still on it, unfinished, and out of habit he had picked up a piece of charcoal and smudged at the paper with it, but he couldn't focus, he couldn't recognize his own capacity. He just stood there holding the charcoal, and saying that he couldn't believe it, he simply couldn't. Petra of all people. *Petra.*

Rachel had been quite silent. She had flopped into the nearest armchair and stayed there, head back, eyes either closed or directed at the ceiling. She had given the boys lobster at lunchtime, specially bought lobster, which she knew they both loved, and had made garlic mayonnaise, and that pudding of crushed meringues and strawberries that had always been Luke's favorite. But nobody had eaten anything much. They'd said, "Great, Mum, thanks," sounding as they did when they were adolescents, and then they'd exchanged glances as if about to confess to a cricket ball through the greenhouse roof, and then Edward had cleared his throat and said, well, actually, there was a reason for their coming, and it wasn't, unfortunately, a very happy reason, and then he started, and Rachel could see, almost from his first words, that Anthony wasn't grasping it, that Anthony couldn't take in what he was being told, that Edward might as well have been talking to him in Mandarin. And then he did understand, suddenly, and he went gray and put down his spoon, and Rachel had felt such fury on his behalf, such protective rage at his betrayed trust, that she had almost leaped out of her chair.

She was calmer now. She was calmer, and exhausted as, she knew, you can only be when you have been literally flooded with anger. And she had been. She had said a great many things about Petra that came straight out of her volcano of outrage, outrage that Ralph's efforts to support his family should be rewarded in such a way, outrage at Petra's conduct, outrage that Anthony's faith in her, real love for her, should be repaid so carelessly.

"She's wicked," Anthony said, bewildered and distressed, red in the face now, his table napkin crumpled into the lobster. "*Wicked.*"

But Rachel knew Petra wasn't wicked. She had, in that first panic of knowing, said terrible things about Petra, but she knew she wasn't wicked. She knew, if she thought about it, if she forced herself right through her violent primitive maternal loyalty to Ralph to the other side, that Petra had come up against something in her marriage that was like hurling oneself against a steel door. It wasn't that Petra had encountered something in her life and in her husband that she could not deal with that got to Rachel; oh no, so much of Ralph, and living with Ralph, was so profoundly intractable. What got to Rachel, what Rachel could neither understand nor forgive, was that, in her trouble, Petra had not come to her and Anthony for help, but had, instead, chosen an alternative solution that was, frankly, disastrous for everybody.

Edward and Luke had described this new man of Petra's as minimally as they could, indicating their distaste for the whole business. Rachel liked their loyalty, liked the sense that no man could be an understandable replacement for their own brother. But she was equally unnerved by how mild this Steve person sounded, how peacefully attractive his work and his interests, how much—this was the worst—the boys seemed to enjoy being with him. Edward had reported that Ralph was as bemused as he was hurt.

"He says Steve's got nothing, really. Rented shared cottage, clapped-out Toyota. But he doesn't mind and Petra doesn't mind. It's all birds and sea and throwing stones on the beach with them. That seems to be all. That seems to be enough."

"Has she been to bed with him?" Anthony demanded.

Luke made a sick noise. Edward said woodenly, "I wouldn't know."

"It won't last," Anthony said. "Flash in the pan. Defiance. I'll go and talk to her—"

"No!" Rachel said loudly and suddenly.

They'd all looked at her.

Anthony said, "But we always talk to her—"

"Not now," Rachel said. "*Not* now."

They'd gazed at her, astonished. She could see that they were all thinking, what's got into Mum, Mum's always rushing in to sort things out, Mum always thinks she's got the answer. Well, this time she didn't have an answer, except to say that they would do nothing, Anthony especially. They would do nothing, Rachel thought, lying in the armchair watching the curious moving patterns behind her closed lids, because, for the first time in decades, Rachel did not know what to do. All that energetic bustling about to try and fix a house in Ipswich for Ralph and Petra now seemed ludicrous, a kind of mad displacement activity for some profound anxiety that she did not care to give a name to. Well, now she knew what that anxiety had been, an anxiety about Ralph's work difficulties causing his strange, opaque, elusive relationship with Petra to dissolve still further, to an extent that no amount of dictatorial external management could shore it up. Petra was Petra. Always had been, slipping in and out of manageableness like a fish in a wet grasp. But really, Rachel thought now, wearily trawling through her jumbled thoughts, I believed I was through to her, I believed that, since Kit was born, we'd got to a steadier place, somewhere where we all knew where we were, where we could rely upon one another. And if she thinks she can get away with treating Anthony like this, after all he's done for her, all his patience and help and affection, well, then she's got another think coming, and a gigantic think at that.

She opened her eyes and looked at Anthony standing by his easel, staring, unseeing, at the cranes. He seemed much older than he had seemed even that morning, his shoulders slightly stooped, his whole demeanor just giving off sadness like a dark vapor.

"Ant?" Rachel said.

He turned slightly, and gave her a halfhearted smile.

"I wondered if you were asleep—"

"No such luck."

She sat up a little straighter, and ran her hand through her hair.

"Tea?" she said.

Anthony ignored her. He said, "What do we do? What do we do, for Ralph?"

Rachel struggled to sit upright.

"We'll ring him. Later. When we've both got our heads a bit more together."

"Yes," Anthony said. "Yes. Poor bloody boy." He raised his arm and added something to a crane's wing. Then he said with some force, "You're right. I'm not ringing *her*. I'm not ringing her, Rachel, ever again."

Luke and Charlotte dropped Edward off at home. He invited them in, but then discovered, from a note on the kitchen table, that Sigrid and Mariella had gone to Indira's house, and would not be back until later, and after he'd made a faint attempt at offering them something to drink, Luke said, well, actually, maybe they ought to get home, and they'd got back into the car, leaving Edward in the late-Sunday-afternoon aimlessness of his own house.

He poured himself a glass of water from the jug in the fridge and took it out onto the deck outside the kitchen. Their little patio garden, always tidied to Sigrid's exacting standards, looked tired and spent. The hornbeams that Sigrid had planted against the back wall—imported, she told Edward, from Italy—were beginning to drop a discolored leaf or two, and such flowers as were left in the wooden planters Sigrid had had specially commissioned looked as if it was simply too much trouble, now, to stay vibrant.

Edward sat down on the edge of a long planter's chair that they had bought with the romantic but unrealistic image in mind of one or other of them in it, with the Sunday papers, or a book from the silently reproachful pile in Edward's study. Sigrid had acquired cushions for it, striped in gray and cream, but those were also in Edward's study and he was sitting on the hard slats of teak, or iroko, or whatever it was made of, and somehow unable to make himself more comfortable.

There had been nothing left, really, to say in the car. Charlotte had been to the sea, she said, and she'd obviously liked it because she seemed quite animated, and chattered away about the beach in Aldeburgh, and when Luke asked her if she'd been to see Ralph she'd given a short laugh, and said, "*Not* a good idea!"

"So you went?" Luke said.

"I did. I rang the bell, and he answered, but he didn't ask me in."

"How was he?"

Charlotte had lowered her voice a little.

"He looked awful—"

"Poor sod. What did he say?"

"Nothing," Charlotte said.

"What d'you mean?"

"He said it wasn't a good time. He didn't want to talk. He wanted me to go away."

Edward had seen Luke put his hand across the gear shift to touch Charlotte's thigh.

"You were a doll to try," Luke said.

Charlotte shrugged.

Edward said, "Did you see Petra and the kids?"

Charlotte's sunglasses turned slightly upwards to meet Edward's eyes in the driving mirror. She said, "They weren't there."

"Oh God," Edward said. "Don't say—"

"Don't think about it," Luke said. "We've all had enough today. More than enough. And you," he said, looking fondly at Charlotte, "have done all the driving."

She'd smiled. She said breezily, "I'd rather drive than throw up," and Edward had had a sudden stab of something like envy at the simplicity of Luke's situation, at his shiny new marriage to this pretty, good-natured, pregnant girl, such a breath of fresh air after an exhausting day of Brinkley dramas.

He turned the water glass in his hands, studying the distorted view of his feet visible through the bottom. He felt that he had done the right thing that day, and doing it had been strangely unsatisfactory, because no solution had emerged, no resolution, only the oddly frustrating sensation that all these tall, clever people were somehow being held to ransom by a slight and enigmatic girl who seemed to have no comprehension of the meaning of obligation or even responsibility. He had had a notion, that night after supper with Ralph in London, that he would go and see Petra, talk to her, explain to her why Ralph was doing what he was doing, and suggest that her support would make the whole process so much easier for everyone, including her. If he had obeyed that impulse, if he had gone all the way to Suffolk to try and reason with Petra, would it actually have made any difference? Would she actually have paid him the slightest bit of attention, or was she always, in her quiet, apparently neutral way, determined to behave in a manner that suited her, and her alone? He shook his head. It was right to feel that his brother was being wronged, that his parents were being treated with extraordinary ingratitude, he was sure it was. But something unsettled him all the same, something that always unsettled him about going back to Suffolk, where the unalteredness of his parents' lives was, weirdly, more of an uneasy disquiet than a consolation.

He was relieved to hear the front door slam. Mariella came skittering down the basement steps, calling out for him.

"Here!" he shouted. "I'm out here!"

She came flying through the kitchen and crashed into him, flinging her arms round him and holding up her face. Her eyebrows were traced with tiny studs of blue glitter.

"I'm an avatar," Mariella said.

Edward bent to reciprocate her embrace.

"So you are. Where's Mummy?"

"Getting stuff out of the car—"

"Did you have a nice time with Indira?"

Mariella pulled free and began to hop round the kitchen table.

"We played airports. For when I go to Sweden."

"Oh," Edward said, not comprehending. "Ready for next time?"

"Yes," Mariella said, still hopping. "Mummy got tickets on the computer before we went to Indira's. She said we'd get the last of the Swedish summer. Before I go back to school."

"I see," Edward said. He felt abruptly slightly sick. The front door on the floor above them opened and closed, and Sigrid's footsteps went across the hall over their heads.

Edward looked at Mariella.

"Am . . . am I coming? Did Mummy get three tickets?"

Mariella had her back to him. She hopped twice more and stopped, balancing unsteadily on one leg.

"Oh no," she said. "Mummy said you couldn't. She said you'd have to stay here, and look after your brothers."

CHAPTER FIFTEEN

There were plenty of reasons why Rachel should find herself in Aldeburgh. There was the bookshop, after all, and the delicatessen, and the need to buy a birthday present for her sister, which always proved so difficult as her sister inferred so much from every present, and was offended by every inference she drew. So it was not at all extraordinary that Rachel should be there, walking slowly and watchfully along the High Street, with her gaze sharpening every time she saw a young woman with a buggy and a small child, or even just a young woman, with disheveled hair and clothes that could never, in a million years, have been dictated by the sartorial requirements of middle-class convention.

She walked and shopped for over an hour. She bought a monograph by Kenneth Clark about the Alde River from the bookshop, and a variety of different olives from the deli, and a striped cotton dressing gown, cut like a kimono, for her sister (would she take offense at the label in the neck being marked "large," meaning large for someone Japanese, but not large at all for a European?) plus a pair of kippers and a loaf of sourdough bread, and stowed them all in the boot of the car. Then she went back to the High Street, and bought a sandwich and a bottle of water, and had a restless small picnic, sitting on the pebbly beach on her spread-out fleece jacket, watching the few late-summer families who were left, and willing one of the small boys she could see to turn out to be Kit: Kit, who would come running up to her, shouting her name with enthusiasm, and thus breaking the ice in whatever conversation she was then going to have with Petra.

She had decided, wrestling with herself as she made the bed or chopped an onion or tied up the toppling stands of Michaelmas daisies in the border, that her entirely justifiable anger would get her nowhere. Anthony was miserably wounded, but yelling at Petra in defense of Anthony would do nothing to influence one or comfort the other. But she could not accept, as much as she had initially felt, when rendered inert by shock, that she could do nothing. She would not shout, or scold, or even reprimand Petra, but she did have to see her and ask her simply why? Why did she not ask for help? Or, if she couldn't ask outright, because of some version of loyalty to Ralph—only a version, surely, in someone who had found herself another man—why had she not at the very least indicated that the idea of changing their lives was half killing her, at an important and most fundamental level?

Rachel had rehearsed her imaginary encounter with Petra every way she could think of. She had visualized Petra defiant, Petra tearful, Petra stubborn and silent, Petra elusive. She had not permitted herself the satisfactory option of Petra relieved and grateful and remorseful, but that seductive scenario had flickered away, beguilingly, at the back of her mind with a persistence that proved to her how much it was the one she longed for. If she gave way, for a second or two, even, she saw Petra back with her in her own kitchen, the boys peacefully playing on the floor, companionably cooking together with Anthony only yards away in his studio, working on the beginnings of a new book, in which project Petra, somehow, was going to collaborate. And then Ralph would appear—this happy scene invariably took place on a Friday—tired but satisfied, in his City suit, and take his family home for the weekend to a house somewhere near that Petra had magically become reconciled to. Even as she luxuriated in this vision, Rachel knew it to be hopeless. To work it required too much improbability and even impossibility. But however much she knew she was fantasizing, she also knew that she could not rest until she had seen Petra, and talked to her.

Petra's mobile phone had been apparently switched off recently. There was no answer-phone message, and sent text messages fell into a black silence. Ralph, readying himself for his departure for London, would not talk about Petra, or reveal her movements or whereabouts. He told his mother that he would be okay if, and only if, he was left to get on with life in his own way. He said he much appreciated his parents' concern—he said this in a voice wholly devoid of appreciation—but that he could only cope if he was left alone. And he meant *alone*. His mobile number, he said, was only to be used in an emergency. Like the children, or something. It wasn't to be used just because Rachel needed news, or reassurance. He hadn't got the energy for that, he had only the energy to do what he had to do for a new job that he didn't want to make a mess of. Get it, Mum, get it?

"Yes," Rachel said, helpless at the receiving end. "Yes. I only wanted—"

"Don't," Ralph said shortly, "don't want anything. Then you won't mind if you don't get it. Like me. Like I have."

And he'd rung off. Rachel had gone out into the garden and shouted at old Dick for stringing up the onions in overlarge bunches, and old Dick had swum up out of the fogs of his blindness and deafness and said that if she spoke to him like that once more he'd be happy to leave her to get on with caring for her vegetable garden all by herself.

She'd said sorry. She'd apologized to old Dick, and she had refrained from worrying Anthony with her call to Ralph, and she had subdued her fury with Petra into a determination merely to seek an explanation. She felt, sitting there on the stony beach watching people crunch and slither their way to the sea, that she, for her, had done pretty well. She had not given way to every impulse and had been penitent about those that had escaped her control. Also, she told herself, she had a right to understand, she was owed an answer. Her and Anthony's relationship with Petra had not been conventional, had not been merely a matter of the effort and manners required by in-laws. They had taken Petra to their hearts. Petra, in turn, had said on several occasions that she did not know what she would do without them.

Rachel got to her feet and shook the sandwich crumbs off her jacket. She would walk, she decided, up and down the High Street one more time, but she would not knock on Petra's front door, and she would not go down to the allotment. The time might come to insist upon a meeting, rather than just hope for it, but that time had not yet come. And if she failed to see Petra, she would never need to confess to Anthony that she had gone to Aldeburgh in the hope of encountering her, and there would be a gratifying honesty in that, at least.

She walked briskly down the High Street, crossed it, and walked equally purposefully back up the other pavement. No Petra. No girls with buggies at all, in fact, they all being, presumably, still involved with toddler lunchtime and toddler naptime. Rachel turned back towards the sea, and the little square where she had left her car, and there was Petra coming towards her, with no buggy, and no children, and her arms weighed down with shopping.

Petra halted, stock-still. She was wearing a kind of gypsy skirt, familiar to Rachel, and her old denim jacket, and her hair was in a rough pigtail, pulled over one shoulder, and tied at the end with a collection of brightly colored woolen bobbles.

"Hi," she said to Rachel. Her voice sounded perfectly normal.

Rachel was hurled into a sudden fluster. It would have been natural, instinctive even, to have kissed Petra, but under the current circumstances that wasn't possible. Nor was smiling, somehow, although Rachel felt her face twist itself into some kind of rictus, like a performing dog. Even her voice, when she managed to say "Hello," sounded unnatural.

Petra was saying nothing, just standing in front of Rachel with her woven grocery bags. Rachel opened her mouth a few times, and made an involuntary gesture or two, trying to indicate a query about where the buggy was, where the boys were. Petra didn't help her.

"How . . . are you?" Rachel said at last.

"Fine—"

"And . . . and the boys?"

"Fine," Petra said.

Rachel got a grip of herself.

"Where are they?" she said. "I don't think I've ever seen you without the boys—"

"They're with Steve," Petra said.

"With . . . with—"

"Yes," Petra said. She sounded as if what she was saying was so ordinary as to be almost boring. "Steve's taken them swimming. They love swimming, so he's taken them." She let a little pause fall, and then she said, "Because I can't swim. Remember?"

And then she smiled at Rachel, politely and remotely, and stepped into the road to walk past her with the shopping bags.

That evening, Rachel rang Edward to describe her encounter with Petra, and to ask if he thought she should tell Anthony.

"Why ever not?" Edward said irritably.

"Well, he's hurt enough already—"

"Exactly."

"And I don't want him picturing his grandsons swimming with this man of Petra's."

"Well, don't tell him then."

"But you said—"

"Mum," Edward said, "Mum. I don't feel like this conversation. I don't want to discuss this. Or think about it. Okay?"

Rachel said sympathetically, "I expect you're missing Sigrid and Mariella."

Edward shut his eyes tightly. He thought he wouldn't reply.

"Are they having a lovely time?" Rachel asked.

Edward didn't open his eyes. Sigrid had been away for four days and he had rung once. There was no phone signal on the island where her parents' summer house was.

"Think so," Edward said.

"Would you like to come up here? The weekend will be grim without them. Come on Friday."

Edward opened his eyes.

"No, thank you, Mum."

"Why not?"

"Because," Edward said, "I want to stay here."

There was a silence. In it, the message signal on Edward's phone beeped. Then Rachel said crisply, "Fine. I'll leave you to be disagreeable in peace. Bye, darling."

The line went dead. Edward scrolled to his message box.

"In Stockholm for 3 nights. Back Sunday. X."

He dialed Sigrid's number. There was a wait while the signal sorted itself out between London and Stockholm, and then her voice-mail message, "This is Sigrid's phone. Please leave me a message and I'll call you back. Thank you."

Edward opened his mouth to say, "Call me," and thought better of it. He threw his phone down on the sofa beside him. She had left, barely kissing him good-bye, declining to account for excluding him from this last-minute holiday, not even offering an explanation for her impulse, withdrawing into a homing Swedishness, which seemed to make her impervious to any consequence of her behavior and certainly to any reaction or emotion of his.

"Will you miss me?" he'd said to Mariella in Sigrid's hearing, despising himself. Mariella had hugged him as if he were a dear old teddy bear, with no human feelings. "A bit," she said. And then they'd left, with a case full of shorts and plimsolls, Sigrid wearing a baseball cap and looking about sixteen, and had gone straight to the island in the archipelago where, Mariella said, they were going to have breakfast in their pajamas and go sailing and make campfires on the beach.

"We're going to sleep together," Mariella said, "in the big bed. Just me and Mummy."

Edward had looked up the weather in southeast Sweden online, and it was beautiful, warm and clear and with low wind speeds. He pictured Sigrid and Mariella in his parents-in-law's house, which was no more than a big cabin, really, white-walled, gray-roofed, furnished with romantic Nordic simplicity, with views on three sides of water and, in the distance, a village of white cottages and a spire on a red-roofed church. He had made love to Sigrid in that cabin, they had cooked fish on flat stones on the beach, she had been thrilled and impressed that he knew how to sail, that he was such a good sailor and handled her father's boat with ease.

234

"You look . . . so right here," she'd said, lying on the beach with her head in his lap.

Well, not right enough, any longer, to be included. Not right enough to accompany her to the island, to see his parents-in-law, with whom he had always got on. Not right enough—oh hell, Edward thought, getting up from the sofa and pacing through to the kitchen, what is going on, what is she playing at, is she going downhill again, what is the *matter*?

He opened the fridge and took out a bottle of beer, slamming it down on the table. Whatever was the matter, whatever Sigrid was up to, he'd just have to bear it. He wouldn't say anything to anyone, certainly not to his brothers, while Ralph was in such a jam himself, and Luke was dealing with all the consequences of a new marriage and all the crossed wires this unexpected pregnancy had caused. And to crown it all, Ralph was coming to stay for the first few days of his new employment, until his room off Finsbury Square was ready, on the first of the month, and he was going to need supporting, wasn't he, not informing that his older brother, to whom he looked for strength and sympathy, was in almost as rocky a place as he was, even if more subtly positioned.

Edward flipped the top off the beer bottle and took a deep swallow. Sigrid would be back four nights from now, full of air and sunshine and happy Swedishness, and, despite all his hurt at her treatment of him, he did not want her to walk back in to a long-faced husband as well as an unexpected-guest brother-in-law. He took another mouthful of beer. No more wallowing, he told himself. No more plaguing myself with imaginings. At least . . . at least, she's coming home.

Sigrid had intended to stay on the island for a week. She had planned on four or five days alone with Mariella, doing all the simple, peaceful, water-orientated things that she had done on the island when she was Mariella's age, and then she had asked her parents to come and join them for the weekend, expecting a gratified agreement since her parents loved the island, and had not seen Mariella, their only grandchild, for seven months. But Sigrid's mother had said that she was so sorry but her father had an important business function in Stockholm on the Saturday night, and so they would be staying in the city.

"Well, *you* come," Sigrid said.

"No, I can't," her mother said. "I'm going with your father. The invitation is for both of us."

"Rather than see Mariella and me?"

"Sigi," her mother said calmly, "you have sprung this trip on us. It is last-minute. We had plans in place."

"But I wanted to see you. For you to see Mariella—"

"Then come to Stockholm."

"But I wanted to be on the island—"

"I must go," Sigrid's mother said. "I leave the decision to you."

Even with the irritation of her parents not changing their plans, Sigrid anticipated loving being on the island. She longed for the familiar, faintly rough texture of the blue-and-white bed linen in the cottage, and the mornings, nursing a mug of tea, still in her pajamas, and watching the sun come up, and the evenings, on the beach, showing Mariella how to gut a fish as her father had shown her and Bengt, and then spearing it on a twig before grilling it. But Mariella did not much like fish, anyway, and certainly didn't want to touch the gluey loops of its innards, and at night, instead of sleeping peacefully and thereby allowing Sigrid to rise, rested and refreshed, to watch the sunrise, she kicked and swiveled in her slumber, seizing the duvet and muttering, to such an extent that Sigrid took herself off to her narrow childhood bed in a separate bedroom, where her feet hit the board at the foot of the bed, and some plumbing pipes cleared their throats at intervals in the wall behind her head, all night long.

The weather was beautiful, but the days on the island were long—long and, frankly, boring. The sailing classes in which Sigrid had hoped to enrol Mariella were finished for the summer, and after a first nostalgic scramble round the rocks, walks were limited. Because Swedish schools returned weeks before English ones, all the families had gone, leaving their houses shuttered and their boats, in some cases, already sheeted for the winter. Mariella knew not to say outright that she was bored, but she did say, now and then, that it was odd to be without a television. It was odd. The whole place felt odd, as if Sigrid's recollection of her childhood there had been conjured out of fantasy rather than out of fact. On the fourth day, watching Mariella building a little cairn of pebbles with one hand, as if she couldn't be sufficiently interested to use both, Sigrid suggested that they return to Stockholm. Mariella scrambled to her feet.

"Oh, *yes!*"

Sigrid smiled at her.

"Is it so very boring here?"

"Well," Mariella said, "it would have been better, really, if Daddy had been here too."

Ralph had laid all his suits for London out on the double bed. He couldn't think of it, anymore, as "our" bed, even though they still shared it, turned away from each other, and lined up along the edges in case a stray foot or knee should touch by mistake. Ralph had considered moving out, to sleep with Kit, or on the sofa downstairs, but anger kept him in his own bed, just as anger was revving him up to leave for London as soon as he possibly could. Edward, sensing this rage, had agreed that he could occupy their small guest room—it doubled as

Sigrid's study—in order to get away from Aldeburgh as soon as possible.

"I'm going crazy," Ralph had said to Edward, "living here. Crazy. And every time I try and talk to her, I get crazier."

The problem was, really, that Petra was hiding nothing.

"Are you still seeing him?"

"Yes."

"Are you"—pause—"sleeping with him?"

"No."

"Are you"—shouting—"going to?"

"Maybe," Petra said.

"What d'you mean, maybe?"

Petra was at the kitchen table, drawing, her hair hanging, her face mostly hidden.

"I don't fancy him much," Petra said to her sketchbook, "but maybe. I dunno."

Ralph placed his hands flat on the table and lowered his shoulders in order to see her face.

"Look at me!"

Slowly, Petra looked up.

"Why," Ralph said, trying to control himself, "do you have to see him at *all*?"

Petra waited a moment, and then she said, "I got lonely."

"Why didn't you tell me that?"

"You couldn't hear me," Petra said.

"Why didn't you tell Mum and Dad?"

Petra bent her head again.

"They'd have wanted to do something. They'd have wanted *me* to do something—"

"But"—shouting again—"you *have* done something!"

"But I chose it," Petra said to her drawing.

Ralph sat down heavily in a chair opposite Petra. He said, "What d'you feel about me?"

"What I have always done."

"Which is?"

"I like you," Petra said. "You're cool."

"But—"

"But you've changed. You want things I don't want now. I can't change, just to suit you."

Ralph sprawled across the table and laid his head in his arms.

"Oh my God—"

Petra said nothing.

Ralph said wearily, "I haven't changed, but if we're going to live and eat, there has to be money, and I've been given a chance to earn some. How are you going to look after the boys without money, for God's sake? And, as you have no job, it has to be me. I cannot believe how . . . how *obtuse* you are."

Petra said, "I don't want that sort of money."

"Christ—"

"I don't need to live in this kind of place. I don't need a car. It's nice to have, but I'd manage. I like things small. I always have."

Ralph said sarcastically, "Oh, so my parents' generosity was repulsive to you, was it?"

Petra looked up. She said sharply, "They wanted to do what they've done."

"Meaning?"

"I'm not a complete fool. They've been lovely to me, but I've suited them."

"You ungrateful little *cow*."

Petra stood up, holding her notebook.

"It's not worth it," she said.

"What isn't?"

"It's not worth people being kind to you. They always want so much back."

"But not," Ralph said, "lover boy."

Petra turned.

"He's easy."

"And I'm not—"

"No. You're not."

"Then why don't you bloody go and live with him!"

Petra began to move towards the doorway to the hall.

"I don't want to. I might, in time, but I don't want to right now. It's just that he's on my side, he doesn't tell me what to do, he just talks to the kids and digs the spuds and I don't have to—" She stopped.

"Don't have to what?"

"*Earn* my existence all the time," and then she'd gone out, and he could hear her going slowly up the stairs and into their bedroom, and then a couple of thuds as she took off her shoes and dropped them on the floor.

He sat there, for a long time, at the kitchen table. He was not going, he told himself, to go back over everything. He was not going to revert to the Ralph who'd come back from Singapore with all those impractical, dreamy notions of sustaining a solitary life, somehow, in an empty cottage on the North Sea, with only wind and gulls for company. Even if he'd wanted to go back, he couldn't, in fact, because the money he had brought with him from Singapore had all gone on his failed business, and all he owned now was a small part of the house in which he now sat, which he no longer wanted—if he ever actually had—and nor did Petra. Most of it belonged to the building society, and in his present mood they were welcome to it. They could have the house and the car and the piecemeal furniture and all he would ask them to leave was the clothes he needed to take to London for this job that was going to give him his life back, his sense of self. And only then, when he was back on top, and not crushed underneath, could he begin the battle to gain custody of his children. Because that's what he wanted. He was sure of that. He wanted his boys. Petra wasn't fit to bring up a . . . *goldfish*.

When he had finally gone upstairs that night, Petra was not in their bed. He found her instead in Kit's bed, and Kit had flung an arm across her in his sleep, and they were lying facing each other, almost nose to nose. Across the room, Barney was snuffling in his cot, stout legs and arms spread-eagled, his thick lashes astonishing on his cheeks.

Ralph stood in the dark bedroom between his sleeping family, and felt something so close to the panic of despair that the only solution he could think of was to force it down with a big hit of anger. It was Petra he was angry with, of course it was, Petra who refused to compromise, refused to understand, refused to be reasonable, refused to *grow up*. It was Petra who had made Kit such a fragile child, it was Petra who had taken all the Brinkleys' open-handed generosity until, on a whim, it didn't suit her to see it as generosity anymore, but only as oppression and control and obligation. It was Petra who couldn't support or admire what he was doing, to look after them all. Hell, she couldn't even iron a bloody *shirt* properly. It was Petra—

He had to stop himself. He was shaking, and his fists had clenched. He could not go on being so furious, it was exhausting him, diverting his vital energies, obsessing him. He couldn't understand Petra any more than she claimed not to be able to understand him, so maybe it was better that they were apart, and the sooner the better. He had to subdue the impulse to hurl her physically out of Kit's bed, and resolved instead to use all that urgent energy towards this new start, that was going to give him, after months of feeling he was fighting under a blanket, focus and purpose and discipline.

He went out of the boys' bedroom and closed the door

behind him. He made himself stand on the landing and breathe slowly and deeply six times. Edward had said he could come up to London on Saturday, but he thought he would ring in the morning and say he needed to come now, *now*, and if Edward couldn't have him, for some reason, then he'd find a hotel. Anything. Anything was better than this.

He took down their only big suitcase from the dusty top of the wardrobe. It bore the bashes of many journeys, and the shreds of old baggage-handling labels. He put it on the bed and opened it. There was an old spray bottle of insect repellent inside, and he picked it up and sniffed it, and the smell made him feel suddenly rather tearful. He threw the bottle towards the wastebin beside the chest of drawers, and began to make rapid, methodical piles of shirts and socks and boxer shorts, emptying drawers with speed, to purge himself of all animation that was other than constructive and forward-looking. And then he got into the half of the bed that wasn't occupied by the suitcase and lay there, panting slightly, and listening to his heart racing away under his rib cage, as if it was just a useful, purposeful muscle, and not the seat, really, of any emotion at all.

CHAPTER SIXTEEN

S igrid tucked Mariella up in the bed that had been hers when she was a child. The bed was now in her mother's study, and used as a daybed, piled with cushions covered in modern graphic designs, but it still had its old wooden headboard with its row of cut-out hearts, and on the wall above it still hung the Carl Larsson prints that Sigrid had loved as a child, depicting idylls of Swedish nineteenth-century country life, complete with apple orchards full of geese and little girls in kerchiefs and pinafores. Otherwise the room was as streamlined and uncluttered as the rest of the apartment. Such papers as were on her mother's desk were in a black lacquered tray, her pens were in a matching pot, the books and files on her shelves upright and orderly. On the walls hung a small abstract oil painting and framed photographs of her family, including Mariella in a life jacket, on her grandfather's knee outside the cottage on the island.

Mariella was leaning back against crisp striped pillows, holding a puzzle made of plastic tubes that her engineer grandfather had made for her. The tubes were linked in such a way that there was only one sequence of separation that could part them, and Sigrid's father had declined even to give Mariella a clue as to how to achieve it. Sigrid had offered to read to—or with—Mariella, maybe something suitably Baltic like Tove Jansson, but Mariella was absorbed in her puzzle. Morfar always set her challenges, just as Mormor always made her an apple cake, and rising to these challenges was something Mariella liked to do. It was, Sigrid supposed, a form of safe family flirting.

She bent and kissed Mariella.

"Sleep tight. I'll send Mormor to kiss you too."

Mariella went on twisting.

"In ten minutes."

"Why ten minutes?"

"I'll have done this by then—"

"Will you?"

"Yes," Mariella said with emphasis.

Sigrid left the study door ajar, and walked down the central corridor of the apartment to the sitting room. It was flooded with soft evening sunlight through the long, floor-length windows, and her mother was sitting by one of those windows, in an armchair upholstered in gray linen, reading the *Aftonbladet* newspaper. She looked up when Sigrid came in and said, "May I go and say good night?"

"In ten minutes. She wants to solve Morfar's puzzle."

Sigrid's mother smiled.

"And he wants her to solve it too."

Sigrid sat down in the chair opposite her mother's. She looked out of the window into the soft dazzle of late sunlight. Her mother looked at her. After a minute or two her mother said, "Were you thinking of coming back to Sweden?"

Sigrid gave a little jump.

"Whatever made you say that?"

"I just wondered," her mother said. "This impulsive trip. Your restlessness. Something . . . unsettled about you."

Sigrid said abruptly, "I can't breathe for those Brinkleys—"

"Ah," her mother said.

"They are like Morfar's puzzle," Sigrid said. "Except that there isn't a way to unlink them."

Her mother put the newspaper down and took off her reading glasses.

"So you were thinking that you could escape them by coming back to Sweden."

Sigrid looked away.

"Only sort of—"

"Well," her mother said kindly, "don't—"

"But—"

"Listen. Listen to me. You've been away too long. It isn't even the country you grew up in. All the people you grew up with have changed with the country, and although you have changed with England you haven't moved on here. How could you? You haven't been here."

Sigrid made a little gesture.

"I could catch up—"

"And there's another thing," her mother said, "a bigger thing. Which I suspect you haven't thought of."

"Which is?"

Sigrid's mother leaned back even more in her chair.

"Me."

"You!"

"Yes," her mother said. "Me. Think of my situation."

Sigrid looked round the room, laughing a little.

"It looks a very comfortable situation indeed—"

"Really?" her mother said. "Really? You think it's so comfortable to have two children, both of whom have chosen to live in other countries?"

"But you don't mind—"

"Who says I don't mind?"

"But—"

"Of course, I am happy you married Edward," Sigrid's mother said. "I adore Mariella. I love your brother dearly, but he will never give me a Mariella. I like his partner, I love your Edward, I am pleased and proud of what my children have achieved, but I don't know their lives. Not as my friends know their children's lives. How can I? You live in different cultures as well as countries."

"Goodness," Sigrid said.

"I have not finished—"

"But—"

"I have had to adjust," her mother said. "And one of the ways I've adjusted to having both my children living in other countries is to throw myself into my work. I work all the time now, as your father does. It suits us. We like it. And when we retire, we will start traveling, and we'll come often to London and we will see more of you, and more of Mariella. But if—" She paused, and leaned forward, fixing her gaze on Sigrid. "If you come back to Sweden now, I couldn't just dump all my patients and become a full-time mother and grandmother. I couldn't. I wouldn't want to. It's too late for that now, and you should realize it."

Sigrid said defiantly, "I'm not sick again—"

"I never said you were. I don't think you are."

"Then why are you talking to me like this? Why are you angry?"

"I'm not angry," her mother said, "but as a mother yourself, I expected that you might have a little more imagination."

Sigrid looked at her lap.

"And," her mother added, "for your mother-in-law too. Didn't she bring up the man you married?"

Sigrid put her hands to her face.

"No crying," her mother said more gently. "We are both too old for that. A bit of frankness between women shouldn't make you cry."

"I'm not crying—"

"Oh?"

"I'm just . . . adjusting. Myself."

Sigrid's mother stood up. She bent forward and gave her daughter's shoulder a squeeze.

"I'm going to say good night to Mariella. Why don't you get us a glass of wine. Friday night, after all."

"Mamma—"

"Yes?"

"I'm not trying to . . . run away—"

Her mother paused, passing her chair. She said, "It never works, Sigi. You just take it all with you, anyway. You can change your situation, but it will be the same one if you don't change yourself. I say this to my patients, over and over. I should have it painted on my surgery wall."

Charlotte's evening sickness was improving. As it diminished, her stomach swelled slightly, but definitely, and her bosom was magnificent. She told her boss at work, who was dramatically unsurprised, that she was pregnant, and was informed that she would have four months' paid maternity leave, plus two further months on half pay, but that her job would not be kept open for her after that automatically. This all sounded fine to Charlotte. It occupied the same realm of improbability as having a baby in the first place seemed to do, and Charlotte thought blithely that it would all somehow just happen, and events would carry her along as if she were a paper boat on a stream, and she would adapt to each new happening as she had adapted, in the past, to school, and work, and London, and men, and then marriage. The early feelings of anxiety, almost fear, that she had felt at being pregnant, finding herself in a tunnel from which only she could exit, had been considerably subdued by seeing how thrilled Luke was about the baby, to the point, she discovered, of buying several pregnancy and baby books, which he read earnestly at night before they went to sleep.

"He'd be having this baby for you if he could," Jed said to Charlotte one day. "It's mental. Just make sure you hand the real Luke back when you're done with the pregnant one."

Jed had brought Charlotte a mug with a stick drawing of a beaming pregnant woman on it, and "Happy Mum" written below the picture. It was very strange indeed to consider herself as a potential mother, to be the kind of person upon whom a much smaller person would shortly depend, a person for whom her responsibility was, her own mother had told her, a lifelong companion from your baby's first breath. Well, Charlotte thought, a sense of responsibility probably arrived along with the baby, just as a different kind of love had appeared when she began to take Luke seriously. A kind of love which, Charlotte suspected, Petra still felt for Ralph and which Charlotte, because of her feelings for Luke, had a great deal of sympathy for.

Since the visit to Petra's allotment, Charlotte had kept in touch with her by text. Petra didn't do Facebook, or Twitter, or even answer her mobile, but she responded sometimes to texts, writing cryptic little messages, often mysterious in meaning, but always signed off with a kiss. Charlotte had half a dozen of these little communications in her phone's memory, and they gave her both the glow and the mild kick of being in some kind of conspiracy. She wasn't quite sure what the conspiracy was for, or when she would tell Luke about it, but it gave her a frisson of secret power all the same, as if she was stealing a march on Luke's family without their knowing it. It wasn't a big disloyalty, she told herself, it wasn't really undermining anything serious, and anyway, didn't Petra have the right to a point of view just as much as any of the Brinkleys?

And so when Luke said, one evening, after Edward had rung

to say that Ralph was due to stay with him, and he sounded pretty down, so could Luke please find time to meet him for a beer in the next day or two, "Ralph's in London. He's actually done it. Maybe that'll bring Petra to her senses," Charlotte said quite forcefully, "Why doesn't anyone in your family consider Petra's point of view?"

They had been clearing up after supper, jostling round each other in the tiny kitchen. Luke had a tumbler in each hand, and a tea towel over one shoulder. He stopped on his way to the shelf where they kept their glasses and said, "What?"

Charlotte was tipping the remains of a chicken korma into a plastic box. She said again, with emphasis, "Why don't any of you think of what it's like for Petra? Why does she get all the blame?"

"She doesn't," Luke said.

"She does. You all go on and on about her ingratitude and not having a grip on real life and wanting everything her own way—"

"Well, she does," Luke said. He put the glasses on their shelf and whipped the tea towel off his shoulder.

"You don't know—"

"What don't I know?"

"What she feels. How she's been treated—"

"Treated?"

"Yes."

"By whom?"

"By you," Charlotte said, snapping the box shut. "By all of you."

Luke picked up a handful of cutlery to dry it. He said, frowning down at the forks in his hand, "Are we that mean?"

"She didn't say anyone was mean. She just said Ralph didn't understand."

Luke looked up.

"*Said?* When?"

Charlotte stood up straight so that she could look directly at Luke.

"When I went to see her."

Luke dumped the forks back on the draining board.

"Oh, Char—"

"I saw her while you were at your parents'. When you went with Edward. I drove to Aldeburgh and I went to their house, but Ralph didn't want to let me in, so I went to find Petra on her allotment."

Luke said sadly, "What good did you think that would do?"

"She deserves a hearing!"

"Are you sure," Luke said, "that you're not just getting even with my mother, somehow?"

"No," Charlotte said too quickly. "She needs someone to be on her side. Don't you think?" She paused, and then she said, "Anyway, we didn't even mention your mother's name."

Luke sighed. He said, "I don't expect you needed to." He glanced at Charlotte. "I don't want a row about this."

"Nor me."

"What did you . . . exactly say to her?"

"I said," Charlotte said, feeling a sudden and disconcerting diminution in her own certainty, "that even if I didn't share everything that's important to her, I understood the importance, and I was, well, I was there for her."

"Shagging the bloke?"

"She isn't shagging him. Why does it always have to be about sex? Why can't she be with someone who isn't always telling her to do things she doesn't want to do?"

"Like what?"

"Like," Charlotte said, gaining confidence again, "like saying he had to be free to go to London, but she wasn't free to see anyone else—"

"He's in London," Luke said, "to earn money to keep her, and the kids."

"That's not how she sees it. It isn't what she wants. She just wants to be left, living by the sea, but not by the standards of . . . of—" She stopped.

"My parents," Luke said.

Charlotte nodded. Luke put the tea towel down in a damp lump beside the forks. He looked out of the window above the sink, his hands in his pockets. Charlotte waited, watching him, uncertain of how she would defend herself, now that she had been found out. Luke didn't turn.

"It always comes back to that," Luke said. "Doesn't it? It always comes back to the fact that you've decided to hate my mother."

Anthony was sorting canvases. He'd been drawing—a sandwich tern in flight, trying to differentiate clearly all the flight-feather groups in its spread wings—but he wasn't concentrating properly, so he left his easel and the bunch of pencils he kept in an old stoneware mustard jar, and climbed a stepladder to haul down, from their unsteady stacks on the rafters, the piles of old boards and canvases, to see which of them might be used again, and which could be taken into the college to be used for his students. It was less than a week until the beginning of term, and Anthony felt a pitiful need for the small structure it gave to his life, the reassurance of familiarity of yet another class of foundation-year students, who were all in love with Jackson Pollock, and Mark Rothko, and could see no point or merit in learning to draw a scene from their grandma's bird table. Anthony thought even of their scorn and reluctance with pleased anticipation.

He had brought down two piles, blown the worst of the dust off them, and sorted through the endless drawings and paintings, years and years of owls and ducks, of storks and swans and geese, of a golden eagle landing on a rock (that had been a good holiday, in the Western Highlands), of gulls and lapwings, and of a dipper swimming as happily as a penguin. He'd paused over a painting of a group of kittiwakes plunging and splashing together in a lake, and thought that it was actually good enough, arresting enough, to do something with rather than leave to molder on the rafters, and he was standing with the painting in one hand and some sketches of herons drawn on thick rough handmade paper in the other when there was a sudden flurry of gravel outside the studio, as if someone was running unsteadily, and the door was flung open, and Kit appeared, panting.

"Gramps!"

Anthony let both pictures fall to the floor. He knelt and held his arms out.

"Kit!"

Kit ran to him. He was laughing. He put his arms round Anthony's neck, and held on, chattering in his ear. Then the gravel crunched again and Petra appeared carrying Barney. She walked through the door, and then halted just inside, looking at Anthony. She didn't speak.

Anthony detached Kit's arms, and got to his feet. Kit clung to his trouser legs, still chirruping. Barney observed his grandfather and leaned forward in Petra's arms, grunting.

Anthony said, "What are you doing here?"

Petra shifted Barney slightly in her arms. She was wearing jeans, and a loose smock made of green Indian gauze, embroidered with mirrors. Her bare feet were thrust into sneakers, whose toe caps were worn into holes.

"I wanted to see you," Petra said.

She bent and deposited Barney on the floor. He began to crawl rapidly towards his grandfather.

"Careful," Anthony said, "there might be drawing pins—"

"I'll look!" Kit shouted. "I'll look! I'll look!"

Anthony dropped to his knees again.

"I was sorting old drawings. They might have fallen out, where a drawing was pinned to a board—"

Petra came a few steps closer.

"We'll all look—"

She dropped to the floor too.

"I'm not sure," Anthony said, "that I have anything to say to you."

Petra found a drawing pin and reached up to put it on the edge of the nearest table.

"Okay—"

"Okay!"

"I didn't think you would," Petra said.

"Then why have you come?"

Petra reached forward to take some nameless small object out of Barney's hand.

"You've been good to me. Always. I wanted you to know that."

"Found one!" Kit said excitedly.

Anthony turned away so that she wasn't in his line of vision.

"I do know it. That's why . . . what you are doing is so hard to understand—"

"I'm not doing anything to you—"

"Ralph is my son. He's hurt. I'm hurt."

Petra sat back on her heels.

"I get that."

"So maybe you will also get that I don't want to see you."

Kit went up to Anthony and offered two drawing pins.

"Thank you," Anthony said. He felt violently disconcerted. He put his hand up to his eyes.

"You crying?" Kit said, peering.

"No—"

"Shall I blow your nose?"

"Kit, old boy, just give Gramps a minute, would you, just let me—"

Kit put his arms round as much of Anthony's trunk as he could manage, as if to haul him to his feet. Petra sat back on her heels and watched while Anthony got up unevenly, clumsily tangled with his grandson.

"There!" Kit said with triumph.

"Thank you—"

Petra stood up, unfolding from the floor in a single movement. She said, "We'll go—"

Anthony spread his arms and hands in a sudden gesture of helplessness.

"Did you see Rachel?"

"I came to see you—"

"Look," Anthony said, "look, I can imagine how wretched this has been for you. I know how tricky Ralph can be. I know you don't want to live in Ipswich or London or wherever, but what . . . whatever *possessed* you to think another man would be the answer?"

Kit began to roam round the studio, investigating things. Barney had found a walnut on the floor that he was trying to insert into a hole in the side of one of the armchairs. Petra watched them both for a while and then she said, "He's not . . . an answer. He's just getting me through."

"But there's *us*! There's always been us! We've always been here to help, you only had to ask, you only had to whisper—"

"I can't go on saying thank you," Petra said.

"We don't want thanks, we don't expect thanks—"

Petra said quietly, "I can't always do what you want. You . . . forget."

"Forget what?"

"That not everybody wants what you want. Some people want much *less*."

"If breaking up something like a marriage is wanting something less—"

"I didn't break it. Not at the beginning."

Anthony looked at her for the first time since she had arrived.

"What do you mean?"

Petra shrugged. She said, "It suited us how we were. It suited us best, at the beginning, with just the cottage and the beach. Then it changed. But I haven't. I want what I've always wanted. I knew it when I first saw the cottage."

"But this *man*—"

Petra bent to heave Barney into her arms again.

"You're all fixated on this man."

"Well, of course!"

Petra looked at him over Barney's head.

"You don't get it, do you?"

"No."

"Well," Petra said, "that's up to you." She looked about for Kit, dawdling round the table on which Anthony's drawing materials lay in a confusion that was completely clear to him. "But I wanted to come and tell you that, whatever happens, I know how good you've been to me, and I'm grateful."

Anthony said hoarsely, "Will you see Rachel?"

Petra shook her head, holding her free hand out to Kit.

"Will you come again?"

"One day," Petra said.

"Petra—"

"Yes?"

Anthony looked at her standing there in her holey sneakers with Barney in her arms, and Kit jigging at her side. He said awkwardly, "I don't know why I should thank you for coming, but thank you for coming."

"I thought you wouldn't see me," Petra said.

Anthony looked at Kit, and then at Barney. He felt weighed down by unhappiness.

"So did I," he said.

"Long time no see!" Marco, the coffee vendor, said to Sigrid.

"One week—"

"One week! Long, long time not to see."

"You Italians—"

"*Bella ragazza*," Marco said on cue, smiling, handing Sigrid her coffee and a small white paper bag containing a biscotto.

She walked down Gower Street holding her coffee. It was a gray day, but the sky was light and high, and there was just a little sharp edge to the air, presaging the end of days when she could walk to work in just a sweater, or a jacket, with bare feet inside her shoes and an abundance of daylight. She had been away only a week, but it had, in its unexpected way, been an intense week, a week that had not turned out in any way as she had planned it, and from which she had returned feeling strangely disorientated, as if she couldn't remember what it was like to live in either Stockholm or London, as if she had abandoned the familiar—or tried to—for something that wasn't at all as she had anticipated it would be when she got there.

Perhaps work would be reassuring. Maybe the lab, and those fragments of wood and cloth and glass that awaited her, would root her again, restore her to the equilibrium that, earlier in the summer, she was sure she had reliably found. Part of her, on the flight home, had felt a twitch of excitement that that equilibrium might be waiting peacefully at home for her with Edward, but when she got home Ralph was there too, gaunt and overanimated, insisting that he wasn't nervous about his first Monday in a new job, but only eager to begin, and there was no opportunity to do more than be a welcoming sister-in-law, and find him a bath towel. Edward had asked, in a slightly forced way, if they had had a good time and Mariella had said, truffling the fridge in search of homecoming favorites, "You know, Daddy, the island was so, so weird, it was like everyone had just *died*," and Edward had laughed with what Sigrid recognized as undisguised relief.

At her station at the bench in the lab, everything looked as she had left it, but with the unmistakable air of having been occupied by someone else who had been careful to restore everything to Sigrid's exacting pattern. Everybody said good morning, and asked politely about Sweden, and the head of the laboratory said he was glad to see her back, as a very interesting specimen had just come in from southern Germany that he knew was squarely in her field. Ginger-haired Philip hovered round her for a while, thinking up things to point out or ask, but then he was summoned to run an errand, and was blessedly absent for two quiet, serious, concentrating hours until he reappeared at Sigrid's elbow and said that there was someone outside to see her.

"It's eleven o'clock," Sigrid said, "I'm working."

"I said that," Philip said. "I told him you'd be working."

"Well, please go and tell him again."

"He says he's your brother-in-law—"

Sigrid looked up from her screen.

"Brother-in-law?"

Philip grinned.

"Luke?" he said hopefully. "Said his name was Luke?"

Sigrid made a little sound of annoyance. She got up from her chair.

"Thank you, Philip?" Philip said.

She glanced at him.

"Thank you—"

"I don't have to do it, you know," Philip said. "I don't have to carry messages and run errands. I've got a perfectly good degree in computing and technology from Nottingham Trent University, and I don't need to be treated like someone from the post room."

"Was I?"

"Yes," Philip said, "always. Even when I give you flowers."

Sigrid put her hands in the pockets of her lab coat.

"Could we have this conversation another time?"

"As long," Philip said, "as we *have* it."

Luke was waiting in the uncompromising reception area of the laboratory building. There was a row of beige-tweed upholstered chairs along the wall opposite the reception desk, but Luke was standing up, his hands in his pockets, looking at a bulletin board where notices of academic meetings and lectures had been pinned with meticulous regularity. He turned round as Sigrid came in.

"Thank you—"

"Is anything the matter?"

"No one's ill," Luke said, "nothing like that. I just—"

"What?"

"Well," he said, "I didn't want to come round to your house because I'd quite like this to be private—"

Sigrid motioned him to sit down.

"Are you in trouble?"

"No," Luke said. "Yes. Well, sort of. It's . . . about Charlotte—"

"Charlotte!"

"She's fine," Luke said, "she's really well. It's . . . it's just her—and my mother."

He stopped. He and Sigrid regarded each other in silence for some time. Then Sigrid sighed.

"Oh," she said. "That."

CHAPTER SEVENTEEN

M arnie did not often go to London these days. In fact, she had hardly been at all since Charlotte's father died, and had only been inveigled to do so on the two days Charlotte had set aside to find her wedding dress. They'd been strenuous days, Marnie remembered, with a sensationally uncomfortable night in between on the sofa in Charlotte's flat, despite Charlotte's flatmate, Nora, kindly finding an extra pillow. The sofa wasn't long enough, the hot water was inadequate, and Marnie was not of an age or generation to do her hair and makeup as girls did, racing about the flat chattering, their phones tucked into their shoulders and hair grips held between their teeth. Marnie was used to a dressing table with a glass top, a triple mirror and a good light. She had felt, standing in Liberty's wedding-dress department after the night on the sofa, that she was in every way disadvantaged. She was just the exhausted, disheveled credit-card carrier.

Today, however, was different. She had prepared herself for today. She had decided the night before what she would wear, and had been delighted to see, when she drew her bedroom curtains back, that the morning weather had obliged her. She had been to the hairdresser in Beaconsfield two days before, there were enough late raspberries for breakfast, and she had rehearsed, both to a mirror and on paper, in her pretty, legible hand, what she was going to say.

She drove steadily and peacefully to the station. There was plenty of time. Her senior rail card secured her a first-class seat at a very reasonable rate, and she bought a newspaper, and a copy of *Country Life*, a magazine ideally constituted for advertising her paintings, or the postcards and birthday cards that they were so well suited to. It struck her, waiting for the train, that what she was about to do was something that she would never have dared to do, something that it would probably never have occurred to her to do, had Gregory still been alive. He would, she was sure, have approved of her idea, but he would have wanted it to be *his* idea; he would have wanted to mastermind it and be applauded for it. Marnie had grown, over the years, very used to applauding Gregory, and skilled at it as well, as it had usually taken a fair amount of time before he was satisfied that he had received all the praise he was due, but it struck her, standing quietly on the station platform with her mind and her person pleasingly ordered, that it was very liberating indeed to feel that every thought and move no longer had to be channeled through, and swallowed up by, another person.

At Marylebone, Marnie took a Bakerloo Line train to Oxford Circus, where she changed to take the Central Line eastwards to Liverpool Street. Gregory—had he still been there—would have insisted she take a taxi, but one of her new freedoms was only sheltering herself when she felt she really wanted to. Also, the small economy of buying a Zone A Underground ticket along with her rail ticket had been very satisfying. Managing money, Marnie had discovered, was satisfying. It was also, if you kept an eye on it, not difficult, especially for someone in her fortunate position of a largely known income. She remembered the hours and hours Gregory had spent snorting over papers in his study, or telephoning his stockbroker. If it was disloyal not to be able to remember his perpetual state of aggrieved agitation about money without smiling, then so be it. It didn't diminish her genuine gratitude that all the huffing and puffing had still left her in a very comfortable place indeed.

At Liverpool Street, Marnie left the train and climbed up to Bishopsgate. The train had been full of refreshingly different people from the kind of people Marnie usually saw, which only contributed to her sense of adventure. People at Liverpool Street station were equally as diverse and interesting, and Marnie had a sudden sense of being extremely conspicuous through conventionality, and was delighted to find that this did not make her feel remotely disconcerted or threatened, but merely mildly exhilarated. A tall Sikh in a turban paused briefly to allow her to get on to the escalator up to the street ahead of him, and smiled when she thanked him, in a way that made her feel she was spreading long-unused wings. How used we become, she thought, to what we have, even if it doesn't suit us.

It was a mild, soft, early September day, warmer in London than it had been in Buckinghamshire. Marnie took off her jacket and folded it over her arm, and then, feeling that this was no way to conduct herself in east London, unfolded it and slung it over her shoulders, pausing in front of the plate-glass window of a vast bank to admire the effect. It looked suitably nonchalant. She turned her jacket collar up, and set off northwards towards Shoreditch High Street, and the intriguingly named Arnold Circus, where Charlotte had told her that she and Luke lived, in a flat the size of a shoe box, five floors above the street.

Jed went down the short flight of stairs from the studio to answer the bell. He found himself face-to-face with a good-looking woman a bit older than his own mother, wearing the kind of clothes his mother wouldn't have been seen dead in. Jed's mother wore jeans, and cowboy boots, and still had hair down her back. This lady looked like Jed's idea of the female half of a Tory Party conference. He wasn't quite sure what to say to her, so he said nothing, just stood there and gawped.

"Is Luke here?" Marnie said.

Jed scratched his head.

"Um . . . well, he might be. You from some charity?"

"No," Marnie said, "I am his mother-in-law, and you are Jed, and you came to his wedding."

Jed felt a dark, hot blush surging up his neck.

"Oh, Jesus—"

"Don't worry," Marnie said kindly, "it's hard to spot people out of context. And you weren't expecting me."

"No—"

"And nor was Luke. Is he here?"

Jed held the door a little wider. He couldn't quite look at her. He had a dim recollection of a big hat who someone said was Charlotte's mother, but the hat had had no face that he could recall.

"Scoot up," Jed said. "He's up there. Sorry."

Marnie gave him a smile that she hoped was as nice as the one the Sikh had given her. She squeezed past him and began to climb the stairs. Jed went outside, letting the door crash behind him. He leaned on the wall and felt for the packet of gum in his pocket. Charlotte's fucking mother! What an earth was she doing here?

"Marnie!" Luke said. He was genuinely absolutely amazed. He got off his stool, and knocked a takeaway coffee cup to the floor.

"Oh—"

"No matter," Luke said, scrambling after it. "Almost fin-ished—"

"I've surprised you."

Luke straightened up, holding the coffee cup.

"Blown me away, Marnie—"

She said, "I thought that if I rang you, you'd have to tell Charlotte."

"Well, I—"

"And I don't want you to tell Charlotte, you see. I want this to be a complete surprise."

Luke said a little awkwardly, "It's certainly a complete surprise."

Marnie looked round.

"Can we talk here?"

Luke said, still awkwardly, "I'm . . . well, I'm working, actually—"

"I'll only be ten minutes."

"Is . . . is it urgent?"

Marnie smiled at him.

"Well, anything to do with Charlotte is important, isn't it? You and I are in complete agreement about that, aren't we?"

"Of course—"

"We could go up to your flat?"

"Yes—"

"I've never seen your flat. Charlotte said I couldn't see it until you'd got some curtains. I don't mind about the curtains, of course I don't, but she wanted it to be perfect for me to see, bless her."

"It's not exactly perfect," Luke said, "but the bed's made, at least. I'd better warn you though, it's a bit of a steep climb. Five floors."

"Game for that," Marnie said brightly.

Luke looked at her. She still played tennis after all.

"Okay," he said.

"Well, then?"

He glanced at his screen. What he was doing wasn't urgent

but it was better uninterrupted, all the same. But now he had been interrupted, and by something and someone about whom he felt more obligation than curiosity. He saved the file.

"We'll go up," Luke said.

The flat, Marnie thought privately, was charming but impossibly small. While Luke made coffee, Marnie washed her hands in the midget bathroom—no bath, only a shower, and the shower curtain missing half its rings—and noticed, fondly, that the only shelf was crowded with Charlotte's hair and beauty products. No change there, then, and how nice of Luke not to mind. Gregory had hated to see anything feminine not confined to a dressing table. He'd loved it all there, as much cut-glass powder-puff nonsense as Marnie liked, there, but the bathroom was a purposeful place in his view: he would never have seen it as synonymous with even an atom of self-indulgence.

Luke had laid out coffee mugs, and a milk jug, and a cafetière on the low table in front of the sofa, and removed several magazines and garments that had been scattered there. Marnie looked at him with approval. Young men of his generation saw nothing dangerous in being domesticated, just as her older sons-in-law were such hands-on fathers, to the point where she had sometimes wanted to urge Sarah and Fiona to remember that those children were their mothers' responsibility too. She sat down on the sofa and looked about her.

"Lovely light room."

Luke began to pour coffee, still standing.

"Makes up for the size—"

"And you two so tall—"

"It's a great location."

Marnie thought of her walk up to Arnold Circus. It had not been through anything that her own upbringing could have described as a great location—there'd even been a sad little secondhand-clothes market happening on the pavement under a railway bridge—but then, things had changed, like this competent young man who was her son-in-law making her coffee with perfect ease, never mind earning his living in a way which had absolutely nothing to do with the settled old professions of Marnie's childhood. She accepted a mug of coffee. It smelled wonderful. She smiled at Luke.

"Thank you, dear."

He sat down on a square upholstered cube opposite her.

"Now," he said.

He looked perfectly friendly, but also slightly in a hurry. Marnie said, "It's about Charlotte and the baby."

Luke took a swallow of coffee.

"Tell me."

Marnie had rehearsed this bit. She sipped her coffee and set it down on the table in front of her. She smiled at Luke again.

"I have been thinking about this baby of yours—"

Luke smiled back.

"Me too."

"And it's lovely that you, especially, are so thrilled about it. So different, I have to say, from my generation where, whatever a man felt about his babies, he wasn't really encouraged to show it."

She paused. Luke waited, still smiling. Marnie said, "I don't want to worry Charlotte, and we all know that she hasn't the best financial brain in the world, but . . . will you be all right for money?"

Luke drank some more coffee. He said, switching his gaze from Marnie to his mug, "A bit strapped. But fine," and then he added, as an afterthought, "thank you."

"Well," Marnie said, her head slightly on one side, "I have a little plan."

Luke didn't look up.

"To your advantage."

Luke glanced quickly at her.

"Just to help you over this stage, just for a little while."

"It's very—"

"No," Marnie said. She leaned forward. "It's not kind. It's what one always wants to do for one's children, as you'll discover for yourselves. The thing is, dear Luke, that Charlotte has always been rather sheltered. Her sisters would call it spoiled, but it's what happens, often, to the baby of the family, especially if that baby is as pretty as Charlotte. And although I know she is in one way thrilled about this baby, I know that part of her is quite nervous, too, scared even, and I thought I could do something to help that, and help you at the same time. I want, you see, to give you a maternity nurse, to help with the baby after the birth, and reassure Charlotte that she is going to be a wonderful mother, as we all know she is going to be, and I think I will engage someone for six weeks, or two months even, to give you both a chance to get back on your feet because a baby's arrival is a big thing, believe me, a very big thing indeed. But—" She held up a hand to prevent Luke saying what he was plainly agitating to say. "But that's not all. You can't possibly fit a nanny in here. You can't, actually, fit a baby in here, not with all the things babies need, especially these days. So I am going to help you. I am going to help you pay for a bigger flat, and one with a lift, you'll find you can't possibly manage all those stairs without a lift, and with a baby, and I shall go on helping you until you are both in a position to help yourselves. I don't want any thanks, or any argument. It is absolutely my pleasure to do this for you and my Charlotte."

She stopped and picked up her coffee and smiled into it, in the sanguine expectation of Luke's relief and gratitude. There was a silence. The silence was, she supposed, because Luke was slightly stunned at the imagination and scope of this offer, but then the silence went on, and on, and she was forced to look up from her coffee to find Luke scowling into his.

"Luke?"

He gave a little jerk, as if he was trying to shake himself into order.

"What do you say, dear?"

Luke looked out of the window. Then he looked at the ceiling. Then he looked at a point slightly to one side of Marnie and said with an effort, "I'm afraid . . . not."

"Not! What *do* you mean?"

Luke managed to drag his gaze on to his mother-in-law.

"I mean, Marnie, that it's really kind of you, but we'll manage."

"Luke, you can't. Charlotte can't—"

"She'll have to learn," Luke said. "Just like me. We'll both have to learn. Like our friends have who've got babies. Like everyone does."

"But there's no *space* here—"

"We'll cope."

"But," Marnie cried, louder now, "there's the stairs, all those stairs—"

"We're looking at other flats," Luke said.

"Then let me help you!"

"No!" Luke said loudly.

There was another, sharper silence. Marnie said with dignity, "Did you just shout at me?"

"I didn't mean to," Luke said. "It's kind of you, but we can't accept—"

"Charlotte might accept—"

"You won't tell Charlotte," Luke said firmly. "You won't go behind my back." He leaned forward a little. "You *won't.*"

Marnie turned slightly to stare out of the window.

"I don't understand your reasons—"

"Don't you?"

"No. It seems to me that you are just being obstinate. Showing male pride. I know all about male pride. I lived with it. I lived with it for almost forty years. You don't want to accept help for the mother of your child because you want to be the only provider."

Luke said, slightly dangerously, "I am so not the same kind of man as Charlotte's father was."

Marnie said nothing, bolt upright on the sofa, staring out of the window. Luke went on, "I don't want to . . . can't accept your offer, for all our sakes. Charlotte and I will never grow up unless we learn how. And we can't be beholden. We have all the right to learn to be independent that you all had. Frankly, Marnie, we can't be *patronized* this way."

Marnie swallowed. She said tightly, "I can only hope you are thinking of Charlotte."

Luke stood up. He had the distinct, and faintly alarming, air of someone bringing an interview to a brisk conclusion. He said, looking down at Marnie, where she sat on the sofa, "It's precisely because I'm thinking of Charlotte that I'm declining your offer."

And then he moved across to the door to the hall, and held it open.

"Why didn't you tell me?" Rachel said.

She was standing in the kitchen, fresh from the garden, with earthy knees to her jeans and her hair held off her face by a spotted handkerchief that Anthony recognized as his own.

"I was going to. I always intended to. I was just waiting until I had marshaled my own thoughts about it—"

Rachel went over to the sink and jammed the kettle roughly under the tap to fill it.

"So I imagine she didn't ask to see me."

"No, she didn't."

"What about the boys?" Rachel said, banging the kettle down on its base and switching it on. "How were the boys?"

"Lovely," Anthony said. "Sweet. They looked fine."

Rachel moved to stand by the sink, gripping its edge, and staring out of the window above it into the garden.

"Why do you suppose she came?"

Anthony went to stand beside her.

"Because," he said, "she isn't without gratitude." He put a hand on Rachel's. "Don't focus on her not asking to see you. Don't take it personally all the time—"

"But I'm *hurt*!" Rachel cried.

"Yes."

"I'm . . . I'm really fond of her. I've been fond of her for years—"

"You love her," Anthony said.

Rachel nodded furiously. She took her hand out from under Anthony's and brushed it across her eyes. She said, "And I was so grateful to her. For taking on Ralph. And letting Ralph be Ralph—"

"Until," Anthony said, "he was too much Ralph."

The kettle clicked itself off.

"Tea?" Rachel said.

"Please—"

"Is she going to live with this man?"

"I don't know. She said he was just getting her through. She didn't sound like someone in love to me, but maybe I just didn't hear that because I didn't want to."

Rachel got two mugs out of the cupboard above the kettle. She said, more calmly, "What exactly did Ralph do?"

Anthony sighed.

"What he always does. What suited Ralph. Not listening. Not listening, ever."

"I don't listen," Rachel said. "I should start with myself. I should hear myself sometimes."

She dropped tea bags into the mugs. She said, "She really didn't want to see me—"

"I think she was afraid to."

"In case I barked. I might well have barked. I've always barked when I'm frightened."

Anthony waited a moment, then he said, "*Are* you frightened?"

Rachel poured boiling water into the mugs, and stirred the tea bags round with a spoon. She said lightly, "Yup."

"Of . . . what exactly?"

Rachel flipped the tea bags out into the sink.

"Of losing my usefulness."

"*What?*"

Rachel walked briskly past him to the fridge and took out a plastic bottle of milk. She said, splashing milk carelessly into the mugs of tea, "What am I for, now, exactly?"

"Rachel!"

"Look," she said, not looking at him. "Look. I've run a house and garden, I've brought up three boys. They've all married. They've produced three children. One to come. And they are doing just what I did, what I wanted to do, which is what I started doing when I came here and married you. Which is to live my own life, start my own family, make my own world. And it's *been* my world. And now it isn't—"

In his studio that afternoon, Anthony had been listening to a radio interview with the Dalai Lama. The Dalai Lama had said, in his light, benevolent way, that as far as he could see most of the public trouble in the world was made by men, and most of the domestic trouble was made by women. Anthony visualized the Dalai Lama, in his spectacles and his maroon-and-ochre robes, sitting at their kitchen table and listening to Rachel describing how her life had outrun its purpose, and wondered what version of Buddhist resignation to the vagaries of the human journey he would recommend.

"Are you listening?" Rachel said.

"Very much—"

"This huge house," Rachel said, "an acre and a half of garden. You and me. At least you've still got the studio."

Anthony said, "You could run cookery courses again."

"I could."

"There was that little shop you thought of, the deli shop, at Snape Maltings."

"Wrong time. It's no time to start something up. Anyway—"

"Anyway?"

"I haven't the heart," Rachel said. "I'm too sad. And too fidgety. I've got to get used to being good at something no one needs me to be good at anymore." She looked at Anthony. She said, "I love being a grandmother."

"I know."

"I miss . . . I miss all that."

"Yes."

"Suppose she takes the children to live with this man—"

"Suppose," Anthony said, "she doesn't." He picked up one of the mugs of tea, and took it to the chair he always sat in, with its blue-checked cushion and view right across the room. He said, "You say you're frightened. Don't you suppose Petra is frightened too?"

Rachel sighed. She put her hands to her head and pushed off the spotted handkerchief.

"I expect she is—"

Anthony took a gulp of tea.

"Well, then," he said.

Charlotte was charmed when Sigrid rang to ask if they could have lunch together. Or coffee, Sigrid said, if she was busy. But she'd love it if they could meet. She gave Charlotte the feeling that this was evidence of how sophisticated a relationship between sisters-in-law could be, when the bond caused by marrying brothers served, in the end, as no more than a beginning to something that had a life of its own.

"Lunch, please," Charlotte said, "I'm always so hungry at the moment. It's such a relief not feeling sick anymore. I'm eating breakfast and elevenses and lunch and tea and supper. So lunch would be lovely."

Sigrid laughed. She said something about how nice it was to hear someone sounding so healthy about being pregnant, and then she suggested that they meet somewhere halfway between their places of work, and why not the first-floor café of a distinguished architectural institute on Portland Place?

So here Charlotte was, slightly early for once, studying the menu with considerable interest, and wondering whether to confide to Sigrid that she had been to see Petra, and had offered her support. She thought that, on balance, she probably would tell Sigrid because Sigrid, after all, even though she had never put a foot wrong as a daughter-in-law, had also suffered from not being the favorite, from not quite ever toeing the Brinkley line. Charlotte didn't know Sigrid very well, and was slightly daunted by what appeared to Charlotte an impressive degree of maturity and togetherness on her part, but then, Sigrid had been the one to suggest lunch, which must mean at least the beginnings of a wish to do a little sisterly bonding. When she saw Sigrid coming up the wide central stairs to the café, she got up, feeling suddenly rather shy, and stood there, waiting to be noticed.

"You look wonderful," Sigrid said. "Being pregnant really suits you. I think the word is blooming, isn't it?"

"I'm going to be like a whale," Charlotte said. "I'm eating like one too. Did you?"

"What—"

"Did you get huge?"

Sigrid took off her jacket and hung it over the back of her chair.

"I was no good at being pregnant."

Charlotte waited. Some instinct kept her from bouncing back at once. Sigrid said, picking up the menu, her voice almost detached, "It nearly killed me, having Mariella."

"Oh!" Charlotte said, horrified.

"But we aren't going to talk about that."

"No—"

"It was nine years ago, and she is wonderful and Edward was a saint." She looked up at Charlotte and smiled. "And you are going to do it beautifully."

"God," Charlotte said, "I hope so. I mean, we never meant this to happen, and if you don't you kind of have to get it more right than if you do. Don't you?"

Sigrid laughed. She said, "Let's order you a big plate of food."

"Yes, *please*."

"Pasta and salad?"

"Perfect."

Sigrid looked up and made a neat little summoning gesture with her menu towards a waitress. Charlotte watched her ordering, with admiration. She looked so in charge of the situation, just as she looked in charge of her appearance, her hair smoothed back into a low ponytail, her white shirt not climbing irrepressibly out of the waistband of her skirt, her lightly tanned hand with its single modern ring holding the menu.

"There," Sigrid said, "food for two adults and almost half a baby. Exciting."

Charlotte buttered a piece of bread lavishly, and told Sigrid how she now felt about the baby, and how she *had* felt, and how sick she'd been, and how great Luke had been and how seriously he was taking the whole baby/fatherhood thing, and how there was an empty flat on the first floor of their building which they'd looked at, and really liked, and it was twice the size, with two bedrooms, but obviously miles more expensive and so they were having to do lots of sums to work out whether they really could afford it, because, quite honestly, their present flat was almost too small for the two of them right now, even without a baby.

Then the pasta and salad arrived, and Charlotte asked Sigrid if she'd had a good time in Sweden, and Sigrid said it was lovely to see her parents, and Charlotte said well, talking of parents, she knew Sigrid would understand why she had done it, but she'd actually, without telling Edward or Luke in advance, gone to see Petra, on the quiet, really, because it must be so awful to be suddenly flung out of the family, like Petra had been, and so Charlotte wanted to offer her some support because oh my God, she needed it, the angel fallen to the ground and all that.

"And Rachel," Charlotte said, spearing rocket leaves on the end of a forkful of tagliatelle, "can be so fierce. I should know." She gave a little laugh. "I mean, I'm not sure I'm quite over it yet, and it was ages ago."

Sigrid took a sip of water.

"It was very difficult with Rachel," Sigrid said, "when Mariella was born."

Charlotte gazed at her, another forkful suspended. She said eagerly, "Was it?"

"I had bad depression. So bad. And I didn't want her to know. I didn't want anyone to know. And Rachel was very angry."

Charlotte put her mouthful in. Round it, she said, "She's good at angry."

Sigrid didn't reply. She sat looking down at her plate, not eating.

Charlotte said energetically, "None of us will ever be good enough for her precious boys, will we?"

Sigrid looked up. She said, "I had such a strange conversation with my mother in Stockholm. It made me think."

"Oh?" Charlotte said. She would have liked to stay on the topic of Rachel, and stoke it up a bit, but there was something about Sigrid's attitude that held her back. She said, "About what?" and ate another mouthful.

"These mothers," Sigrid said, "these mothers of ours."

"Mine's a doll—"

"Maybe. But she's also a person. They are all people. They were our age once. They went through a lot of the things we are going through."

Charlotte gave a little snort. She said, "Well, Rachel's forgotten half of it—"

Sigrid said slowly, "She's not a witch, you know."

Charlotte stopped eating. She said, "She doesn't like me, she doesn't much like you—"

"Oh, I think she does," Sigrid said, "and if she hasn't in the past, she will now. She only is as she is because no one ever opposed her, no one ever challenged her position as the only woman in a circle of men. Petra certainly didn't. But now she is having to learn something new, and she must learn to hold her tongue, and that comes hard with her."

Charlotte put her fork down.

"Wow—"

"Think about it," Sigrid said. "Ralph is very difficult, I don't think anyone could have brought up Ralph any differently, but even he is a good father. And the others, our husbands, Rachel brought up good men for us. She did that, you know."

Charlotte pushed her plate away. She looked down at the table, and the crumbs and smears she had left on it.

"We can't gang up on her," Sigrid said. "It's lonely for her now. My mother said she had coped with her own loneliness by working. She's a doctor. Rachel isn't a doctor, she's never worked properly, she is a homemaker, and now . . . well, I don't know what she is. I expect she is terrified she will lose her grandchildren."

"But—"

"I think that's why she's angry," Sigrid said. "She is a very tactless person, and now she is angry too. But I don't think she doesn't like us. And I don't think she would want her sons back, even if we offered them to her. I think she has new ways to learn, and she is angry with herself for that too." She smiled at Charlotte. "Think now. If Rachel was a bad woman, wouldn't Luke be bad too?"

Charlotte said, "What, exactly, are you telling me?"

"Oh," Sigrid said, "I wouldn't tell you anything. I would only describe how I see it now."

"But you were so lovely to me that day in our flat, about the baby—"

"Of course," Sigrid said, "it was an unprovoked attack. Rachel was in the wrong, everybody saw that. I expect she saw that, too, even if she could never say so. But after this Petra thing, we have all moved round in the dance a little, we are all in a slightly different place. So is Rachel."

Charlotte picked up her fork again, and pulled her plate back towards her. She opened her mouth to protest the continuing validity of her own grievance, and found she hadn't got the heart for it. She wound a final mouthful of tagliatelle round her fork, and then she paused and looked at Sigrid.

"Okay," Charlotte said with a reasonableness that quite surprised her. "Okay. Point taken."

CHAPTER EIGHTEEN

S teve Hadley was not a man given to restlessness. All his life
he had gone steadily from activity to activity, every waking hour, moving without hurry from one practical task to
another, to a point where he was almost unable to think unless
his hands were busy with something. His mother, he knew,
would say it was inherited. His father was unable to think, or
hold a significant conversation unless physically occupied with
something else. Steve remembered his father's halting attempts
to tell him the facts of life being conducted with both of them
lying under the old jacked-up Alvis his father was restoring,
until Steve plucked up the courage to admit, passing his father
a spanner, that he knew about it already.

He did not say that he had tried it, too, at thirteen, with a
fifteen-year-old from year eleven who was, depending upon
your point of view, either very generous or a bit of a slapper.
And even if he hadn't actually done it, he'd had a frustrating
glimpse of how hugely exciting and satisfactory it was going
to be when he did, and three years later, he had succeeded, and
in his own view had never looked back. He'd had innumerable

brief relationships, and one steady one (she'd ended it, when she went away to college, in Scotland) and in all cases he had known, in his unshowy, steadfast, unremarkable way, that he gave sexual satisfaction. It was in his nature. Sex was a good thing to do in his view, so why not learn to do it properly? He was no god to look at, for heaven's sake, but that didn't stop him from being an attractive proposition as a lover. He had, consciously, made sure of that.

Except that, at the moment, his unquestioned competence seemed to be of no use to him. Petra plainly liked him, liked his company, had done nothing to discourage him, but was not so much refusing to sleep with him as seeming to be oblivious to the idea in the first place. In Steve's view, sex was a natural progression after you got to know someone a bit and were confident, after a kiss or two, that they fancied you back, but Petra, although apparently happy to be kissed, and to be touched significantly here and there as they passed each other or sat next to each other in Steve's car, seemed somehow to evaporate when Steve's movements began to shift the situation into another gear. He supposed that he should simply ask her outright about it, but that kind of conversation didn't come easily to him, and he kept waiting for a moment when it would be entirely natural to say, in so many words, what the hell do you think you're playing at?

He had asked himself, moving steadily round the endless tasks of repair and renewal at the nature reserve, why he went on with Petra anyway. She wasn't the first mother he'd had a relationship with, and she wasn't the best-looking, or the liveliest, or the most enticing hard-to-get girl he'd ever pursued, but she had something that chimed with something in him, this profound appreciation of the sea and shore and bird life that amounted, he was surprised to find himself thinking sometimes, almost to a shared religion. She was unusual too, and he revered her artistic talent to a point way beyond mere admiration; her ability, with less than half a dozen pencil lines, to make him feel he was looking not at a drawing but a living bird, roused in him a degree of respect that bordered on awe. And he liked her kids. He liked little kids anyway, but these two were especially great, particularly the older one with his imagination and his fears. Steve had few fears, and it intrigued him that someone of only three had the capacity somewhere in his brain to have so many. All in all, there was, definitely, something in Petra that made him disinclined to give up and turn his attention instead to one of the girls who worked in the reserve's café, and who had made it more than plain that he could have pretty much anything he wanted.

He was blithely confident, too, about Petra's marital situation. There was this husband in the background, but Steve had never seen Petra other than alone, and she almost never mentioned her husband, only saying, once, that he had gone to London, in a way that suggested that he had gone for good, and not just for a few days, or a while even. Steve had picked up the distinct impression, too, that Petra and her boys' father came from very different backgrounds, and although that was in no way a handicap, it did mean that neither could rely as a given on shared assumptions. Petra was a kind of orphan, it appeared, with no immediate family left alive in England, and that family never cohesive or supportive when it was around anyway. Petra had learned to fend for herself when she was still at school, and this situation aroused in Steve a protectiveness that was all the stronger for being unfamiliar to him. To be abandoned by both your family and then your husband, but not to seem to resent either seemed to Steve evidence of a remarkable nature. It was just how to get such a remarkable nature to focus on him as someone who might be an all-round answer, that was Steve's current preoccupation.

And then an opportunity arose at work. In the internal e-mail bulletins that went round the organization, any job vacancies going were advertised. It was how Steve had found his present job. He scanned these bulletins regularly, rather in the way that someone who is perfectly content with their own home cannot help, all the same, glancing through property columns. A vacancy caught Steve's eye, a vacancy on an island off the northwest coast of Scotland, an island famous in the bird world for its corncrakes. The job required several practical skills as well as knowledge of bird conservation, and the terms included a tied cottage at the southern end of the island. There was only a small community on the island itself but on the sister island, merely a short, tidal causeway away, there was a school. Steve was not someone given to romantic fantasies of any kind, but this possibility seemed, all of a sudden, to offer a potential solution to the intriguing and thwarting problem of what to do about Petra.

He closed his laptop and moved to look out of his living room window. It was dusk, and the vast stretches of shingle, dotted with domes of sea kale, shone faintly in the fading light. Steve had never been to Scotland, let alone the West Highlands, but as he stood there gazing at the North Sea darkening beyond the beach, he conjured up in his mind a calendar-picture image of how the place might be, all hills and streams and long white beaches, sprinkled with cowrie shells. It might, just might, be the answer.

Jed was alone in the studio. Luke had gone out to buy a new design component for their shared digital camera, and Jed was idly tinkering with something they had both been working on that day when the key turned in the lock, and Jed said, "You were quick," to be answered by Charlotte saying, "It's Charlotte."

Jed jumped off his stool.

"Hi there, pregnant lady! Wasn't expecting you!"

"No," Charlotte said, "I wasn't expecting me, either. But I wanted to see Luke about something."

Jed jammed his fists in his pocket.

"He's gone to get a whatsit."

Charlotte looked round vaguely, as if Luke might really still be in the room.

"Doesn't matter. Will he be long?"

"Shouldn't think so," Jed said. "Want a coffee?"

"I'm not drinking coffee—"

"Will caffeine stunt its growth?"

"I'm not taking any risks," Charlotte said. "And Luke—"

"Don't tell me about Luke," Jed said. "Impending fatherhood has made a right old woman of Luke. Talking of old women—I mean, not *old* but older—I made a complete prat of myself the other day, with yours."

Charlotte was unwinding a long linen scarf from round her neck.

"My what?"

"Your mother."

Charlotte stopped unwinding and stared at Jed.

"My mother? Where on earth—"

"She came here," Jed said airily. "To see Luke. And I . . . I did not," Jed continued, spacing the words out for emphasis, "I did not recognize her. I was only a guest at your wedding, I was only one of the ushers, wasn't I, and do I recognize the mother of the bride when she turns up under my very nose? No. No, I do not."

"Why did she want to see Luke?" Charlotte said.

"Search *moi*. I was too busy feeling a prize idiot to worry. She was very cool about it."

Charlotte began to wind her scarf again.

"Did they talk?"

"Who?"

"Mummy and Luke."

"They went up to your flat," Jed said. "All those stairs. They were gone for most of an hour." Jed leaned forward a little, head jutting, and peered at Charlotte.

"Didn't Luke say?"

"Why didn't you say?" Charlotte said later.

She was slicing tomatoes, in Luke's huge white bathrobe after a shower.

"You weren't supposed to know. I forgot to shut that utter plonker Jed's mouth—"

"Why wasn't I?"

Luke leaned against the kitchen door frame. He folded his arms and looked at the floor.

"Because I said no."

Charlotte stopped slicing. She said, "No to what?"

Luke said steadily, still looking at the floor, "To an idea—an offer—your mother made."

Charlotte put the knife down. She ran her hands under the tap and dried them off on the front of Luke's bathrobe. Then she came and stood right in front of him, almost touching him.

"What offer?"

Luke raised his head slowly.

"It doesn't matter now. It's over. She meant well, but it wouldn't work. It doesn't matter."

"It does!" Charlotte said sharply.

"I don't want it to turn into a big deal—"

"It'll only be a big deal," Charlotte said, "if you won't *tell* me! I shall go and ring my mother whom I suppose you've sworn to silence?"

Luke put out a hand and gripped Charlotte's nearest wrist.

"Okay, okay. But don't scream at me—"

"Would I?"

"Yes," Luke said.

He turned, still holding Charlotte's wrist, and towed her to the sofa.

"Sit down."

Charlotte sat. Luke sat down beside her, and dropped her wrist in order to take one of her hands in both his. He said, "You'll hear me through to the end?"

"Yes."

"Right to the end, so I can tell you why I said what I said to your mother?"

"Okay," Charlotte said.

"Look at me, then. Look at me all the time."

"I'm looking."

"Your mother," Luke said, "had hatched a plan. She wanted to surprise you. Her plan was to organize and pay for some nanny, or something, for six weeks after the baby's born, and to pay, also, the difference in rent between this place and somewhere bigger, because she thinks this place is too small for two people, let alone three, and she thinks we'll never manage the stairs. And I said—well, I said thank you, of course—but I said no."

Charlotte opened her mouth. Luke took one hand away in order to hold it up in a silencing gesture.

"One minute, babe. One minute. I said no because I don't want help. I don't want to be treated like some half adult who can't manage now his wife's pregnant. I also said no because we've got to be grown-up about this; it's our baby, our marriage, we've got to do it without bleating for help every time things get a bit demanding. I said no because we can't be beholden to your mother, and because she's got to realize that you're mine now, not hers, and you've got to realize that, too, especially with a baby coming. And I said no because—"

"Stop," Charlotte said.

"You said you wouldn't—"

"I've heard enough."

"Well, think about what I said, think about what it means if . . . we go on being dependent, letting our parents—"

"I *have* thought," Charlotte said.

Luke gave a faint groan. He took his hands away from Charlotte's, and briefly covered his eyes.

"Okay, then," he said tiredly.

"I have thought," Charlotte said again. "And even though I expect Mummy was pretty hurt after she'd been so generous, I think you were right."

"You *what*?"

Charlotte rearranged the tie belt of the bathrobe. Then she smiled at Luke.

"You heard me. I said . . . I think you were right."

For Ralph, the first two weeks of work had been, quite frankly, surreal. Waking in his strange, impersonal room by six at the latest was novelty enough, but being at his desk an hour later, showered, shaved, dressed, and equipped with a takeaway coffee and a muffin, was almost the stuff of film or fantasy. Seven o'clock was the hour when companies published the announcements that served as the basis for the analyses that Ralph was required to make on behalf of his clients, and if seven o'clock in the past had meant the first reluctant awareness that Kit and Barney were suddenly and completely awake, now it meant a bank pretty well full of its employees, all at their desks, all focused on the first adrenaline rush of the day. The first three days, Ralph had been so knackered by lunchtime that he wondered how any of them made it, full tilt, till early evening, but then an infectious collective acceleration caught him up, and carried him through, as if he'd been riding a giant wave.

The wave then, of course, dropped him with a thud. He had planned all manner of exciting, if vaguely visualized, ways that he might spend the evenings, but the reality was that he was simultaneously too wired and too tired to focus on anything constructive. He could see why his colleagues drank, and spoke of their drug dealers with such elaborate nonchalance, because it was, quite simply, so difficult to know how to manage oneself once the engine of the day's roller-coaster ride had been switched off. He had fallen asleep in the cinema and at Sigrid and Edward's kitchen table, he had drunk too much with work colleagues and with Luke, he had bought tickets for performances he had failed to make, and even a football game at the Emirates Stadium, which he missed because he was still working at the time of the kickoff, and he had subsisted, as well as on coffee and muffins and alcohol, on ready-meals in polystyrene trays banged into the microwave in the flat's small unhelpful kitchen, which he then ate with a fork, or even a spoon, lying on his bed with both his shoes and the television on.

And then there was Petra. He had told Kit, in Petra's hearing, that he would telephone every night at six. He would ring even at weekends, when he clearly could not now, on account of Petra's obstinacy and behavior, come home. He told Kit, inappropriately, that he did not know where he would now be at weekends, but that he would ring from wherever he was each night at six. Some nights, he did indeed ring at six, but most nights, whatever was going on at his desk meant that he rang at half past, almost seven, when Kit was querulous with tiredness, and cried on the phone and said where was he, where was he, and why wasn't he there in Kit's house? After these calls, Ralph felt as miserable as he had ever felt about anything, but, because of the extreme and involving oddity of his days, was unable to stoke up quite the pure flame of rage and resentment against Petra that he had felt before he left Aldeburgh. He missed that fury: it had made everything so simple and straightforward, almost clean. It had seemed to him, in the white-hot cauldron of anger, that he would apply himself to

this enticing, but fundamentally uncongenial job with a fero-
cious energy driven by his central purpose of gaining custody
and control of his children, whom he would then bear into
some as yet undefined but decent and structured future. He had
felt, at times, almost crusading in his zeal, as if he were actually
rescuing Kit and Barney from darkness and disorder.

But the reality was not so clear-cut. The reality was that
working like this—if, indeed, this was how one had to work,
to make visible money—was too disorientating, too detached
from the world of simply trying to be alive at the end of the
day, and too, even if disconcertingly, beguiling to imagine
how one could possibly incorporate into it responsibility for
two very small boys, one of whom could barely as yet walk.
He told himself that he was no less angry with Petra, merely
confused now about his anger. He would, he was sure, get the
hang of this new life, and he would, when Kit answered Petra's
phone, as he always did—"Daddy?" he said, "Daddy, Daddy,
Daddy"—ask to speak to Petra, and he would say to her that
she still had a great deal to fear from him, and that his inten-
tions were in no way subdued by the hours or the commit-
ments of the new life.

He told himself fiercely that he had no desire to speak to
Petra otherwise. He was thankful to be away from the dreamy
muddles of her life, her propensity to stop halfway through
cooking a meal to draw a giraffe for Kit ("Can they eat the
stars?"), and then not resume cooking because she felt inclined
to dawdle down to the allotment, or the beach. He was relieved
to be in a world of crisp, conventional clothing, sharp haircuts
and prevalent technology. He missed nothing, *nothing* about
his life in Aldeburgh except his children, and he was going to
prove to everyone—family, colleagues, friends—that he had
lost not one iota of the sureness of touch that led to his being
implored to stay in that position in Singapore.

* * *

Edward closed the door on Mariella after their good-night conversation. Mariella said she did not want to be read to, and she did not want to read, she just wanted her father to talk to her. Edward was delighted to talk to her, but discovered that what she really wanted was to talk to him. She wanted to tell him about Sweden—lovely, except for those gray curled-up little fish in oily vinegary stuff all the time, yuck—and how she felt about being back at school, and whether she and Indira would still be best, *best* friends, and now that she had had to give up the idea of having a dog, and probably a baby, could she have tap-dancing lessons or go to drama club or maybe have a hamster. Or a rabbit.

Edward sat on the edge of her bed and watched her. While she talked, she played with the ingenious puzzle her Swedish grandfather had made her, so that Edward could regard her uninterruptedly, and think what an extraordinary joy she had been to him since she came home, and how painfully flattering it had been to hear her say that Sweden would have been so much better if he had been there, and how pathetically needy he was of her good opinion. When she said that he could go now, because she needed to think about the hamster/rabbit/tap-dancing priorities, he had bent down to kiss her, and she'd dropped the puzzle and put her arms round his neck and pulled him down until her cheek was against his. She'd held him there silently for a while, and then she said that actually his cheek was a bit prickly, and released him abruptly, and he went out of the room, laughing, closing the door on her, intent once more on her puzzle.

Sigrid was watching the news on television, her feet up on the low table in front of the sofa. She picked up the remote, and turned the volume down. She said, "Did you hear the phone?"

"No," Edward said.

"It was your mother—"

287

"Oh God. What's happened now—"

"Nothing," Sigrid said.

"That *can't* be true—"

Sigrid patted the sofa cushion beside her.

"Sit down. I think . . . that's why she rang. Because nothing's happened."

Edward sat.

"So . . . so you felt like talking to her this time?"

"I did," Sigrid said. "We spoke for ten minutes. I think she is very sad."

"About Petra?"

"Well, yes. But really because she is now out of touch with everyone. Of the six of us, only one is left in Suffolk, and they are not speaking. She sounded . . . well, she sounded lost."

Edward glanced at Sigrid.

"You sound almost . . . *sorry* for her."

"I am," Sigrid said.

Edward waited a moment, and then he took Sigrid's hand. He said hesitantly, "May . . . I ask what's brought this on?"

Sigrid didn't take her hand away.

"She doesn't work," Sigrid said. "She never has, not really. My mother said to me that when both her children left Sweden, her work saved her. She didn't put it quite that way, but that is what she meant. I have been thinking about what she said ever since I came home."

Edward said nothing. He interlaced his fingers with Sigrid's, and squeezed her hand.

"My mother said also a bit later that although she knew our children are lent to us, they do not belong to us, she still found it very difficult to let go. She said we would find it so with Mariella, and that we must make sure we have interesting work and . . . and enough between us, enough relationship so that we are not begging Mariella for the time

and attention she should give to her own life. She said—"
Sigrid stopped.

She did not take her hand away from Edward's, but she put
her free hand up to her eyes briefly, and then she said, not quite
steadily, "My mother said you were a good man."

Edward made a little self-deprecating noise in his throat. It
was, in a way, wonderful when Sigrid was in one of her serious, almost melancholy Scandinavian moods, but it was also
awkward to know quite how to respond to them without
sounding embarrassingly theatrical, so he sat there beside her
holding her hand and feeling at once both pleased and foolish,
and then abruptly she leaned sideways, kissed him full on the
mouth, and said with fervor, "And you *are*."

Petra sat on the floor by Kit's bed with her arms round her
knees. Kit was asleep, flung across his pillow with his arms
above his head. Across the room, peering at her through the
bars of the huge, heavy, old-fashioned cot that Ralph and his
brothers had once slept in, Barney lay on his side not moving,
his eyes round with the effort of keeping them open.

Both boys had been very quiet at bath time, playing docilely
in the water without fighting or splashing and then making no
fuss when it was time to get out, Barney even lying peacefully
on the bath mat while Petra put his nappy on, without squirm-
ing over and onto all fours, so that he could crawl rapidly
away out of the door and down the landing. And when Ralph
had rung, quite close, this time, to six o'clock, Kit hadn't cried,
or shouted for him to come home, but had simply sat there,
holding Petra's phone against his ear and nodding, but not saying anything, not responding.

She hoped they hadn't frightened them, she and Steve, when
they had their argument. It hadn't been the kind of argument
she had with Ralph, when Ralph shouted, or banged out of the

house slamming doors, but the atmosphere had been strained enough for someone like Kit to pick it up, and react to it, and for that reaction to be passed on to Barney, who could not be distracted by another slice of toast and jam, but who crawled to her feet, whimpering, and pulled himself up to lean against her knees, staring up into her face with eyes enormous with distress. He was still staring now, as if he feared that if he closed his eyes she might not be there when he opened them again, as had happened with Ralph.

She was appalled at herself. Why had it not struck her, all those dozy, hazy weeks of avoiding facing the inevitable, that she might have been alarming her children—and herself—into the bargain? Why hadn't she thought of that? Why hadn't she seen something like Steve's proposal coming? Why hadn't she broken out of her own stupid head for just long enough to see that, whatever all this was about, it wasn't just about how *she* felt at this moment, in these precise circumstances, it was about something much broader, and with a future, and you couldn't just go back to what you knew, like Barney sucking his thumb, because nothing was the same when you went back to it, because you weren't the same. And what had struck her that afternoon, sitting on the windy shingle while Steve told her his plans, and told her what he wanted, and told her that they could really make a go of things, if only she'd stop messing him around, was that she was no longer in the place in her own heart and mind where she could just say, oh wow, cool idea, let's all go and conserve corncrakes on an island.

She couldn't do that anymore. Clutched now by a kind of horror at her dangerously sleepwalking state these past weeks, she wondered if, in fact, she ever could have. She took a breath and held it, to fight down a rising panic.

Then, still hardly breathing, and to give herself time to calm down, she'd let him talk. She'd let him describe this new job, this new idea, she'd let him go on, in his steady, unhurried way, about what they had in common, about how he felt about the boys, and she'd looked round her, at the great sweeps of tawny pebbles and the quietly heaving expanses of the sea, and she had waited to feel what she always felt there, the sense of belonging, the sense of reassurance and homecoming. She gazed and gazed . . . and nothing came. And then her gaze had traveled to rest on the little boys, Kit scrambling on a slope above the sea, Barney sitting in a hollow he had made throwing stones tiny distances with ecstatic, jerky movements, and it was all she could do to stay still, listening to Steve, and not race to pick up her children and stumble away with them, away from this alarming prospect of embarking on a new life in an unknown place with someone, she realized, whom she hardly knew anyway.

She had taken some deliberately deep breaths. Then she said, as emphatically as she could, "I'm married."

Steve glanced at her.

"When did that stop you seeing me?"

Petra looked down.

"You've been really good to me," she said. "Really good. I shouldn't—"

"Shouldn't what?"

"I shouldn't have let you. I shouldn't have let you be so good to me. I should have told you."

"Told me what?"

Petra picked up a pebble. She could not say that she had, all along, been watching, hoping for Ralph to look her way again, that she would have given anything, anything right then to have heard the crunch of approaching footsteps behind her, and turned to see that it was Ralph coming to collect them all, and take them home. So she said instead, mustering her courage, "I should have told you that I wouldn't leave him."

"I thought he'd left you."

"That's different," Petra said. "Ralph's different. He does things differently. He's got a temper."

Steve looked out to sea. He said, "You're lucky I haven't."

"I am." She looked at him. "I haven't been playing with you."

"Okay," he said. He got to his feet. He called to the boys, "Teatime."

Petra had thought, slightly dazedly, that that was that, that she had survived the bomb blast going off under her feet, and that there would be no repercussions. But once they were in Steve's kitchen, and the business of settling the boys and giving them toast was done, Steve started on Petra.

He didn't raise his voice. He didn't yell or shout or slam round the kitchen. He simply told her, in a low, steady, furious monotone, what he thought of her, what he thought of her morals, and her cowardice, and her conduct, and her selfishness, and her immaturity. He told her she had used him, and that he didn't like being used, and that she had allowed him to believe all kinds of things that could never happen, and presented herself as a rejected outcast, not some right little cow who wanted to have her cake and eat it, which is what she, in fact, was. He called her all sorts of names, and all the time he was talking she sat by the table, motionless, until Barney came miserably to her knee and roused her as if from a trance. She'd bent down to pick him up, and then she'd stood up, and Kit had scrambled off his chair to be close to her, and she had looked directly at Steve.

"You can call me all the names you like," Petra said. "But it takes two to tango, and you know it. And now I'm going home."

"You'll have to walk," Steve said. "I'm not driving you another yard."

"We'll walk, then," Petra said. She'd taken Kit's hand. She

hoped he wouldn't speak, she hoped he wouldn't make a move towards Steve. Barney had his arms round her neck, and his face buried in her hair. His face was hot through her hair, and he was breathing heavily. She let go of Kit long enough to sling her bag over her shoulder, and then she walked past Steve, out of the kitchen, not even pausing when he tried to catch at her as she went by, and said, in quite a different, more urgent voice, "Please stay."

In the little rough parking space by the entrance to the beach, an elderly couple were urging their spaniel into the back of their car. Petra paused beside them.

"Excuse me—"

They looked up at her, standing there in her gypsy skirt with tousled hair, a child in her arms and another beside her holding on to a fold of her skirt with both hands.

"Could you please do me a favor?" Petra said. "Could you drive us some of the way, at least, back towards Aldeburgh?"

CHAPTER NINETEEN

The bar was full. Luke, holding two pint glasses unsteadily above his head, and conscious of occasional little splashes of beer down his hands, made his way through the hubbub to where Ralph had managed to corner a couple of galvanized bar stools next to a long shelf running across the wall.

Ralph had taken his jacket off and loosened his tie. He looked exhausted, and thin, but he'd had a haircut, Luke noticed, and even if his nails were bitten he had links in his shirt cuffs and his shoes were polished. Despite Ralph's clothes, and despite Luke only being in his work uniform of black combat trousers, black T-shirt, and baseball boots, Luke felt very much in charge of the occasion, very much, he was surprised to find, older than his older brother.

He put the glasses down on the shelf in front of Ralph. Ralph said, "Is this welcome, or is this welcome—"

He ducked his head, and slurped the first mouthful of beer without touching the glass. Then he lifted his head and wiped his mouth with the back of his hand.

"Magic."

"You look right manky," Luke said.

"I'm okay—"

Luke grunted. He picked up his glass and took a long swallow.

"So," he said. "How's it going?"

"Good," Ralph said, "I'm good. Got given two new clients this week."

"You don't get a cut of the profits, do you—"

"Nope," Ralph said. "That's the quantitative-trader guys. But I'll be in line for a bonus."

Luke watched him drink. Then he said, "And what'll you spend it on?"

Ralph put his glass down and stared into it. After a pause, he said, "A house for the boys and me. And legal fees."

"Don't be daft," Luke said.

Ralph glanced at him.

"What's daft—"

"That kind of talk. What are you playing at? Are you going to take your children away from their mother and bring them up on your own?"

Ralph didn't look at him. He said to his drink, "That's the idea, yes."

Luke said calmly, "You are insane."

Ralph was silent.

"You couldn't do it," Luke said. "You don't have a case. No court is going to take two little children away from a perfectly okay mother just because you don't want to admit that this is as much your fault as Petra's."

Ralph said angrily, "She's the one who—"

"She hasn't," Luke said. "She hasn't had an affair. It's a funny old relationship, but it's not sex. She told Charlotte."

Ralph said, "You don't have to have sex for it to be disloyal—"

"And," Luke said, interrupting, "you don't have to throw your wife downstairs to be an abusive husband."

"I'm not abusive!" Ralph yelled.

A group of drinkers nearby looked round, and there was a sudden pool of silence in their corner.

"I'm not abusive," Ralph said again quietly.

"Depends on how you define abuse—"

Ralph said, leaning forward to hiss his words at Luke, "I am here doing this fucking job, to *keep* them all."

Luke looked back at him. He waited a moment, and then he said, "So you are. Heroically battling to pay the bills. Having previously buggered up your online work and kept Petra in the dark about it, and then just telling her what you were going to do next, never asking her, or including her, just frightening her with your sudden plans and turning her whole life upside down. That's all."

There was an astonished pause, and then Ralph said, "You've changed your tune!"

"I've had time to think," Luke said. "Stuff's happened. You've just let Mum and Dad shove you around all the time, and then, when things go wrong, you take it out on Petra. It's not her fault. It's not her fault that she does what everyone wants until she just can't anymore, and does some stupid bloody thing, like this bloke, and we all go apeshit about it."

"So," Ralph said sarcastically, "you do everything Charlotte wants all the time, do you? If she wants it, then it must be right?"

"Actually," Luke said, taking no notice of his brother's tone, "not."

Ralph picked up his beer glass and put it down again. He said, "Well, there *is* this guy. And I don't know what's going on except he sees my kids and I don't like it."

"Well," Luke said. "*You're* not seeing them."

"I told you. I *told* you. I'm working my arse off because—"

"Bullshit," Luke said.

Ralph made a little jerky movement as if he was going to scoop up his jacket, slip off his stool, and fight his way through the crowd without another word to Luke. But he hesitated. He took his hand off his jacket.

"You like doing this job," Luke said. "You like being good at it. Fair enough. But don't pretend it's to put bread into the mouths of your starving children, don't give me all that noble, self-sacrificing *crap*. Just don't. And don't make a complete and utter idiot of yourself, talking about fighting for the custody of your children." He looked at Ralph. "God, bro," he said, "don't *embarrass* yourself."

Ralph turned away slightly, and hunched himself over his beer glass. He was silent for a minute or two, and then he said grumpily, not looking at Luke, "So what d'you think I should do?"

Luke picked up his drink and drained it, then set it down on the shelf with a bang.

"Go home," he said.

Petra decided to travel by bus. It would, apart from all other considerations, be cheaper than a train, and the thought of driving in London, even with her renewed spirit of enterprise, made her heart fail a little. Ralph had sent her a check—thrust inside an envelope, with no note accompanying it, and her name and address typed on a computer-generated label—but she didn't feel she could use it. She had put it under a jar of peanut butter on the table and hoped it would just somehow vanish in all the clutter, and not persist in troubling her. She didn't want the money, and Ralph's signature on the check upset her. She put the peanut-butter jar actually on his signature so that she didn't have to look at it.

She had a few notes put away in a teapot they never used. She'd done that all her life, since she was small, squirreling money in pockets and boxes and pillowcases, because money had always meant an escape to her. You didn't need much, but you needed enough on hand to get away, to obey your own instincts for flight, or food—or drawing lessons. And if they all went on the bus from Ipswich, Petra reckoned that, with Barney being only a baby, and choosing a less popular time of day for traveling, she could probably get them all there for under twenty pounds. And once they were there, she could figure out what to do next.

She wasn't, especially, troubled by what to do next. In her present mood—a mood she recognized with relief, as the one that carried her resourcefully through her grandmother's leaving and those dodgy but successful years of hand-to-mouth jobs and art school—she was pretty sure that she would have an idea when she needed one. It was like, she thought, being woken from a long sleep, and finding that, not only were you free to choose, but you had to choose, because no one was going to choose for you.

She took the teapot down from the shelf where it had been since they moved in, and blew the dust off it. There were fingerprints on the lid—hers, where she had opened it to put money in—and a rag of cobweb hanging down from the spout. She blew at it, took the lid off, and tipped it upside down over the table.

"Money!" Kit said appreciatively. He was in his Spider-Man T-shirt, ready for the journey, his digger in his Bob the Builder rucksack.

Petra counted the money.

"Sixty-three quid," she said to Kit. "Plenty. Plenty for what we're after."

"In a rocket?" Kit said hopefully.

"No. In a bus. But a high-up bus, with steps."

Kit considered this. He said, "Where are we going?"

Petra looked at him. He had never been a rosy-cheeked child, but the last week or so he had grown especially wan, and now, with his hair still unbrushed from the night before, and a smear of something or other from breakfast around his mouth, he looked pathetic indeed. It was tempting, she thought, so tempting, to bring a light to his face by telling him that she was making an attempt to get back to a place familiar to him, a place she should never have contemplated leaving, with Kit and Barney to consider, but, as the chance of failing seemed pretty considerable to her, it wasn't fair to kindle even the smallest hope in him. So she went on moving the mess around the kitchen table—the check, though not visible, glowed through the layers like a burning coal—and said, with enough energy to make it sound like an adventure, "London!"

Kit said nothing. He picked up a spoon lying in front of him and began to bang it rhythmically against the nearest table leg. He had done that the day before, too, with a wooden spoon, when Steve had turned up, just before the boys' bedtime, and tried to say sorry. Petra had at first considered saying sorry, too, as was her instinct, but then something else had taken over, something she had recognized from long ago, when she had first learned to stand up to her grandmother, and she would just stand there in her grandmother's kitchen, mute and unresponsive, refusing either to engage or to give in.

Kit had been, at first, excited to see Steve, had rushed forward, his mouth still full of his supper. But Barney remembered. Barney remembered the scene in Steve's kitchen, and twisted round in his high chair to hold his arms up to Petra, begging to be lifted up, away from whatever turbulence Steve might have brought with him this time. Petra picked him up, and held him, and said nothing. She stood, with the table between her and Steve, and Barney in her arms, and without speaking held her ground. And Kit faltered. He paused, inches away from Steve, and looked back at his mother. Then he retreated, step by step, until he was within clutching distance of her nearest leg. He held on to her jeans, still chewing.

"I'm saying I'm sorry," Steve said.

Petra nodded.

"I don't know what got into me," Steve said. He spread his hands. "Suppose I—well, I suppose you mean more to me than I thought you did. I—I shouldn't have called you names. Not those names. I shouldn't have done that."

Petra shifted Barney a little on her hip. She put her hand on Kit's head. Very faintly, she could feel the vibration of his moving jaws through her palm.

"I've come to apologize. I've come to ask you to forgive and forget."

Petra said nothing.

"Please," Steve said. He made an effort. "*Please.*"

There was a silence. Then Petra said, without heat, "Forgive, yes. Forget, no."

"But—"

"If it's in you, it's in you," Petra said. "You'd do it again."

"I swear—"

"I'm not interested," Petra said.

"*Please.*"

She shook her head.

"Just a month. Just a week more—"

"I'm not interested," Petra repeated.

"So what'll you do?"

Petra said to Kit, "Spit it out. You can't keep on like that. Spit it in the bin."

Kit turned towards the wastebin. Petra looked at Steve.

"Good-bye, then."

"Don't do this—"

Behind her, Kit spat vigorously.

"You mean it," Steve said.

Petra nodded again.

"Okay." He looked at Barney. He bent sideways to see Kit, still occupied by the waste bin. "Bye, boys."

Barney put his face into Petra's neck.

"Say good-bye, Kit," Petra said.

Kit looked up.

"Bye," he said. He trailed back to his place beside Petra, extracting a wooden spoon from the muddle on the table in front of them. He began to bang it rhythmically on the nearest table leg.

"I'll miss you—"

"Bye," Petra said.

"Have a . . . good life. Hope things work out—"

He retreated to the outside door, and stood on the worn mat, holding the handle. He said awkwardly, "I meant . . . all the good stuff. I did. I meant it."

He opened the door and paused, waiting for Petra to say something. Kit went on with his spoon on the table leg, bang, bang, bang, as if he was signaling something.

Petra didn't take her eyes off Steve, and she didn't speak. "Take care," Steve said, and left.

When the door had closed behind him, and his footsteps had retreated down the cement path away from the house, Petra bent down to insert Barney back into his chair. Then she put a hand on the wooden spoon.

"Enough, hey?"

She did it again now with the cereal spoon.

"Enough, big guy."

Kit held on to the spoon, glaring at Petra.

"Listen," Petra said, "listen." She bent towards Kit. Maybe

it was okay to take a small gamble, offer just a little promise of better things.

"Who lives in London?" Petra said.

Kit thought. He pressed the spoon into one cheek, pushing his mouth sideways.

"Spider-Man?" he suggested.

Petra smiled at him.

"Mariella," she said.

Mariella had been amazed. She was not allowed to open the front door to anyone, but she was allowed to drag one of the hall chairs across to the door, in order to stand on it and be able to see, through the fish-eye spy-hole at adult height, who was standing on the step outside. She would then, ignoring the intercom, call penetratingly down to her mother, and Sigrid would come up to open the door to visitors either amused or disconcerted by how Mariella had described them. But this time, Mariella could hardly believe what she was seeing, to such an extent that she could scarcely speak, but merely stood there balancing on her chair, and staring at Petra and the boys, huddled on the doorstep outside and gazing at her with the expressions you saw on African babies when there were videos about world poverty in assembly at school. Then she'd started shrieking, she was shrieking, "Mummy, come, Mummy, *come*, it's them, it's them, it's *them*!" and Sigrid had come running up the stairs from the kitchen, where she'd been starting to get supper, and she'd peered through the fish-eye too, and gasped, and then the door was flung open and there was a great confusion of arms, and bags, and crying, and Kit wanting her to look at his digger as if she hadn't seen it a million times before, and Barney refusing to let go of Petra for an instant and Sigrid saying, "There, there," and, "Don't worry, don't worry," and then they were all downstairs in the kitchen, and the boys were beginning to laugh, and shout a bit, and then Edward came home and all the confusion started again. It was, Mariella made a note to tell Indira on Monday, just *crazy*.

But it was happy, too. Everything got noisy and sticky very quickly, but it felt right, Mariella thought, it felt really okay to have everyone there, and spilt yogurt on the table, and Petra sitting on the floor as if she knew the house really well, instead of being practically a stranger in it, and Edward giving her a glass of wine and ringing Luke and Charlotte to come over too, and Charlotte arriving with a bag of pick-and-mix sweets which weren't healthy at all, being all sugar and chemicals, but which were so yummy all the same, and Charlotte sat on the floor, too, and Sigrid started cooking pasta for everyone, and it suddenly felt like a party and it just got better and better until Edward said above the racket, really loudly, "I'm ringing Ralph," and it was like someone had shut a door or popped a balloon or said it was bedtime when it really, really wasn't— and everything stopped.

"Please," Petra said from the floor.

Edward looked at her. He was standing, holding a wine-glass. She was below him, holding Barney.

"Please no, or please yes?" he said.

"Please yes," Petra said.

"Good," he said. "Good." He looked quite stern. "I wouldn't have accepted please no."

Mariella glanced at her mother. Sigrid was looking at Edward. Mariella knew, from long experience, that her father's expression was one he wore when he was being the responsible eldest son of the family, the one who had to listen on the phone when Granny rang up with a problem. And when her father got tense, her mother usually got tense too, and Mariella emphatically didn't want anyone getting tense when everything was being so fun, and, more important, being so fun right here in this kitchen, which was normally so dull. So she watched while her mother began to walk across to her father, obviously to say something to him quietly, and before she got there Luke looked up from fitting chestnuts out of Sigrid's nut bowl into the bucket of Kit's digger and said, "I'll go and get him."

"But—" Edward began.

Luke stood up.

"Much the easiest. I'll call him and say I'm picking him up from work for a beer. And if he's already out having one, I'll go and find him."

"Don't tell him why," Charlotte said from the floor. She had now enticed Barney onto her knees. He was eating dolly mixtures out of her cupped hand.

"Wouldn't dream of it—"

Edward said, "Are you sure?"

"Quite sure."

"But—"

"I'm sure," Luke said, "I'm doing it." He bent and aimed a kiss at the top of Charlotte's head. "I'm gone."

Mariella looked at her father. He looked dazed, then he shook himself slightly and glanced at Sigrid. She was smiling. She held out her wineglass.

"More, please," she said.

"I'm fagged out," Ralph said to Luke.

He had gone down to the deserted reception area to let Luke into the building, through all the security systems, past all the empty desks where people were free to go home because their work didn't depend on the American market, which still had four or five hours' life left in it yet.

Ralph thought he might get away by nine, nine thirty anyway, and then he'd probably mooch off with a few of the others and have some drinks, and a Chinese, maybe, and get back to his room—his landlord and girlfriend had gone to Barcelona for a city break—when he'd be too past it to do anything but crash out. And then here was Luke, saying come to Ed's, come on, come on, turn that thing off, and come to Ed's.

"Why?" Ralph said. "I'm fagged out."

"It's Friday, man. Friday night is downtime night. Sigrid's cooking pasta."

Ralph began, very slowly, to close the programs on his computer.

"I don't want any lecturing—"

"Nobody will lecture you."

"I don't want—"

"Bro," Luke said, "stop mingeing and *come*. You need time off and feeding. It's an impulse supper at Ed's and we want you there."

"We?" Ralph said suspiciously.

"We. Char and me. Ed and Sigi. Put your jacket on."

In Luke's car, driving up to Islington, Ralph told Luke about his week. He said that one of his clients was someone really tricky, a right fucker no one else wanted to touch, but with a five-hundred-million-dollar turnover, so worth getting to grips with, and everyone on the team thought that Ralph was the man for a tricky client as he was so tricky himself. Luke let Ralph talk. It was a boring story, but it kept Ralph's mind occupied and, if he just grunted now and then, he wouldn't be in any danger of giving the game away. And if that happened, if Ralph got even a hint that he was being cornered, coerced, presented with something he couldn't escape dealing with, then he might just bolt. Luke thought that he couldn't actually relax until he'd got Ed's front door shut behind him, with Ralph safely inside.

Edward plainly had the same thought. He opened the door to them, and then he stationed himself on Ralph's other side, almost as if he and Luke were a personal police escort, and they went down the stairs in that formation, Edward leading, Ralph in the middle, Luke bringing up the rear, and halfway down you could hear the little boys' voices suddenly, and Ralph stopped and said loudly, "What *is* this, what is—" and Edward turned back and took his arm and led him on down until they were there in the kitchen, and only Sigrid was looking their way because everyone else, wired on sugar and wine, was burying Charlotte with cushions from the TV sofa and screaming.

Ralph halted. Luke waited for him to turn round and accuse him of betrayal and kidnap. But he didn't. He just stood there and stared at his children, at Petra stopping Barney from crawling ecstatically and heedlessly across Charlotte's face.

Edward gave Ralph a little push.

"Go on," he said. "Go on. Go on in and join them."

They put the little boys to bed on improvised mattresses on the floor of Mariella's bedroom. She was very gratified by this, and lent them several of her plush animals each as a favor, keeping watch from her superior position on the bed until at last, and despite, in Barney's case, the novelty and excitement of not being caged in a cot, they fell asleep, Barney snoring on his back, his arms flung above his head. When Ralph came in to see if they were okay, she made it plain to him that she was perfectly capable of being in charge.

"Sorry, *ma'am*," Ralph said to her, smiling.

She nodded. He looked so much better when he smiled. She did her Swedish puzzle twice before she put the light out. She could do it so deftly now that it was time to ask Morfar to make her another. And planning that seemed to Mariella, very oddly, the only thing left to plan in the whole wide world right now.

* * *

Once or twice, during supper, Edward had managed to catch Sigrid's eye. He had wanted to convey to her his surprise and satisfaction at having, for the first time, both his brothers and both their wives round his and Sigrid's kitchen table, with all three children safely asleep in the same bedroom, and a weekend ahead. But Sigrid, although she had smiled at him, although she was plainly enjoying herself, enjoying being the provider, the one who could produce extra pillows, and supper, and a bath toy for Barney as if she did such things every day of the week, was not going to allow Edward to point out, or emphasize, what a rarity this evening was. She was behaving as if it was all perfectly normal, as if Petra often came up to London on the bus as a matter of course, as if there had been no estrangement between Ralph and Petra, no complicity between Charlotte and Petra, no break in the step of her and Edward's married march together. And she is right, Edward thought, she is right not to make a big deal of it, because even if it's a first it's only a beginning, and there is a long, long way to go.

For a start, Ralph and Petra were at opposite ends of the table from one another. They had not touched all evening; they had scarcely spoken directly to one another and Ralph had announced quite early in the evening that he was going back to his room at the end of it. Petra hadn't flinched. She appeared, Edward thought, remarkably composed and able to look at Ralph in a way he couldn't—yet, anyway—look at her. Charlotte and Luke were flirting across the table, monopolizing the noise and the energy, and Edward observed that Petra was watching them with every sign of ease and pleasure, wearing the expression she'd worn watching her boys with the sofa cushions, almost indulgent. Funny girl, he thought, funny, odd girl, but we shouldn't underestimate her, me especially, Ralph in particular. Just because someone doesn't know exactly what you know doesn't mean that what they *do* know isn't as important. Or even more important. She's got where she's got all by herself, we shouldn't forget that, we shouldn't ever forget how sheltered we've been, compared to her. He had a lump in his throat. He picked up his wineglass to take a swallow in order to dislodge it. God, he was getting as sentimental as his father.

His father! He raised his hand to his head and smacked his forehead with his palm. The parents! They should tell them, they ought—no, he ought—to ring Anthony and Rachel and say that everyone was here together, and fine. He hadn't given them a second thought. That was awful, really awful. He half rose. He'd go and do it now in the study, right now.

"Where are you going, man?" Luke said. He was leaning half across the table, among all the dirty plates and glasses, so that he could hold Charlotte's hand.

Edward's face assumed the faintly careworn expression familiar to Sigrid.

"I just remembered. I ought to ring the parents—"

"No," Sigrid said. "Sit down—"

"Honestly," Luke said, "honestly. Why spoil a really good evening?"

"But they'll—"

Luke let go of Charlotte's hand. He leaned sideways and put the hand on Ralph's shoulder.

"I'll do it."

"What—"

"I'll ring Mum and Dad," Luke said.

"But—"

"In the morning," Luke said. "Not now. We're celebrating now. I'll ring them tomorrow and tell them we were all together." He squeezed Ralph's shoulder. "Okay, bro?"

"Okay," Ralph said.

Sigrid was leaning back in her chair.

"There," she said to Edward, "there. Luke will do it. No need for you to do anything."

She was smiling at him. He didn't know when he'd seen her so relaxed. He smiled back, and lowered himself into his chair again. He picked up the nearest wine bottle and held it against the light. Empty. How had that happened? Better get another—

"I'll get another," Ralph said, taking the bottle out of his hand.

"They're in the—"

"I know," Ralph said. He stood up. "I know."

Edward looked round the table. He said, "What's happening?"

Sigrid was laughing now, and so were Petra and Charlotte. Luke folded his arms on the table, and leaned towards Edward.

"All change," Luke said. He looked about sixteen, Edward thought, but a very welcome sixteen. He gave Edward the thumbs-up sign. "All change."

CHAPTER TWENTY

The light was fading fast. Every year, Anthony was increasingly taken by surprise at how, once summer was over, the evenings drew in so rapidly, and he had to adjust himself to a winter schedule of only being able to rely on natural light, if it was a bright day, for four or five hours. In the past, the winter had been his time of dissection and observation, reconstructing bird skeletons with meticulous reference to diagrams, and wiring them up as if these ghostly creatures were still stepping or pecking or turning in flight. The studio shelves were crammed with skeletons as well as those wired to the roof beams, mostly fractured now, a broken ossuary of past life, past movement. They were ghoulish in their way, particularly the eyeless, beakless skulls, but they were hard to throw away all the same, representing as they did all that learning, all that progress, evidence, if he needed it, that he could represent a bird in two dimensions because he knew exactly how its body worked in three.

Every early autumn, Anthony surveyed his skeleton collection, vowed to do something to at least rationalize it, and did nothing. Rachel said to him, annually, that it was most unfair on the boys never to attempt to clear out some of the deep litter of the studio, but just to slide round such a monumental task knowing it would inevitably fall to them, once Anthony was dead.

"They can chuck it all," Anthony said. "All of it. It won't mean to them what it means to me. And I won't be there to mind what it means anymore. Will I?"

"But it'll be such a depressing task for them. Bags and bags of bones. Why subject them to anything so gloomy?"

But they're not gloomy, Anthony thought now, standing surveying the shelves as the early dusk thickened the light in the studio. Not gloomy at all. They are interesting, every one, and valid. They represented a journey for me, my journey. I never thought I could make a life and a livelihood out of being an artist, nor did my parents. But I did. I have. I've kept it all going, and brought up three boys, and educated them, because not only can I see, but I can, with this hand and this brain, translate what I see in such a way that other people can see it too. I can make birds live on paper. And these old bird bones, as Rachel calls them, were part of that process, part of the looking and looking, until you really understand how something works and can then reproduce it in a way, now, that I don't even have to think about. He raised his right arm involuntarily, his fingers holding an imaginary pencil, and sketched something in the air. There you are, he told himself. There. The power of the unconscious mind. I've drawn a lapwing taking off, and I didn't even have to think what to do before I did it. I *knew*. I knew, because there's a lapwing up there, somewhere, on those shelves, and I expect its head has fallen off and it's missing a wing rib or two, but once I knew every bone in its body and that knowledge is now as deep in me as my DNA. The boys won't mind clearing off these shelves. They'll get it.

They'll know that, if their mother's kitchen was always the engine room of the house, of family life, this place was the lookout. It was in here, Anthony said, almost out loud, where we didn't just focus on what had to be done—very necessary, admit that—but what *might* be done. And even if she'd rather die than admit it, I think Rachel knows that too, in her heart of hearts, and is afraid of it in her way, because it's something she can't control.

Like Ralph. Had they ever been able, really, to control Ralph? If he conformed, as a boy, it was because he wanted to, or it suited him, never because he felt the smallest necessity to be obliging. And because of this innate perversity, Ralph had always exercised a peculiar fascination for his mother. She didn't—Anthony was sure of this—love him any more than she loved Luke or Edward, but she was, in a way, spellbound by him, always had been, this creature who had always lived on the edge of, or entirely outside, her dominion. So that when he did seem more pliable these last few years, when he had submitted to her brisk, practical organizing of his life—the marriage to Petra, the move to the house in Aldeburgh—there was bound to be a price to pay in the end. And that price had turned out to be the mess of this summer, the upsets in the family, the creeping sense—so evidently painful for Rachel—that they, the parents, were no longer at the hub of things, were not being visited as much, or told as much, or seen as naturally involved in whatever was going on. They were now, Luke had made it plain when he had telephoned yesterday morning, to be informed of everything that was going on, but they weren't any longer central to the discussion of what should happen next. The three brothers, Luke had implied, in his emphasis on their heady London-weekend togetherness, now had their own priorities, the priorities of their lives, their children, their wives.

"We're all here," Luke said cheerfully. "We're all spending

the day together, all nine of us. Everyone's fine. You're not to worry. Everyone's happy. Barney even walked four steps this morning. He's a riot."

It was Anthony who had picked up the phone when Luke rang. He was alone in the kitchen. He stood there, staring out of the window above the sink, while Luke described the evening before and how Ralph had had no idea that he would find Petra and his children at Ed's house, how Petra has clearly come to her senses and done the sensible thing and just got on a bus, with boys and baggage. If Rachel had been in the room, she would have seized the phone and fired questions, but she was out, buying milk and matches and a crab for supper, if she could find one, and so it was left to Anthony to say, "Good. Good, lad. I'm so pleased, I'm so thankful—" and then to stand there, the phone in his hand after Luke had rung off, and think dazedly, "What *was* all that? What was it?"

When she heard, Rachel wanted to ring, at once, for confirmation. She had her phone in her hand, lifting it to her ear, when Anthony took it from her by force.

"No."

"But I've got to, I've got to be sure—"

"Leave them!"

"I can't, I must know—"

Anthony flung her phone across the kitchen. It hit the far wall and fell behind a chair, clattering against the skirting board.

"Leave them, I tell you."

He waited for her to scream at him, but she didn't. She said, as if wrestling with tears, "I need to know if they're okay—"

Anthony was breathing heavily.

"Never better. Luke sounded like he sounded on his wedding day."

"But Ralph. Ralph and Petra—"

313

"Together. No need to suppose anything other."

"But . . . but *really* together?"

"I don't know."

"I *must* know," Rachel said, starting across the room to retrieve her phone.

Anthony caught her wrist.

"You'll know when they choose to tell us. Not before."

"Whose side are you on?" Rachel demanded.

"No one's," Anthony said untruthfully.

Rachel stood there for a minute or two, not making any attempt to move. And then she said with an effort, "If no one has rung by tomorrow night, by Sunday night, can I ring then?"

But Ralph came. They were clearing up a desultory lunch that had taken place with the welcome companionship of the Sunday newspapers when they heard wheels on the gravel outside.

"Who—?"

Rachel flung down the tea towel she was holding and made as if to dart for the door.

"Wait," Anthony said.

"But—"

"Wait!"

She paused, almost quivering, like a dog thwarted of chasing after something unimaginably tempting.

"Whoever it is," Anthony said, "we can see them here."

It was Ralph. He was thinner than when they had last seen him, a month ago, and he had dark circles under his eyes, but he had an air of energy they hadn't seen in him in ages. Beside him, Anthony could feel Rachel collect herself. She reached up to kiss Ralph's cheek.

"My goodness, darling," she said in an entirely normal voice, "a haircut."

Ralph grinned. He lifted one foot towards her.

"And a shoeshine—"

Anthony said, not smiling, just looking straight at Ralph, "Where are the children?"

"At home."

"In Aldeburgh?"

"Of course," Ralph said. "Where else?"

"And . . . and Petra?"

"With them. Where else would *she* be?"

Rachel turned towards the table.

"Sit down. Sit down, and I'll make some coffee."

"Not for me, thanks," Ralph said, "I'm rather pushed for time. I'm going back to London tonight."

"Going back—"

"But we thought—"

Ralph said calmly, "I'll be down next weekend. And the weekend after. Until we let the house."

Rachel lowered herself carefully into a chair as if she had a bad back. She said faintly, "Let the house?"

Ralph took a chair opposite.

"Yes."

Anthony leaned on the table.

"Could you explain—"

Ralph smiled at him. He seemed in a sunnier mood than Anthony could ever remember. He said, "Why else d'you think I'm here?"

"We don't know," Rachel said. She sounded close to tears again. "We don't know anything—"

"You do," Ralph said. "You do know. Luke rang you. Didn't he?"

"But we don't know *enough*—"

There was a small silence. Then Ralph said, "I'll tell you."

Anthony straightened up and moved round the table to sit

next to Rachel. He had an instinct to take her hand, and a conflicting one to show no reaction whatsoever. So he sat there, his own hands clasped loosely on the table in front of him.

"Tell us."

"We're going to let the house for the winter," Ralph said. "I'm going to be in London in the week, and back at weekends, till we've let it. Petra is going to see the agent in the morning. Then we'll go to London for the winter. We'll find somewhere near Luke and Charlotte, playgroups for the boys; Petra can work a bit in the cafés and places round Columbia Road. Then we'll come back to Suffolk for the summer."

Rachel said, "You're . . . leaving Suffolk?"

"For the winter, Mum. It's called a compromise."

"So you and Petra—"

"None of your business, Mum," Ralph said pleasantly.

"Can't I even know if you're no longer planning a *divorce*?" Rachel cried.

Ralph tipped his chair back. He said carelessly, "No. We've made this plan. We'll try it. We'll see if it works."

"But when will we see the boys?"

"When you come to London."

"London," Rachel said disgustedly.

"You'll have to learn to like it," Ralph said. "You both will. We'll all of us be there."

Anthony said slowly, "But Petra . . . in London?"

"Sure," Ralph said. "Why not? She'll find her feet again."

"Does . . . does she like this plan?"

Ralph looked directly at his father.

"She suggested it."

"And—"

"And," Ralph said, "Sigi suggested you come to London and stay with them. Regularly. You'll want to, anyway, when the baby comes, won't you?"

"Of course," Anthony said. He glanced at Rachel. She was looking fixedly at the far end of the table, the place where Anthony always sat when the table was full, full of people, full of food and noise and activity.

She said, with just an edge of sarcasm in her voice, "And Charlotte? Did Charlotte have a message for me, too, as to how I might live my life in the future?"

"She sent her love," Ralph said. "She sent it twice, actually."

He stood up. He said, looking down at his parents, "Petra would send hers, too, if she did that kind of thing. But she doesn't. You know she doesn't. She never has. But it doesn't mean she doesn't feel it. She feels a lot, in fact, she's more honest than all of us in what she feels. True to herself." He paused, and then he said, "We've got to learn to do things differently, both of us." Then his gaze sharpened, and he said with emphasis, looking straight at his father, "Just as you and Mum have got to do. Differently. Okay?"

They sat there for a long time after he had gone, side by side at the table in the quiet kitchen. Various little village cries and calls filtered in from the outside, and a car or two went by, but inside the house it was like being under a bell jar, suspended out of time and the turning of the world. Anthony didn't know how long they sat there, didn't know if he was actually thinking or was just allowing his mind to float, unfettered, across what Ralph had said, and what he had implied. In either case, he was startled when Rachel said abruptly, "Well, I suppose I could revive the bed-and-breakfast idea."

He stared at her.

"*What?*"

"You know," Rachel said. "Ages ago. I thought I'd do bed-and-breakfast in the summer. It would mean tarting up upstairs a bit. The bathrooms are the complete reverse of state-of-the-art, whatever that means."

"Could . . . could you face it?"

She turned to look at him.

"Oh yes. If I have to. And . . . and now, maybe I do?"

He leaned sideways, and kissed her cheek.

"Good girl."

"Don't patronize me."

"I'm admiring you—"

"Well," Rachel said, getting up, "go and admire me in the studio. I'm going to spread the stuff out on the table, and think. I'm going to think how to do whatever it is the boys want us to do."

"Just like that?"

"No," she said. She gave a little smiling grimace. "With difficulty." And then she said, "And you can do a difficult thing too. You can get rid of those bird bones."

But I can't, Anthony thought now. I can't and I shouldn't. Getting rid of them has nothing to do with changing this stage of fatherhood; it has to do with something essential in me, something that makes me who I am. Ralph said Petra was true to herself. I don't know if that means merely unaffected, or something deeper. But I am a painter of birds, in my true heart, and I need my bones.

It was full dusk now. There were oblongs of pale, filtered light from the high north windows, and smaller rectangles from the windows along the west wall, but the rest of the studio was softly dark, only the easel standing high above the surrounding bulky shapes of the furniture, like a crane on a building site. There was a board on the easel, on which Anthony had pinned a sheet of rough, handmade paper preparatory to drawing all the birds that came to the bird table that Rachel kept supplied outside the kitchen window, the robins and tits and dunnocks, even the occasional goldfinch, which he would draw in charcoal, then paint in watercolor, choosing poses that indicated where each bird intended to move next. Maybe he would include a wren. *Troglodytes, troglodytes,* nine centimeters long, nine grams in weight, two broods a year in little dome-shaped nests made of moss. Wonderful.

He smiled up at the shelves where the bird bones still glimmered faintly in the gloom. There'd be the wren up there too, what there was of it. He went slowly across the room in the darkness, avoiding all obstacles out of familiarity, and laid his hand upon the doorknob. He looked back. It would all be there in the morning, dusty and disordered to all eyes but his own, which saw it, either in reality or in recollection, as a place of evolution and a place of promise.

He went slowly across the gravel to the house. A huge yellow September moon had hoisted itself among the trees behind the roof, and there was a little sharp edge to the air, a little bite, that was as invigorating as brushing one's teeth. The kitchen window was a warm golden square, and through it he could see Rachel bending over a sea of brochures and folders on the kitchen table. He stood and watched her for a while, his wife, the woman he had married, yet not that woman, as he was not that long-ago man.

He opened the back door. A surge of warmth came out to greet him.

"Anthony?" Rachel called, not turning.

He closed the door behind him. He remembered Ralph.

"Who else?" he said.

ABOUT THE AUTHOR

JOANNA TROLLOPE is the author of sixteen highly acclaimed bestselling contemporary novels. She has also written a study of women in the British Empire, *Britannia's Daughters*, and, under the name of Caroline Harvey, a number of historical novels.

Joanna Trollope was born in Gloucestershire, and now lives in London. She was appointed OBE in the 1996 Queen's Birthday Honours List.

Daughters-in-Law

Introduction

Rachel Brinkley has devoted herself fiercely to her three sons and continues to do so now that they are all grown-up. But when her youngest, Luke, marries Charlotte, Rachel finds that her control begins to slip away. Charlotte and Rachel butt heads almost immediately, but when Rachel's son Ralph discovers his wife's affair, that quickly takes center stage. Even Edward, the eldest and most settled son, finds his marriage to Sigrid troubled by the family drama.

As these rifts rise to the surface, the Brinkley family is forced to find new loyalties and call old assumptions into question, while Rachel must find a way to preserve the relationships she holds most dear.

For Discussion

1. The novel opens with Anthony fixating on his soon-to-be daughter-in-law's figure. How does this affect your opinion of him? Does it set any expectations for him as a character or for the book as a whole?

2. Early in the novel, Petra is regarded as the standard by which the other daughters-in-law are judged. Who suffers most from this comparison: Petra, Charlotte, or Sigrid?

3. The daughter-in-law relationship is traditionally more fraught than that of the son-in-law. Why do you think this tension exists? Whom did you identify with the most? The daughter-in-law or the mother characters? Why?

4. The novel shifts perspective many times. How do the varying viewpoints shape your reading experience? Did you like certain characters better than others? Would you have preferred more from a particular viewpoint?

5. How does the author avoid stereotyping the characters? How realistic are the ways in which the characters grow and change throughout the novel? How would you characterize Ralph as a father and husband in comparison to Edward and Luke?

6. Did you find yourself taking sides with any of the characters? Which incidents were the most polarizing? How did your sympathies for the characters shift throughout the novel? Did you understand Rachel's outburst over Charlotte and Luke's announcement? Why or why not? Was her reaction forgivable? How would you have responded if your mother or close family member acted similarly?

7. How large a role does proximity and distance play in the family relationships in *Daughters-in-Law*? Would Sigrid be frustrated with her own family if they were closer, as Edward argues? How large a role does distance play in your own family?

8. How did you react to Luke's refusal of Marnie's help? What would you have done if it were you?

9. How much of a role does obligation play in Petra's relationship with Rachel and Anthony? With the rest of the family?

10. How understandable and/or forgivable were Petra's actions regarding Steve? Is it an affair even if they never had sex?

11. Steve goes from being a source of comfort to Petra to being verbally abusive. Did you predict this shift? Were you surprised by their argument or by Petra's response to his proposal?

12. Do you think there are any heroes or villains in the book? If so, who are they?

A Conversation with Joanna Trollope

Daughters-in-Law **portrays women from several different generations, ranging from Rachel and Marnie to Petra and Charlotte. How did you go about finding their voices?**

I suppose finding the voices of women of different generations is a function of the imagination. While I'm actually writing, I am describing a movie running in my head, complete with sound track, and I'm also conscious of inhabiting each head as a character speaks. So I suppose that what I'm doing is somehow *being* each person as I make them speak, irrespective of their age or gender.

What are the challenges and conveniences of telling a story from multiple perspectives? How do you decide which viewpoint to tell a certain incident from? For example, why did you focus on Mariella during the lunch debacle at Luke and Charlotte's?

Just as changes of pace are important in a novel in order to refresh the reader as she or he goes along, so are changes of viewpoint—it's hard work to read only from one person's point of view for three hundred pages. It also, I think, gives a novel vividness and charm to surprise the reader sometimes with an unexpected viewpoint, and when adults are behaving badly—as in the scene the question cites—that point can be subtly and powerfully made by seeing their conduct through more innocent (though not less knowing!) eyes. So each scene, in my opinion, is enhanced by being given, as it were, to an often unexpected character as the filter—it gives the narrative validity and energy.

You have written more than fifteen novels. How has your creative process changed over the years? Do you see an arc or progression in your work?

I don't think the way I write has changed hugely—still the months of research, still the same plotting of the first quarter and then the end, still the handwriting—but I think my style has evolved, rather than changed, and is possibly more economical and lighter now. And that, I'm sure, is a direct response to the loyalty of readers that has (over what is now decades!) given me the confidence to pare everything down a bit and emerge with a way of writing that has more impact and less elaboration.

Daughters-in-Law **is full of women who find their strength. For example, Petra and Marnie are very different characters who both unexpectedly take control of their lives. Is this a theme you return to often in your work?**

I love female strength and the female capacity for endless self-reinvention as themes for novels. It never ceases to amaze me how women can go on evolving all their lives, and how many of them go on opening their minds to new ideas and fads and fashions at almost any age. And of course, the longer you live, the more you turn into a person flavored by decades of experience, which in turn often rewards you with the confidence that growing up in a largely (still . . .) male-dominated society (however lovely a lot of those men are!) isn't there at the beginning. So, acquiring control is still a huge achievement for many women and makes a wonderful topic for fiction, as it's no less than a kind of real triumph.

You once said that you did not see yourself as a feminist writer. What kind of writer do you identify yourself as?

A contemporary writer. If I'm doing anything, I'm trying to chronicle the way we live now—i.e., how we live as shaped and sometimes dictated by modern customs and morality. And as modern culture affects all of us, I don't really think my novels are gender, or sociologically, specific.

Anthony and Petra both turn to nature to find comfort and inspiration. What are your own sources of inspiration?

Other people. I can't get enough of them, whether it's people known to me or perfect strangers observed on public transport. All fascinating and illuminating.

Are you an artist yourself? What kind of research did you do for Anthony and Petra's drawing scenes?

Oh, I wish! I can't draw and I can't sing and I can't dance, which is why I am so completely beguiled by people who can! I studied a number of well-known bird artists for this novel . . . and learned a very great deal, but I simply can't *do* it myself.

The novel has a marked lack of villains, with the possible exception of Steve. Do you believe there are ever true villains in real life, or are there always extenuating circumstances?

It's not so much malevolence that makes villains in real life (though there are beasts out there, I know . . .) as muddle. And I think most people are complicatedly shades of gray rather than black and white, good or bad. I don't even think Steve is a villain. I think he's an inarticulate man who resorts to anger when frustrated and doesn't have the words or emotional maturity to express himself any other way. The aim was to make him credible, rather than a simple hate figure, which would have been unbelievable and clumsy—someone who arouses fear because he isn't fully in control of his stronger feelings.

Is there any kind of message you hope readers will take away from *Daughters-in-Law*?

Only what I hope emerges from all my books, which is that a bit of empathy towards our fellow humans makes living with ourselves and other people a more successful business!

Why did you choose to focus this novel on the relationship between mothers and daughters-in-law?

Most women have, or are, a daughter-in-law, even in the loosest sense, and also I can't help noticing that mothers behave differently to their daughters-in-law than they do towards their sons-in-law—even if this last statement is a generalization! And I like to investigate topics that apply to very many of us—I am more interested in the common ground than in any arcane situation that only concerns a very few. . . . And I'm at an age where very many of my friends are mothers-in-law!

Enhance Your Book Club

1. Petra, Anthony, and Marnie are artists in their own right. Plan an art-related activity for the group. Consider visiting a local gallery or museum, taking a drawing class, or visiting a nature preserve to sketch with your book club members.

2. The Minsmere reserve, where Petra meets Steve, is a real place. Find photos, maps, and information about the bird species at Minsmere by visiting www.rspb.org.uk/reserves/guide/m/minsmere/index.aspx.